D0758928

A CROWNING MERCY

A CROWNING MERCY

Susannah Kells

The Viking Press   New York

Library of Congress Cataloging in Publication Data
Kells, Susannah
  A crowning mercy.
  I. Title.
PS3561.E3926C7   1983   813.'54   83-47869
ISBN 0-670-20068-9

Printed in the United States of America
Set in Times Roman

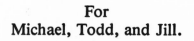

For
Michael, Todd, and Jill.

Matthew, Mark, Luke and John,
The bed be blest that I lie on.
Four angels to my bed,
Four angels round my head.
One to watch, and one to pray,
And two to bear my soul away.

Thomas Ady

Prologue
1633

The boat slammed into a wave. Wind howled in the rigging and brought water stinging down the treacherous deck, driving the shuddering timbers into the next roller.

'Cap'n! You'll take the bloody masts out of her!'

The captain ignored his helmsman.

'You're mad, Cap'n!'

Of course he was mad! He was proud of it, laughing at it, loving it. His crew shook their heads; some crossed themselves, others, Protestants, just prayed. The captain had been a poet once, before all the troubles, and all poets were touched in the head.

He shortened sail an hour later, letting the ship go into irons so that it jerked and rolled on the waves as he walked to the stern rail. He stared through the rain and windspray, stared for a long while at a low, black land. His crew said nothing, though each man knew the sea-room they would need to weather the low, dark headland. They watched their captain.

Finally he walked back to the helmsman. His face was quieter now, sadder. 'Weather her now.'

'Cap'n.'

They passed close enough to see the iron basket atop the pole that was the Lizard's beacon. The Lizard. For many this was their last sight of England; for too many it was their last sight of any land before their ships were crushed by the great Atlantic.

This was the Captain's farewell. He watched the Lizard till it was hidden in the storm and still he watched as though it might suddenly reappear between the squalls. He was leaving.

He was leaving a child he had never seen.

He was leaving her a fortune she might never see.

He was leaving her, as all parents must leave their children, but this child he had abandoned before birth, and all that wealth he had left her did not assuage his shame. He had abandoned her, as he now abandoned all the lives that he had touched and stained. He was going to a place where he promised himself he could start again, where the sadness he was leaving could be forgotten. He took only one thing of his shame. Beneath his sea-clothes, hung about his neck, was a golden chain.

He had been the enemy of one king and the friend of another. He had been called the handsomest man in Europe and still, despite prison, despite wars, he was impressive.

He took one last, backward look and then England was gone. His daughter was left behind to life.

PART 1

1643
The Seal of St Matthew

1

She first met Toby Lazender on a day that seemed a foretaste of heaven. England slumbered under the summer heat. The air was heavy with the scent of wild basil and marjoram, and she sat where purple loosestrife grew at the stream's edge.

She thought she was alone. She looked about her like an animal searching for enemies, nervous because she was about to sin.

She was sure she was alone. She looked left where the path came from the house through the hedge of Top Meadow, but no one was there. She stared at the great ridge across the stream, but nothing moved among the trunks of heavy beeches or in the water meadows beneath them. The land was hers.

Three years before, when she had been seventeen and her mother dead one year, this sin had seemed monstrous beyond imagination. She had feared then that this might be the mysterious sin against the Holy Ghost, a sin so terrible that the Bible could not describe it except to say it could not be forgiven, yet still she had been driven to commit it. Now, three summers later, familiarity had taken away some of her fear, yet she still knew that she sinned.

She took off her bonnet and laid it carefully in the wide, wooden basket in which she would carry back the rushes from the pool. Her father, a wealthy man, insisted that she worked. St Paul, he said, had been a tentmaker and every

Christian must have a trade. Since the age of eight she had worked in the dairy but then she had volunteered to fetch the rushes that were needed for floor-coverings and rushlights. There was a reason. Here, by the deep pool of the stream, she could be alone.

She unpinned her hair, placing the pins in the basket where they could not get lost. She looked about her again, but nothing moved in the landscape. She felt as solitary as if this was the sixth day of creation. Her hair, pale as the palest gold, fell about her face.

Above her, she knew, the Recording Angel was turning the massive pages of the Lamb's Book of Life. Her father had told her about the angel and his book when she was six years old, and it had seemed an odd name for a book. Now she knew that the Lamb was Jesus and the Book of Life was truly the Book of Death. She imagined it as vast, with great clasps of brass, thick leather ridges on its spine and pages huge enough to record every sin ever committed by every person on God's earth. The angel was looking for her name, running his finger down the ledger, poised with his quill dipped in the ink.

On the Day of Judgment, her father said, the Book of Life would be brought to God. Every person would go, one by one, to stand before His awful throne as the great voice read out the sins listed in the book. She feared that day. She feared standing on the floor of crystal beneath the emerald and jasper throne, but her fear could not stop her sinning, nor could all her prayers.

A tiny breath of wind stirred the hair about her face, touched silver on the ripples of the stream and then the air was still again. It was hot. The linen collar of her black dress was tight, its bodice sticky, the skirts heavy on her. The air seemed burdened by summer.

She put her hands beneath her skirts and unlaced her stocking tops just above her knees. The excitement was thick in her as she looked about, but she was sure she was alone. Her father was not expected back from the lawyer in Dorchester till early evening, her brother was in the village with the vicar, and none of the servants came to the stream. She pulled her heavy stockings down and placed them in her big leather shoes.

Goodwife Baggerlie, her father's housekeeper, had said she should not dally by the stream because the soldiers might come. They never had.

The war had started the year before in 1642 and it had filled her father with a rare, exalted excitement. He had helped to hang a Roman Catholic priest in the old Roman amphitheatre in Dorchester and this had been a sign from God to Matthew Slythe that the rule of the Saints was at hand. Matthew Slythe, like his household and the village, was a Puritan. He prayed nightly for the King's defeat and the victory of Parliament, yet the war was like some far-off thunderstorm that rumbled beyond the horizon. It had hardly touched Werlatton Hall or the village from which the Hall took its name.

She looked about her. A corncrake flew above the hayfield across the stream, above the poppies, meadowsweet and rue. The stream surged past the pool's opening where the rushes grew tallest. She took off her starched white apron and folded it carefully on top of the basket. Coming through the hedged bank of Top Meadow, she had picked some red campion flowers, and these she put safely at the basket's edge where her clothes could not crush the delicate five-petalled blossoms.

She moved close to the water and was utterly still. She listened to the stream, to the bees working the clover, but there was no other sound in the hot, heavy air. It was the perfect summer's day; a day devoted to the ripening of wheat, barley and rye; to the weighing down of orchard branches; a day of heat hazing the land with sweet smells. She was crouching at the very edge of the pool, where the grass fell away to the gravel beneath the still, lucid water. From here she could see only the rushes and the tops of the great beeches on the far ridge.

A fish jumped upstream and she froze, listening, but there was no other sound. Her instinct told her she was alone, but she listened for a few seconds more, her heart loud, and then with swift hands she tugged at her petticoat and the heavy, black dress, pulled them up over her head, and she was white and naked in the sun.

She moved swiftly, crouching low, and the water closed about her cold and clean. She gasped with the shock and the pleasure of it as she pushed herself into the deep place at the pool's centre, giving herself up to the water, letting it carry her, feeling the joy of fresh cleanness on every part of her. Her eyes were shut and the sun was hot and pink on them—for a few seconds she was in heaven itself. Then she stood on the gravel, knees bent so that only her head was above the water and opened her eyes to look for enemies. This pleasure of swimming in a summer stream was a pleasure she must steal, for she knew it to be a sin.

She had found she could swim, an awkward paddling stroke that could take her across the pool to where the stream's swift current tugged at her, turned her, and drove her back to the pool's safety. This was her sin, her pleasure, and her shame. The quill scratched in the great book of heaven.

Three years ago this had been something indescribably wicked, a childish dare against God. It was still that, but there was more. She could think of nothing, nothing at least that bore thinking about, that would enrage her father more than her nakedness. This was her gesture of anger against Matthew Slythe, yet she knew it to be futile for he would defeat her.

She was twenty, just three months from her twenty-first birthday, and she knew that her father's thoughts had at last turned to her future. She saw him watching her with a brooding mixture of anger and distaste. These days of slipping like a sleek, pale otter into the pool must come to an end. She had stayed unmarried far too long, three or four years too long, and now Matthew Slythe was finally thinking of her future. She feared her father. She tried to love him, but he made it hard.

She stood now in the shallow part of the pool and the water streamed from her, making her hair cold against her back. She brushed water from her breasts, her slim waist, and she felt the touch of the sun on her skin. She stretched her arms up and then her body, feeling the joy of freedom, the warmth on her skin, the sleekness of water around her legs. A fish jumped.

It jumped again, then a third time, and she knew it was no fish. It was too regular. Panic swept her. She waded to the pool's edge, scrambled desperately on to the bank and fumbled with her petticoat and dress. She pulled them over her hair and down, forcing the heavy, stiff material about her hips and legs. Panic was coursing through her.

The splashing came again, closer now, but she was decent, even if dishevelled. She removed the wet hair from within her collar, sat down and picked up her stockings.

'Dryad, hamadryad, or nymph?' An easy voice, full of hidden laughter, came from the stream.

She said nothing. She was shivering in fear, her wet hair obscuring her view.

He smiled at her. 'You have to be a nymph, the spirit of this stream.'

She jerked her hair away from her eyes to see a smiling young man, his face framed with unruly dark red curls. He was standing in the stream, but curiously bent forward so that his hands and fore-arms were beneath the water. His white shirt was unbuttoned, tucked into black breeches that were soaking. Black and white, the colours of a Puritan's sober dress, but she did not believe the young man to be a Puritan. Perhaps it was the fineness of the linen shirt, or the hint of black satin where the breeches were slashed, or perhaps it was his face. She decided it *was* his face. It was a strong-boned, good face, full of laughter and happiness. She should have been frightened, yet instead she felt her spirits rise at the sight of the stooping, wet man. She disguised her interest, putting defiance into her voice as she challenged the trespasser. 'What are you doing here?'

'Stealing Slythe's fish. What are you doing?'

There had been something so cheerful in his admission of poaching that she smiled. She liked his face. It was crossed by the odd reflections of the sunlight from rippling water. She saw that he had no rod or net. 'You're not fishing.'

'You're calling me a liar!' He grinned at her. 'We Lazenders don't lie. At least, not much.'

A Lazender! That made everything more fitting somehow for this private place where she defied her father. Sir George Lazender was the Member of Parliament for the northern part of the county, a great landowner, a knight, and a man of whom her father had a low opinion. Sir George Lazender supported Parliament in its war against the King, but Matthew Slythe believed that support to be lukewarm. Sir George, Matthew Slythe believed, was a man too cautious in the great fight. There was worse. Sir George, it was rumoured, would keep the bishops in a Protestant church, would keep the Book of Common Prayer for its services, and Matthew Slythe believed both to be the works of the Papist devil.

The young, red-headed man bowed clumsily in the stream. 'Toby Lazender, nymph. Heir to Lazen Castle and stealer of fish.'

'You're not stealing fish!' She was hugging her knees.

'I am!' He proved it by slinging a bag from his back and showing her a half dozen trout. Yet he had no fishing gear with him.

She smiled. 'How?'

He told her. He waded to the bank, lay on the grass a few feet from her, and described how to catch fish with bare hands. It was, he said, a slow business. First he immersed his hands and forearms in the water and left them there until they had chilled to the temperature of the stream. Then, very slowly, he walked upstream still keeping his hands under the water. He explained that trout were lazy fish, lying in the thick weed and swimming only enough to hold their position against the water's flow. He said she could creep into the weeds and, moving slow as thistledown, feel with spread fingers for the presence of a fish. He grinned at her. 'You don't feel the fish, at least not at first. You just feel the pressure of it.'

'The pressure?'

He nodded. 'I don't know. It's just there. The water's thicker.'

'And then?'

'You stroke.' He showed her how he worked his fingers back and forth, closing on the strange pressure until he could feel the fish's belly. Because his fingers were as cold as the water, and because they moved with infinite slowness the fish suspected nothing. He told her how to stroke the fish, always stroking backwards and always gently, until the hands knew precisely how the trout lay in the water. Then he pounced. The fish was jerked out of the weed, faster than it could twist away, and he would send it spinning to the bank. 'Then you hit its head.' He grinned.

She laughed. 'Truly?'

He nodded. 'On my honour. Were you swimming?'

She shook her head and lied. 'No.'

His legs were bare, his wet breeches rolled up. He smiled. 'I'll look the other way while you finish dressing.'

She felt a pang of fear. 'You shouldn't be here!'

'Don't tell anyone and I won't.'

She looked about her, but could see no one watching. She put on stockings and shoes, her apron, and laced up her dress.

Toby made her laugh. She felt no fear of him. She had never met anyone with whom it was so easy to talk. Her father's absence meant time was not pressing on her and they talked all afternoon. Toby lay on his stomach as he told her of his unhappiness with the war and of his wish to fight for the King rather than his father's side. She felt a chill go through her when he proclaimed his loyalty for the enemy.

He smiled at her, teasing her gently, but asking an unstated question at the same time. 'You wouldn't support the King, would you?'

She looked at him. Her heart was beating loud. She smiled back shyly. 'I might.'

For you, she was saying, I might even change the loyalty in which I was reared.

She was a Puritan girl, protected from the world, and she had never been allowed more than four miles from home. She had been raised in the harsh morality of her father's angry religion, and though he had insisted that she learn to read, it had been only so she could search the scriptures for salvation. She was ignorant, kept deliberately so, for the Puritans feared the knowledge of the world and its seducing power, yet not even Matthew Slythe could rein in his daughter's imagination. He could pray for her, he could beat her, he could punish her, but he could not, though he had tried, stop her dreaming dreams.

She would say later that this was love at first sight.

It was, too, if love was a sudden, overwhelming urge to know Toby Lazender better, to spend time with this young man who made her laugh and feel special. She had been walled in all her life, and the result had been that she dreamed of the wild world outside, seeing it as a place of laughter and happiness, and now, suddenly, this emissary from beyond the wall had broken in and found her. He brought happiness and she fell in love with him there and then, beside the stream, making him the object of all the dreams that were to come.

He saw a girl more beautiful than any he had seen before. Her skin was pale and clear, her eyes blue, her nose straight over a wide mouth. When her hair dried it fell like spun gold. He sensed a strength in her that was like fine steel, yet when he asked if he could come again she shook her head. 'My father won't allow it.'

'Do I need his permission?'

She smiled. 'You take his fish.'

He looked at her in astonishment. 'You're Slythe's daughter?'

She nodded.

Toby laughed. 'Dear God! Your mother must have been an angel!'

She laughed. Martha Slythe had been fat, vengeful and bitter. 'No.'

'What's your name?'

She looked at him, sadness in her. She hated her name and she did not want him to know it. She thought he would think less of her because of her name's ugliness, and as she thought that, so the realisation struck her that she would never be allowed to meet him again. Her name could never be Toby's business.

He persisted. 'Tell me?'

She shrugged. 'It doesn't matter.'

'But it does!' He exclaimed. 'More than the sky, the stars, the heavens, more than my dinner tonight! Tell me.'

She laughed at his ridiculous ebullience. 'You don't want to know my name.'

'I do. Otherwise I shall just have to invent a name for you.'

She smiled as she stared over the stream. She was embarrassed. Perhaps the name he would invent would be worse than her real name. She could not look at him as she spoke it aloud. 'My name's Dorcas.'

She expected him to laugh, but there was silence, so she turned a defiant stare on him. 'Dorcas Slythe.'

He shook his head slowly, looking serious. 'I think we must find you a new name.'

She had known he would hate her name.

Toby smiled, then leaned over to her rush basket. He picked up one of the pink-red campion flowers and slowly twirled the blossom in front of his eyes. He stared at it. 'I shall call you Campion.'

She liked it immediately, feeling as if all her life she had waited for this moment when someone would tell her who she was. Campion. She said the name over and over in her mind, Campion, and she savoured it, liking it, and knowing it was a hopeless dream. 'My name is Dorcas Slythe.'

He shook his head, slowly and deliberately. 'You're Campion. Now and forever.' He drew the flower towards his face, staring at her over the petals, then kissed it. He held it towards her. 'Who are you?'

She reached for the flower. Her heart was beating as it did before she swam. Her fingers trembled as she took the stalk, shaking the petals, and her voice was low. 'Campion.'

It seemed to her, that moment, as if nothing existed in all creation except herself, Toby, and the fragile, beautiful flower.

He looked at her, his own voice low. 'I shall be here tomorrow afternoon.'

The hopelessness rushed in to spoil the moment. 'I won't, she said. 'I can't.' The rushes were cut only once a week, and she had no other excuse for visiting the stream. The thought reminded her that she was late, that she must hurry.

Toby still watched her. 'When will you be here?'

'Next week.'

Toby sighed. 'I'll be in London.'

'London?'

He nodded. 'My father's sending me to learn some law. Not much, he says, just enough to know how to avoid all lawyers.' He looked up at the sky, gauging the time. 'I'd rather be fighting.' He was twenty-four and men much younger were fighting.

'Would you?'

He sat up. 'It will be a dull place if the Puritans take over.'

She nodded. She knew. The Puritans already controlled her life. She pinned her hair up. 'I'll be in church on Sunday.'

He looked at her. 'I'll pretend I'm a Puritan.' He made a grim, glum face and she laughed.

He had to go. He had come to the next village to buy a horse and the horse was being shod for him. It was a long journey back to Lazen Castle, but he would do it swiftly with a dream in his head of a girl he had met by a stream.

'Till Sunday, Campion.'

She nodded. Even talking to him was a sin, or so her father would say, but she wanted to see him again. She was in love, a hopeless, romantic, helpless love because there was nothing she could do about it. She was her father's daughter, at his command, and she was Dorcas Slythe.

Yet she yearned, now, to be Campion.

Toby cut the rushes for her, making it all a game, and then he left. She watched him walk north along the stream and she wished she was going with him. She wished she was anywhere but at Werlatton.

She carried the rushes home, hiding the campion flowers in her apron while, unknown to her, her brother, Ebenezer, who had watched all afternoon from the shadows under the great beeches, limped to the Dorchester road and waited for their father.

She was Dorcas and she wanted to be Campion.

2

The leather belt cracked on to her back.

Matthew Slythe's shadow was monstrous on her bedroom wall. He had brought candles to her room, unbuckled his belt and his big, heavy face was burdened with God's anger.

'Whore!' Again his arm descended, again the leather slammed down. Goodwife Baggerlie whose hands were in her hair, was pulling Campion across the bed so that Matthew Slythe could whip her back.

'Harlot!' He was a huge man, bigger than any man who worked for him, and he felt a thick fury within him. His daughter naked in a stream! Naked! And then talking to a young man. 'Who was he?'

'I don't know!' Her voice came in sobs.

'Who was he?'

'I don't know!'

'Liar!' He brought the belt down again, she screamed with the pain and then his anger took over. He thrashed her, shouting that she was a sinner. He was in a blind fury. The leather tip of the belt lashed on the wall and ceiling and still he drove his arm so that her screams stopped and all he could hear were her hopeless sobs as she lay curled at the pillow end of the bed. Her wrist was bloody where the belt had caught it. Goodwife Baggerlie, her hands still tangled in Campion's hair, looked at her master. 'More, sir?'

Matthew Slythe, his short dark hair dishevelled, his big, red face distorted in anger, gasped great lungfuls of air. The fury was still on him. 'Whore! Harlot! You have no shame!'

Campion wept. The pain was dreadful. Her back was bruised, bleeding in places, and the leather belt had strapped her on legs, belly and arms as she had scrambled away from his fury. She said nothing; she could hardly hear her father.

Her lack of response angered him. The belt whistled again, she called out and the lash cut into her hip. The black dress hardly dulled any of the force.

Matthew Slythe's breath was hoarse in his throat. He was fifty-four now, yet still an immensely strong man for his age. 'Naked! Woman brought sin into this world, and a woman's shame is her nakedness. This is a Christian house!' He bellowed the last words as he brought the belt down again. 'A Christian house!'

An owl hooted outside. The night wind stirred the curtains, wavered the candle flames, made the great shadow on the wall shiver.

Matthew Slythe was shaking now, his fury subsiding. He put the belt about his waist and buckled it. He had cut his hand on the buckle but he did not notice. He looked at Goodwife. 'Bring her down when she's tidy.'

'Yes, sir.'

This was not the first beating she had been given; she had lost count of the times that her father had harnessed God's wrath to his right arm. She sobbed, the pain blurring everything and then Goodwife Baggerlie slapped her face. 'Get up!'

Elizabeth Baggerlie, who had been honoured by Matthew Slythe with the name Goodwife after the death of his wife, was a short, fat-waisted woman with a shrewish, raw-boned face and small red eyes. She ruled Werlatton Hall's servants and she devoted her life to the extermination of the Hall's dust and dirt as her master devoted his to the extermination of Werlatton's sin. The servants were driven about Werlatton Hall by Goodwife's shrill,˙ scouring voice, and Matthew Slythe had given her also the governance of his daughter.

Now Goodwife thrust Campion's bonnet at her. 'You should be ashamed of yourself, girl! Ashamed. There's a devil in you, that's what there is! If your dear mother had known, if she'd known! Hurry!'

Campion pulled the bonnet on with nerveless fingers. Her breath came in great, sobbing gasps.

'Hurry, girl!'

The household was awesomely quiet. The servants all knew that the beating was taking place, they could hear the belt, the screams, the terrifying anger of their master. They hid their feelings. The beating could happen to any of them.

'Stand up!'

Campion was shaking. The pain was as it always was. She knew she would not be able to sleep on her back for at least three or four nights. She moved like a dumb thing, knowing what was to happen, submitting to the inescapable force of her father.

'Downstairs, girl!'

Ebenezer, one year younger than his sister, sat reading his Bible in the great hall. The floor shone. The furniture shone. His eyes, dark as sin, dark as his Puritan clothes, looked unfeelingly at his sister. His left leg, twisted and shrunk at birth, stuck out awkwardly. He had told his father of what he had seen and then listened with quiet satisfaction to the searing cracks of the belt. Ebenezer was never beaten. He sought and gained his father's approval by quiet obedience and hours of Bible reading and prayer.

Campion still cried as she came down the stairs. Her beautiful face was smeared with tears, her eyes red, her mouth twisted.

Ebenezer, his black hair cut short in the fashion that had given rise to the nickname 'Roundheads', watched her. Goodwife nodded to him, and he acknowledged the recognition with a slow, stately inclination of the head. At nineteen he was old beyond his years, bitter with his father's bitterness, envious of his sister's wholeness.

Campion was taken to her father's study. Outside the door, as ever, Goodwife pushed down on her shoulder. 'Down!' Then Goodwife knocked on the door.

'Come in!'

The ritual was always the same. After the punishment, forgiveness, and after the pain, prayer. She crawled in on hands and knees as her father demanded of her and Goodwife shut her in with Matthew Slythe.

'Come here, Dorcas.'

She crawled to his chair. She hated him at this moment. She submitted because she had no choice.

The big hands closed on her tight-fitting bonnet. She hated the feel of them. The fingers pressed on her skull.

'Oh God our Father! Almighty God!' The fingers pressed tighter and tighter. His voice rose in powerful prayer, as Matthew Slythe hectored his God asking Him to forgive his daughter, to cleanse her, to make her whole, to take away her shame, and all the while the hands threatened to crush her skull. He pushed at her head, shaking it, seeking in a paroxysm of power to convince God that Dorcas needed His grace, and when the prayer was over he leaned back, exhausted, and told her to stand up.

He had a strong face, big-boned and fierce, a face heavy with God's anger. He looked at Campion with his usual distaste and his voice was deep. 'You are a disappointment to me, daughter.'

'Yes, father.' She stood with head bowed, hating him. Neither he nor her mother had ever kissed her, ever hugged her. They had beaten her, prayed over her, but never seemed to love her.

Matthew Slythe rested his hand on his Bible. He breathed heavily. 'Woman brought sin into the world, Dorcas, and woman must ever bear that disgrace. A woman's nakedness is her shame. It is disgusting to God.'

'Yes, father.'

'Look at me!'

She raised her eyes. His face was twisted with dislike.

'How could you do it?'

She thought he would hit her again. She stood still.

He opened the Bible, his fingers seeking the book of Proverbs. He read to her, his voice grating. ' "For by means of a whorish woman a man is brought to a piece of bread." ' The page turned. ' "Her house is the way to hell, Going down to the chambers of death." ' He looked up at her.

'Yes, father.'

He seemed to growl. He had beaten her again and again, but he had never crushed her and he knew it. He could see the flicker of challenge in her soul and he knew that he would never destroy it. Yet he would never stop trying. 'You will learn the seventh and eighth chapters of Proverbs by heart by this time tomorrow night.'

'Yes, father.' She already knew them.

'And you will pray for forgiveness, for grace, for the Holy Spirit.'

'Yes, father.'

'Leave.'

Ebenezer still sat in the hall. He looked at her and smiled. 'Did it hurt?'

She stopped and looked at him. 'Yes.'

He still smiled, one hand holding the pages of his Bible flat. 'I told him.'

She nodded. 'I thought you might have done.' She had always tried to love Ebenezer, to give him the love she had not been given, to protect a small, weak, crippled boy who was her brother. He had always rejected her.

Now he sneered. 'You disgust me, Dorcas. You're not fit to be in this house.'

'Good night, Eb.' She climbed the stairs slowly, her back hurting and her mind filled with the bleakness and horror of Werlatton Hall.

Matthew Slythe prayed when she was gone, prayed as he often prayed with a furious, twisting intensity as if he thought God would not hear a quiet plea.

Dorcas was a curse to him. She had brought him wealth beyond his dreams, but she was, as he had feared when the wealth was offered, a child of sin.

She had never, in truth, been bad, but Matthew Slythe did not see that. Her sin was to be strong, to be happy, to show no signs of fear of the awful, vengeful God who was Matthew Slythe's master. Dorcas had to be crushed. The child of sin must become a child of God and he knew he had failed. He knew that she called herself a Christian, that she prayed, that she believed in God, but Matthew Slythe feared the streak of independence in his daughter. He feared she could be worldly, that she could seek out the pleasures of this world that were damned, pleasures that could be hers if she found his secret.

There was a jewel hidden, a seal of gold, which he had not looked at in sixteen years. If Dorcas found it, if she learned what it meant, then she might seek the help of the seal and uncover the Covenant. Matthew Slythe groaned. The money of the Covenant belonged to Dorcas but she must never know. It must be tied up by a will, by his wishes, and above all, by a marriage settlement. His daughter, with her dangerous beauty, must never know she was rich. The money which had come from sin must belong to God, to Matthew Slythe's God. He drew a sheet of paper towards him, his head throbbing with the echoes of prayer, and wrote a letter to

London. He would settle his daughter once and for all. He would crush her.

Upstairs, in the bedroom she had to share with one of the maids, Campion sat on the wide window-sill and stared into the night.

Once Werlatton Hall had been beautiful, though she did not remember it thus. Its old, stone walls had been hugged by ivy and shaded by great elms and oaks, but when Matthew Slythe had purchased the estate he had stripped the ivy and cut down the great trees. He had surrounded the Hall with a vast lawn that took two men to scythe smooth in summer, and about the lawn he had planted a yew hedge. The hedge was tall now, enclosing the clean, ordered world of Werlatton and keeping at bay the strange, tangled outside world where laughter was not a sin.

Campion stared at the darkness beyond the hedge.

An owl, hunting the great ridge of beeches, sounded hollow across the valley. Bats flitted past the window, wheeling raggedly. A moth flew past Campion, attracted by the candle and causing Charity, the maid, to squeal in alarm, 'Shut the window, Miss Dorcas.'

Campion turned. Charity had pulled out the truckle bed from beneath Campion's. The girl's pale, frightened face looked up. 'Did it hurt, miss?'

'Always does, Charity.'

'Why did you do it, miss?'

'I don't know.'

Campion turned back to the rich, sweet darkness. She prayed every night that God would make her good, yet she could never please her father. She had known it was a sin to swim in the stream, but she did not understand why. Nowhere in the Bible did it say 'Thou shalt not swim', though she knew that the nakedness was an offence. Yet the temptation would come again and again. Except that now she would never be allowed to the stream again.

She thought of Toby. Her father, before he beat her, had

ordered her to be confined to the house for the next month. She would not be in church on Sunday. She thought of stealing away, going to the road that led north to Lazen, but knew she could not do it. She was always watched when she was forbidden to leave the house, her father guarding her with one of his trusted servants.

Love. It was a word that haunted her. God was love, though her father taught of a God of anger, punishment, wrath, vengeance and power. Yet Campion had found love in the Bible. 'Let him kiss me with the kisses of his mouth: for thy love is better than wine'. 'His left hand is under my head, and his right hand doth embrace me'; 'And his banner over me was love'; 'By night on my bed I sought him whom my soul loveth'. Her father said the Song of Solomon was merely an expression of God's love for his church, but she did not believe him.

She looked into the dark over the Werlatton valley and she thought of her father. She feared him when she should love him, yet the fear had never struck at the very centre of her. She had a secret, a secret that she clung to day and night. It was like a dream that never left her, and in the dream it was as if she was a disembodied soul merely watching herself in Werlatton. She smiled. She now found she was thinking of the disembodied soul as Campion, watching Dorcas be obedient, or trying to be obedient, and she had the sense that somehow she did not belong here. She could not explain it, any more than Toby Lazender had been able to explain how the cold fingers knew the pressure of a fish in the water, yet the sense of her difference had been the sense that enabled her to resist the savage fatherhood of Matthew Slythe. She fed her soul on love, believing that kindness must exist somewhere beyond the tall, dark hedge of yew. One day, she knew, she would travel into the tangled world that her father feared.

'Miss?' Charity was shrinking away from the fluttering moth.

'I know, Charity. You don't like moths.' Campion smiled.

Her back hurt as she bent over, but she cradled the large moth in her hands, feeling its wings flutter on her palms, and then she threw it to the freedom of the dark where the owl and the bats hunted.

She closed the window and knelt beside her bed. She prayed dutifully for her father, for Ebenezer, for Goodwife, for the servants, and then she prayed, a smile on her face, for Toby. The dreams had been given fuel. There was no sense in it and little hope, but she was in love.

Three weeks later, when the corn was the colour of Campion's hair and the summer promised a harvest richer than England had known for years, a guest came to Werlatton Hall.

Guests were few. A travelling preacher, his tongue burdened with hatred for the King and preaching death to the bishops, might be offered hospitality, but Matthew Slythe was not a gregarious man.

The guest, Dorcas was told, was called Samuel Scammell. Brother Samuel Scammell, a Puritan from London, and Charity was excited at the visit. She came to Dorcas in the bedroom as the sun was dying over the valley. 'Goodwife says you're to wear Sunday best, miss. And the rugs are down in the hall!'

Campion smiled at Charity's excitement. 'The rugs?'

'Yes, miss, and master's ordered three pullets killed! Three! Tobias brought them in. Goodwife's making pie.' Charity helped Campion dress, then adjusted the white linen collar over her shoulders. 'You do look well, miss.'

'Do I?'

'It was your mother's collar. It mended ever so nice.' Charity twitched at the edge of it. 'It looks so much bigger on you!'

Martha Slythe had been fat and tall, her voice competing with Goodwife Baggerlie's for mastery over the dirt of Werlatton Hall. Campion lifted the edge of the collar. 'Wouldn't it be nice to wear something pretty just once? Do you remember that woman in church two years ago? The one the Reverend Hervey told off for dressing like a harlot?' She laughed. The woman had worn a lace collar, pretty and soft.

Charity frowned. 'Miss! That's a wicked lust!'

Campion sighed inwardly. 'I'm sorry, Charity. I spoke without thinking.'

'God will forgive you, miss.'

'I'll pray for that,' Campion lied. She had long learned that the best way to avoid God's wrath was to pay Him frequent lip service. If Charity had told Goodwife about Campion's wish to wear lace, and Goodwife had told her master, then Matthew Slythe would punish Campion. Thus, Campion thought, to avoid punishment she had been taught to lie. Punishment is the best teacher of deceit. 'I'm ready.'

Matthew Slythe, his two children and the guest ate their supper at the far end of the great hall. The shutters of the tall windows were left open. Dusk was bringing gloom to the wide lawn and hedge.

Samuel Scammell, Campion guessed, was in his mid-thirties and there was a fleshiness to him that betokened a full diet. His face was not unlike her father's. It had the same bigness, the same heaviness, but where her father's face was strong, Scammell's seemed somehow soft as though the bones were malleable. He had full, wet lips that he licked often. His nostrils were like two huge, dark caves that sprouted black hair. He was ugly, an ugliness not helped by his cropped, dark hair.

He seemed eager to please, listening respectfully to Matthew Slythe's growled remarks about the weather and the prospect for harvest. Campion said nothing. Ebenezer, his thin face darkened by the shadow of beard and moustache, a darkness that was there even immediately after he had shaved, asked Brother Scammell his business.

'I make boats. Not I personally, you understand, but the men I employ.'

'Sea-going ships?' Ebenezer asked, with his usual demand for exactness.

'No, no, indeed, no.' Scammell laughed as though a joke had been made. He smiled at Campion. His lips were flecked with the pastry of Goodwife's chicken pie. More pastry clung to his thick black broadcloth coat, while a spot of gravy was smeared on his white collar with its two tassels. 'Watermens' boats.'

Campion said nothing. Ebenezer frowned at her, then leaned forward. 'Watermens' boats?'

Scammell put a hand to his stomach, opened his small eyes wide, and tried, unsuccessfully, to stifle a small belch. 'Indeed and indeed. In London, you see, the Thames is our main street.' He was addressing Campion again. 'The watermen carry cargoes and passengers and we build most of their craft. We also serve the big houses.' He smiled at Matthew Slythe. 'We built a barge for my Lord of Essex.'

Matthew Slythe grunted. He did not seem over-impressed that Samuel Scammell did business with the general of Parliament's armies.

There was a silence, except for the scraping of Scammell's knife on his plate. Campion pushed the stringy chicken to one side, trying to hide it under the dry pie crust. She knew she was being rude and she sought desperately for something to say to their guest. 'Do you have a boat yourself, Mr Scammell?'

'Indeed and indeed!' He seemed to find that funny, too, for he laughed. Some of the pastry scraps fell down his ample stomach. 'Yet I fear I am a bad sailor, Miss Slythe, indeed and indeed, yes. If I must travel upon the water then I pray as our Dear Lord did for the waves to be stilled.' This was evidently a joke also, for the hairs in his capacious nostrils quivered with snuffled laughter.

Campion smiled dutifully. Her brother's feet scraped on the boards of the floor.

Her father looked from Campion to Scammell and there was a small, secret smile on his heavy face. Campion knew that smile and in her mind it was associated with cruelty. Her father was a cruel man, though he believed cruelty to be kindness for he believed a child must be forced into God's grace.

Matthew Slythe, embarrassed by the new silence, turned to his guest. 'I hear the city is much blessed by God, brother.'

'Indeed and indeed.' Scammell nodded dutifully. 'The Lord is working great things in London, Miss Slythe.' Again he turned to her and she listened with pretended interest as he told her what had happened in London since the King had left and the rebellious Parliament had taken over the city's government. The Sabbath, he said, was being properly observed, the playhouses had been closed down, as had the bear gardens and pleasure gardens. A mighty harvest of souls, Scammell declared, was being reaped for the Lord.

'Amen and amen,' said Matthew Slythe.

'Praise His name,' said Ebenezer.

'And wickedness is being uprooted!' Scammell raised his eyebrows to emphasise his words. He told of two Roman Catholic priests discovered, men who had stolen into London from the Continent to minister to the tiny, secret community of Catholics. They had been tortured, then hanged. 'A good crowd of Saints watched!'

'Amen!' said Matthew Slythe.

'Indeed and indeed.' Samuel Scammell nodded his head ponderously. 'And I too was an instrument in uprooting wickedness.'

He waited for some interest. Ebenezer asked the required question and Scammell again addressed the answer to Campion. 'It was the wife of one of my own workmen. A slatternly woman, a washer of clothes, and I had cause to visit the house and what do you think I found?'

She shook her head. 'I don't know.'

'A portrait of William Laud!' Scammell said it dramatically. Ebenezer tutted. William Laud was the imprisoned Archbishop of Canterbury, hated by the Puritans for the beauty with which he decorated churches and his devotion to the high ritual which they said aped Rome.

Scammell said the portrait had been lit by two candles. He had asked her if she knew who the picture represented, and she did, and what is more had declared Laud to be a good man!

'What did you do, brother?' Ebenezer asked.

'Her tongue was bored with a red hot iron and she was put in the stocks for a day.'

'Praise the Lord,' Ebenezer said.

Goodwife entered and put a great dish on the table. 'Apple pie, master!'

'Ah! Apple pie.' Matthew Slythe smiled at Goodwife.

'Apple pie!' Samuel Scammell linked his hands, smiled, then cracked his knuckles. 'I like apple pie, indeed and indeed!'

'Dorcas?' Her father indicated that she should serve. She gave herself a tiny sliver that brought a sniff of disapproval from Goodwife, who was bringing lit candles to the table.

Samuel Scammell made short work of two helpings, gobbling the food as though he had not eaten in a week, and swilling it down with the small beer that was served this night. Matthew Slythe never served strong drink, only water or diluted ale.

The pie was finished without further talk and then, as Campion expected, the conversation was of religion. The Puritans were divided into a multiplicity of sects, disagreeing on fine points of theology and offering men like her father and Brother Scammell a splendid battleground for anger and condemnation. Ebenezer joined in. He had been studying Presbyterianism, the religion of Scotland and much of England's Parliament, and he attacked it splenetically. He leaned into the candlelight and Campion thought there was something fanatical in his thin, shadowed face. He was speaking to Samuel Scammell. 'They would deny our Lord Jesus Christ's saving grace, brother! They would dispute it, but what other conclusion can we draw?'

Scammell nodded. 'Indeed and indeed.'

The sky had gone ink black beyond the windows. Moths flickered at the panes.

Samuel Scammell smiled at Dorcas. 'Your brother is strong in the Lord, Miss Slythe.'

'Yes, sir.'

'And you?' He leaned forward, his small eyes intent on her.

'Yes, sir.' It was an inadequate answer, one that made her father stir in suppressed wrath, but Scammell leaned back happy enough.

'Praise the Lord. Amen and amen.'

The conversation, thankfully, passed from the state of her soul to the latest stories of Catholic atrocities in Ireland. Matthew Slythe warmed to the subject, anger giving his words wings, and Campion let the phrases hammer unheard about her head. She noticed that Samuel Scammell was stealing constant looks at her, smiling once when he caught her eye, and she found it unsettling.

Toby Lazender had said she was beautiful. She wondered what he did in London, how he liked a city 'cleansed' by the Puritans he so disliked. She had asked Charity, three weeks before, if a visitor had been in church and Charity had said yes. A strong young man, she said, with red hair, who had bellowed out the psalms in a loud voice. Campion was sad. She guessed Toby must have thought she did not want to see him again. She saw Samuel Scammell staring at her again and it reminded her of the way other men looked at her, even, though she found it hard to believe, the Reverend Hervey. Scammell seemed to eye her as a bull might a heifer.

The owl that hunted the beech ridge sounded in the night.

Samuel Scammell excused himself from the table and walked down the stone-flagged passage that led to the close-chamber.

Her father waited till his footsteps stopped, then looked at his daughter. 'Well?'

'Father?'

'Do you like Brother Scammell?'

Her father did, so her answer was obvious. 'Yes, father.'

Scammell had not closed the chamber door and she could hear him urinating into the stone trough, a sound just like that of a horse staling in the stable-yard. It seemed to go on for ever.

Ebenezer scowled at the candles. 'He seems sound in his beliefs, father.'

'He is, son, he is.' Matthew Slythe leaned forward, his face gloomy as he stared at the remains of the apple pie. 'He is blessed of God.'

The splashing still sounded. He must have the bladder of an ox, Campion thought. 'Is he here to preach, father?'

'Business.' Her father gripped the table top and seemed to brood. A pulse throbbed at his forehead. The sound of Scammell's pissing stopped, started again, then faded in spurts. Campion felt sick. She had hardly eaten. She wanted to be out of this room, she wanted to be in her bed where she could lie and dream her private dreams of the world beyond the high yew hedge.

Samuel Scammell's footsteps were loud in the passage. Matthew Slythe blinked, then put a welcoming smile on his face. 'Ah! Brother Scammell, you're back.'

'Indeed and indeed.' He waved a pudgy hand towards the passage. 'A well-appointed house, brother.'

'Praise God.'

'Indeed and indeed.' Scammell was standing by his chair, waiting for the mutual praise of God to cease. Campion saw a dark, damp patch on his breeches. She looked at the table instead.

'Sit down, brother! Sit down!' Her father was forcing jollity into his voice, a heavy-handed jollity that was only used with guests. 'Well?'

'Yes, indeed yes.' Scammell hitched up his breeches, scooped his coat aside and scraped his chair forward. 'Indeed.'

'And?'

Campion looked up, alerted by the inconsequential words. She frowned.

Scammell was smiling at her, his nostrils cavernous. He wiped his hands together, then dried them on his coat. ' "Who can find a virtuous woman? For her price is far above rubies. The heart of her husband doth safely trust in her, so that he shall have no need of spoil. She will do him good and not evil all the days of her life." '

'Amen,' Matthew Slythe said.

'Praise the Lord,' Ebenezer said.

'Indeed and indeed,' Samuel Scammell said.

Campion said nothing. A coldness was on her, a fear at the very centre of her.

Her father looked at her and quoted from the same chapter of Proverbs. ' "Favour is deceitful, and beauty is vain: but a woman that feareth the Lord, she shall be praised." '

'Amen,' said Brother Scammell.

'And amen,' said Ebenezer.

'Well?' asked Matthew Slythe.

Samuel Scammell licked his lips, smiled, and patted his stomach. 'I am honoured by your offer, Brother Slythe, and have laid it prayerfully before the Lord. It is my fervent belief that I must accept.'

'Amen.'

Scammell looked at Campion. 'We are to be united as husband and wife, Miss Slythe. A happy day, indeed and indeed.'

'Amen,' said Ebenezer.

Scammell looked at Ebenezer. 'We are to be brothers, Ebenezer, in family as in God.'

'Praise Him.'

She had known, she had known, but she had not dared accept the knowledge. Her fear burned, tears pricked at her, but she would not cry in front of them. Her father was smiling at her, not in love, but as an enemy might smile when he sees his foe humiliated. 'Brother Hervey will read the banns beginning this Lord's Day.'

She nodded, incapable of fighting him. She was to be married in one month. She would be Dorcas for ever. Dorcas Slythe would become Dorcas Scammell, and she could never be Campion.

'Amen and amen,' said Samuel Scammell, 'a happy day!'

3

'You must be happy.' Goodwife's words before breakfast sounded to Campion like an order.

'I'm so happy for you,' Charity had said glumly, wishing herself to be married.

'Praise be, Dorcas,' Myrtle said and Myrtle was perhaps the only happy person in Werlatton Hall, for the dairy maid was half-witted.

'You're much blessed in your intended,' said Ebenezer, his dark eyes unreadable.

She knew she had no right to be unhappy. She had always known that she was a chattel, to be disposed of as her father wished. That was the way of fathers and daughters, and she could not expect anything different. Yet even in her darkest moods she would not have dreamed of Brother Samuel Scammell.

After morning prayers, when she turned to the door to go to the dairy, her father checked her. 'Daughter.'

'Father.'

'You are betrothed now.'

'Yes, father.'

He stood, big and powerful beside the lectern, Scammell a few paces behind. Light from a stair window slanted on to Matthew Slythe's dark and ponderous face. 'You will no longer work in the dairy. You must prepare yourself for marriage.'

'Yes, father.'

'You will acquaint yourself with the household accounts.'
He frowned. 'You have the freedom now to walk to the
village in Brother Scammell's company.'

She kept her head low. 'Yes, father.'

'You will walk there this morning with him. I have a letter
you must give to Brother Hervey.'

They walked between hedgerows heavy with cow parsley
and ragwort, away from Werlatton Hall and down the slope
to where lady's smock and meadowsweet grew. Beyond the
stream, where a bank climbed towards the beech trees,
Campion could see the blaze of pink-red where the campions
grew. The sight almost made her cry. She was now to be
Dorcas for ever, the mother of Samuel Scammell's children.
She wondered if she could ever love children who had his
fleshy lips, his lumpen face, his gaping nostrils.

Stepping stones crossed the stream beside the ford and
Scammell held a hand towards her. 'May I help you?'

'I can manage, Mr Scammell.'

'Samuel, my dear. You should call me Samuel'.

The water ran fast over the gravel between the stepping
stones, flowing north, and she glanced upstream and saw the
dark, quick shape of a fish. This was the stream in which she
swam. She almost wished that she had drowned yesterday,
that her body had floated above the long weeds, a white and
naked corpse drifting towards Lazen Castle.

The road turned south to negotiate the end of the high
ridge. It was another hot day with white clouds far to the west
and Campion's long skirts stirred dust from the track.

Scammell walked heavily, leaning forward into each step.
'I want you to know, my dear, that you have made me a very
happy man.'

'So you said at prayers, Mr Scammell.'

'A very happy man. It is my intention that we shall be
happy.'

She said nothing in reply. The wheatfield on her left was
thick with poppies and she stared at them, blind to what she
saw. She had always known this would happen, that her

father would marry her to whomsoever he pleased, and she was surprised that he had waited so long. He had said that he would wait until she showed signs of Christ's redemptive grace working in her, but she did not think that was the only reason. Ebenezer was Matthew Slythe's heir, but Ebenezer's survival had never been certain. He had always been weak, sickly and crippled, and Campion had always known that the man her father would choose as her husband might well become the heir to Werlatton. She supposed that Matthew Slythe had taken his time in searching out the right godly merchant.

Scammell cleared his throat. 'It is a beautiful day, my dear. Indeed and indeed.'

'Yes.'

She had always known this would happen, that marriage and childbirth were the events to follow her childhood, so why, she wondered, was she so saddened and horrified by the prospect? It was not as if any alternative had ever been offered to her, except in her own flimsy dreams, so why this sudden desolation at a fate she had been expecting for so long? She glanced at Scammell, provoking a nervous smile, and she could not believe that she was to marry him. She thrust the thought away. Her sense of difference was the basis of her daydreams and it was a sense that had betrayed her. She was neither special nor different, just a daughter to be disposed of in marriage.

Where the road turned north at the tip of the ridge there was a shadowed space beneath the great beeches, a place of old leaves, for beech leaves are slow to decay, crossed by a fallen trunk. Scammell turned into the shade. 'May we pause, my dear?'

She stopped at the edge of the road.

Scammell wiped the sweat from his brow with a handkerchief, then brushed at the smooth, barkless wood of the fallen trunk and gestured for her to sit down. She could see that he planned to sit beside her, close beside her, so she shook her head. 'I will stand, Mr Scammell.'

He pushed the handkerchief into his sleeve. 'I wished to talk with you.'

She said nothing. She stood at the road's edge in the bright sunlight, refusing to go into the green shadows with him.

He smiled his unctuous smile. The sun was behind her, making it difficult for him to see her. He stood awkwardly. 'It will be a joy once more to have family. My dear mother, God bless her, passed away last year to be buried with my father. Yes, indeed.' He smiled, but she did not respond. He moved heavily from one fleshy leg to the other. 'So you see I am quite alone, my dear, which means my joy is doubled by uniting myself with your dear family.' He sat down, plumping his large bottom up and down on the fallen trunk as if to demonstrate the comfort of the smooth wood. He subsided slowly as he realized that the gesture would not entice her from the dusty road. 'Indeed and indeed.' He seemed to sigh.

I could run now, she thought, run through the poppies and the wheat to the great stand of oaks that marks the southern boundary of father's land, and then keep running. She had the thought of sleeping wild like the deer that sometimes came to the stream, of feeding herself, and she knew she could not run. She knew no one outside Werlatton, she had never travelled more than four miles from the house; she had no money, no friends, no hope.

Scammell leaned forward, elbows on knees, hands clasped as if in prayer. He was sweating in the heat with his thick broadcloth clothes. 'Your father suggested I talk to you of the future.'

Still she said nothing.

He smiled hopefully. 'We are to live here in Werlatton with your dear family, so you will not have to leave home. Indeed, no. Your father, alas, gets no younger and he desires assistance with his affairs. Of course, when dear Ebenezer—I think of him already as a brother—is of age then our help may not be needed and then, perhaps, we shall return to London.' He nodded, as if pleased with himself. 'We have put all this before the Lord in prayer, my dear, so you may be sure that it is the wisest course.'

He frowned suddenly, shifting his buttocks on the trunk. He kept his concentrated frown and leaned forward in silence. It struck her that he was passing wind and she laughed aloud.

He leaned back, relaxing. 'You are happy, my dear?'

She knew she should not have laughed, but she could feel the temptation to be cruel to this man. He waited for her answer which came in a low, modest voice. 'Do I have a choice, Mr Scammell?'

He looked uneasy, unhappy, frowning again at her reply. There seemed small profit to him in answering her. He smiled again. 'Your father has been most generous, most generous in his marriage settlement. Indeed and indeed. Most generous.' He looked for a response, but she was still and silent in the sunlight. He blinked. 'You know of the Covenant?'

'No.' Against her will her curiosity was touched.

'Ah!' He sounded surprised. 'You are a fortunate woman, my dear, to be blessed by the Lord with wealth and, dare I say, beauty?' He chuckled.

Wealthy? Covenant? She wanted to know more, but she could not bring herself to ask. If she had to marry this man then so be it, she had no choice, but she would not force herself to show a happiness and eagerness that she did not feel. She would resist the temptation to be cruel and maybe the love would grow, but she could feel the tears stinging her eyes as she looked over his head at the sunlight carving through the beeches on to the leaves of the previous autumn. By the time the leaves fell again she would be married, sharing a bed with Samuel Scammell.

'No!' She had not meant to speak aloud.

'My dear?' He looked eagerly at her.

'No, no, no!' She could feel the tears now and she rushed her words, hoping the speech would hold them back, as her resolve to submit with silent dignity broke almost as soon as it was born. 'I want to marry, sir, and I want to marry in love, and have my children in love, and raise them in love.' She stopped, the tears flowing now, and she knew the futility of her words, the unreality, and her head throbbed with the horror of marriage to this slack-lipped, piss-splashing, wind-passing man. She was angry, not at him, but because she had broken into tears in front of him. 'I do not want this marriage, I do not want any marriage, I would rather die . . .' She stopped. She would rather die than have her children raised in Matthew Slythe's house, but she could not say so for fear the words would be passed back to him. Despite her incoherence and her tears, she was seething with anger at Scammell.

He was aghast. He wanted this marriage, he had wanted it ever since Matthew Slythe had proposed the settlement, because marrying Dorcas Slythe would make Samuel Scammell into a very rich man. Then, last night, he had seen her and he had wanted the marriage even more. Matthew Slythe had not described his daughter and Scammell had been astonished by her beauty.

Last night he had not believed his good fortune. She was a girl of astounding beauty and of calm presence who stirred the fleshly lust in him. Now that same grave, dutiful girl had turned on him, scorned him, and he stood up, frowning.

'A child must be obedient to its parents, as a wife is obedient to her husband.' He had adopted his preacher's voice, stern and full. He was nervous, but Matthew Slythe had impressed on him the need for firmness. 'We live in God's love, not an earthly love of flesh and pleasure.' He was in his stride now, as if talking to the congregation of Saints. 'Earthly love is corruptible, as flesh is corruptible, but we are called to a heavenly love, God's love, and a sacrament holy to Him and his Son.' She shook her head, helpless against the Puritan harangue, and he stepped towards her, his voice louder. ' "Whom the Lord loveth he chasteneth!" '

She looked at him, bitterness in her soul, and she gave him a text in return. ' "My father hath chastised you with whips, but I will chastise you with scorpions." '

Scammell glared at her. 'Am I to tell your father that you reject his wishes?'

She was beaten and she knew it. If she rejected this man then her father would lock her in her room, feed her on bread and water and then, as the sun faded in the west, he would come to her, the thick leather belt in his hand. He would flail it at her, bellowing that this was God's will and that she had sinned. She could not bear the thought of the bruises and the blood, the whimpering beneath the whistling lash of the belt. 'No.'

Scammell rocked back and forth. He dropped his voice to a whining, unctuous level. 'It is understandable that you are upset, my dear. Women are prone to be upset, indeed and indeed. The weaker sex, yes?' He laughed, to show that he was sympathetic. 'You will find, my dear, that God has made a woman's way easy through obedience. Let the woman be subject to her husband. In obedience you will be saved the unhappiness of choice. You must see me now as your shepherd, and we will live in the house of the Lord for ever.' He leaned forward, magnanimous in victory, to kiss her on the cheek.

She stepped back from him. 'We are not yet married, sir.'

'Indeed and indeed.' He saved his balance by stepping forward. 'Modesty, like obedience, is pleasing in a woman.' He felt bitter. He wanted this girl. He wanted to paw at her, to kiss her, yet he felt a fear of her. No matter. In a month they would be married and she would be his property. He clasped his hands together, cracked his knuckles, and walked on to the road. 'Shall we continue, my dear? We have a letter for Brother Hervey.'

The Reverend Hervey, vicar of the parish of Werlatton, had been christened Thomas by his parents, but in the sudden religious zeal that had swept England in recent years, a zeal that had erupted into war between King and Parliament, he had taken a new name. Like many Puritans he felt that his name should be a witness to the truth and he had prayed long and hard over the choices. One of his acquaintances had adopted the name of And I Shall Bind Them In Fetters Of Iron Smith, which the Reverend Hervey liked, but thought a little over long. There was also the Reverend His Mercy Endureth For Ever Potter who dribbled and had the shakes, and if Potter had been called to glory then Hervey might have taken that name, despite its length, but the Reverend Potter lived up to his adopted name by living into a sickly and senile ninth decade.

Finally, after much searching of the scriptures and much frenzied prayer seeking God's guidance, he settled on a name that was neither too long nor too short, and which he felt was distinguished by force and dignity. He had made a name for himself and the name would make him famous and all England would know of the Reverend Faithful Unto Death Hervey.

For indeed, the Reverend Faithful Unto Death Hervey was a man of vaunting ambition. He had been fortunate, five years before, when Matthew Slythe had plucked him from an unhappy curacy and offered him the living of Werlatton. It was a good living, paid for by the Hall, and Faithful Unto Death received no less than thirty pounds a year from Matthew Slythe. Yet he yearned for more, for his ambition was overpowering, and he suffered torments of jealousy when other divines gained the fame that was denied to him.

He was now thirty-two years old, unmarried, and, despite his fashionable change of name, quite unknown outside the county. This was not entirely Faithful Unto Death's fault. Two years before, in 1641, the Irish Catholics had rebelled against their English overlords and sent a shiver of horror through Protestant England. This shiver, Faithful Unto Death decided, would become the wave that would sweep him into prominence. He wrote a pamphlet, that lengthened to a book, that became a manuscript equal to two books, purporting to be an eyewitness account of 'The Horrors of the Late Massacres Perpetrated by the Irish Catholicks Upon

the Peacefulle Protestants of That Lande'. He had not been to Ireland, nor was he acquainted with anyone who had, but he did not see this as a hindrance to his first-person account. God, he knew, would guide his pen.

He equipped himself with a map of Ireland from which he drew the names of towns and villages, and had he kept his account brief and bloody, then he might well have been rewarded by the fame he sought so eagerly. Yet brevity was not within his power. Feverishly he wrote, night after night, his pen embellishing his nightmare thoughts. Rape came easily to his imagination, though at too great length, and by the time his catalogue of ravished Protestant virgins reached the London book publishers, two other men had already printed their own histories and had offered them for sale. The Reverend Faithful Unto Death Hervey had missed the tide. His book was returned, unprinted.

If the ignorance of the world of his own abilities was one disappointment to Faithful Unto Death, then there was another equal sadness in his life. A clergyman with thirty pounds a year should not have lacked for a bride, but Faithful Unto Death had fixed his ambition on just one girl, a girl he thought a fit and meet companion for his rising life and a girl who could endow him with worldly goods. He wanted to marry Dorcas Slythe.

He had wanted her for five years, watching her from his low pulpit and seeking every opportunity to visit Werlatton Hall and stare at her beauty. The absence of other suitors had encouraged him to approach Matthew Slythe and propose himself as her husband, but Slythe had scorned him. He had been short, brutal, and unmistakable. The Reverend Faithful Unto Death Hervey was never to speak of the matter again. Yet Slythe's dismissal had not diminished Hervey's lust. He wanted Dorcas so much that it hurt.

Now, sitting in his garden making notes on the sermon he must preach on Sunday, she was announced to him. His dream bride in person, come with her betrothed.

It was a bitter moment for Faithful Unto Death, bitter as

gall, but he had no choice but to welcome them. He fussed about Samuel Scammell, knowing that one day this man could be his paymaster, and he hated inwardly what he fawned on outwardly. 'Fine weather, Brother Scammell.'

'Indeed and indeed. I was saying so to dear Dorcas.'

Dear Dorcas was staring at the grass, saying nothing. She did not like Hervey, had never liked him and she did not want to look at his raw, lugubrious face with its long neck and wobbling Adam's apple. Hervey ducked to look at her face. 'You walked here, Miss Slythe?'

She was tempted to say that they had come on broomsticks. 'Yes.'

'A fine day for a walk.'

'Yes.'

Matthew Slythe's letter was laid on the sundial while Faithful Unto Death fussed about bringing a bench from the house. Campion sat on the bench, moving away from the pressure of Scammell's bulging thigh, while Hervey scanned the letter. 'So the banns are to be read?'

'Yes.' Scammell fanned his face with his black hat.

'Good, good.'

The religious turmoil of England might have driven the Book of Common Prayer from many parishes, but the forms were kept up for marriages and deaths. The law would be complied with, and the banns would be read on three successive Sundays, giving the parishioners a chance to object against the marriage. No one, Campion knew, would raise an objection. There were no objections to be raised.

The two men discussed the service, choosing which psalms would be sung and at what hour of the morning it should take place. Campion let their voices pass her by like the buzzing of the bees who worked the blossoms of Faithful Unto Death's garden. She was to be married. It seemed like a judgement of doom. She was to be married.

They stayed an hour and left with many statements of mutual esteem between Brother Hervey and Brother Scammell. They had knelt for a brief prayer, ten minutes only, in which Faithful Unto Death had drawn the Almighty's attention to the happy pair and asked Him to shower blessings on their richly deserving heads.

Faithful Unto Death watched them walk away through the village, his guts twisted up inside with envy. Hatred rose in him: for Matthew Slythe who had denied him his daughter and for Samuel Scammell who had gained her. Yet Faithful Unto Death would not give up. He believed in the power of prayer and he returned to his garden and there looked up verses in the book of Deuteronomy: 'When thou goest forth to war against thine enemies, and the Lord thy God hath delivered them into thine hands, and thou hast taken them captive, and seest among the captives a beautiful woman, and hast a desire unto her, that thou wouldest have her to thy wife; then thou shalt bring her home to thine house.'

He prayed for it to come true, his thin face screwed tight in concentration, praying that one day Dorcas Slythe would be his captive. It was thus that his friend Ebenezer Slythe found him a half hour later when he arrived for his daily talk.

'Brother Hervey?'

'Ebenezer! Dear Ebenezer!' Faithful Unto Death struggled to his feet. 'Wrestling with the Lord!'

'Amen and amen.' They blinked at each other in the sunlight, then settled down with open scriptures and bitter hearts.

Campion dreamed of an escape that she knew was impossible. She thought of a red-headed man who had laughed in the stream, who had relaxed beside her on the grass, who had talked to her as though they were old friends. Toby Lazender was in London and she did not know if he would even remember her. She thought of running away, but where was she to run? She had no money, no friends, and if, in her desperation, she thought of writing to Toby Lazender, she knew no one who could be trusted to carry the letter to Lazen Castle.

Each passing day brought new reminders of her fate.

Goodwife Baggerlie approved of the marriage. 'He's a good man, God be praised, and a good provider. A woman can want no more.'

Another day, listening to Goodwife list the possessions of the house and where they were stored, she heard another part of her future being planned. 'There's good swaddling clothes and a crib. They were yours and Ebenezer's, and we kept them in case more should be born.' 'We', to Goodwife, always referred to herself and Campion's mother, two bitter women united in friendship. Goodwife looked critically at Campion. 'You'll have a child before next year's out, though with your hips I'll be bound it will be trouble! Where you get them I don't know. Ebenezer's thin, but he's spread in the hips. Your mother, God rest her soul, was a big woman and your father's not narrow in the loins.' She sniffed. 'God's will be done.'

Faithful Unto Death Hervey read the banns once, twice and then a third time. The day came close. She would never be Campion, never know love, and she yearned for love.

'By night on my bed I sought him whom my soul loveth.' And by night on her bed Campion tossed in an agony of apprehension. Would Scammell take her as a bull took a heifer? She cringed from her imagination, hearing his grunts, feeling the hanging weight of his great body as he mounted her. She imagined the fleshy lips at the nape of her neck and she cried out helplessly in her bed. Charity stirred in her sleep.

Campion saw her own death as she gave birth, dropping a sleek, bloody mess as she had seen cows drop. Sometimes she thought it would be simpler to die before the wedding.

Her father spoke to her only once about her wedding and that three days before the ceremony. He came upon her in the pantry where she was slapping butter into great squares for the table. He seemed surprised to see her and he stared at her.

She smiled. 'Father?'

'You are working.'

'Yes, father.'

He picked up the muslin that covered the butter jar, twisting it in his huge hands. 'I have brought you up in the faith. I have done well.'

She sensed that he needed reassurance. 'Yes, father.'

'He's a good man. A man of God.'

'Yes, father.'

'He will be a tower of strength. Yes. A tower of strength. And you are well provided for.'

'Thank you, father.' She could see that he was about to leave so, before he could disentangle his hands from the muslin, she asked the question that had intrigued her since Scammell had spoken to her beneath the beech trees. 'Father?'

'Daughter?'

'What is the Covenant, father?'

His heavy face was still, staring at her, the question being weighed in the balance of his mind. A pulse throbbed in his temple.

She would always remember the moment. It was the only occasion when she knew her father to lie. Matthew Slythe, for all his anger, was a man who tried to be honest, tried to be true to his hard God, yet at that moment, she knew, he lied. 'It is a dowry, no more. It is for your husband, of course, so it is not your concern.'

The muslin had torn in his hands.

Matthew Slythe prayed that night, he prayed for forgiveness, that the sin of lying would be forgiven. He groaned as he thought of the Covenant. It had brought him riches beyond hope, but it had brought him Dorcas as well. He had tried to break her spirit, to make her a worthy servant of his harsh God, but he feared for her if she should ever know the true nature of the Covenant. She could be rich and independent and she might achieve that effortless happiness that Slythe sensed in her and feared as the devil's mark. The money of the Covenant was not for happiness. It was, in Matthew Slythe's plans, money to be spent on spreading the fear of God to a sinful world. He prayed that Dorcas would never, ever, discover the truth.

His daughter prayed, too. She had known, she did not know how, that her father had lied. She prayed that night and the next that she would be spared the horror of marrying Samuel Scammell. She prayed, as she had ever done, for happiness and for the love God promised.

On the eve of her wedding it seemed that God might be listening.

It was a fine, sunny day, a day of high summer, and, in the early afternoon, her father died.

4

'Apoplexy,' Dr Fenderlyn said.

'Sir?'

'Apoplexy, Dorcas.' Fenderlyn stood beside his horse at the entrance to Werlatton Hall. 'Too much blood, child, that's all. I could have bled him last week, if I'd known, but he wouldn't come to me. Power of prayer!' He said the last scornfully as he slowly climbed the mounting block. 'Urine, child, urine! Send your physician urine regularly and you might have a chance, you might . . .' He shrugged, drawing in a hiss of breath that suggested everything was doomed anyway. 'You're not looking well, child. Too much yellow bile in you. I can give you an emetic, it's better than prayer.'

'No, thank you, sir.' Campion had been given one of Fenderlyn's emetics in the past, dark brown and slimy, and she could still remember the desperate breath-stealing vomit that had erupted to the doctor's grave approval.

He gathered the reins of his horse, swung his leg across the saddle and settled himself. 'You heard the news, Dorcas?'

'News, sir?'

'The King's taken Bristol. I suppose the Royalists will win now.' He grunted approvingly. 'Still, I suppose you've got other things on your mind. You were to be married tomorrow?'

'Yes, sir.'

'Not now, child, not now.' Fenderlyn said it gloomily, but the words were like an angelic message in her head. The doctor pulled his hat straight. 'It'll be a funeral not a wedding. Fine weather, Dorcas! Bury him soon. I suppose he'll want to rest beside your mother?'

'Yes, sir.'

'I'll make sure Hervey opens up the grave. Heigh ho. Another one gone.' He looked up at the eaves of the Hall where the house martins had their nests. 'It comes to us all, child, comes to us all. Apoplexy, the stone, strangury, the gout, epilepsy, leprosy, botches, plague, fistula, cankerworm, dropsy, gut-twisting, rupture, goitre, fever, the pox, tetterworm, the sweat, gripes.' He shook his head, relishing the list. 'It's only the young who think they'll live for ever.' Dr Fenderlyn was seventy-eight years old and had never had a day's illness in his life. It had made him a cheerless man, expecting the worst. 'What will you do, Dorcas?'

'Do, sir?'

'I suppose you'll marry Mr Scammell and breed me more patients?'

'I don't know, sir.' There was a joy in Campion, a leaping joy because she did not know what the future held. She knew only that the marriage had been postponed and she felt as a condemned prisoner must when the gaoler announces a reprieve.

'I'll bid you good day, Dorcas.' Fenderlyn touched his whip to the brim of his hat. 'Tell that brother of yours to send me some urine. Never thought he'd survive weaning, but here he is. Life's full of surprises. Be of good cheer!' He said the last miserably.

Ebenezer had found his father dead, slumped over his study table, and on Matthew Slythe's face was a snarl that had been there so often in life. His fist was clenched as if, at the last moment, he had tried to hold on to life and not go to the heaven he had looked forward to for so long. He had lived fifty-four years, a good length for most men, and death had come very suddenly.

Campion knew she should not feel released, yet she did, and it was an effort to stand beside the grave, looking down at the decaying wood of her mother's coffin, without showing the pleasure of the moment. She joined in the 23rd psalm, then listened as Faithful Unto Death Hervey rejoiced that Brother Matthew Slythe had been called home, had been translated into glory, had crossed the river Jordan to join the company of Saints and even now was part of the eternal choir that hymned God's majesty in the celestial skies. Campion tried to imagine her father's dark browed, ponderous scowl in the ranks of the angels.

After the service, as earth was shovelled on to her father's coffin, Faithful Unto Death Hervey took her to one side. His fingers gripped her arm tightly. 'A sad day, Miss Slythe.'

'Yes.'

'Yet you will meet in heaven.'

'Yes, sir.'

Hervey glanced back at the mourners, out of earshot. His straw-coloured hair fell lank on his thin, pointed face. His Adam's apple bobbed up and down as he swallowed. 'And what, pray, will you do now?'

'Now?' She tried to pull her arm away, but Faithful Unto Death kept firm hold of it. His eyes, pale as his hair, flicked left and right.

'Grief is a hard burden, Miss Slythe.'

'Yes, sir.'

'And not one that should be borne alone.' His fingers tightened on her upper arm, hurting her. He smiled. 'I am the shepherd of this flock, Miss Slythe, and I stand ready to help you in any way I can. You do understand that?'

'You're hurting me.'

'My dear Miss Slythe!' His hand leaped from her arm then

hovered close to her shoulder. 'Perhaps together we can pray for the balm of Gilead?'

'I know you will pray for us, Mr Hervey.'

It was not the answer Faithful Unto Death wanted. He was imagining emotional scenes in the Hall, Campion perhaps prostrate on her bed with grief while he administered comfort, and he began to blink rapidly as his imagination stirred thick with the image.

Samuel Scammell walked over to them, breaking Hervey's thoughts, and thanked the minister for the service. 'You'll come to the Hall tomorrow, brother? Mr Blood has the will, indeed yes.' He licked his lips and smiled at Hervey. 'I think our dear departed brother may have remembered your good works.'

'Yes. Yes.'

The household waited for Scammell and Campion beside the farm cart that had brought Slythe's body to the churchyard. Ebenezer was already mounted beside the cart, drooping in the saddle, his twisted left leg supported by a specially large stirrup. He held Scammell's horse. 'Brother Scammell?' He held the reins out, then looked at his sister. 'You'll go in the cart with the servants.' His voice was harsh.

'I shall walk, Ebenezer.'

'It is not seemly.'

'I shall walk, Ebenezer! I want to be alone!'

'Leave her, leave her!' Scammell soothed Ebenezer, nodded to Tobias Horsnell, who had the reins of the cart-horse, and Campion watched them go.

It took all of her control not to run across the ridge down the hayfields and the stream, and there to strip naked and swim in the pool for the sheer, clean joy of it. She dawdled instead, relishing the freedom of being alone, and she climbed part way up through the beeches and felt the wings of her soul stretching free at last. She hugged one of the trees as though it was animate, clinging to it in joy, feeling the seething happiness because a great weight was gone from her.

She put her cheek against the bark. 'Thank you, thank you.'

That night she slept alone, ordering Charity from her room, insisting on it. She locked the door and almost danced for the joy of it. She was alone! She undressed with the curtains and windows open and saw the touch of the moon on the ripening wheat. She leaned on the sill, stared into the night, and thought her joy would flood the land. She was not married! Kneeling beside the high bed, hands clasped, she thanked God for her reprieve. She vowed to Him that she would be good, but that she would be free.

Then Isaac Blood came from Dorchester.

He had a white face, lined with age, and grey hair that hung to his collar. He was Matthew Slythe's lawyer and, because he had known Slythe well and knew what to expect at Werlatton Hall, he had brought his own bottle of malmsey wine which he eked into a small glass and sipped often. The servants faced him, sitting on the benches where they gathered for prayers, while Samuel Scammell and Faithful Unto Death flanked Campion and Ebenezer on the family bench. Isaac Blood fussed at the lectern, arranging the will over the family Bible, then fetched a small table on which his wine could stand.

Goodwife Baggerlie, in memory of her good, loyal and God-fearing service, was to receive a hundred pounds. She dabbed her red-rimmed eyes with her apron. 'God bless him! God bless him!'

Faithful Unto Death had been surprised at the legacy. It was an enormous amount. His eyes watched Goodwife and he assumed that Slythe would be more generous with a man of God than with a house-servant. He smiled to himself, and waited as Isaac Blood sipped malmsey and wiped his lips.

'To our Brother Faithful Unto Death Hervey,' Isaac Blood began reading again, and Scammell leaned forward on the bench and smiled at the vicar. Hervey kept his eyes on the lawyer. 'I know,' went on Blood, 'that he will not wish distraction from his humble toiling in God's vineyard, so we will not burden him beyond his desires.'

Hervey frowned. Blood sipped his wine. 'Five pounds.'

Five pounds! Five! Hervey stiffened on the bench, aware that all the servants were watching him, and he felt the agony of insignificance, of virtue unrewarded, of hatred for Matthew Slythe. Five pounds! It turned out to be the same sum that went to Tobias Horsnell and some of the other servants. Five pounds!

Blood was unaware of the seething indignation to his left. 'To my beloved children, Samuel and Dorcas Scammell, go those properties described in the marriage settlement.'

Scammell grunted in satisfaction and nudged Campion beside him on the bench. The truth was slow to dawn on her. The marriage settlement? It was part of her father's will, so that his death had solved nothing. She began to feel the despair, of the last few weeks return. Even from the grave Matthew Slythe would control her.

Werlatton Hall, its farms, fields, and all the tenancies attached, went, as expected, to Ebenezer. Her brother did not move as he listened to the wealth shower on him, except to smile at Scammell when the will dictated that Brother Samuel Scammell would administer the wide estate until Ebenezer was of age. If Ebenezer should die without issue, then the Werlatton properties passed intact to Samuel Scammell.

There was little more to the will, except a homily on righteousness that Isaac Blood read tonelessly. It was Matthew Slythe's last sermon in this hall. Campion did not listen. One thing only was clear to her; that she was a chattel, disposed of in her father's will, bequeathed to Samuel Scammell.

The sermon over, Isaac Blood folded the stiff papers and looked at the servants. 'It was Matthew Slythe's wish that you all continue in service here. I assume that is your wish too?' He asked the question of Scammell, who smiled, nodded, and made a vague gesture of welcome towards the benches.

'Good, good.' Blood sipped his malmsey. 'And now I would ask the immediate family to stay here alone.' He indicated Scammell, Ebenezer and Dorcas who waited on their bench as the servants filed obediently from the room. Faithful Unto Death, unhappy to be lumped with the household servants, hovered expectantly, but Isaac Blood chivvied him politely from the room. The lawyer closed the door and turned back to the family. 'Your father's will had one more instruction. If you will be so good as to wait.' He went back to the lectern and laboriously unfolded the papers again. 'Ah! Here it is.'

He cleared his throat, sipped some wine and held the paper up to his bloodless face. 'I was instructed to read this to you in private, and I shall now do so. "My duty to the Covenant is discharged by appointing Samuel Scammell, my son-in-law, to be the holder of the seal in my possession. Should he die before my daughter has reached the age of twenty-five, then the guardianship of the seal will pass to my son, Ebenezer, who will, I know, obey the terms of the Covenant." ' Isaac Blood glanced sternly at Campion, then looked back at the paper. ' "Should my daughter, Dorcas, die before her twenty-fifth year and leave no issue, then whoever is the holder of the seal will direct that the monies of the Covenant be used for the spreading of the Gospel to the unenlightened." There, I've read it now.' Blood looked at Scammell. 'You understand, Mr Scammell?'

'Indeed and indeed,' Scammell smiled and nodded vigorously.

'Master Ebenezer?'

Ebenezer nodded, though Campion could see a small frown on his face as though he did not fully understand.

'Miss Dorcas?'

'No, I don't understand.'

This was unexpected, for Isaac Blood started with some surprise, and then looked annoyed. 'You don't understand?'

Campion stood and walked towards the north-facing windows. 'What is the Covenant, Mr Blood?' She felt that her wings had been mangled, torn, bloodied, and she was plummeting helpless to earth. Her father's death had solved nothing, merely delayed the wedding.

The lawyer ignored her question. He was bundling his papers together. 'If you will permit some small advice? I would suggest a quiet wedding in the near future. Six weeks perhaps? It would not be unfitting.' He peered heavily at Samuel Scammell. 'You understand, Mr Scammell, that the will supposed your marriage, and your position in the household is dependent upon it?'

'I do understand, yes.'

'And, of course, it would be Matthew Slythe's wish that the happy event was not overlong delayed. Things must be regular, Mr Scammell. Regular!'

'Indeed and indeed.' Scammell stood to show the lawyer out.

Campion turned from the window. 'Mr Blood, you did not answer my question. What is the Covenant?'

Her father had been embarrassed by the question, but the lawyer shrugged dismissively. 'Your marriage portion, Miss Slythe. The estate, of course, was always destined for your brother, but your father made arrangements for your dowry. I fear I know little more. It was handled by a lawyer in London, but I suspect you will find yourself generously provided for.'

'Indeed,' Scammell nodded at her, eager for her to be pleased.

There was a brief silence. Campion's question had been answered and it had offered her no hope of escaping marriage with Scammell. Then Ebenezer's grating voice was loud in the room. 'What is "generously"? How much is the Covenant worth?'

Isaac Blood shrugged. 'I do not know.'

Scammell raised his eyebrows archly, fidgeted, and looked pleased with himself. He was bursting with his news, eager to impress the beautiful, golden-haired girl whom he wanted to embrace. He wanted Campion to approve of him, to like him, and he hoped that his next words would break the dam of her withheld feelings. 'I can answer that question, indeed I can.' He smiled at Campion. 'Last year, as near as we can judge, the Covenant yielded ten thousand pounds.'

'Dear God!' Isaac Blood held on to the lectern.

Ebenezer stood up slowly, his face animated for the first time that day. 'How much?'

'Ten thousand pounds.' Scammell said it humbly, as though he were responsible for the profit yet did not want to sound boastful. 'It fluctuates, of course. Some years more, some less.'

'Ten thousand pounds?' Ebenezer's voice was rising in shocked anger. 'Ten thousand?' It was a sum of such vast proportions that it was scarcely conceivable. A King's ransom, a fortune, a sum far in excess of Werlatton's income. Ebenezer might expect £700 a year from the estate and now he was hearing that his sister had been given far, far more.

Scammell giggled with pleasure. 'Indeed and indeed.' Now, perhaps, Campion would marry him with a glad heart. They would be rich as few in this world are rich. 'You're surprised, my dear?'

Campion shared her brother's disbelief. Ten thousand pounds! It was an unthinkable sum. She was grasping for understanding and failing, but she remembered the words of the will and ignored Samuel Scammell. 'Mr Blood? Do I comprehend the will to mean that the money becomes mine when I am twenty-five?'

'Quite so, quite so.' Isaac Blood was looking at her with a new respect. 'Not, of course, if you are married, for then the monies will be your dear husband's, as is proper. But should he predecease you,' here Blood made an apologetic motion towards Scammell, 'then, of course, you will take the seal into your own keeping. That much, I think, is clear from the will.'

'The seal?' Ebenezer had limped close to the lectern.

Blood was pouring the last of the malmsey into his glass. 'It merely authenticates the signature on any paper dealing with the Covenant.'

'But where is it, Mr Blood? Where is it?' Ebenezer was unusually animated.

The lawyer drank the sweet wine, then shrugged. 'How would I know, Master Ebenezer? I assume it is in your father's belongings.' He stared regretfully into the empty wine glass. 'You should look for it. I recommend a diligent search.'

He left, after expressing perfunctory but profound sympathies for their sad loss, and Ebenezer and Scammell escorted the lawyer to his horse. Campion was left alone. The sun slanted through leaded windows on to the polished, waxed floorboards. She was still a prisoner here; the fortune of the Covenant changed nothing. She did not understand all the legalities; she only understood that she was trapped.

Samuel Scammell came back into the hall, his shoes squeaking on the boards. 'My dear? Our fortune surprised you?'

She looked wearily at him. 'Leave me alone. Please? Leave me alone.'

It was August now, a high, ripening August that promised better crops than for years past. Campion walked through the scented fields, avoiding those where anyone worked, seeking always the solitary places where she could sit and think. She ate alone, slept alone, yet her presence pervaded Werlatton Hall. It was as if her father's force, his ability to impose a mood upon the house, had passed to her. Goodwife Baggerlie resented it most. 'She's got a devil in her, master, you mark my words!'

'Grief is hard,' Scammell said.

'Grief! She's not grieving!' Goodwife crossed her arms and stared defiantly at Scammell. 'She needs a beating, master, that's all! A good beating! That'll teach her her place. Her father would have beaten her, God rest his soul, and so you should.' Goodwife began vigorously dusting the hall table where Scammell was finishing a lonely lunch. 'She's lacked for nothing, that girl, nothing! If I'd been given her advantages . . .' She tutted, leaving it to Scammell's imagination what heights Goodwife might have scaled had she been Matthew Slythe's daughter. 'Give her a beating, master! Belts aren't just for holding up breeches!'

Scammell was master now, doling out the servants' wages and collecting the estate's rents. Ebenezer helped him, sharing the work and always seeking to ingratiate himself with the older man. They shared a concern, too. The seal of the Covenant could not be found.

Campion did not care. The existence of the Covenant with its extraordinary income did not help her. She was still trapped in a marriage she did not want and neither ten pounds nor ten thousand would reconcile her to Scammell. It was not, she knew, that he was a bad man, though she suspected he was a weak man. He might, she supposed, make a good husband, but not for her. She wanted to be happy, she wanted to be free, and Scammell's flabby lust was inadequate compensation for the abandonment of her dreams. She was Dorcas and she wanted to be Campion.

She did not swim again—there was no joy in that now—yet she still visited the pool where the purple loosestrife was in flower and remembered Toby Lazender. She could not summon his face in her imagination any more, yet she remembered his gentle teasing, his easy manner, and she daydreamed that one day he might come back to the pool, and rescue her from Werlatton and its crushing rule of the Saints.

She was thinking of Toby one afternoon, a smile on her face for she was imagining him coming, when there were hoofbeats in the meadow behind and she turned, the smile still there, and watched as Ebenezer rode towards her. 'Sister.'

She held the smile for him. 'Eb.' She had hoped, for one mad, exhilarating second, that it was Toby. Instead her brother's face scowled at her.

She had never been close to Ebenezer, though she had tried

so hard. When she had played games in the kitchen garden, safe from her parents' prying eyes, Ebenezer would never join in. He preferred to sit with his open Bible, memorising the chapter ordained by his father for the day, and even then he had watched his sister with a jaundiced, jealous gaze. Yet he was her brother, her only relative, and Campion had thought much about him during the week. Perhaps Ebenezer could be an ally. She patted the grass beside her. 'Come and sit down. I wanted to talk to you.'

'I'm busy.' He frowned on her. Since their father's death he had adopted an air of burdened dignity, never more evident than when he shared the ministration of household prayers with Samuel Scammell. 'I've come for the key to your room.'

'What for?'

'It's not for you to ask what for!' His anger showed as petulance. He held out a hand. 'I demand it, isn't that enough? Brother Scammell and I wish to have it! If our dear father was alive you would not be skulking behind locked doors!'

She stood up, brushing the grass from her skirt and unhooked the key from the ring at her waist. 'You can have it Eb, but you'll have to tell me why you want it.' She spoke patiently.

He glared at her, his face shadowed by his wide-brimmed, black hat. 'We are searching, sister, for the seal.'

She laughed at that. 'It's not in my room, Eb.'

'It isn't funny, Dorcas! It isn't funny! It's for your benefit, remember, not mine! I don't get ten thousand a year from it!'

She had held the key towards him, but now she withdrew her hand. She shook her head. 'You don't understand, Eb, do you? I don't want ten thousand pounds. I don't want anything! I just want to be alone. I don't want to marry Mr Scammell. We can look after the money, Eb. You and I. We don't need Mr Scammell!' The words were tumbling out now. 'I've thought about it Eb, I really have. We can live here and you can take the money and when you marry I'll go and live in a house in the village, and we can be happy, Eb! Happy!'

His face had not moved as she spoke. He watched her sourly, disliking her as he always had because she could run while he could not; she could swim naked in a stream while he dragged his twisted, shrunken leg behind him. Now he shook his head. 'You're trying to tempt me, aren't you? You're offering me money, and why? Because you dislike Brother Scammell. The answer is no, sister. No.' He threw up a hand to stop her interrupting. 'It sounds so good, just you and me, but I know what you'd do! You'd run away with the money as soon as you were twenty-five. Well you won't, sister, because you're going to marry, and when you're married you'll learn that Brother Scammell and I have an agreement. We will share the money, Dorcas, all three of us, because that's what Brother Scammell wants. It's what our father would have wanted and have you thought of that? You think that because he's dead all his hopes are to be destroyed? That all he prayed for should be destroyed?' Ebenezer shook his head again. 'One day, Dorcas, we will meet him again and in a better place than this, and I want him to thank me on that day for being a good and faithful son.'

'Eb?'

'The key, sister.' He thrust his hand out again.

'You're wrong, Eb.'

'The key!'

She gave it to him, then watched as he wrenched violently at the horse's rein, rowelled savagely with his right spur, and galloped towards the house.

She sat again, the stream placid in front of her, and she knew that her dreams were vain. Ebenezer disliked her, she did not know why, and she suspected that he enjoyed her misery. Ebenezer had inherited more than anger from his father, he had taken too the streak of cruelty that had been in Matthew Slythe. She remembered when Ebenezer was ten how she had found him in the orchard, Clark's *Martyrologie* open beside him. The page showed Romish priests disembowelling a Protestant martyr, and she had screamed in anger because, tied to an apple tree, was a small kitten on which Ebenezer was copying the torture, tearing at its tiny, soft stomach with a knife. She had dragged him away from the blood-soaked tree, away from the yowling kitten, and Ebenezer had spat at her, clawed at her, and shouted spitefully that this was the tenth kitten he had so killed. She had been forced to kill the kitten herself, cutting the little throat, and she could remember Ebenezer laughing.

Now Ebenezer was in league with Samuel Scammell. Her marriage portion was to be divided between them and she would have no say in the matter.

There was nothing for her in Werlatton. She watched where the stream ran strong and calm past the pool's entrance, and she thought that she must leave. She should go with the stream, seeing where it led, and even though she knew that it would be impossible to run away, she knew too that it would be impossible to stay.

She stood up, sad in the afternoon sun, and walked slowly back towards the house.

She entered through the side passage that led past her father's study. The lawn was pungent with the smell of newly scythed grass, the sunlight so bright that she was temporarily blinded when she walked into the darkness of the passage. She did not see the man who stood in the door of her father's room.

'The bowels of Christ. Who are you?'

Her shoulder was gripped, she was pushed against the wall, and the man grinned at her. 'Sweet God! A little Puritan maid. Well, well.' He tilted her chin up with his finger. 'A ripe little piece of fruit.'

'Sir!' It was Samuel Scammell's voice. He hurried out of the study. 'Sir! That is Miss Slythe. We are to marry!'

The man let her go. He was big, as big as her father had been, and his face was scarred and ugly. It was a broad face, hard as leather, with a broken nose. At his side was a sword, in his belt a pistol, and he looked from Campion to Scammell. 'She's yours?'

'Indeed, sir!' Scammell sounded nervous. The man frightened him.

'Only the best, eh? She's the answer to a Puritan's prayer, and no mistake. I hope you know how damned lucky you are. Does she have it?'

'No!' Scammell shook his head. 'Indeed, no!'

The man stared at Campion. 'We'll talk later, miss. Don't run away.'

She ran. She was terrified of him, of the smell of him and the violence that he radiated. She went to the stable-yard that was warm in the sunlight and sat on the mounting block and let the kittens come to her. They rolled about her hand, fur warm and sharp-clawed, and she blinked back tears. She must run away! She must go far from this place, but there was nowhere to go. She must run.

There were footsteps in the archway to the yard, she looked left, and there was the man. He must have followed her. He came swiftly towards her, his sword clanging against the water trough, and before she could move he had seized her shoulder and pushed her once more against the wall. His breath stank. His leather soldier's jerkin was greasy. He smiled, showing rotten, stained teeth. 'Now, miss, I've come all the way from London so you're going to be nice to me, aren't you?'

'Sir?' She was terrified.

'Where is it?'

'Where's what, sir?' She was struggling, but was helpless against his huge strength.

'God's bowels, woman! Don't play with me!' he shouted, hurting her shoulder with his hand. Then he smiled again. 'Pretty little Puritan, aren't we? Wasted on that bladder of a man.' He stayed smiling as his right knee jerked upwards, forcing her legs apart, and he pushed it up between her thighs, reaching down with his free hand for the hem of her skirt.

'That's enough, mister!' The voice came from her right. Tobias Horsnell, the stable-man, stood easily in a doorway, the musketoon that was used to kill sick beasts held in his hand. 'I doubt this be good, mister. Let her go.'

'Who are you?'

'I'm the one who should be asking that.' Horsnell seemed unconcerned by the man's crude and violent air. He twitched the gun. 'You take your hands off her. Now what be this about?'

The man had stepped back, releasing her. He brushed his hands as if she had been filthy. 'She has something I want.'

Horsnell looked at Campion. He was a thin man, his wiry forearms burned black by the sun. He was taciturn in household prayers, though he was one of the few servants who had learned to read and Campion had watched him laboriously mouth the words of the Bible. 'Is that true, Miss Dorcas?'

'No!' She shook her head. 'I don't even know what it is!'

'What is it, mister?'

'A seal.' The man seemed to be gauging whether he would have time to pull the pistol from his belt, but Tobias Horsnell kept his musketoon steady and his voice neutral. 'Do you have the seal, Miss Dorcas?'

'No.'

'There, mister. That be your answer. I think you should go.' The musketoon added force to his polite suggestion and Horsnell kept the weapon levelled till the stranger had left the yard. Only then did he drop the muzzle and give her a slow smile. ' 'Twasn't loaded, but the Lord looks after us. I hope you told the truth, Miss Dorcas.'

'I did.'

'Good, God be praised. He was an ungodly man, Miss Dorcas, and there be plenty like him outside these walls.'

She frowned at the words. She had spoken little with Tobias Horsnell, for he was a man who stayed away from the house except for prayers, yet he seemed to have divined her intention of running away. Why else would he have stressed the dangers outside Werlatton's estate?

She smoothed the collar of her dress. 'Thank you.'

'You thank your Lord and Saviour, miss. In times of trouble He'll be at hand.' He had stooped to pick up and fondle one of the kittens. 'I could tell you tales of His mercy, Miss Dorcas.'

'And tales of His punishment, Mr Horsnell?'

It was a question she would never have dared put to her father, nor would her father have given her the answer that his stable-man now gave. He shrugged, and spoke as matter-of-factly as if he were talking of hoof-oil or dung shovels. 'God loves us, miss, that's all I do know. Wind or blow, Miss Dorcas, He loves us. You pray, miss, and the answer will be there.'

Yet she knew the answer already and had been too blind to see it. She knew what she had to do. She had to do what the strange man had failed to do, what her brother had failed to do, and what Samuel Scammell had failed to do. She must find the seal and hope that it would be the key to a door which led to freedom. She smiled.

'Pray for me, Mr Horsnell.'

He smiled back. 'Nigh these twenty years, Miss Dorcas, I've done that. Reckon I won't stop now.'

She would find the seal.

5

Campion began that same evening, announcing that she would tidy up the mess which the stranger had made in her father's study. The man had gone, saying he would visit Isaac Blood, though it was Blood's signature on a letter of introduction that had let him into Werlatton Hall. He had shocked Ebenezer and Scammell by the violence and savagery of his search, but he had gone as quickly and mysteriously as he had arrived. The seal did not seem to exist.

Scammell was pleased that Campion seemed to be emerging from her week-long oppression. He unlocked the study door and offered to help her. She shook her head. 'Do you have the key to my room?'

He gave it to her. He looked past her at the mess she had first glimpsed when the man had seized her in the passageway. 'It's a big job, my dear.'

'I can manage.' She took the key to the study too, shut the door, and locked herself in.

Almost at once she realized that her impetuosity had led her into a mistake. This room had been searched more than once and it was unlikely that she would discover anything that her brother or Scammell had missed, yet now that she was inside she was overcome with curiosity. She had never been allowed in this room on her own. Her father had spent hour after hour in it, far into the night, and as she looked about the spilled wreckage she wondered what he had done in here. She wondered whether the scattered papers and books would yield a clue, not to the mystery of the seal, but to the mystery of her father. Why had a Christian man scowled through life? Why had he been so angry with his God, so brutal with his love? It seemed to her, standing in the musty smell of the room, that this was also a secret which needed to be uncovered if she was to be free.

She worked all evening, leaving the room only once to stalk stealthily to the kitchen. She fetched two apples, some bread and a lit candle with which she could light the thick candles on her father's table. On her return to the study, Scammell was standing silent at the door, his eyes gloomy, observing the mess. He smiled hopefully at her. 'You're clearing up.'

'I said I would.' She waited for him to leave which, obedient, he did. There were times now when she almost felt sorry for him. She was stronger than he was and she knew that he had come to Werlatton Hall expecting so much, only to be plunged into the misery of the household. She knew, too, that he still wanted her. He still stared at her with hopeless, lusting eyes and she knew that if she married him then he would be obedient and eager to please. Exchanging her body for obedience seemed a bad bargain.

She lit six of the big candles and saw Goodwife's face pressed against a window. Goodwife rapped on the glass, asking what she thought she was doing, but Campion simply drew the thick, heavy curtains, blotting out the mean, angry face. The candles and the shut, curtained windows made the room stuffy. She stripped to her petticoat, took off her bonnet, ate her food, then settled to her task again.

A quarter of the papers were long, rambling essays on God. Matthew Slythe had tried to plumb the mind of God as Campion now tried to plumb Matthew Slythe. She sat with her long legs crossed on the floor and frowned over his tight, crabbed handwriting. He had despaired of God as a master impossible to please. Campion read wonderingly of his fear, of his desperate attempts to appease his unpleaseable God. There was no mention in the essays of God's love; for Matthew Slythe it did not exist, only God's demands existed.

A greater part of the papers seemed to be explorations in mathematics and those she put aside because she had discovered bundles of letters that promised to be far more interesting. She felt like an eavesdropper as she read them, these letters that stretched back to the year of her birth, but through them she could trace the story of her parents' lives and learn things they had never told her.

The first letters were dated 1622 and they surprised her. They were from her mother's parents to Matthew and Martha Slythe, and they contained not just godly advice, but admonitions to Matthew Slythe that he was a poor merchant who must work harder to gain God's favour and prosper. One letter refused to lend him any more money, saying that enough had already been proffered, and hinting that he must examine his conscience to see if God was punishing him for some sin. At that time, the year of her birth, her parents had lived in Dorchester where her father, she knew, had been a

wool merchant. Evidently, from the letters, a poor one.

She read three years of letters, skipping the passages of religious advice, reading swiftly through the stilted news that John Prescott, her maternal grandfather, wrote from London. She came to a letter that congratulated Matthew and Martha on the birth of a son, 'a cause of great rejoicing and happinesse to wee all'. She paused, trying to pin down an errant thought, then frowned. There was not one mention of her in any letter, except for general references to 'the childrenne'.

The letters of 1625 introduced a new name to her: Cony. Letter after letter talked of Cony; 'a goode man', 'a busie man', 'Cony has written you, wee believe', 'Have you replied to Mr Cony? Hee deserves your answer', yet not one of the letters gave the smallest hint why Mr Cony should be 'busie' for Matthew Slythe or John Prescott. One letter, evidently written after Matthew Slythe had visited London, spoke of 'the busienesse wee had words on'. Whatever the business, it was too important to entrust to letters.

Then, after 1626, there were no more references to Matthew Slythe's inability to manage his financial affairs. Now the letters spoke of Slythe's riches, of 'God's bounteous grace to you, for which wee give manifold Thankes', and one of the letters looked forward to 'oure visit to Werlatton'. So her father, sometime between 1625 and 1626, had moved from Dorchester. She would have been three years old at the most and could not remember the move. Werlatton Hall was all she had known. She skipped through more letters, seeking a clue to her father's sudden wealth, but there was none. One year he had been a struggling merchant, the next master of this huge estate with its great Hall.

A letter from 1630 was in a different hand, telling Matthew Slythe of his father-in-law's death and Slythe had written in the letter's margin a laconic note recording the death of his mother-in-law a week later. 'The Plague' was the brief explanation.

Someone knocked loudly on the study door. Campion put

the letter down and ran fingers through her unpinned hair. The knock came again. 'Who is it?'

'Ebenezer. I want to come in!'

'You can't. Go away.' She was half undressed, her hair undone, and she could not let him in.

'What are you doing in there?'

'You know what I'm doing. Tidying up!'

'No you're not! I've been listening.'

'Go away, Eb! I'm reading the Bible.'

She waited till she heard his footsteps disappear, heard him grumbling down the passage and then got stiffly to her feet to light more candles. She thought Ebenezer might try to enter the room through the window, or spy on her through the crack in the curtains. She stood between the curtain and the window, in the darkness of the night, watching to see if Ebenezer's curiosity would take him into the garden. An owl bellied its call in the darkness, bats flickered above the lawn, but Ebenezer did not appear. She waited, listening, and could hear nothing. She remembered the many, many nights when she would lie awake in childhood's cold bed, listening for the voices of this house raised in anger, and she would know, with a child's sense, that when her parents fought with each other they would expend their venom on her.

The letters told her nothing, offered no explanation, mentioned no seal. The only papers left were those covered in mathematics and she picked them up wearily, spread them out and bent again to her reading. These, evidently, were the papers that had driven Matthew Slythe to the long nights in this room, that had forced him into writhing, wrestling prayer with his God. She looked in amazement at the work.

Her father had believed that the Bible contained two messages; the first open to anyone who cared to read, the second hidden by means of secret numbers disguised in the text. As the alchemists struggled to turn mercury into gold, so Matthew Slythe had tried to prise God's secrets from the scriptures.

'Praise bee for this!' began one page, and Campion saw

that he had been working from the book of Revelation where the number of the beast, the anti-Christ, the Pope of Rome, was given as 666. He had tried to divide it by twelve and, because it was impossible, he was pleased. Twelve, it seemed, was a godly number, indeed the fourteenth chapter of Revelation said that 144,000 people would stand on Mount Zion and her father had excitedly divided that number by twelve (the 'apostles and tribes of God') and received the answer 12,000. For some reason that seemed to be significant for he had underscored the number twelve times, and then listed further subdivisions. By three, the number of the Trinity, by four 'for that bee the corners of this world', and by six, described merely as 'halfe twelve'.

Yet for each such success, there were horrid failures. The book of Daniel foretold the world's end, the abomination, as being 2,990 days after the 'end of sacrifice'. Matthew Slythe had struggled with that number and it had yielded nothing, its secret intact, and in desperation he had copied a verse from the same chapter of Daniel that expressed his disillusion: 'for the words are closed up and sealed till the time of the end.'

Sealed. She shrugged and smiled at the word. It had not been important to her father, instead he had underlined the words 'closed up'. Closed up. She frowned, the paper forgotten, because something tugged at her memory, something she could not place, and she said the words aloud. 'Closed up. Closed up.' She felt as she knew Toby Lazender must feel when his fingers felt the pressure in the cold water and he knew that a fish was between his hands, but she could still not place the words. Closed up.

Cony, Covenant, closed up.

She rubbed her temples and tried to take from the words their hidden meaning, just as her father had struggled with the Bible's numbers. Yet the more she thought, the more elusive was the answer. Closed up? Why had that triggered her?

She stood up, pulled the curtain back, and opened one of the two windows. The lawn was pale in the moonlight, the hedge dark, and she could see the smear of stars above her. Closed up. It was quiet now, the whole household asleep, but then the owl sounded again, hunting the beeches on the ridge. Cony, Covenant, closed up.

She thought suddenly of Toby Lazender and had a sudden, clear vision of his face, a vision that had eluded her for weeks. She smiled into the darkness, for she was intent now on running away, and she thought that he would be the person she would run to. Perhaps he would remember her, but even if not, surely he would help her for he had been kind, generous and a friend if only for one afternoon. Then she felt the hopelessness of it. How could she reach London without money?

She sighed, closed the window, and was suddenly utterly still. Closed up. She remembered it now! She remembered her mother's funeral, four years before, and she remembered the weeping in the womens' pews, the long, long sermon from Faithful Unto Death Hervey in which he had likened Martha Slythe to the Martha in the Bible, and she also remembered the words 'closed up'. Her father had prayed at the funeral, an extemporaneous prayer in which he had tussled with God, and he had used the words in the prayer. Not that there was anything special in the way he used them, more, she remembered, in the manner in which he spoke them.

He had paused just before those two words. The echo of his voice was fading between the stone pillars and embarrassment was spreading through the congregation for they thought that Matthew Slythe had broken down. The silence stretched. He had said something like, 'her life on this earth is ended, her affairs . . .' and then he had embarrassed them by a long silence. She remembered the feet shuffling on the floor, the sobbing from Goodwife, and she had raised a head to steal a glance at her father. His face was turned up to the beams, one fist was raised, and she realised, as the pause went on, that he had not broken down. He had simply lost the thread of his words and thoughts. It was nothing more. She saw him shake his massive head and then he had simply

finished the sentence by saying, 'closed up'.

That was all. Yet at the time it had struck her as strange, as if some remnants of her mother's life had been locked in a cupboard. She remembered little else of the funeral, except singing the doleful words beside the raw grave as the snow whirled off the high ridge. Closed up.

It was not much, yet the letters had come from Martha Slythe's parents, and Cony, whoever he was, had appeared in their lives just at the time when Matthew Slythe came into his fortune, and she wondered if the seal, the secret of the seal, was hidden, not here, but in her mother's room. Closed up still? Waiting?

She dressed quickly, blew out the candles and turned the key in the lock. It scraped as it yielded, she froze, but there was no sound from the passageway. She would search upstairs, in her parents' bedroom that was empty, awaiting her marriage with Scammell that was confidently expected before her birthday in October.

The servants, except for Goodwife, all slept at the far end of the house where her own bedroom was. Scammell was in a room above the main entrance, and she could hear his snores as she paused at the top of the private stairs. Goodwife was the closest, in a bedroom that opened directly from her mother's dressing room, and Campion knew she would have to move with desperate silence. Goodwife would wake at the smallest sound and then emerge, bristling with anger, to face the intruder. Campion crept on stockinged feet down the short passageway and into the large, silent room where her parents had shared their unhappy bed.

The room smelt of wax. The bed was covered with a heavy flax sheet, rucked where the poles went up to the dark canopy. To her right was her father's dressing room, to her left her mother's, and she hesitated.

It was dark in the room. She wished she had thought to bring a candle, but the curtains were open and slowly her eyes became accustomed to the gloom. She could hear her own breathing. Every sound she made seemed magnified; the rustle of skirts and petticoat, the tiny scuff of her bare feet on the wooden floor.

She looked to the right, hearing even her hair as it moved on her shoulders, and she saw the mess in her father's dressing room. Someone had been here before her, had turned out the chest and pulled clothes from the shelves. She suspected her mother's room would have had the same treatment. The door was ajar.

She crept towards it, letting her weight gently on to each foot, freezing at the slightest creak of a board, and then her hand was on the door, she pushed and it swung ponderously, silently open.

Moonlight showed her the small room. A door at the far end gave directly into Goodwife's bedroom. It was shut. If anyone had searched this room they had left it tidy or, more likely, Goodwife had been in after them. It was used now to store the heavy flax sheets that were pale on the shelves. The room smelt of rue which, Goodwife said, repelled moths.

Closed up. Her mother's big chest stood, its lid open, against the wall.

Campion was nervous. She listened. She could hear the creak of timbers in the old house, she could hear her own breathing, she could hear the far, muffled rumble of Scammell's snoring.

She was close, she knew she was. She remembered playing hunt-the-thimble with their old cook, Agnes, in the kitchen garden, and Campion knew that at this moment she was warm. Over the years she suddenly heard Agnes's voice: 'You'll burn yourself, child, you're that close! Look, child! Go on with you!'

She was utterly still, drawn to this room by instincts sharpened by her long immersion in her father's papers. She imagined him hiding something. What would he have done?

Secret places. Closed up. Then it came to her, so simple, and again she was listening to her father's voice. He had preached each Sunday to his household in the days before Faithful Unto Death had come to Werlatton parish, and now

Campion was remembering one of those sermons. It had been his usual two-hour length, the servants and family expected to be still on the hard benches as he preached, and she remembered the sermon about the secret places of a man's heart. It was not enough, her father had said, to be an outward Christian, praying much and giving much, because there were secret places in a man's heart where evil could lurk. It was in those secret places that God looked.

It is like, Matthew Slythe had preached, a strong box. When the lid is open a thief in the night will see only an ordinary chest, but the owner knows that there is a secret layer at the bottom of the chest. God is the owner, and he knows what is in the secret part of each person's life. Campion remembered the story and turned slowly, knowing that her father drew his stories and examples from his own life.

It would not be this chest but his own, and Campion went soft as the night across the floor, like a thief in the darkness, into the room that was strewn with his clothes, pulled the untidy mess out of the huge wooden chest and made a pile of clothes on the floor.

She searched the bare, wooden box, finding nothing, but always hearing the voice across the years from the kitchen garden. 'Look, child!'

She tried to lift the chest, but it was impossibly heavy, and she probed at its corners, pushed each knothole in the wood. Nothing moved, nothing gave, yet still she knew she was warm.

In the end it was simple. The base of the chest was surrounded by a thick skirting board of varnished wood which she had tugged and pushed. Then she thought that it might be easier to lift the chest at one end, jam a pair of her father's great shoes beneath, and thus feel the chest's base. She shuffled slowly to the right-hand side of the huge chest, moved a pair of her father's breeches out of the way, and saw something she had missed in the thick darkness of the room. There was a handle cut into the skirting board, presumably to facilitate the lifting of the heavy chest, and she knelt in front of it, gripped the simple handle, and tried once more to lift the chest.

It would not move. It was simply too heavy, but the skirting board moved. Only the smallest fraction, but she knew she had not been deceived, and she hauled on it again, and again she felt the tiny movement.

There was a small window behind her, its wooden shutter open, and she was aware that the sky was lightening. Dawn would come soon.

She frowned, the tiredness heavy on her, as she contemplated the skirting board with its cut-out handle. It had moved, but it revealed nothing, and she tugged it again, knowing the effort to be useless, and trying to think what she should do.

She put her hand into the hole and felt with her fingers at the back of the board. There was something cold there, something made of metal, and her long fingers explored the metal, found a ring, and she tugged on it.

She heard the sound of a bolt sliding open. She froze, half expecting the small sound to bring Goodwife from her room, but the house was still.

Campion's heart was beating as it did before she went naked into the water.

She gripped the handle again, pulled, and this time the skirting board moved easily, sliding out as the front of a shallow, secret drawer, and then the runners of wood shrilled and she froze again.

She bit her lip, closed her eyes, as if those actions might lessen the noise, and pulled again.

The drawer opened. She had found her father's secret place and she knelt there, not exploring the contents, waiting to see if anyone in the house stirred.

The first birds were calling outside. Soon, she knew, Werlatton would be busy, and the knowledge made her hurry.

Two bundles were in the drawer. She lifted the first,

hearing the clink of money, and she guessed that this had been her father's secret reserve of cash. Most houses, even the poorest, tried to keep a little money hidden against the bad times. Agnes had told her that her mother had pushed a leather purse of two gold coins into the eave of the thatch, and this heavy bag was Matthew Slythe's equivalent. She put the purse on to one of his shirts, then lifted out the smaller, lighter package.

Then, holding her breath, she pushed the drawer home. There was no need for anyone to know she had been there. Her fingers found the ring of the bolt, pushed, and the chest looked innocent again.

Somewhere a pail clanged against stone; she heard the creak and groan of the yard pump, and she knew Werlatton was about to wake up. She wrapped the shirt about the two packages, crept from the room, then went on silent feet to her own bedroom.

There were fifty pounds in the purse, more money than most men would ever dream of owning. Fifty golden pounds, each with the head of King James on them, and she looked at the money on her bedroom table and she knew now she could run away. She smiled at the thought that the money which her father had saved against calamity would be used to take her away from Werlatton. Carefully, slowly, she placed the coins back in the purse, putting each heavy piece of gold in separately so that the noise would not alert any of the servants.

The second packet was tied tight with string. She cut the knot with the scissors she used for her sewing, then unwrapped the old, yellow linen that hid her father's secret.

Inside was a pair of gloves.

She frowned, lifting them, seeing two other things still in the package, and she saw that the gloves were made of lace, delicate and beautiful, fragile as thistledown, and as unlikely in a Puritan's house as a drunken game of cards would be. They were women's gloves, made for someone with long, slender hands, and Campion gently pulled one of them on and held her hand out to the window light. The glove was old and yellowed, but still beautiful. At the wrist was a ring of small, sewn pearls. Sheathed in the lace glove, it seemed to her that her hand belonged to someone else. She had never worn anything beautiful, anything pretty, and she stared at her lace-covered hand and smiled at the effect. She could not understand why something so lovely should be described as sinful.

She carefully pulled the glove off, folding it on its partner, and picked up the second object. This was a piece of parchment, its folds crackling and stiff, and she feared that the paper might break as she opened it. It was a letter, written in an ornate and bold hand, and she sat on her window-seat to read it.

'You have been sent the Jewell by the Jewe, tell mee if this bee not so. Thou *knowest* its importance. I have long worked for this, and its power bee in *your* disposall at least till the girl be of twenty-five years. The Covenant is secure if the jewell bee secure.

'It is important that you sende an impression of the Seale to the name I furnished you with, and I doe earnestlie require that you *Marke* the Seale in a Privatt way that wee bee not undone by counterfeiting. Wee have not seen the Seales of Aretine and Lopez, though they *have* seen oures, and this device of a Secrett Marke I have made a parte of oure Agreement. Doe *not* fail mee in this.

'Guard the Jewell well. It is the key to great Wealth, and though the Other Seales are needed too, you may bee sure that One Day this Jewell will bee much sought.

'The Gloves are of the Prescott Girl. You may have them.

'Guard the Jewell.'

It was signed Grenville Cony.

Cony, Covenant. She read the letter again. 'Till the girl be of twenty-five years' must, she knew, refer to herself. Isaac Blood had said that the monies of the Covenant would be hers at twenty-five, unless she was married. 'The Prescott Girl' had to be her own mother, Martha Slythe, whose

maiden name had been Prescott, but Campion could not imagine her fat, bitter mother ever owning lace gloves. She picked up one of the gloves, seeing the pearls hanging at its wrist, and she wondered by what mystery her mother had owned them.

The letter raised more mysteries than it solved. 'Aretine and Lopez', whoever they were, were names that meant nothing to Campion. 'You may bee sure that One Day this Jewell will bee much sought.' That had come true. Ebenezer and Scammell had ransacked the house, the strange man had come from London and thrust his leg between hers, and all for the last object in the packet.

Grenville Cony, in his letter, had described the seal as a jewel. She lifted it, marvelling at its weight. The jewel was made of gold, suspended from a gold chain so it could be worn as a necklace, and Campion, brought up in the rigours of her father's religion, had never seen an object so beautiful.

It was a cylinder of gold, banded by tiny, glowing stones that were white like stars and red like fire. The whole pendant was the size of her thumb.

On its base was the seal, duller than the gold of its setting, and she guessed it was made of steel. It had been cut by a craftsman who had made the seal into a work of art, as beautiful as the gold jewel itself.

Light was flooding the cornfields, touching grey silver on the bend in the stream far to the north, and Campion held the seal up to the dawn light from her window.

The rim of the seal was chased with an ornate design. In the centre was an axe, short handled and wide bladed, and on either side of the axe's handle were small letters in mirror-writing: 'St Matt'.

This was the Seal of St Matthew, showing the axe which legend said had cut off the disciple's head.

She fingered the heavy gold, wondering at it, looking at it in her hands when, just as the skirting board had moved, so now the seal seemed to give in her fingers. She frowned, tried to repeat what she had just done, and realized that the seal was in two halves, the joint concealed cunningly by one band of the precious stones. She unscrewed the two halves.

The half of the cylinder which bore the seal of St Matthew fell away in her right hand. She lifted the other half into the light. The jewel, on its long golden chain, held a secret.

There was a tiny carving inside the cylinder, a carving that had been made with exquisite skill and cast in silver so that the gold cylinder enclosed a tiny silver statue. The statue shocked her. It was a symbol of such ancient power, a symbol of all that she had been taught to hate, and it had been in this house. Her father would have abominated this, yet he had kept it, and Campion stared at it, fascinated and repelled. It was a crucifix.

A crucifix of silver in a cylinder of gold, a seal made into a jewel, the key to great wealth. She looked at the letter again, noting once more the urgent appeal for Matthew Slythe to mark the seal. She lifted the jewel into the light and saw that her father had scratched a line across the face of the axe-blade. To stop counterfeiting, the letter said, but who was the man to whom the impression had to be sent? Who was Aretine? Lopez? Her discovery of the seal had uncovered new mysteries and she knew the answers did not lie in Werlatton.

The answers would be in London. The letter was signed Grenville Cony, and beneath his signature he had written, simply, 'London'.

London. She had never seen a town, let alone a city. She was not even sure which was the road that led from Werlatton towards London.

Grenville Cony was in London, whoever he was, and Toby Lazender was certainly in London, and Campion looked at her table and saw the heavy, leather purse with her father's hoard of gold. That could take her to London! She gripped the jewel in her hands, stared at the flooding of the summer light into the valley, and she felt the excitement rise within her. She would run away, away from Ebenezer and Scammell, from Goodwife and Werlatton, from all the people who wanted to crush her and make her into what she was not. She would go to London.

PART II
The Seal of St Mark

6

Sir George Lazender, Toby's father, was a worried man.

He had friends who thought him always worried, gnawing at problems when the meat was long gone from the bone, but, as August ended in 1643, Sir George had real reasons for concern.

He had hoped to forget his worries for a morning. He had taken a boat from the Privy Stairs and landed in the city. Now he was in the precincts of St Paul's Cathedral indulging his passion for books, yet his heart was not in it.

'Sir George!' It was the bookseller, coming crabwise behind his stall. 'A fine day, Sir George!'

Sir George, ever courteous, touched the brim of his hat in response to the bookseller's greeting. 'Mr Bird. You're well, I hope?'

'I am, sir, though trade is bad, indeed it is, Sir George. Very bad.'

Sir George picked a random book from the table. He could not face a long discussion of the new taxes which Parliament had imposed and for which, as a member of the House of Commons, he was partly to blame. Yet it would be discourteous to ignore the bookseller, so he waved at the cloudless sky. 'The weather is on your side, Mr Bird.'

'I thank God it's not raining, Sir George.' Bird had not even needed to bring out the canvas shelters for his tables. 'Bad news from Bristol, Sir George.'

'Yes.' Sir George opened the book and stared, unseeing, at the pages. Even less than he wished to discuss trade did he wish to discuss the war. It was the war which was his chief worry.

'I shall let you read, Sir George.' Mr Bird, thankfully, had taken the hint. 'That copy is a little foxed, Sir George, but still worth a crown, I think.'

'Good! Good!' Sir George said absent-mindedly. He found he was reading Harington's translation of *Orlando Furioso*, a book he had owned for twenty years, yet by burying his nose in the poetry he might escape the greetings of his many friends and acquaintances who used the bookstalls at St Paul's.

The King had taken Bristol and that, in a very strange way, worried Sir George. It worried him because it suggested that the Royalists might be gaining the upper hand in the Civil War, and if Sir George changed sides now, then there were many men who would say he did it out of fear, deserting Parliament in a cowardly attempt to join the winning side, and that was not true.

Sir George wanted to change sides, but his reasons had nothing to do with the fall of Bristol.

War had begun the previous year and Sir George, as a loyal Parliamentarian, had no doubts then. He had been offended, deeply so, by King Charles's use of illegal taxation, and the offence had become personal when the King had forced loans out of his richer subjects. The loans, Sir George knew, would never be repaid and he was among the men who had been robbed by his monarch.

The argument between King and Parliament had drifted almost imperceptibly into war. Sir George continued to support Parliament for its cause was his cause; that the kingdom should be ruled by law and that no man, not even the King of England, was above that law. That doctrine pleased Sir George, made his support of the rebellion firm, yet now he knew that he was changing sides. He would support the King against Parliament.

He moved to one of the great buttresses of the medieval Cathedral and leaned against the sun-warmed stone. It was not, he thought, that he had changed, it was the cause that had changed. He had entered the rebellion convinced that it was a political fight, a war to decide how the country should be governed, but in opening the gates of battle Parliament had released a plague of monsters. The monsters took religious shapes.

Sir George Lazender was a Protestant, stout in the defence of his faith, but he had little time for the Ranters, the Fifth Monarchy Men, the Anabaptists, the Familists, the Mortalists, or any of the other strange sects that had suddenly emerged to preach their own brand of revolutionary religion. Fanaticism had swamped London. Only two days before he had seen a stark naked woman parading in the Strand, preaching the Rantist sect, and the extraordinary thing was that people took such nonsense seriously! And with the religious nonsense, that might be harmless, came more insidious political demands.

Parliament claimed that it fought only against the King's advisers. That, Sir George knew, was a nonsense, but it gave Parliament a shred of legality in its revolt. The aim of Parliament was to restore the King to his throne in Whitehall, a throne that was meticulously maintained for his return, and then to force him to rule England with the consent and help of his Parliament. There would, of course, be great changes. The bishops would have to go, and the archbishops, so that the Church of England would appear a more Protestant church and, though Sir George was not personally offended by bishops, he would sacrifice them willingly if it meant a King ruling a kingdom according to law and not whim. Yet Sir George no longer trusted that Parliament, if it defeated the King, could control the victory.

The fanatics were fuelling the rebellion, changing it. They spoke now not just of abolishing the bishops, but of abolishing the King as well. Men preached an end to property and privilege and Sir George remembered with horror a popular verse of the previous year:-

> Wee'l teach the nobles how to crouch,
> And keep the gentry downe.

Well, Sir George was a gentleman, and his eldest child, Anne, had married the Earl of Fleet who was a noble. The Earl of Fleet, a good Puritan, believed that the fanatics could be contained, but Sir George no longer did. He could not support a cause that would, in the end, destroy him and his children, and so he had decided, reluctantly, to fight against that cause. He would leave London. He would pack his precious books, his silver, his pewter and his furniture, and he would abandon London and Parliament, to return to Lazen Castle.

He would miss London. He looked up from the Harington and stared fondly at the cathedral precinct. This was the place where unemployed house servants came to look for new employers, it was where the booksellers could set up their stalls, and it was where virulent sermons were preached beneath St Paul's Cross. It was a place of life, colour, movement, and crowds, and Sir George would miss it. He liked the sense of life in London, its crowded streets, the never-ending noise, the long conversations, the feeling that things happened here because they were forced to happen. He would miss the politics, the laughter, and the house near Charing Cross from which, on the one side, he could look into green fields, and from the other into the smoky heart of the great city. Yet London was the heart of Parliament's rebellion and he could not stay if he changed sides.

'Sir George! Sir George!' The voice called to him from the direction of Ludgate Hill. 'Sir George!'

Reluctantly he put the book back on the table. This was a man he could not brush off by pretending to read. 'My dear John!'

Only minutes before Sir George had been thinking of his son-in-law, the Earl of Fleet, and now the Earl, red-faced and sweating, pushed his way through the midday crowds. 'Sir

George!' he called out again, fearful that his father-in-law might yet escape.

Sir George was fifty-five, counted an old man by his colleagues, yet he remained alert and spry. His hair was white, yet there was a liveliness to his face that made him seem younger than his years. The Earl of Fleet, on the other hand, though twenty years Sir George's junior, had the burdened face of a man old before his time. He was a serious man, even, Sir George suspected, a tedious man. Like many other aristocrats he was a confirmed Puritan who fought for Parliament. 'I thought I might find you here, father-in-law, I've come from Whitehall.'

He made it sound like a complaint. Sir George smiled. 'It's always good to see you, John.'

'We have to speak, Sir George, a matter of utmost importance.'

'Ah.' Sir George looked about the precinct, knowing that the Earl would not wish to be overheard in such a public place. Reluctantly Sir George suggested that they share a boat back to Whitehall. It was odd, Sir George thought, how no one minded being overheard by watermen.

They walked down to St Paul's wharf, down the steep street that was noisy with trade and shaded by washing strung between the overhanging upper stories. They joined the queue waiting for the watermen, keeping to the right for they needed a two-oared boat and not the single sculls that sufficed a lone passenger. The Earl of Fleet frowned at the delay. He was a busy man, preparing to leave in a week's time for the war in the west country. Sir George could not imagine his portly, self-important son-in-law as a leader of troops, but he kept his amusement to himself.

They shuffled down the stone quay as the queue shortened, and Sir George looked to his left at the sunlight on the houses of London Bridge. It was a pity, he thought, that the houses burned at the city end of the bridge had never been rebuilt, it gave the great structure a lopsided look, but the bridge, with its houses, shops, palace, and chapel built above the wide river, was still one of the glories of Europe. Sir George felt the sadness of loss. He would miss the sun glinting on the Thames, the water thronged with boats, the skyline below the bridge thicketed with masts.

'Where to, genn'l'men?' a cheerful voice shouted at them and the Earl handed Sir George into the boat.

'Privy Stairs!' The Earl of Fleet managed to sound as if their business was of vast importance.

The watermen spun their boat, leaned into the oars, and the small craft surged into the stream. Sir George looked at his son-in-law. 'You wanted to talk, John?'

'It's Toby, Sir George.'

'Ah!' Sir George had been worried that the Earl might have guessed his wavering loyalty, but instead he wished to speak about Sir George's other concern: his son. 'What's he done now?'

'You don't know?'

Sir George tipped his plain hat back so that the sun could warm his forehead. To his right the wall of London ended at Baynard's Castle, beyond which was the old Blackfriar's Theatre. Sir George decided innocence was his best defence against the Earl. 'Toby? He's at Gray's Inn, you know that. I think he should know something of the law, John, enough to steer well clear of it later. Mind you, I think he's bored. Yes, very bored. It makes him boisterous, but I was boisterous once.' He looked at his son-in-law. 'Young men should be boisterous, John.'

The Earl of Fleet frowned. He had never been boisterous. 'You will forgive me, Sir George, but it is not that he is boisterous.' Water splashed on his coat and he ineffectually flapped at the black cloth. 'I fear you will not be happy, father-in-law.' The Earl was obviously distressed at being the bearer of bad news.

Sir George spoke gently, 'I'm rather in suspense at this moment.'

'Quite so, quite so.' Fleet nodded vigorously, then took the plunge. 'Your son, Sir George, is actively striving for our enemies. He pretends otherwise, but it is so.' The Earl spoke ponderously, poking his finger into his knee as if to emphasise his words. 'If his activities reach the ear of the competent authorities then he will be arrested, tried, and doubtless imprisoned.'

'Yes,' Sir George still spoke softly. He looked away from his companion at the crowd waiting for boats at the Temple Stairs. Sir George knew of Toby's activities, because his son had told him of them, but how on earth had the Earl of Fleet discovered them? 'I hope you're sure of this, John.'

'Quite sure.' The Earl of Fleet was genuinely upset at being the bearer of bad news. 'It is, I fear, quite certain.'

'You'd better tell me, then.'

The Earl began at the beginning, as Sir George feared he would, and he pedantically described Toby's activities. It was all, Sir George knew, correct. Toby had become embroiled in a Royalist conspiracy, a conspiracy that Sir George knew was doomed to failure. There were rich merchants in London who were not supporters of Parliament, but whose businesses prevented them from leaving the city. Some had sent word to the King in Oxford that, if he were to ask it, men might flock to his standard raised in the centre of London. They planned a rebellion against the rebels, an uprising in the heart of London, and Sir George knew that Toby had been charged with discovering their exact strength and ascertaining how many men would follow the Royalist merchants.

Sir George knew because Toby had told him. There was a great deal of respect and love between father and son, and though Sir George did not wholeheartedly approve of Toby's clandestine activity, he could not find it within his uncertain loyalties to forbid it.

The Earl of Fleet turned his round, serious face to Sir George. 'One of the men Toby spoke to has a secretary, a man strong in the Lord, and the secretary reported it to the minister of his congregation. The minister, knowing of my relationship with you, laid the matter before me. And now I have come to you.'

'And I thank you for that.' Sir George was sincere. 'It's put you in an awkward position, John.'

The boat was turning south round the great bend. To their left was the empty untidiness of Lambeth Marsh, to their right the rich houses of the Strand. The Earl lowered his voice. 'I must act soon, Sir George, I must.'

'Of course you must.' Sir George knew that his son-in-law, an honest man, would be forced to go to the proper authorities within a few days. 'How long, John?'

The Earl did not reply at once. The boat had gone to the Surrey bank where the current was weaker, but now the watermen were beginning the wide turn that would bring them smoothly downstream to the Privy Stairs at Whitehall. The Earl frowned at his damp coat. 'I must report this by next Lord's Day.'

Six days till Sunday. 'Thank you, John.' Six days to remove Toby from London, to send him to safety at Lazen Castle. The thought made Sir George smile. His wife, the formidable Lady Margaret Lazender, would welcome her husband's change of allegiance. She would doubtless wholeheartedly approve of her son's secret actions for the King.

Sir George paid the stroke oar, then climbed on to the stairs. He walked beside his taller son-in-law along the right of way that led through the royal Palace, under the archway, and into King Street. 'I'm for home, John.'

'And I for Westminster.'

'You'll come and dine before you leave London?'

'Of course.'

'Good, good.' Sir George looked at the blue sky above the new Banqueting Hall. 'I hope the weather lasts.'

'A good harvest, yes.'

They parted, and Sir George walked slowly home. Whitehall had never looked better. He would miss it, though he acknowledged pleasure at the thought of rejoining Lady Margaret in Lazen. His wife, whom Sir George loved, refused to travel to London, saying it was a viperous den of lawyers, thieves and politicians. Sir George hated being away from the city. Perhaps, he admitted to himself with a smile, that was why their marriage had been so good. Lady Margaret loved him from Dorset, while he loved her from London.

He crossed the road to avoid a virulent Puritan member of the Commons who was bound to detain him twenty minutes to tell him the latest gossip about the King's flirtation with the Roman Catholics. Sir George touched his hat once, in reply to a similar greeting from Sir Grenville Cony who passed in his coach. A powerful man, Sir Grenville, deep in the inner councils of Parliament and paymaster to half the rebel army. Sir George had the uncanny impression that Sir Grenville, in a single smiling glance from his coach, had divined Sir George's wavering loyalty.

Sir George stopped at Charing Cross, looking over at the Royal Mews, because a stage wagon, come from the west, blocked his path. The wagon had huge, broad wheels to negotiate the muddy, rutted roads, though this summer the going had been dry and easy. The coach roof was piled with luggage and passengers, but Sir George's eye was caught by a girl who stared with awe and wonder through the leather-curtained window. His breath almost caught in his throat. She was more beautiful than any girl he had seen in years. He caught her eye unintentionally and raised his hand in a polite salute so she would not take offence.

If I were thirty years younger, he thought, and the desire amused him as he crossed towards his house. He envied the girl. Her expression seemed to convey that this was her first sight of London, and he was jealous of all the experience that lay before her. He must leave the great city.

Mrs Pierce opened the door to him. 'Master.' She took his hat and cane. 'Master Toby's upstairs.'

'He is? Good!' Sir George glanced at the staircase. He must pack his son off to safety in the next six days, send him far away from the vengeance of the Saints. Toby must return to Lazen, and his father would follow. Sir George slowly climbed the stairs.

Campion saw the elderly man salute her with his cane, she almost smiled in return, but then her fear of the unknown, her dread of the great city, overtook her and the moment passed.

She had reached London, and the enormity of her achievement had astonished her even as it scared her.

If a child is punished often and punished cruelly, and if a parent has such an all-embracing concept of sin that even the most innocent acts can lead to punishment, then the child will learn early to be cunning. Campion had learned early and learned well, and it had been cunning that had brought her this far.

Cunning and more than a little luck. She had waited one more day, then left the house well before dawn. She was dressed in her sober best and carrying a bundle of food, coins and one spare dress. The seal was about her neck, hidden beneath her bodice, while the pearled gloves and the letter were in her bundle.

She had walked east, towards the dawn, and for a time she had been exhilarated. Two hours later, as the sun flooded the fields and woods, the exhilaration had ended. She was walking into a sheltered valley where the road crossed a stream when a filthy beggar erupted from a ditch. He had possibly meant her no harm, but the bearded face, the grunting sounds, and the single, reaching, clawing hand had terrified her and she had run, easily outstripping him, and thereafter she had walked cautiously and warily, fearing the dangers that this strange world contained.

An hour later, when she was already tired and dispirited, a farmer's wife who drove a wagon offered her a ride. The wagon was heavy with flax, the stalks rustling as the horses dragged it, and even though the flax was going south-east Campion accepted the ride because the woman's company was a protection against danger. Campion told the woman that she was being sent to London to work for her uncle, and when the woman asked scornfully why she was travelling alone, Campion invented a story: her mother had suddenly

.been evicted from her cottage, Campion was the only hope of raising money and her mother had begged her to accept her uncle's offer of employment. Her mother, Campion said, was sick. She told the story well and the farmer's wife sympathized, and did not abandon Campion when the wagon reached its destination at Winterborne Zelston.

A carrier was in the village, going to Southampton with a string of mules, and the farmer's wife arranged for Campion to go with the man and his wife. The carrier, like so many travelling people, was a Puritan and Campion was glad of it. She might find their religion oppressive and cruel, but she knew they would also be honest and trustworthy. The carrier's wife clucked as she heard Campion's story. 'You poor thing, dear. You'd best come to Southampton, then on to London. It's safer that way nowadays.'

She slept that first night in the public room of an inn, sharing the room with a dozen women, and there were times in the reaches of the night when she wished she was back home in Werlatton. She had launched herself on the stream, and its current was already taking her to strange, frightening places where she did not know how to behave. Yet the thought of Scammell, of his flabby, heavy desire of her, of being forced to mother his children, made her determined to endure.

In the cold dawn she paid for her lodgings with a gold coin, causing raised eyebrows, and she had to trust that she was given the correct coins in change. The womens' privy was an empty pigsty, open to the sky. It was all so strange. The broadsheets pasted on to the wall of the tavern told of Puritan victories against the King, for this was an area loyal to Parliament.

The carrier's wife, having settled her own bill, took her out into the street where her husband had already strung the mules into their chain. They walked into the dawn again and Campion's spirits soared to the sky for she had survived one whole day.

The carrier, Walter, was a taciturn man, as stubborn as

the mules that made him a living. He walked slowly at the head of his string, his eyes on his Bible that his wife proudly told Campion he had recently learned to read. 'Not all the words, mind you, but most of them. He reads me nice stories from the scriptures.'

It clouded over that day, great clouds that piled from the south, and in the afternoon it rained. That evening, in a tavern on the edge of the New Forest, Campion dried herself in front of a fire. She drank small beer and stayed close to Walter's wife, Miriam, who protected her from the men who tried to flirt with the beautiful, shy girl beside the hearth. Miriam tutted. 'Your mother should have married you off.'

'I think she wanted me at home.' She instantly feared that Miriam would ask why, in that case, her mother had sent her to London, but the carrier's wife was thinking of other things.

'It's not a blessing, dear.'

'What?'

'To be fair, like you. You can see the disturbance in the men. Still, the Lord didn't make you proud, and that's a blessing. But if I were you, dear, I'd marry and marry soon. How old be you?'

'Eighteen,' Campion lied.

'Late, late. Now I was wed to Walter at fifteen, and a better man God could not have shaped in His clay, b'aint that be, Walter?'

Walter, puzzling his way through Deuteronomy, looked up and grunted shyly. He went back to his scriptures and his pot of ale.

Campion looked at Miriam. 'Don't you have children?'

'Lord bless you, child, but the children be growed. Them that God let grow. Our Tom now, he be married, and the girls are in service. That's why I travel with Walter, to keep him company and out of trouble!' She laughed at her own joke and Campion was surprised to see a warm smile soften Walter's stern face. The joke was evidently an old one between them, a comforting one, and Campion knew she was with good, kind people and wished that she did not need to deceive them.

They crossed the New Forest the next day, travelling in company with two dozen other people, and Walter pulled out a great pistol that he stuck in his belt and laid a sword across the leading mule's packs. They were not troubled in the forest though, except by more rain that soaked the path and dripped from the trees long after the showers had stopped. By afternoon the sun shone again and they were coming close to Southampton where Campion must leave Miriam's company.

Each stage of her journey loomed ahead to worry her. She had reached Southampton safely, and she was further from home now than she had ever dreamed of going, but there was still the largest obstacle to be cleared; the journey to London itself. Miriam asked if she had much money and Campion said yes, about five pounds, and Miriam told her to take the stage wagon. 'It's the safest way, child. Is your uncle expecting you?'

'I think so.'

'Well, you take the wagon. Who knows, maybe he'll pay for you?' She laughed, then took Campion to the huge inn where the wagons left, and kissed her farewell. 'You're a good girl, I can tell. The Lord protect you, child. We'll pray for you.'

And perhaps the prayers worked, for at Southampton Campion met Mrs Swan, and although Mildred Swan was not the likeliest person to be God's instrument, she was undoubtedly effective. Within minutes of seeing Campion, lost and frightened, she had taken the girl under her wing. They shared a bed and Campion listened to the interminable story of Mildred Swan's life.

She had been visiting her sister who was married to a clergyman in Southampton and was now returning to her own home in London. The story, interrupted by sleep, was picked up the next morning as they waited in the cobbled yard. 'I'm a widow, dear, so I knows about sorrows and troubles.' She had a huge, untidy bundle on the ground, next to a basket filled with pies and fruit. As she turned to check on their safety she saw an ostler loitering near her belongings. 'Get your thieving eyes off them! I'm a Christian woman travelling defenceless! Don't you think you can thieve from me!' The ostler, astonished, made a hasty retreat. Mrs Swan, who liked to arrange the world about her, smiled happily at Campion. 'You must tell me about your mother, dear.'

Mildred Swan was a plump, middle-aged woman, wearing a dress of faded blue, with a gaudy, flowered scarf about her shoulders and a bright red bonnet crammed on unruly, fair hair. She did not wait for Campion to answer, instead she wanted to know whether Campion planned to travel on top or inside the coach. Campion said she did not know.

'You'd better travel with me, dear. Inside. Then we can protect each other against the men.' The last words were spoken loudly enough for a tall, gloomy looking minister to hear. Mrs Swan watched him to make sure the words had registered, then looked back to Campion. 'So?'

Campion had changed her story a little. She had kept a sick, failing mother, but now she claimed to be travelling to London to see a lawyer about an inheritance. It was close enough to the truth, for Campion had conceived the idea that Grenville Cony must be the lawyer who had arranged the Covenant.

By the time Campion had explained about the inheritance they were inside the wagon, perched on a cushioned bench, and Mrs Swan had jostled the other passengers unmercifully to make herself ample space. The minister, a Bible now in his hands, sat opposite Campion by the window.

Mrs Swan was fascinated by Campion's sick mother. 'She's got thin blood, has she, dear?'

'Yes.'

'Buttercups, dear, buttercups. Buttercups work for thin blood, dear. My mother had thin blood. She died, of course, but it wasn't just the thin blood. Oh no.' She said the last words darkly as though they enshrined a terrible secret. 'What else does she have, dear?'

For two hours, as the wagon rumbled and lurched northwards, Campion heaped upon her mother the troubles of a female Job, each ailment more terrible than the last, and for each Mrs Swan had a remedy, always infallible, though she also always knew of someone who had died despite them. The conversation, though tiring on Campion's imagination, was a very heaven for Mrs Swan. 'The ague, dear? My grandmother had the ague, God bless her, but she didn't die of it. No. She was cured, but then she prayed to St Petronilla. Can't do that now, of course, thanks to some I won't name.' She glowered at the minister to whom she had taken an irrational dislike. 'Does she have sore breasts, dear?'

'Very.'

'She would, she would,' Mrs Swan sighed heavily. 'I had sore breasts, dear, when my husband was alive, but then he was a sailor. Yes. He brought me the image of St Agnes from Lisbon and, do you know, it worked like a charm, but then it was a charm, of course.' She was raising her voice to provoke the minister. 'Mind you, dear, they were sore. And there's plenty of them to hurt!' She pealed with laughter at the thought, her eyes unblinking on the man of God who, sure enough, reacted. Whether it was the talk of Romish saints or the discussion of breasts that had offended him, Campion could not tell. He leaned towards Mrs Swan.

'You are indecent in your talk, woman!'

She ignored him and smiled at Campion. 'Does she have long ears, dear?'

'No.'

'God be thanked for that, dear, 'cos there's no cure for long ears except a clouting. A good clouting!' She turned to the minister, but he had already leaned back in defeat, his eyes on Ecclesiastes. Mrs Swan tried to rouse him again. 'Has she got the falling sickness?'

'Oh, yes.'

'Yes. My aunt had that, God rest her. One moment she was on her feet, the next she was flat on the floor. Just like that. St Valentine cures that, dear.' The minister stayed silent.

Mrs Swan settled back on the bench. 'I'm going to sleep now, dear. If anyone molests you,' and here she looked hard at the travelling preacher, 'you just wake me up.'

Mrs Swan was her guide, her mentor, her protector, and now, as they alighted at the end of the Strand, her landlady too. She would not hear of Campion seeking lodging in an inn, though she had not been slow to make clear that her hospitality was not free. 'Not that I'm greedy, dear, no. No one can say that of Mildred Swan, but a body has to look after a body.' With which gnomic words the deal had been made.

Even though Charing Cross and the Strand were not London proper, but just the westward extension of the houses built outside the old walls of the city, it seemed fearful to Campion. The eastern sky was hazed dark with the smoke of innumerable chimneys, a haze pierced by more church towers and spires than Campion could have dreamed possible; the whole overshadowed by the great cathedral on the hill. The houses in the Strand, down which Mrs Swan led her, were huge and rich, their doors guarded by armed men, while the street was filled with cripples and beggars. Campion saw men with empty, festering eye-sockets, children with no legs who swung themselves along on strong arms, and women whose faces were covered with open sores. It stank.

Mrs Swan noticed none of it. 'This is the Strand, dear. Used to be a lot of gentry along here, but most have gone, more's the pity. It's all Saints, now, and Saints don't pay like the gentry.' Mrs Swan had been left money by her sea-captain husband, but she augmented her income by embroidery, and the Puritan revolution in London had lowered the demand for such decorative work.

A troop of soldiers marched from the city, long pikes over their shoulders, their barred helmets bright in the sunlight. People were thrust unceremoniously from their path. Mrs Swan shouted scornfully at them. 'Make way for the Lord's anointed!' An officer looked sternly at her, but Mildred Swan was not a woman to be overawed by the military.

'Watch your step, Captain!' She laughed as the officer hastily
dodged a pile of horse-dung. She made a dismissive gesture at
the soldiers. 'Just playing, they are. Did you see those boys at
the Knight's Bridge?' The coach had been stopped at the
bridge in the fields to the west of London, and the soldiers
had searched the travellers. Mrs Swan snorted. 'Little boys,
they are. That's all! Shave their heads and they think they can
rule the world! This way, dear.'

Campion was led into an alley so narrow that she could not
walk alongside Mrs Swan. She was lost now, confused by the
maze of tiny streets, but at last Mrs Swan reached a blue door
which she laboriously unlocked, pushed Campion inside, and
Campion reflected, as she settled into the small parlour, that
she had reached her destination. Here, in this great,
confusing city, she might find the answer to the seal which
hung between her breasts. Here too was Toby Lazender, and
in a world where her only friend was Mrs Swan, he suddenly
loomed large in her thoughts. She was in London at last, free.

Mrs Swan sat heavily opposite her, pulled up her skirts and
took off her pattens. 'Oh, my poor corns! Well, dear! We're
here.'

Campion smiled. 'We're here.' Where the mystery could
be solved.

7

Campion's behaviour, before she ran away from Werlatton,
had been so solitary and eccentric that her absence on the first
morning provoked nothing more than grumbles and self-
satisfied noises from Goodwife saying that she had always
known the girl could not be trusted. By mid-afternoon the
grumbles had turned to alarm in Scammell's head and he
ordered a horse saddled and rode himself about the bounds
of the estate.

Even when it was realized that Campion had disappeared, their imagination could not encompass anything so dramatic as a journey to London. On the second day, at dawn, Scammell ordered Tobias Horsnell to search the villages to the north, while he and Ebenezer went south and west. By then the trail was long cold, and that evening, in the great hall, Samuel Scammell felt the stirrings of fear. The girl was his passport to riches beyond dream and she had gone.

Goodwife Baggerlie took pleasure in Campion's disappearance, much as bad news will always cheer a prophet of doom. Goodwife had joined eagerly in the Slythes' persecution of their daughter, a persecution that was rooted in a distaste for her looks, her spirit, and her apparent unwillingness to subdue her soul to the tedious boredom of Puritan existence. Now that Campion had fled, Goodwife dredged from the past an endless catalogue of trivial sins, each magnified in Goodwife's sullen mind. 'She has a devil, master, a devil.'

Faithful Unto Death Hervey, who had joined the search, looked at Goodwife. 'A devil?'

'Her father, God bless him, could control it.' Goodwife sniffed and dabbed at red eyes with her apron. ' "He that spareth his rod hateth his son: but he that loveth him chasteneth him betimes." '

'Amen,' said Scammell.

'Praise his word,' said Ebenezer, who had never been beaten by his father, though he had often watched as his sister was lashed with the great belt.

Faithful Unto Death Hervey steepled long fingers in front of his bobbing Adam's apple. ' "As a jewel of gold in a swine's snout, so is a fair woman which is without discretion." '

'Indeed and indeed.' Scammell searched his mind for a suitable verse of scripture so he would not be left behind in this company. Nothing came to mind except inappropriate words from the Song of Solomon, words he dared not say aloud: 'Thy two breasts are like two young roes that are twins.' He groaned inwardly. He wondered what her breasts were like, breasts that he had yearned to fondle, and now, perhaps he would never know. She had gone, taking her beauty with her, and taking, too, Scammell's hope of wealth. 'We must watch and pray.'

'Amen,' Ebenezer said. 'Watch and pray.'

Campion's supposition was right. Grenville Cony was, indeed, a lawyer, only now, according to Mrs Swan, much more. 'He's a knight, dear, Sir Grenville, and he's so high and mighty that he doesn't notice the likes of you and I. He's a politician. A lawyer and a politician!' Her words left no doubt as to her opinions of both categories. Lawyers, to Mrs Swan, were the lowest form of life. 'Killing's too good for them, dear. Bloodsuckers, dear. If God hadn't invented sin, then the lawyers would, just to line their own purses.' She expounded further so that her life, to Campion, seemed to have been a perilous journey between the dangers of various illnesses on the one side, and the plottings of predatory lawyers on the other. 'I could tell you stories, dear,' said Mrs Swan, and proved it by doing so; many of the stories of a complexity that would have done credit to a lawyer, but all distinguished by endings in which Mrs Swan, single-handedly, confounded the entire legal profession.

Yet Campion could see little choice but to visit Sir Grenville Cony and here, once more, fortune smiled on her. A neighbour of Mrs Swan, a French tailor, knew Sir Grenville's address which turned out to be one of the massive houses in the Strand.

Mrs Swan was pleased. 'That's convenient, dear, nice and close.' She was threading coloured silks on to fine needles. 'You tell him, dear, that if he wants any embroidery then he doesn't have far to go.'

So, on her second afternoon in London, Campion walked to the Strand. She dressed soberly, her hair covered with a bonnet, but even so she was conscious of the glances men gave her and glad of the company of the tailor. Jacques was elderly and fine-mannered, helping her across the busy Strand, gracious in his words to her. 'You will find yourself successfully home, Miss Slythe?'

'You've been very kind.'

'No, no, no. It is not every day that I walk the streets with such beauty. You have given me pleasure, Miss Slythe. This is it.'

Cony's house was not as large as some on the Strand, not to be compared with Northumberland or York House, but it was impressive nonetheless. It was built in dark brick, its stories rising to a high, stone balustrade with carved beasts guarding the corners. The tall mullioned windows were masked by velvet curtains. The door to the house was guarded by an armed man, a pike at his side, who smirked at Campion and was rude to Jacques Moreau. 'What do you want?'

'The lady has business with Sir Grenville.'

'Business, eh?' He looked Campion up and down, taking his time. 'What sort of business, eh?'

She had come determined to be humble, a favour seeker, but the man's attitude annoyed her. 'Business Sir Grenville would not want discussed with you.'

It was evidently the right answer, delivered in the right tone, for he sniffed, jerked his head towards the side of the building, and spoke with a little more respect. 'Business is down the alley.'

She said farewell to the tailor on the corner, then went into the narrow, high alleyway. It ran to the river, and she could see the sheen of the sun on the water and, beyond it, the dreariness of Lambeth Marsh.

A small porchway was two-thirds of the way down the alley, close enough for her to smell the river, and she presumed this was the door where those with business visited Sir Grenville Cony. There was no guard here. She knocked.

No one answered. She could hear voices from the Strand, the sound of wheels on stone, and once there was a splash from the river, but the house seemed to exude silence. She was nervous suddenly. She felt the seal beneath her dress, and the touch of the gold on her skin reminded her that this house might hold the secret of her future, the secret of the Covenant that might free her from her father's stranglehold imposed by his will and marriage settlement. Emboldened, she knocked again.

She waited. She was about to knock a third time, indeed was looking back into the alley for a loose cobblestone that could make more noise on the wooden door, when a tiny shutter banged up.

'Don't you know there's a bell?' a voice demanded.

'A bell?'

'To your right.'

She had not seen it in the shadows, but now she saw an iron handle hanging from a chain. The irritation of the person behind the tiny shutter seemed to demand an apology, so she made one. The man was slightly mollified. 'What do you want?'

'I want to see Sir Grenville Cony, sir.'

'To see Sir Grenville? Everyone wants that! Why don't you watch him pass in his coach, or in his private barge? Isn't that sight enough?'

She could not see the man to whom the petulant voice belonged, she could only make out the glitter of one eye and the half shape of a nose pressed against the iron grille that barred the small opening. 'I have business with Sir Grenville, sir.'

'Business!' The man seemed never to have heard of the word. 'Business! Put your petition here. Hurry!' The eye and nose were replaced with fingers reaching for her petition.

'I don't have a petition!'

She thought the man had gone, for there was silence after the fingers disappeared, but then the glittering eye came back. 'No petition?'

'No.'

'Does Mr Cony know you?' The question was asked grudgingly.

'He knew my father, sir.'

'Wait!'

The shutter dropped with a smart click, leaving the house in silence again, and Campion walked back into the alley and stared down at the river. A heavy barge was crawling across her narrow view, propelled by long, wooden sweeps that were rowed by men standing on its decks. One by one, three heavy cannons came into view, lashed to the barge's deck, a cargo going westward to war.

The shutter snapped up. 'Girl!'

'Sir?'

'Name?'

'Dorcas Slythe.' This was no time for fanciful, self-adopted names. She could hear the scratch of quill on paper.

'Your business?'

She hesitated, provoking a tut from the grille. She had half expected, having been told to wait, that she would be invited into the house, and so she was not prepared with a message. She thought quickly. 'The Covenant, sir.'

'The what?' There was no interest in his voice. 'Covenant? Which one?'

She thought again. 'St Matthew, sir.'

The quill scratched beyond the door. 'Sir Grenville's not here, girl, so you can't see him today, and Wednesday is the day for public business. Not this Wednesday, though, because he's busy. Next Wednesday. Come at five o'clock. No. Six. In the afternoon,' he added grudgingly.

She nodded, appalled at the time she would have to wait for any answer. The man grunted. 'Of course he may not want to see you, in which case your time will have been wasted.' He laughed. 'Good day!' The shutter snapped down, abandoning her, and she turned back to the Strand and to Mrs Swan.

In the house she had left, in a great comfortable room that overlooked the Thames, Sir Grenville Cony stared at the barge which lumbered away from him around the Lambeth bend. Guns for Parliament, guns bought with money that had probably been lent by Sir Grenville himself at twelve per cent interest, but the thought gave him no pleasure. He felt his belly gingerly.

He had eaten too much. He pressed his huge belly again, wondering if the small pain in his right side was simple indigestion and his fat, white face flinched slightly as the pain increased. He would summon Dr Chandler to the house.

He knew his secretary was at the House of Commons so he walked himself to the clerk's room. One of the clerks, a weedy man named Bush, was coming through the far door. 'Bush!'

'Sir?' Bush showed the fear that all the clerks felt of their master.

'Why are you away from your desk? Did you seek permission to wander through the land on my time? Is it your bladder again? Your bowels? Answer me, you beast of Belial! Why?'

Bush stuttered, 'The door, sir. The door.'

'The door! I heard no bell! Correct me, Sillers,' he looked at the chief clerk, 'but I heard no bell.'

'They knocked, sir.' Sillers dealt laconically with his master, yet never without respect.

'Who knocked? Strangers at my door, dealt with by Bush. Bush! Who was this lucky man?'

Bush stared in fear at the short, fat, grotesque man who stalked him. Sir Grenville Cony was grossly fat, his face had the appearance of a sly white frog. His hair, white after his fifty-seven years, was cherubically curly. He smiled on Bush, as he smiled on most of his victims.

'It was not a man, sir. A girl.'

'A girl!' Sir Grenville feigned surprise. 'You'd like that, Bush, wouldn't you? A girl, eh? Have you ever had one? Know what they feel like, eh? Do you? Do you?' He had backed Bush into a corner. 'Who was this slut who has put you into such a fever, Bush?'

The other clerks, fourteen of them, smiled secretly. Bush

licked his lips and brought the paper up to his face. 'A Dorcas Slythe, sir.'

'Who?' Cony's voice had changed utterly. No longer flippant and careless, but suddenly hard as steel, the voice that could ride down committees in Parliament and silence courtrooms. 'Slythe? What was her business.'

'A Covenant, sir. St Matthew.' Bush was quaking.

Sir Grenville Cony was very still, his voice very quiet. 'What did you tell her, Bush?'

'To come back next Wednesday, sir.' He shook his head and added in desperation, 'they were your instructions, sir!'

'My instructions! Mine! My instructions are for you to deal intelligently with my business. God! You fool! You fool! Grimmett!' His voice had been rising, till his final call became a shrill scream.

'Sir?' Thomas Grimmett, chief of Grenville Cony's guards, came through the door. He was a big man, hard-faced, utterly fearless in his master's presence.

'This Bush, Grimmett, this fool, is to be punished.' Cony ignored the clerk's whimpers. 'Then he is to be thrown out of my employment. Do you understand?'

Grimmett nodded. 'Yes, sir.'

'Sillers! Come here!' Sir Grenville Cony stalked back into his room. 'Fetch the papers on Slythe. We have work, Sillers, work.'

'You have the Scottish Commissioners to see, sir.'

'The Scottish Commissioners can bubble the Thames by farting, Sillers. We have work.'

The punishment was administered during Cony's dinner, so that Sir Grenville could watch while he ate. He enjoyed it. Bush's squeals of pain made a better sauce for the lamb, chicken, prawns and beef than anything his kitchen could provide. He felt better afterwards, much better, so he no longer regretted that he had forgotten to summon Dr Chandler. After dinner, when Bush had been taken away to be hurled into some gutter, Sir Grenville graciously allowed the Scottish Commissioners to see him. They were, he knew, all fervent Presbyterians, so he prayed aloud with them, praying for a Presbyterian England, before settling to his work with them.

The girl. He thought of her, wondering where she was in London, and whether she would bring him the seal. Above all he wondered whether she would bring him that. St Matthew! He could feel the excitement of it, the joy of a long-ago plot well laid. He sat up late that night, drinking claret before the darkened river, and he raised his glass to the grotesque reflection in the diamond paned window, a window that broke his squat, heavy body into a hundred overlapping fragments. 'To the Covenant,' he toasted himself. 'To the Covenant.'

Campion could only wait. Mrs Swan seemed genuinely glad of her company, not least because Campion could read the news-sheets aloud to her. Mrs Swan did not see the 'point' in reading, but she was avid for news. The war had made the news-sheets popular though Mrs Swan did not approve of the London sheets which naturally, supported Parliament's cause. At heart Mrs Swan supported the King and what she felt in her heart emerged easily on to her tongue. She listened as Campion read the stories of Parliamentary victories, and each one was greeted with a scowl and a fervent hope that it was not true.

Not much news that summer brought relief to Parliament. Bristol had fallen and there had been no great victory by which the balance of that defeat could be redressed. There were numerous small skirmishes, enlarged by the news-sheets into premature Armageddons, but the victory Parliament wanted had not come. London had other reasons to be gloomy. In their search for money to prosecute the war, the Parliament had raised new taxes, on wine, leather, sugar, beer and even linen, taxes that made King Charles's burden on London look light. Mrs Swan shook her head. 'And coal's short, dear. It's desperate!'

London was warmed by coal brought by ship from

Newcastle, but the King held Newcastle so the citizens of London faced a bitter winter.

'Can't you move away?' Campion asked.

'Dear me, no! I'm a Londoner, dear. Move away! The thought of it!' Mrs Swan peered closely at her embroidery. 'That's very nice, though I say it myself. No, dear. I expect King Charles will be back by winter, then everything will be all right.' She shifted closer to the window light. 'Read me something else, dear. Something that will cheer a body up.'

There was little to cheer anyone in the news-sheet. Campion began reading a vituperative article which listed those members of the Commons in London who had still not signed the new Oath of Loyalty that had been demanded in June. Only a handful had not signed and the anonymous writer claimed, 'that tho it bee said sicknesse bee the cause of their ommission, yet it bee more likelie a sicknesse of the courage than of the bodie'.

'Can't you find something interesting, dear?' Mrs Swan asked, before biting a thread with her teeth. Campion said nothing. She was frowning at the ill-printed sheet so intently that Mrs Swan's curiosity was aroused. 'What is it, dear?'

'Nothing. Really.'

Such an answer was a challenge to Mrs Swan, who could extract from nothing enough material to fill three happy mornings in gossip. She insisted on an answer, but even she was surprised that the subject of Campion's interest was merely that Sir George Lazender was one of the Members who had not signed the new oath. Then a thought suggested itself. 'Do you know Sir George, dear?'

'I met his son once.'

The embroidery went down. 'Did you now?'

Campion endured a relentless cross-examination, confessing to her one meeting, though not the circumstances, and ending by slyly admitting that she wanted to see Toby again.

'Why not, dear? So you should. Lazender, Lazender. Well-off, are they?'

'I think so.'

Mrs Swan smelt a customer, if nothing else, and in the last evening light before the candles were lit she bullied Campion into borrowing paper, ink and a quill from Jacques Moreau. She wrote a simple message, merely saying that she was in London, staying with Mrs Swan ('gentlewoman', Mrs Swan insisted on that, and made Campion trace out the letters one by one to her satisfaction), and that she was in the house with the blue door in Bull Inn Court to which Toby would be a welcome visitor. For a moment she wondered how to sign the letter, uncertain if he would remember the fanciful name he had given her by the stream, but then she found she could not write her true, ugly name. She signed herself Campion. The next morning they both walked to Westminster. Mrs Swan took her to Parliament itself, pushing through the booksellers of Westminster Hall, past the crowded lawyers' offices, to leave the message, care of Sir George, with a clerk of the Speaker. Then Campion was forced to wait with even more apprehension than she felt about Sir Grenville Cony and the mystery of St Matthew's seal.

Even the diversions of London could not erase the expectations from her heart. Mrs Swan insisted on showing her the city, but every minute Campion was away from Bull Inn Court was a moment during which Toby might call, and she might miss him.

On the second evening after they had delivered the letter, they went to Jacques Moreau's house where three households had gathered together for music. The French tailor played the viol, his wife the flute, and it should have been a happy evening, but Campion was racked with apprehension. Perhaps he would call this evening, when she was not in the house? Then she wondered if he would bother to call at all. Perhaps he would not remember her, or if he did he would dismiss the letter with a laugh, pitying her, and in those moments she wished she had not written to him. She convinced herself, listening to the music, that he would not come, so she tried to persuade herself that she did not want him to come. Then she wondered, if he did come, whether she would still like him. Perhaps it would all be a terrible, embarrassing mistake, and she tried once more to believe she was indifferent to his response. Yet every time there were footsteps in the Court she would look anxiously out of the window.

Perhaps, she thought, he was not in London. She invented a hundred reasons why he could not come, yet she still waited for the footsteps; she hoped, she feared, she waited.

She had met him once, only once, and in that one meeting she had fixed on him all her hopes, her dreams, her imagination of the word 'love', and she knew it was foolish, yet she had done it, and now she was frightened that he would come and she would discover that he was ordinary after all. Just another man who would stare at her as the men in London stared.

The next morning her hopes faded. So much time seemed to have passed since the letter was given to the clerk at Westminster, and it was impossible for her hope, fear and apprehension to stay at the same pitch. Campion was helping Mrs Swan's maid in the small kitchen, plucking two scrawny chickens that had been bought that morning. She plucked with short, hard tugs while the maid was drawing the first bird, her hand plunged up to the wrist in entrails. There was a knocking on the door. The maid went to rinse her hand in the bucket, but Mrs Swan called that she was by the door and would answer.

Campion's heart was racing. It could be just a customer, come to fetch a cushion cover or curtain square, and she tried to calm her hopeless expectancy. He would not come. She tried to persuade herself of that. There were voices in the hall but she could make out neither the words nor the speakers.

Mrs Swan's voice grew louder and most distinct. She was talking of the chickens bought that morning. 'Prices, dear! You wouldn't believe it! I remember when you could feed a family of eight on five shillings a week, and good food too, but now you couldn't give a man a square meal for that. Oh dear, my hair! If I'd known you were coming I'd have worn a cap.'

'My dear Mrs Swan, you beauties obviously attract each other.'

It was he! The voice crashed on her with such sudden familiarity that it seemed she could never have forgotten. It was Toby, and she could hear him laughing, and Mrs Swan offering him the best chair, refreshment, and she hardly heard his reply. She had been pulling at the last, obstinate small feathers on the chicken and her apron was fluffy with the small wisps. She took her bonnet off and her hair hung loose. She knew she was blushing. She brushed desperately at the small feathers, twitched her hair transferring the feathers to her head, and then there was a shadow in the doorway. She looked up and he stood there, grinning at her, and the grin turned into a laugh, and in that one moment she knew it was all right. She had not been wrong about him, she would never be wrong about him again.

She wondered how she could ever have forgotten his face with its easy smile, its curly red hair falling either side of the strong lines of jaw and cheek. He looked her up and down. 'My little feathered angel.'

She almost threw the chicken at him. She was in love.

8

For two days, it seemed, they did nothing but talk. Mrs Swan was an easy chaperone, always ready to put her feet up and 'let you young things go on without me,' though if anything truly interesting was promised she was assiduous in accompanying them. On the second evening they went to a play together. The theatre had been banned by the Puritans, but dramas were still privately staged in some large houses, and Campion was astonished by the experience. The play was

Bartholomew Fayre, and there was an added spice to the occasion for they could all have been arrested simply for watching the actors.

Campion had never seen a play and did not know what to expect. Her father had preached that such things were spawned of the devil and the performance was not without moments of sharp guilt for her. Yet she could not but find it amusing. The audience, unsympathetic to London's new masters, revelled in Ben Jonson's mockery of the Puritans. Campion had never known that the mockery existed, that people despised and hated men like her father, yet even she could see that the character Zeal-of-the-land Busy was both typical and ridiculous. The audience roared their approval when Zeal-of-the-land Busy was finally clapped in the stocks, and for a moment Campion was appalled by the hatred she sensed around her. Then the actor who played Zeal-of-the-land Busy made such an amusing face, one that reminded her of her father's scowl, that she laughed out loud. Toby, who was sensitive to her moods, relaxed beside her.

Campion was luckier than she knew. Toby's father, who was a sensible man, often thanked God for his fortune in his only son. Toby Lazender was someone to be proud of. He had inherited his mother's independence and spirit, but he had also taken his father's intelligence and sympathy. Toby knew that his parents would disapprove of Campion, his father would say Toby must marry money, for the sake of Lazen's roof, and preferably well-born money, while what Lady Margaret would say, Toby could not predict; his mother being a lady difficult if not impossible to predict. Campion's parents, her birth, her station, all conspired against Toby, yet he would not give her up. To his own mind their first meeting had seemed as fortuitous and miraculous as it had to Campion, and now on this second meeting it seemed instantly that they had shared a lifetime, so much did they have to say. Even Mrs Swan, who was rarely short of a word, marvelled at their loquaciousness.

Toby would inherit Lazen Castle with all its fertile lands in the Lazen valley and its flocks in the higher land to the north. He was twenty-four now, more than ready for marriage, and he knew that his mother kept a memorized list of girls suitable to take her place in Lazen Castle. Toby now dismissed them all. It was foolish, he knew, wildly impractical, yet nothing now would deflect him from the Puritan girl he had met beside a summer stream. He had fallen in love with all the unexpectedness, suddenness and impracticality that love is capable of, and Mrs Swan, observing it, was delighted. 'It's like Eloise and Abelard, it is, and Romeo and Juliet, and Will and Beth Cockell.'

'Who?' Campion asked. They were alone in the house, late at night.

'You wouldn't know the Cockells, dear. He was a baker in St Sepulchre's and he took one look at Beth, he did, and his yeast was up for life, dear.' She sighed romantically. 'Very happy they were, too, till he died of the stone, poor man. Broken-hearted, she was. She went a week later. Said she couldn't live without him and she just took to her bed and faded away. So what did he say to you today?'

They were in love, and the hours when they were not together were like endless nights, while the hours they shared flew like minutes. They planned a future that took no notice of the present, and they talked of their lives as though they would be spent in an eternal summer beneath an unmarred sky. In those days Campion discovered a happiness so great she thought her heart could not contain it, yet reality was remorseless in its pursuit of them.

Toby spoke of her to his father. As he expected, but with a force that was quite unexpected, Toby had been told that Campion was unsuitable. She would not do, she must be forgotten, and Sir George would not even agree to meet her. His opposition was absolute. There was more. Toby had to leave London, on pain of possible arrest and imprisonment, three days before Campion's appointment with Sir Grenville. Toby shook his head. 'I won't leave.'

'You must!' Campion was terrified for him.

'I'm not leaving without you.' He was adamant. 'I'll wait.'

Mrs Swan, with her gossip-sharpened acuteness, quickly divined that Toby was of Royalist sympathy. She liked him for it. 'I remember Queen Bess, young man, and I tell you they were good days. Ah me! They were good days!' In truth Mrs Swan had been a toddler when Queen Elizabeth had died, though she claimed to remember being held up in her father's arms to see the royal coach go by. 'There weren't so many Saints then, I can tell you. A man prayed in his bedroom or in his church and there wasn't all this caterwauling in the streets and gloom in the pulpits. We were happier then.' She sniffed in disapproval. 'The country's got drunk on God since then, and it don't make for happiness.'

Toby smiled. 'And the sun always shone on good Queen Bess?'

Mrs Swan knew she was being teased, but she liked being teased by good-looking young sons of the gentry in her own parlour. 'It's a funny thing, Mister Toby, but it did. If that doesn't show God approving of us, I don't know what does.' She shook her head and laid her work on the table. 'We used to have such fun! Tom and me went to the bear baiting, and the plays, and there was a puppet man in the Paris Garden who could make you roll on the grass! He really could! There was no harm in it. There were no Roundheads then, telling us what we could and couldn't do, not when the Queen was in London. I don't know why they don't all go to America and leave us in peace. They're welcome to America! They can all be gloomy there and let us be happy here.'

Toby smiled. 'You could be arrested for saying that.'

Mrs Swan snorted in derision. 'From what you say, Mister Toby, you could be arrested just for showing your nose in the street. I don't know what the country's coming to, I really don't!'

Toby did not leave London on Sunday, nor on Monday. He would wait till Campion had seen Sir Grenville Cony, for Toby, like Campion, believed that in some way the lawyer would point her towards freedom. They speculated endlessly about the seal, the letter, even the pearled gloves, but in all their speculation they did not find a solution that convinced them. Sir Grenville Cony had the answer, if any man did, and Toby would not leave London till he had learned it. He would not, he said, leave Campion either. Together they planned their improbable, impossible future as if love could conquer everything.

Yet Toby was wanted. A description had been circulated to the watch, to the soldiers in the city, and Campion was appalled at the risks he took. He walked openly in the streets with her, his dark red curls obvious beneath his wide-brimmed hat, and on the Tuesday, the day before her appointment with Sir Grenville, he came close to being caught.

They were walking from St Giles, both soberly dressed, though Toby insisted on having black satin beneath his slashed sleeves. He was laughing at some joke he had made when a burly man stepped into their path. The man raised a hand to Toby's chest. 'You.'

'Sir?'

The man's face was twisted with anger and inner hatred. 'You're him, aren't you? The Lazender scum!' He stepped back, raising his voice. 'A traitor! A traitor!'

'Sir!' Toby's voice was just as loud. People were watching, ready to side with the burly man, but Toby made them listen. He let go of Campion's arm and pulled up his sleeve, pointing to a great white scar that ran ragged on his left forearm. 'I took that wound, sir, last year on Edgehill field. Where were you, sir?' Toby stepped a pace forward, his right hand now dropping to his basket-hilted sword. 'I drew this sword for the Lord, sir, and I did not have you at my side when the forces of evil surrounded me!' Toby shook his head sadly. 'Praise the Lord, brothers and sisters, for He delivered me, Captain Scammell, from the Papist hordes of that man Charles. A traitor, am I? Then I am proud to be a traitor for my Lord and Saviour! I have slain for the Lord, brethren, but was this man with me?'

Toby's imitation of the Puritan rabble-rousers was so convincing that the small crowd were now all in sympathy with him. The burly man, taken aback by Toby's pious vehemence, was eager to offer apologies and beseeched Brother Scammell to kneel in prayer with him. Toby, to Campion's infinite relief, was magnanimous in victory, declining to pray, and pushing his way through the dispersing crowd with many expressions of piety. Once they were clear he grinned at her. 'I got that scar two years ago, falling off a horse, but it comes in useful.'

She laughed, but there was a desperate worry in her. 'They'll find you, Toby!'

'I'll put on a disguise, like those actors.'

'Be careful!'

Toby was taking some precautions, however. He had stopped sleeping at his father's house, using instead the rooms of a friend in the city itself, but the experience with the angry man in St Giles had worried him. 'There's only tomorrow.'

'Then what?'

They had paused outside Mrs Swan's house. He smiled down at her; the gentle, amused smile she liked so much. 'Then we'll marry.'

'We can't.'

'Why not?'

'Your father!'

'My father will fall hopelessly in love with you.'

'Toby! You said he won't even meet me!'

Toby smiled again, one finger on her cheek. 'He will. He'll have to. He can't refuse to meet my wife, can he?'

She looked at him, a small frown on her face. 'Are we mad, Toby?'

'Probably.' He smiled. 'But all will be well, I promise you. All will be well.'

She believed him, but then she was in love, and lovers always believe that fate is on their side.

★

Sir George Lazender, alone in his upstairs parlour of the house he would leave in two weeks' time, lit a pipe of his beloved tobacco and wished that the popular belief, that the tobacco-leaf was a dangerous substance giving rise to unnatural fervour and strange fancies, was true. He faced too much reality, too many problems.

He was about to alienate his son-in-law and his eldest daughter. He did not think the enmity would run deep, but they would undoubtedly become enemies.

Now he had estranged Toby.

Twice the soldiers had searched the house for his son, and twice Sir George had truthfully said that he did not know Toby's whereabouts. He suspected his son was staying in the city and he hourly dreaded the news that Toby had been arrested and imprisoned.

It was the girl's fault. The Slythe girl. Sir George felt anger. She must be a conniving, ambitious girl to have snared his son.

He walked to the eastern window and stared down into the street. It was dark, the lights of a few torches fitful. Two soldiers, their helmets catching the red glare of the flames, paced towards the Royal Mews. An empty cart went the other way.

And what a story she had told Toby to snare him! Tales of a Covenant, of a seal, of a fortune so big that it belonged to a child's imagination. Yet Toby believed her! He had spoken to his father of Sir Grenville Cony, of Lopez and Aretine, of a jewel on a chain. It was all nonsense.

Sir Grenville Cony was a respected member of Parliament, a Chancery lawyer who had done brilliantly and who now moved the levers of power in the Committees of Parliament. What could Sir Grenville have to do with a country Puritan?

Lopez. Sir George knew of a dozen Lopez's, Spanish Jews all, and none were left in England, though Sir George suspected that a few Jews lived quietly and untroubled within the city. Lopez. What could a Spanish Jew have to do with a girl from Dorset?

And Aretine. Sir George admitted to a twinge of pleasure at the memory. Christopher Aretine, always known as Kit, friend of Jack Donne, and dead, Sir George supposed, these many years. Kit Aretine was the only Aretine Sir George knew of, though it was possible there were more. Lady Margaret would know; she knew all the leading families.

Sir George had never met Kit Aretine, though he had heard him spoken of a hundred times in his youth. The wildest man in England, Jack Donne used to say, a man who could outfight, outwit and outlove any man in England. A rogue with the ladies, a wit, a poet, and a man who had been put in the Tower by King James. Somehow he had got himself out, but only at the price of perpetual banishment from England.

Sir George puffed at his pipe, wreathing himself with smoke, and tried to remember what else he knew of Aretine. A bad poet, Sir George seemed to remember, too much passion and not enough discipline. He must be dead now. Once a man got into print, Sir George knew, he developed a taste for more, and Aretine had not published these twenty years or more. Dear God! What could a dead poet have to do with the Slythe family?

Toby said the girl was beautiful, and Sir George made a scornful noise at the memory. Any girl was beautiful if you were twenty-four, just as any food looked appetising to a hungry man. Sir George walked back to his chair, regretting the empty bookshelves about him. The volumes were packed away, ready to travel.

At least Toby had promised him one thing. He would return to Lazen Castle as soon as this foolish business with the girl was done. Sir George feared, feared mightily, that his son might marry the Slythe girl on the way, but Toby had promised to talk to his mother first. Sir George smiled.

Lady Margaret Lazender would end the girl's hopes. Sir George almost felt sorry for her, pitted against such a formidable enemy. Sir George had sent a letter with the Earl of Fleet, that would reach Lazen Castle long before Toby did. It forewarned Lady Margaret, and a forewarned Lady

Margaret was even more dangerous.

'The girl is, bye Tobie's owne Account, quite Unlettered except in the Scriptures. She knoes No Manners except Those of the Puritans, and her Birthe ye knowe as well as I.

'The Girl has Persuaded Tobie, bye Means I scarce credit, that she must inherit Monie. It is a Fancifull tale, a romance as headie as Tobie's braines.'

Sir George remembered the letter. Did his son not know he must marry money? Dear God! The Old House at Lazen needed tiling and the watermill must have a new shaft. Sir George knew what the old shaft had cost in his grandfather's time and he dreaded to think what it must be at today's prices. If Toby did not marry money then the rents at Lazen would have to be raised and that was a step Sir George and Lady Margaret shrank from.

It was not simply a question of money. Toby must marry birth, breeding, a girl whose manners were equal to Lazen's responsibilities. Sir George shook his head sadly.

'He has promised mee, Faithfullie, That He will seeke you Before he marries the Girl. I beg you to Deale Firm with them.' That sentence, he knew, would bring a smile to his wife's lips, wondering why her husband had not dealt more firmly. 'The Girl must be sent Back to Werlatton, and If She must be Paide for her Silence, Then I knoe you will bee Discreet. Tobie, as hee desires, Must goe to Oxford to Fight for His Majestie.

'I sende this Letter with John, who does not knoe my Minde on Matters of State. I beg you not to tell him, but waite Upon my arrivall.'

Sir George puffed his pipe. Toby would recover from this infatuation and the girl would too. She would marry someone, some canting Puritan who would make her fat on babies and trade. Lady Margaret would deal with it, as she always dealt with problems. Sir George could leave it in her capable hands.

Toby came for Campion at five o'clock the next afternoon.

He had adopted a simple disguise, donning the leather jacket of a soldier and covering his distinctive red curls with a greasy, leather helmet-liner. He had not shaved that morning, so that he looked faintly sinister and brutal. It was an effect he liked. Campion was already aware of his penchant for play-acting. He loved to mimic, to pretend to be other than he was, and she had seen, with the man in St Giles, how useful that talent could be. Today, though, she stopped him as he played the part of a brutal soldier in the Strand. 'If you don't calm down, Toby, I'll walk on the other side of the street.'

He had been growling and giving combative stares to innocent passers-by. He grinned. 'I'll obey orders, ma'am, simple soldier that I am.'

She stopped when she saw the strange stone beasts on the cornice of Sir Grenville Cony's house. 'I'm nervous.'

'Of what?'

'What do I say to him?' Her blue eyes stared guilelessly at Toby, who laughed.

'We've talked about it for a week. You know what to say.'

'But suppose he won't answer?'

'Then we go to Lazen, get married, and forget all about it.'

She moved into the doorway of a building to avoid the crowds who pushed past them. 'Why don't we do that anyway?'

'Do you want to?'

She smiled. 'Yes. But.'

'But you're curious. So am I!' For a moment Toby was tempted. They could walk away, they could run away, and they could abandon the Covenant and the seal as part of a world Campion wished to forget. They could find a priest, get married and Toby did not care one whit for the opposition of his parents, so long as he was with this golden, calm-faced beauty.

She looked shyly at him. 'If I truly had ten thousand pounds a year, would your father approve of me?'

'He would for a thousand!' Toby laughed. 'The roof of the

Old House will overcome any of his principles.'

She looked past him at Sir Grenville Cony's house. 'Perhaps he won't want to see me.'

'So find out.'

'I wish you could come in with me.'

'So do I, but I can't.' He smiled. 'He's an important Parliament man, remember? He'd have to arrest me on the spot, and I don't think that would help you.'

She looked at him decisively. 'I'm being stupid. What can he do to me? Either he tells me or he doesn't.'

'Correct. And I shall wait for you outside.'

'Then Lazen?'

'Then Lazen.'

She smiled. 'I'll get it over with.'

'One minute!' He had been holding a leather bag which he had not explained to her, but which he now picked up, unlaced, and drew out what it held.

It was a cloak of powder blue, a silvery touch to the threads, and he held it up so she could see the silver clasp at its throat. 'For you.'

'Toby!' It was lovely. The cloth had a sheen that made her want to touch it, to wear it, and he tenderly put it about her shoulders, then stepped back.

'You look beautiful.' He meant it, too. A woman, passing the doorway, looked at Campion and smiled.

Toby was pleased. 'It's your colour. You should always wear that blue.'

'It's wonderful!' She wished she could see herself, but even to the touch it felt luxurious. 'You shouldn't have done it!'

'I shouldn't!' He mocked her gently.

'I like it.'

'It's your travelling cloak.' He twitched it unnecessarily. It hung to perfection on her slim, tall body in long folds. 'You can wear it down to Lazen. Now give it back to me.'

'No!' She smiled in delight. 'I shall wear it now. I shall wear it in Cony's house and I'll know I have something of yours.' She clutched the edges of the cloak. 'May I?'

He laughed. 'Of course.' He held out his arm to her, a strangely courteous gesture from such a villainous looking man, and escorted her across the Strand.

She had half expected the alleyway beside Cony's house to be crowded with petitioners. Today, she had been told, was the day when Sir Grenville dealt with the public, but to her mild surprise the narrow, dark alley was as deserted as before. The river gleamed at the far end.

'Toby!' She had stopped short of the porchway.

For a moment he thought her nerve had failed her, but then he saw her hands busy at her throat. 'What is it?'

'Here.' She held something to him. 'I want you to have something of mine while I'm in the house.'

It was the Seal of St Matthew, golden in the rancid alleyway, its chain swinging from Toby's palm. He shook his head. 'No.'

'Why not?' She would not take it back.

'Because you might need it in there. Maybe it's the proof he'll need to give you some answers.'

'Then I'll come and get it from you.'

'But it's yours! It's valuable!'

'It's ours! Keep it for me.'

'I'll give it back when you come out.'

She smiled. 'All right.' He put it about his neck, inside his shirt and leather jerkin, and he was glad she had given it to him. He needed something of hers at this moment, for lovers need talismans, and the gold felt good against his skin.

'I'll wait for you.'

They kissed, as they had kissed a thousand times in the week, and then she walked purposefully towards the door and pulled the iron-handled chain. She was early, but she wanted this meeting done quickly. She had a life to live, a life she had only dared dream of in the unhappiness of Werlatton, and once this meeting with Sir Grenville Cony was over, she could leave with Toby.

The bell had sounded deep inside the house.

She turned to Toby. 'I'll think of you.'

'I love you.'

The shutter snapped open. 'Yes?'

She turned. 'I'm Miss Slythe, to see Sir Grenville Cony.'

'You're early.' The voice was ungracious. The shutter snapped down and for a moment Campion thought she would not gain entry, but then came the sound of bolts being withdrawn, a bar being lifted and the wooden door swung open.

A thin, sallow young man stood there. He beckoned her inside. She turned once, smiled at Toby, and went into the dark passageway.

Toby saw the cloak swirl splendid in the gloom, saw her start to climb a brief flight of stone steps, and then the door slammed shut.

He listened to the echo of the door die away and, for an instant, it seemed that the house was utterly and strangely silent.

Then came the sound of the bolts being shot to, of the bar dropping into its iron brackets, unnaturally loud in the dark alley. He frowned, spoke Campion's name aloud, but the house was again silent.

9

Campion was shown into a spacious, empty room. It was quite silent, almost as if this was the heart of the strange quietness that emanated from the house. Even the clerks, in their gloomy, unseasonably chill room, seemed to make no noise as they put quills to curled papers. The man who had opened the door, evidently one of the clerks himself, had left, saying Sir Grenville would be with her soon. Then, disturbingly, he had locked the door behind him.

She hesitated, wondering whether she ought to wander free in such a private, silent chamber, but the view from the great mullioned windows drew her soundlessly across the deep carpet. The room looked on to the River Thames, and the silence within the house was made even more strange by the evidence of busy life upon the river. A score of boats were within sight, yet not one sound reached this rich, quiet room. Below her, entered from the floor beneath, was a garden of espaliered pear trees, of neat flowerbeds surrounded by gravel walks, all leading to a private pier that jutted into the river.

Alongside the pier was a barge, white-painted and beautiful. In it four oarsmen sat erect, their white-bladed oars upright, as if on display or under the watchful eye of a harsh master. In the boat's stern was a wide, cushioned thwart where she imagined Sir Grenville sitting in state.

She turned from the tall, velvet-curtained windows. The room, though rich, was sparsely furnished. In front of the window was a huge table, covered in papers which she supposed was Sir Grenville's desk. Behind it, facing the room, was an immense chair, its arms splayed, the whole upholstered in shining leather. In the room's centre, facing the desk, was a single, spindly chair that looked out of keeping with the rest of the room which was dominated by a huge, carved marble fireplace on the wall facing the window. Logs were laid for a fire that would not, she guessed, be lit till autumn. The room's single picture was vast above the fireplace.

It was a picture that could be concealed by wooden shutters, limewashed oak like the panelling of the room, but which now were folded back to show the large, gorgeous, and shocking portrait. A young man sat naked in a sunlit glade of a dark forest. His body was slim, muscled, and hard. His skin was tanned by the sun. Campion found herself thinking that Toby's naked body would look as tough and beautiful, and she was embarrassed by the thought. It shocked her, as much as it pleased her, but then she forgot such speculations for she was entranced by the face of the young man.

It was an extraordinary face, a splendid, arrogant, pagan

face. That face, she thought, ought to be framed by a gilded helmet and be staring at a conquered land. The young man had golden hair, falling either side of a wide, cruel mouth. She had never imagined that any man could be so handsome, so frightening, and so desirable.

The naked man was not looking out of the picture, but rather staring down at a pool hidden among rocks. The painter had showed the pool by letting its reflections gild the fine face, just as the sun was reflected by the Thames in liquid light ripples that moved on Sir Grenville Cony's ceiling.

The face still held her. She wondered if she would want to meet such a man, and then she tried to tell herself that no man could be so handsome, so golden, so arrogant, so perfect. This was a painter's fantasy, no more, yet still she could not take her eyes from the startling features.

'You like my painting.' She had not heard the second door, the door by the desk, open. She turned, startled, and in the doorway was one of the strangest figures she had ever seen. She was staring at a grotesque man, of stunning ugliness, who seemed to smile derisively at her.

Sir Grenville Cony, she supposed it must be he, was short. His monstrously fat belly was supported by thin, spindly legs that looked unequal to the task of holding such obscene grossness. His face was uncannily like the face of a frog, with a wide, mirthless slash of a mouth beneath bulging, pale eyes. His hair was white and curly. His brown, rich clothes were taut on his huge belly. He looked from her to the painting, to the life-size naked figure above her head. 'It is Narcissus in love with himself. I keep it to remind myself of the dangers of self-regard. You would not want me, Miss Slythe, to turn into a flower?' He chuckled. 'It is Miss Slythe?'

'Yes, sir.'

The bulging eyes stared at her. 'You know who Narcissus was, Miss Slythe?'

'No, sir.'

'Of course you don't. You're a Puritan. You know your Bible stories, no doubt?'

'I hope so, sir.' She felt Sir Grenville was mocking her. He smiled.

'Narcissus was a young man of such beauty, Miss Slythe, that he fell in love with himself. He would spend hours gazing at his own reflection and, as a punishment, he was turned into a flower, that flower we now call the narcissus. Do you think he is handsome?'

She nodded, embarrassed by the question. 'Yes, sir.'

'And so he is, Miss Slythe, so he is.' Sir Grenville was staring at his painting. 'That picture is also a punishment.'

'A punishment, sir?'

'I knew the young man, Miss Slythe, and I offered him my friendship, but he chose to be my enemy. I had his face put on to that picture as revenge, so that everyone would think that he was my friend, would believe that he had posed like that.' He was looking at her, laughing at her. 'You don't know what I'm talking about, do you?'

'No, sir.'

'Such innocence. All you need to know, Miss Slythe, is that I make a wonderful friend, and a very bitter enemy. Well?'

The last word was not addressed to Campion, but to a tall, well-built young man who had come into the room and now waited by the desk with a handful of papers. He gestured with the papers.

'The Manchester monies, Sir Grenville.'

Sir Grenville Cony turned. 'Ah! My Lord of Manchester's loan. I thought I had signed those papers, John.

'No, Sir Grenville.'

Sir Grenville walked to the table, took the sheaf of papers, and looked through them 'Twelve per cent, yes? What people will pay for money now! Is he importunate?'

'Yes, Sir Grenville.'

'Good. I like my debtors to be importunate.' He reached for a quill, dipped it in ink, and signed. Then, without turning round, he spoke to Campion. 'Are you not warm in that cloak, Miss Slythe? My secretary will take it. John?' He gestured for the young man to take Campion's cloak.

'I'll keep it, sir. If I may,' she added lamely.

'Oh, you may, Miss Slythe, you may.' Sir Grenville was still looking at papers. 'You may do as you like, it seems.' He plucked one paper from the desk. 'John, tell my Lord of Essex that if we put a tax upon saltpetre he will have no powder for his guns. I suppose we must treat him as a simple soldier. He seems intent on being one.' He thrust the papers at his secretary. 'Good. Now leave us alone. Miss Slythe and I do not wish to be disturbed.'

The secretary left and, once again, there was the ominous sound of a door being locked. Sir Grenville Cony ignored it, thrusting his huge belly between the angle of table and wall, and then settling in the vast leather chair. 'So you are Miss Dorcas Slythe.'

'Yes, sir.'

'And I, as doubtless you have surmised, am Sir Grenville Cony. I am also a busy man. Why have you come to see me?'

She was unsettled by his abruptness, by the distaste on his extraordinarily ugly face. The meeting was not at all as she and Toby had imagined it.

'I wished to ask you some questions, sir.'

'Meaning you wish me to supply you with answers? About what, pray?'

She forced herself to speak clearly, even boldly. There was something about the small, fat man that was unnerving. 'About my father's will, sir, and about the Covenant.'

He smiled, the wide mouth curving malevolently. 'Sit down, Miss Slythe, sit down.' He waited until she was perched precariously on the spindly chair. 'So, you wish some answers from me. Well, why not? I suppose that's what lawyers are for. Preachers for opinion, Miss Slythe, poets for fancy, and lawyers for facts. So, ask me your questions.'

Sir Grenville had begun a strange action as he spoke to her. His left hand was moving with stealthlike slowness along the surface of the table. It crawled like a crab, as if his white, pudgy fingers were small legs, and she saw that the hand was travelling towards a china dish in which were the remains of a fruit pie. His eyes stayed on Campion.

'Well, go on, girl!'

The hand distracted her. It had reached the dish now and the fingers were sidling slyly over the rim. She forced her eyes away and tried to think. 'My father's will, sir, seemed mysterious . . .' She tailed off lamely, her nervousness increasing with each second.

'Mysterious? Mysterious!' Cony's voice was oddly harsh for such a small, fat man. 'The will was read to you, was it not, by a lawyer? I will agree that Isaac Blood is merely a country lawyer, but I would have thought him competent to read a will! The hand had reached the remnants of pie now and was moulding pastry and fruit into a compact ball.

'He did read the will, sir.' Campion was trying to compose her thoughts, but still the sight of the hand, now on its slow way back from the dish, disconcerted her.

'I am so glad, Miss Slythe, so glad. For a moment I had thought you found our profession wanting, but it seems Mr Blood is spared this charge. So what, pray, was so mysterious? I found your father's will touchingly simple.' He smiled again, as if to soften his sarcasm and then, with an oddly ceremonious gesture, brought up his hand and popped the ball of crushed pie into his mouth.

He seemed to smile at her as he chewed, as if he knew he had succeeded in unsettling her. His left hand, freed of its first burden of pie, was once more creeping down the table.

Campion forced herself to look at the pale, unblinking eyes. 'In my father's will, sir, there was mention of a Covenant, and of a seal. Mr Blood was not able to give me details.'

He nodded, swallowed, and smiled again. 'So you have come all this way to find out?'

'Yes, sir.'

'Good, good!' The hand was almost at the dish again. He turned. 'John! John!'

The door was unlocked. Campion supposed that the secretary would be asked to fetch some papers, maybe even the Covenant itself, but instead he brought two shallow dishes on a tray. Sir Grenville waved towards Campion and the tray was offered to her. She took one dish, the thin china fearfully hot. She was forced to put the dish on the carpet, and saw that it contained a dark, transparent liquid in which some brown scraps floated.

Sir Grenville had taken the second dish, after which the secretary left, closing and locking the door. Sir Grenville smiled. 'Tea, Miss Slythe. Have you ever drunk tea?'

'No, sir.'

'You poor deprived child. You have never heard of Narcissus, and you have never drunk tea. It is a drink, Miss Slythe, brought from the Orient at considerable risk to mariners' lives, merely so we can enjoy it. Don't worry,' he had raised a pudgy hand, 'it contains no spiritous liquor. You may drink it in the knowledge that your soul is quite safe.' He bent over the dish of tea and slurped it noisily, straining it between his thin lips, and still his eyes seemed fixed on her. 'Try it, Miss Slythe. It is most expensive, and I will be offended if you spurn my kindness.'

She used the edges of her silver-blue cloak to carry the dish to her mouth. She had heard of tea, but never seen it, and the taste was strong and nauseating. She made a face.

'You don't like it, Miss Slythe?'

'It's bitter.'

'So many things in life are, don't you think?' It seemed to Campion that Sir Grenville was trying to be friendly now. She had stated her business, he must approve, and now he seemed to want to put her at her ease. His left hand crept once more towards the pie dish, which at last he acknowledged. 'It is a quince tart, Miss Slythe. Do you like quince tart?'

'Yes, sir.'

'Then you must try Mrs Parton's quince tarts. She makes them in a small house by Lambeth Stairs, from where they are conveyed to me, quite fresh, each morning. Have you brought me the seal?'

The question surprised her, startled her, so much that she

spilt some of the tea on to her beautiful, new cloak. She cried out in dismay, and the distraction gave her a second or two to think. 'No!'

'No what?'

'I have not brought the seal.' She was astonished at the vigour of his attack.

'Where is it?'

'I don't know!'

Sir Grenville Cony stared at her. She had the sensation that his pale, bulging eyes saw clean through her, into the recesses of her soul. She still held the tea-dish, her face still bore her distress at the stain on her new cloak. Suddenly he had seemed friendly, the offer of tea convincing her that he was prepared to deal kindly with her, yet now she realized that Sir Grenville was far better prepared for this interview than she was. He had not needed to tell his secretary what he wanted, the tea had been prearranged, and just as she was relaxing he had hit her with his fast questions. She put the tea unsteadily on to the carpet. Sir Grenville's voice was still harsh.

'You know what the seal is?'

'Yes.'

'Yes, sir.'

'Yes, sir.'

'Tell me.'

She thought quickly. She must reveal no more than what Isaac Blood had revealed on that day when he read the will. She spoke carefully. 'It authenticates a signature on any papers dealing with the Covenant, sir.'

Cony laughed. 'Very good, Miss Slythe, very good! So where is the seal?'

'I don't know, sir.'

'What does it look like?'

'I don't know, sir.'

'Really?' He put another ball of pie into his mouth and chewed as he stared at her. She wondered if he ever blinked and, just as the thought occurred to her, he did so. He blinked slowly, like a strange animal, and then his row of chins heaved as he swallowed the quince and pastry. 'You do not know what it looks like, Miss Slythe, yet when you first sought admittance to my house you described the Covenant as being that of St Matthew? Yes?'

She nodded. 'Yes, sir.'

'And how, pray, did you know about St Matthew?'

'My father told me, sir.'

'He did? He did, Miss Slythe?' The left hand was crawling again. 'Tell me, did you have a happy relationship with your father?'

She shrugged. 'Yes, sir.'

'Really, Miss Slythe? A pleasant father and daughter, were you? He talked with you, yes? Shared his problems? Told you all about the Seal of St Matthew?'

'He mentioned it, sir.'

He laughed at her, disbelieving, and then, quite suddenly, he seemed to change again. He leaned forward. 'So you want to know about the Covenant. Very well, Miss Slythe, I shall tell you.' He seemed to be thinking, staring over her head at the naked Narcissus while his left hand, that appeared to have a life of its own, groped and moulded at the fruit and pastry.

'Some years ago, Miss Slythe, your father and I, together with some other gentlemen, embarked upon a commercial venture. It does not matter now what it was, all that matters is that it was successful. Indeed! Very successful. I dare say we all surprised ourselves and even enriched ourselves. It was my thought, Miss Slythe, that the monies we had jointly made might be sufficient to keep us in our respective old ages, to make us comfortable in our dotage, and so the Covenant was formed. The Covenant was a convenient arrangement whereby one man could not cheat on his partners, and thus it has proved. We now severally limp into our dotage, Miss Slythe, those of us who survive, and the Covenant ensures our comfort during the winter of our lives. And that, Miss Slythe, is all there is to it.' He ended triumphantly, celebrating by another ceremonious gesture with a crushed ball of pie.

He had lied, just as her father had lied. If the Covenant had been a simple piece of business, why had her father not shared the monies with Ebenezer as well as herself? And she remembered the letters from her father's parents-in-law, letters that described Matthew Slythe as failing in his business. Yet Sir Grenville Cony would have her believe that her father had somehow attracted London merchants and Cony himself into some venture of unbelievable success. She looked at Cony. 'What was the business, sir?'

'None of your affair, Miss Slythe, none at all.' He had spoken harshly, and she was provoked by his tone.

'Yet the seal becomes mine, sir, when I am twenty-five. Surely that makes it my business.'

He was laughing at her now, his shoulders heaving up and down and his chins wobbling above his tight, white collar. 'Your business, Miss Slythe! Your business! The seal becomes yours, girl, because it is pretty! That is a woman's business, the procreation of children and pretty things, no more. You say you have not seen a seal?'

'No, sir.'

His shoulders still moved with laughter as he beckoned at her. 'Come here.'

She walked to the table as Cony struggled with the pocket of his waistcoat. His belly distended the brown cloth so much that he was unable to extract whatever he was looking for. She stared over his white, curly hair and saw that the boatmen still sat like statues in the barge, their white blades pointing at the blue sky. She thought of Toby in the alley, and wished he were with her. She was sure he would not be awed by this frog-like man who alternated between sarcastic friendliness and disdain.

'There.' The lawyer pushed something over the table.

It was exactly like the seal Toby held in the alleyway. Campion picked it up, surprised again by the weight of the gold. She saw the delicate banding of diamonds and rubies. Like the seal of St Matthew, this one too had a long, gold chain so that it could be worn as a pendant. She turned the seal to the window light and saw the same ornately chased border on the steel impression. She held it close and saw, in place of the axe, a beautifully carved winged lion. The mirror writing spelt 'St Mark'.

Holding this second seal, so like the first, once again she felt their mystery. She remembered the letter which described the seals as keys to great wealth, and somehow this sight of the second seal made the power of the gold cylinders seem far more real. She understood now that men would want these seals and that the lawyer across the desk was her enemy so long as she possessed one. She had thought her adventure was love, and now it was danger.

Sir Grenville's voice was light and careless. 'You should see what is inside.'

He so nearly caught her. The meeting of the seal's two halves was so cunningly hidden that it was not apparent that there was any interior to the cylinder, yet on his carefully contrived words her fingers moved automatically to unscrew the two halves. She remembered, even as her fingers took hold, and she kept her hands moving, as if all she wanted to do was dangle the seal by its long, heavy, gold chain. 'It's beautiful!'

Sir Grenville paused a long time. She could see the cylinder of gold reflected in his pale, glaucous eyes. He blinked slowly. 'I said you should see what is inside.'

She pretended innocence. She pulled at the seal, frowned, then shook it close to her ear.

'It unscrews.' He sounded disappointed.

She made a small, girlish sound of achievement as the cylinder came apart. For a second she thought it contained a crucifix, as did her father's, for she could see a similar human figure with arms spread wide.

Yet this was no religious symbol of ancient power. It was a depiction of a power far older than Christ's, as old as humanity itself. It was a woman, arms spread wide, her legs, too, splayed apart. Her head was back, her hips thrust forward and, tiny though the statue was, there was a hint of lust and abandon about the small, naked figure. Sir Grenville chuckled. 'Distasteful, is it not?'

She carefully joined the two halves, hiding the naked woman in her pleasure. 'My father would have disliked it, sir. Perhaps that is why he threw his away.'

He held out a pudgy, white hand for the seal and, reluctantly, Campion dropped it into his palm. He smiled. 'Threw it away?'

'We looked for it, sir. Everywhere. We couldn't find it.'

He waved her wearily towards the chair. 'Sit down.'

She obeyed him. She was feeling proud of herself. She might not have succeeded in finding out the truth from Sir Grenville Cony, but she had avoided his traps. She had not betrayed her own seal, and though she still did not know why the seals were important, she had learned that this rich, powerful man desired to possess them.

Sir Grenville tucked the Seal of St Mark carefully and laboriously away. 'You are right, Miss Slythe, that the Seal of St Matthew was to be yours on your twenty-fifth birthday.' His left hand had begun its surreptitious journey once more. 'In that year our little Covenant expires, our agreement is no more, and the seals become worthless. Apart from their intrinsic value, of course, which is not inconsiderable.' He smiled at her. 'I thought the seals were pretty, a bauble a young lady might want, and so I persuaded your father to give you the Seal of St Matthew at the end of its useful existence. He had one daughter, and why, I thought, should that daughter not possess one thing of beauty? Your father was not happy, but he agreed, humouring me no doubt. It was too good to be thrown away, but perhaps you are right. Perhaps, in a fit of virtuous wrath, he discarded the seal. Such a shame.' He shrugged. 'Was that all you came to see me about?'

It was not, but she was sure the truth was not to be found here. She was hot in her new cloak, and the sight of the river sparkling beyond Cony's windows had made her want to be out of this house. She wanted to be with Toby. She gathered the skirts of her cloak in her hands and nodded. 'That is all, sir.'

'How very curious, Miss Slythe, that you should come all the way from Werlatton to ask me such simple questions. And I note you have not finished your tea! Do so, child! Do so! Worry not, you will leave soon.' He smiled at her as she settled back on the uncomfortable chair. His hand, she saw, had stopped its journeys to and from the pie.

'Tell me, Miss Slythe, are you not betrothed to a Mr Samuel Scammell?'

She nodded.

He smiled. 'That was your dear father's wish, was it not?'

'Yes, sir.'

He stared at her, still smiling. 'Tell me, Dorcas, you don't mind me calling you Dorcas?'

'No, sir.'

'Then tell me, Dorcas, for I am ever curious, do you want to marry Mr Scammell?'

She hesitated, seeing the bulging eyes staring at her, seeing into her, and she wondered whether the truth would do her harm. She frowned. 'No, sir.'

'Ah!' He sounded surprised. 'How odd, how singularly odd. I never married, Dorcas. No. I have devoted my life to the harsh taskmastership of the law, of Chancery law, and of late, no doubt because I am not burdened with a wife, I have been asked to add my humble opinion to those who guide our ship of state. I understand, you see, much of law, and much of public policy, but little, I fear, of marriage. However, I always believed that young ladies such as yourself had little interest in anything but marriage. Do you not wish to be married, Dorcas? Do you desire, like myself, to devote yourself to the law?'

She nodded and spoke slowly. 'I would like to marry, sir.'

'Ah!' He held up a hand in mock surprise. 'I understand! It is Mr Scammell who is the problem, yes? You are not, perhaps, I think the vulgar phrase is "in love"?'

'I do not love Mr Scammell, sir.'

'Ah! You poor child. You poor, poor child. You want to be in love! You want the stars spread beneath your feet in a carpet of light, you want flowers in your heaven, and you want to meet a twin soul, breast on breast, and live in harmony and gold. Is that right?' She did not answer, and he chuckled. 'You have, I presume, read the marriage settlement?'

'Yes, sir.'

'Yet still you want love? Ah, but of course, you are not a lawyer as I am. True, I must divide my time between the councils of state and the Court of Chancery, but I still retain a few scraps of useful law in my old head. Mr Scammell, I believe, has signed the marriage agreement?'

'I believe so, sir.'

'Your belief is well founded. I assure you he has! He has moved from his London house, from his business of creating river-craft, and he has hired a man to keep his place of business going, and all so that he could devote himself to you! And now, because you want the stars at your feet, Mr Scammell must be disappointed! He has spent money on this marriage, Dorcas, he has made sacrifices, and in return he has been promised much! He is like a man who, having paid his price, is denied the goods! Do you not think, dear child, that Mr Scammell might now have recourse to the lawyers?'

His voice mocked her, taunted her, yet she could not take her eyes from the grotesque face that leered at her, smiling. He paused, she made no reply, and he chuckled.

'Suppose now, child, that Mr Scammell takes himself and his marriage agreement to the Court of Chancery. He complains that Miss Dorcas Slythe is fickle, that she prefers the stars and the sun and the moon to his own solid virtues. Shall I tell you what will happen? I shall! Nothing!' He laughed. 'To my own certain knowledge the Court of Chancery has of this day twenty-three thousand cases pending . . . twenty-three thousand! I would not have thought there was that much ink in the land, let alone lawyer's breath, but yet more cases come each day! Your case will be heard, Dorcas, it will be heard, but by that time you will be old, wrinkled and shrivelled and your money, such as it is, will have been drained from you by clever lawyers. And who, my child, will marry a fading flower whose future is tied up in Chancery?'

Campion said nothing. Mildred Swan had talked of 'being baked in a lawyer's pie', and now she knew what it meant. Her future with Toby, that endless summer beneath a seamless sky, was being shredded and soiled by the frog-like, laughing man. He leaned forward, his voice a conspiratorial whisper.

'You want to be free of Mr Scammell?' She said nothing. He looked dramatically into the corners of the room, as if someone might be listening. 'Do you want to be free of Mr Scammell, Dorcas, without the threat of Chancery either? Do you?'

She nodded. 'Yes, sir.'

'Then give me the seal, Dorcas. Give it to me.'

'I don't have it, sir.'

'Then you must marry Mr Scammell!' He spoke as if she were a small child, a singsong intonation in his voice. 'You'll have to marry Brother Scammell!'

'No!'

He leaned back, smiling at her, and his voice became friendly. 'My dear, dear Dorcas. What is it? Is it that you do not wish to make the beast with two backs with Brother Scammell? Is that it!' He laughed. 'I can see you now, so happy in your bedroom.' His voice rose, became harder, and he flayed her with a graphic and grotesque description of Scammell mounting her. She tried to blot her ears, she shook her head, she moaned, but his voice was relentless in its obscene, sweaty vision of her future. He mocked it by calling it 'love', and his words painted a picture far worse than her own thoughts had been of Scammell clambering on her as a bull reared on to a heifer. She was in tears when he had finished. He watched her cry, waited till the sobs were gentler.

'You want to avoid that, Dorcas?'

'Yes!'

'Then give me the seal.'

'I don't have it!'

'Then you must marry Mr Scammell.'

'No!' It was half a sob, half a cry of protest.

Sir Grenville Cony watched her shrewdly. 'One more chance, Dorcas, just one. You give me the seal of St Matthew, and I will give you a hundred pounds, yes, a hundred pounds! Enough for you to live on, child, while you find someone you care for more than you do for Mr Scammell.'

'No!' She had hardly listened, the image he had put in her head blotting out his words, but she dared not now reveal that she had lied. She would be questioned more, punished maybe, as her father had punished her, and so she gripped to her story. 'I don't have the seal!'

'Then you must marry Samuel Scammell.'

'I will not!'

She was recovering now, wanting to fight back if only with words.

He laughed, his wide mouth opening to show stained teeth. 'Oh, but you will, Dorcas, you will. I am a lawyer, remember? I can do most things, child, and even Chancery will move with unaccustomed speed when Sir Grenville Cony calls.' He was smiling hugely, and his left hand moved, not towards the pie, but to a piece of paper which he held up above the desk. She could see black writing on it, and a great, red seal dependant at its base.

'Shall I tell you what this is? It is a document, a legal document, and I took the trouble of collecting it this morning. I knew you might visit me, Dorcas, and I told the court of your plight. Ah! Such a plight! An orphan, not yet twenty-one, alone, away from home, and the court was touched. Yes! Truly touched. She needs a guardian, I said, as does her brother and, do you know, Dorcas, you are both now wards of court.' He laughed. 'Your brother seems happy enough, and I'm sure you will be. You're a ward of the court and I, Grenville Cony, am your guardian. Your future, child, is entirely within my capable hands.' He put the paper down, leaned back in triumph, and laughed.

She had listened, appalled, as her dreams had collapsed. She saw his white, round face split by the laughing mouth, tears blurred her vision, then she heard him call to his secretary.

'John! Open the door, John!'

There was gleeful anticipation on Cony's face. 'Come in! Come in! All of you!'

The room suddenly seemed filled with people, with faces staring at her in curiosity, in dislike, and she shook her head as if to clear it of a nightmare. 'No!'

'But yes!' Cony was standing now. 'You met Thomas Grimmett, I believe. He is my chief guard and a noble servant.' The man who had held her against the stable-block wall at Werlatton, who had thrust his knee between her legs, leered down at her. A boil was livid on his broad, broken-nosed face.

Cony's voice was relentless. 'Your dear brother, Ebenezer. Such a fine young man! I have offered him employment. And Goodwife! Loyal Goodwife, how pleased you must be that your errant chick is restored.'

Goodwife's spiteful face seemed about to spit at her. Ebenezer looked scornful.

Cony laughed. 'And Brother Scammell! Lo! Your bride, restored! What joy there is in the practice of law!' Samuel Scammell smiled at Campion, bobbed his shorn head, and she could feel the great clamps of law and duty and religion and punishment close on her soul. Her hopes, her love, her freedom, all were going, even as the light began to fade over the river. She bowed her head, she cried, and the tears dropped on to the fine, silvered threads of her cloak.

Sir Grenville Cony made a sympathetic noise. 'Ah! See how moved she is? She cried! Is there not more joy in heaven when one sinner repents?'

'Amen,' Scammell said.

'And amen!' Sir Grenville Cony said it fervently. 'Now, Ebenezer! Goodwife! Brother Scammell! Take dear Dorcas next door. Thomas will join you soon. Go now! Goodbye, dear Dorcas! I am glad you visited me, yes, very glad!'

She was taken from the room, Goodwife's hands spiteful on her, and when she was in the secretary's room Cony moved and slammed the door leaving him alone with his henchman Thomas Grimmett. Cony rubbed his eyes. 'The girl's got spirit.'

'Has she got the seal, sir?'

Cony edged round the table and sat down. 'No. I thought she might, but I don't think so.' He laughed. 'I offered her a price she couldn't refuse. No. She hasn't.' He looked up at the huge Grimmett. 'It's still in that damned house, Thomas. Search it again. Pull every damned stone down, dig up the garden if need be, but find it.'

'Yes, sir.'

'But first,' Cony pushed papers about on his desk until he came up with what he wanted, 'that's Scammell's marriage certificate, dated this morning to make it legal.' Sir Grenville sounded tired. He looked up again. 'She has to be married, Thomas, she has to be! You understand?'

'If you say so, sir.'

'I don't say so, Thomas, the law says so. The will says so, the marriage settlement says so. If she's married then Scammell is the seal-holder, and Scammell will give the seal to us.'

'You know that, sir?'

'I know it, Thomas, because you will stay with Brother Scammell until he does give it to you.'

Grimmett smiled. 'Yes, sir.'

'So get them married. Tonight! And make it legal. A priest, the prayer book, none of Scammell's ranting Puritans. You can fix that?'

Grimmett thought for a second. 'Yes, sir. Where?'

'In Brother Scammell's house.' Cony invested Scammell's

name with derision. 'Take her there in the boat, then do what you have to do.'

'Get them married, sir.' Grimmett grinned.

'Yes. And afterwards, Thomas, not before, because I want this legal, make damned sure she's no longer a virgin. I don't want her claiming the marriage isn't valid and opening her legs to prove it. If that damned Puritan doesn't know how to do it, then you stand over him.'

'Do it myself, sir?'

Sir Grenville looked up, curious.

'You like her?'

'Very pretty, sir.'

'Then you do it. It will be your reward.' He laughed at the huge, leather-jacketed man. 'The hardships you endure for me, Thomas.'

Grimmett laughed.

Cony waved at the door. 'Go on, then. Enjoy yourself. Leave the boy here, I've got a use for him. Come to me in the morning, Thomas. I want to hear all about it!'

Sir Grenville watched as the small party embarked in his barge. The girl, in her distinctive blue cloak, was struggling, but Grimmett easily subdued her with one hand. The servant, Goodwife, seemed to be slapping and pinching the girl who was beneath Grimmett's grip. Samuel Scammell walked behind, his hands flapping in impotent helplessness, and Cony shook his head and laughed.

He had been worried for a while, thinking the girl might have gone to Lopez, but he need not have worried. She was here, and the seal would turn up in a few days. All was well, indeed, more than well for Ebenezer was here. Sir Grenville, on first meeting Ebenezer, had seen the boy's need for a cause, had seen the bitter look on the cripple's face. There was no love there, either, for his beautiful sister. Cony smiled. It was time to educate Master Ebenezer, that gift from the gods to Cony's plans.

The sky had its first touch of red. The bargemen, the girl finally safe in the boat, pushed away from the pier. The oars dipped down, went forward, and the white-painted boat moved easily on to the darkening stream. Light flashed from the widening ripples at its stern. Sir Grenville Cony was tired, but happy. The Scots, he knew now, would come into the war against the King and that was good for Cony's investments, but this news was better. The seals would be his. He turned away from the river, looked up at the naked Narcissus bending over his pool, then threw open the anteroom door. 'My dear Ebenezer! My dear boy! We have so much to talk about. Bring that wine!'

Sir Grenville Cony was a happy, happy man.

10

James Alexander Simeon McHose Bollsbie knew, as did Sir Grenville Cony, moments of pure happiness. Bollsbie was a clerk in holy orders, a minister of the Church of England, ordained as such by the Bishop of London, licensed to preach, to administer the sacraments, to bury the dead, and, of course, to join Christian souls in holy matrimony.

The Reverend James Bollsbie was also a drunkard.

It was that circumstance, rather than any desire to witness for the Lord, which had prompted the nickname 'Sobriety'. Sobriety Bollsbie he had been for two years now. His drunkenness, in addition to supplying him with a new name, was also responsible for those moments of happiness he was given to enjoy. He also had moments of fearful despondency, but new every morning was the ale-given joy.

It had not always been so. He had once been known as a preacher of fire and conviction, a man who could start hysteria in the nearest pews and spread it back down the church. He specialized in sermons of hell fire, and had been known in a score of parishes as a man who could frighten sinners from their ale-houses into true repentance. He

preached against alcohol, yet the enemy had laid seige and broken into his citadel. Sobriety Bollsbie preached no more.

Yet even as a finished man, a broken drunkard in his late forties, Sobriety Bollsbie had his place in society. He had always been an adaptable man, ready to trim the sails of his belief to the prevailing wind of theological fashion; thus when Archbishop Laud had been supreme and had demanded church services modelled on the hated Papist ritual, Sobriety had been the first to deck his altar cloths and illuminate his choir with candles. When he saw that he had miscalculated, and that the pathway to heaven lay in a plainer, Puritan service, he had not been shy in his conversion. Not for him the sly change or the slow dismantling of ritual. He advertised his change of allegiance. He invited the Puritans to witness the destruction of his gaudy altar, the burning of his altar rails, and the shredding of his embroidered vestments. He preached a sermon in which he likened his enlightenment to the conversion of St Paul and thus, in one service, became the darling of the Puritan faction as a witness to their truth.

That adaptability he had carried into his fall and disgrace. Such was the entwinement of church and state that lawyers, such as Sir Grenville, were often in need of a willing priest to add God's imprimatur to their own. Bollsbie was such a priest.

Bollsbie lived now in Spitalfields, in a miserable room where Thomas Grimmett, having safely delivered Campion to Scammell's house, discovered the priest drunk. Grimmett manhandled Bollsbie downstairs.

'Leave me, good sir! I am a priest! A priest!'

'I know you're a damned priest. Hold on, Sobriety.' Grimmett picked up a pail of filthy water and poured it over the straggle-haired man. 'Sober up, you bastard!'

Bollsbie moaned. He rocked to and fro, miserable and damp. 'Oh God!'

Grimmett squatted at his side. 'When did you last eat, Sobriety?'

'Oh, God!'

'You're a miserable bastard. You've got a wedding, your reverence. Understand? A wedding.'

'I want to eat.'

'You'll eat. Now fetch your book, Sobriety. We're going.'

Grimmett helped the priest find his old cassock, a filthy scapular, and his prayer book, then he half carried the preacher into the lane which led to Bishopsgate. He stopped at the first pie-stall and forced two beef pies into Bollsbie, then primed him with a tot of rum. 'There, your Holiness. Remember me now?'

Sobriety smiled. 'It's Thomas, isn't it?'

'That's it, your reverence. Sir Grenville's man.'

'Ah! Good Sir Grenville! Does he do well?'

'You know Sir Grenville, reverend, he doesn't do badly. Now come on, we've got work to do.'

Bollsbie looked hopefully at the bag of bottles Grimmett carried. 'You want me as a witness? Yes?'

'I told you, Sobriety, a damned wedding. Now come on!'

'A wedding! How pleasing! I like weddings. Lead on, good Thomas, lead on!'

Toby Lazender grew bored. The alley was a cheerless place to wait. After an hour he walked to the Strand, persuading himself that Campion might be leaving by Cony's front door, but there was no life there except for the guard who leaned against the brick archway. Toby went back to the alleyway, down to the very end where the cobbles became a stinking river-washed ramp of littered mud. The wall of Cony's garden extended deep into the water and there was no way he could peer round its end. He went back to the porch, leaned against the opposite wall, and stared up at Cony's blank, featureless house. He must wait. Soon, he consoled himself, very soon, Campion would come through the door and they would be together.

He was in love, and he saw the world through the distorting glass of that love. Nothing mattered except that he should be with Campion, and his father's disapproval had seemed irrelevant. He had seen her first at the stream and, with the fear of love, he had thought she might not want to see him again. He had cursed himself for not going back, even though his return would have been impossible once he was in London, but then she had written to him and he had left his father's house within minutes of the letter's arrival. His life before he had met Campion, the hours he spent without her, both seemed an irrelevance. He was in love. His father, and doubtless his mother too, disapproved. By birth and education she was unsuitable, but Toby did not care. There was something in Campion's soul that intoxicated him, he would not be without it, and even the dank, sunless alley seemed brighter because of it.

He touched the seal, feeling it as a lump beneath his leather coat and shirt. It had touched her skin, now it touched his, and even that triviality was turned by the distorting glass into an omen of brilliant hope.

He heard her before he saw her. He was leaning against the wall, dreaming the dreams of the shadowless future, when he heard her shriek. He turned, catching one glimpse of the silver-blue cloak in the boat's stern, and then the oarsmen bent forward again, pulled, and the barge surged out of sight.

'Campion!' He ran to the water's edge, but already she was gone, the river current carrying her away. 'Waterman! Waterman!'

Damn, damn and damn again! There was never an empty boat when you needed one!

He ran up the alley, his boots loud between the walls, and he turned east into the Strand. He tried to think of the nearest stairs to the river. Exeter Street! The Temple Stairs! He pushed past people, careless of their complaints, and he knew that with each second his loved one was going further from him.

Scammell! It had to be Scammell! Campion had told him the whole story and he had made her tell it again and again as he searched for an escape within the legal tangle of will,

Covenant and marriage settlement. He wondered, as he pushed through the evening crowds, whether it was another name from the letter, Lopez perhaps, who had seized her, but if he was to rescue her then he had to make his own fateful decision about which of her enemies had taken her and his instinct said Scammell. A maker of boats, she had said, and the barge on which she had gone looked lavish and fitting for a boat-maker.

He turned off the Strand, banging into a solid merchant who shouted at him, and then he was taking the steps of Exeter Street down towards the line of people who waited for watermen.

A pikestaff slammed across the narrow street, stopped him, and a breastplated soldier moved in front of him. Two more came up behind him. 'In a hurry, lad?'

'Yes!' God damn! A patrol! One of the many that Parliament put into the streets to search for deserters.

They had him against the wall now. The other people using the street sidled at the far side, not wishing to be involved in any kind of trouble. The soldier who had stopped him looked Toby up and down. 'Who are you, lad?'

He thought quickly, snatching the name of the son of one of his father's colleagues. 'Richard Cromwell, Oliver Cromwell's son.'

'In a hurry, were you?' The soldier frowned, uncertain now.

'Yes. My father's business.'

'Let him go, Ted,' one of the other two said, but the third was frowning.

'Red 'air.' He sniffed. 'Strong build, red 'air. That's what the captain said we was to look for.' He snatched at the leather helmet-liner, tugging it clear of Toby's head. 'There you are! Red 'air!'

The first soldier was impressed, but still a little uncertain, 'Lazender?'

Toby forced himself to relax, even to smile. 'My name is Richard Cromwell. Take me to your captain. Who is he?'

The first man shifted uneasily. 'Ford, sir. Captain Ford.'

'Ah! Ford!' Toby laughed. 'I know Ford! Let's go and see him. Come on! You have your duty to do.' He smiled at the first man. 'What's your name?'

'Wiggs, sir. Edward Wiggs.' Wiggs looked pleased.

'Let's get it done then, Wiggs, then I can be about my father's business.'

Wiggs was quite prepared to let Toby go there and then, but the other two decided that a walk to Ludgate, their guardhouse, would be a welcome break in the monotony.

Toby contained himself. It was maddening, but to do the wrong thing was to invite disaster. He must pick his spot, and he watched the corner of Essex House coming closer as he carefully rehearsed his actions in his mind. Wiggs was on his left, saying that a word in the right place would be most welcome, thank you sir, while the other two trailed behind. They were all relaxed, lulled by Toby's cheerful co-operation, and then they were at the corner, the archway to Fleet Street on their right, and Toby pointed to the roof of the arch and laughed. 'Look at the stupid man!'

They looked, of course, and Toby brought his right knee about into Wigg's crotch, snatched the falling pike, and then ran. He heard the bellow of pain behind him and then started shouting himself, 'Make way! Make way! Stop him!'

The crowd assumed he was a soldier. They parted before the blade and looked round for the man he was chasing. The illusion was helped by Wigg's two colleagues who came shouting behind.

Toby was far fitter than the London apprentices who made up the city's garrison. He sprinted into the centre of the Strand, going away from the city, away from Campion, and then he twisted to his right into one of the foetid alleyways that lay to the north. He dropped his pike so he could go faster through the narrow maze. The shouts faded behind him.

He slowed at each corner, walking unconcernedly if he saw people ahead, greeting them casually, then running when an alley was clear. He knew now that he had escaped the soldiers, but he was tormented for Campion.

He paused at the corner of Bull Inn Court. The hue and cry was fifty yards away, lost in the complex of alleys, as he knocked on the blue door.

'Mister Toby!' Mrs Swan's eyes widened.

'Sh!' He put a finger to his lips, stepped past her, then bent over in the hallway to let his breath come in great gasps. 'I'm not here, Mrs Swan.'

'Course not, dear. Never seen you.' She shut the door. 'Tell me!'

'In a minute.' He straightened up, smiling at her. 'I think I need your help.'

'I think you do too, dear. Where's Campion?'

In trouble, Toby thought, in desperate trouble. And he had to rescue her.

Thames Street was the longest in the city, running three-quarters of a mile from the Customs House beside the Tower to the decaying walls of Baynard's Castle at Ludgate. Scammell's yard was almost in the centre of the street, built where a tangle of wharves and buildings jostled to the river bank.

Throughout the journey to the yard Goodwife was triumphant. She hit at Campion, pinched and scratched her, her voice slicing at the girl like a saw-blade. Goodwife brought up every misdeed of twenty years, every small sin, every disappointment to her parents, and every ounce of grief was squeezed from this catalogue of evil. It was counterpointed by verses of scripture from Scammell. Cony's boatmen watched, their faces impassive, while Grimmett smirked in the stern of the boat.

Goodwife tugged at the pale blue cloak. 'What's this? What's this? You were brought up in the ways of the Lord, and you dress like this?'

Samuel Scammell knew his cue. His voice was mournful. 'A woman with the attire of an harlot, and subtil of heart. She is loud and stubborn; Her feet abide not in her house.'

'Amen,' Goodwife leaped on to the end of the verse. 'A disgrace you are! A disgrace to your parents, to me, to Mr Scammell, to your Lord and Saviour, and what will Sir Grenville think of us? Tell me that! What will he think of us?' This last, despairing question was asked at a shriek that invited worried looks from passing boats.

They arrived at last, the boat pulling into a narrow slip between two piers, and Campion was pushed up steps into a yard piled with timber, stinking of tar and crammed with half-finished small boats. Scammell left Grimmett and Goodwife to guard her while he cleared the area of his workmen. They were curious, his foreman especially so, but Scammell chivvied them away. Cony's barge backed into the river, turned, and disappeared upstream.

On one side of the yard were tall sheds, filled with timber, and on the other Scammell's big, gloomy house. Campion was pushed inside, then into a small room that led from the hall. She was locked in, alone, and the sound of the key reminded her of the times when her father would punish her, locking her first in her room while he worked himself into a state to perform God's vengeance on a child.

The shutters of the room were locked closed, yet after a while her eyes adjusted to the gloom and she guessed she was in Scammell's old study. The shelves were empty now, but there was a table which still held some religious pamphlets. She tore one of them into shreds, but knew the futility of the gesture. It was not a pamphlet she wanted to tear up but this whole house. She wanted to scream, to cry, to pound her fists on the door in frustration, yet she would not give her enemies the satisfaction of seeing her utterly defeated.

Yet defeated she was. She knew it and, standing in the room, tense and frightened, she knew she was plunging into a great oppression of spirit. She fought back tears, hatred giving her strength, and she listened to the voices in the hall. Grimmett was explaining something, she could not hear what, and Scammell's voice was raised first in surprise, then expostulation, and finally agreement. The front door sounded and then there were only the voices of Scammell and Goodwife.

She hated hearing voices far away in a house. It reminded her of childhood, of listening to the anger of her parents, that harbinger of cruel punishment. She used to pray on those nights, pray desperately with her fingers clenched tight for one single, small sign of Jesus's love. Yet the only answer would be the wind about Werlatton, the darkness pressing on the great lawn, and the mutter of voices far off.

Time passed. She was panting now, though she did not know it, as if her body needed great draughts of air to calm it. And calm she did, slowly. Night was falling outside. She tried to open the shutters but her fingers were powerless against the locked metal bars.

She prayed. She prayed for deliverance. She knew God was there and she knew Jesus was love and, despite the evidence of her childhood, she insisted on believing that there might be goodness and love in God. She prayed, not to the Puritan God of punishment, but to a God of love. Her prayers, even as she uttered them, seemed hopeless.

The key turned. It was impossible for that sound not to awaken the terrors of childhood as the door opened and a candle appeared, just as it would when her father came late at night to beat her, his face heavy with God's burden as he despatched the maid, Charity. This time, though, it was Samuel Scammell who appeared.

He shut the door behind him, placed the candle on the table, and smiled at the girl who stood by the window. 'Shall we pray, Dorcas?'

She said nothing.

He beckoned her to come round the table and gestured at the floor. 'I thought if we knelt together and took our troubles to Him, it might help.'

The calmness of her voice surprised her. 'He tumbled the walls of Jericho. Do you have a trumpet?'

He flinched from the scorn in her voice. 'You don't understand, Dorcas. You're not well.' He kneaded the air with his hands, desperate for her understanding. 'Your father's death, it must be hard. Dr Fenderlyn said you should be physicked. You must rest, my dear, in Dorset.' He shook his head stupidly, then dropped into the language of Zion which saved him from thinking too deeply. 'Our Lord and Saviour Jesus Christ will help, Dorcas. Put your cares on Him, and your trust in Him.' His voice grew stronger as he fell into the cadences of worship. 'Though we be troubled, Dorcas, though we be afflicted, yet He is there! I know it! I've proved it in my life, through His saving grace, through the blood of the Lamb, Dorcas!'

'Be quiet!' She screamed it at him. 'Be quiet!'

Goodwife had advised him to beat Campion. She had said it would solve all his problems and he wondered if she was right. He blinked. He knew he was not a strong man, otherwise he might have resisted Grimmett's insistence that they be married this night. Scammell had protested that a marriage performed at night was illegal, but Grimmett had laughed. 'Leave that to Sir Grenville, sir. He knows what's legal.'

This then was Samuel Scammell's wedding night, the night when he would take on Matthew Slythe's sacred charge to lead Dorcas in the path of salvation. Scammell's religion had brought him to this night, to this bride, and though his flesh cried out for her, he was appalled at her strength of will. Perhaps Goodwife was right. Perhaps he should beat her into submission. He tried one more time.

'Are you truly saved, Dorcas?'

She despised him. She stood straight and tall by the barred shutters. 'I believe in Jesus Christ.'

His response was automatic. 'Praise Him. Praise Him.'

'I'm not your kind of Christian, though.'

He looked puzzled. One finger scratched at a cavernous nostril. 'There is only one kind, Dorcas.'

'And what kind is that?'

He was pleased that, at last, she was talking to him. Maybe he would not have to unloop the thick belt that held up his breeches. He smiled, his thick lips gleaming in the light of the single candle. 'A Christian is someone who has taken Jesus as their Lord, who obeys His commandments.'

'Which were to love one another, and to do unto them as you would have them do to you.' She laughed at him. 'Is that what you're doing? Forcing yourself on me is to obey one of His commandments?'

He shook his head impatiently. 'No, no, no. If a man is chosen of God, Dorcas, if a man is strong in the Lord, then he has a duty, yes, a duty to guide others. No one said that being a Christian is easy, Dorcas, yet we have to be shepherds to the flock. We have to guide them.'

There was an infinity of scorn on her face. 'And I am one of "them"? I have to be guided?'

He nodded, eager for her to understand. 'Women are weak, Dorcas, they are more flesh than spirit. Yet a woman's way is easier, because it lies in obedience. If you would submit yourself to obedience then you would not be troubled. I come to you, Dorcas, only in the spirit of God, in a desire to lead you in a goodly path. You should submit prayerfully, Dorcas, knowing that this is His will.'

She leaned forward on the table and he flinched from the anger in her face. Her words lashed at him. 'Submit! Obedience! That's all you know. Punishment, hate, that's your religion. If Christ were to come back today do you know what you'd do? You'd be running for the hammer and nails and shouting for someone to build a cross.' She straightened up. 'You're not marrying me out of Christian duty, Samuel Scammell. You're marrying me because it will make you rich, and because you want this!' She drew the hems of her cloak apart, showing her soberly clothed body. She spat on his religious tracts. 'That's for your greed, and that's for your lust.'

The anger was thick and hot in him, an anger fed by the memories of his own mother's treatment of him. Goodwife had been right! She should be beaten! He was humiliated in his own house and he would not suffer it. The anger gave him courage, his hands fumbled to pull his belt free, and the words shouted from him, 'You're a blasphemer, woman! A sinner! But you will be saved. You will!' The belt swung free and to Campion it was as if her father's mantle, together with his money, had dropped on to Scammell's shoulders. He cracked the belt in his right hand, bubbling incoherently in his wrath, and then stretched back to lash at her across the table.

She had gripped the table's edge and now, with a strength she did not know she possessed, she heaved up and kept heaving so that the candle and tracts slid towards him, the light flickering, until the table crashed over into sudden darkness and the edge struck with all its weight on to Scammell's foot.

He bellowed like a clumsily gelded calf, and the bellowing turned to self-pitying yelps. There was a rapping at the door.

'Master! Master!' It was Goodwife.

'Dear God! My foot's broken!'

Campion stayed still.

'Master! Master!' Goodwife shouted.

'I'm coming!' Scammell blundered in the darkness, whimpering as he tripped again, and then fumbled at the door.

It opened to show him crouching, his face, twisted in pain, turned up to the candle Goodwife carried. 'My foot's broken!'

'Never mind that, sir.' Goodwife looked over the room at Campion and on her face was triumph. 'The priest's here, master. Book and all.'

Scammell half straightened, turned to look at Campion then back to Goodwife. 'The priest?'

'Yes, master. For your wedding.' She looked at Campion, smiling with vindictive pleasure. 'For Dorcas's wedding. A happy night!'

There were voices in the hall. Campion shook her head. 'No!'

'Yes.' Goodwife came into the room, putting the candle on

a shelf. 'Off you go, master, prepare yourself. I'll stay with Dorcas. There'll be no trouble.'

Campion's day had begun in the sunlight of love with Toby, planning a future of love, yet now she was in utter darkness, and tonight she would be a bride. Scammell's bride.

Twice Toby tried to leave Bull Inn Court and twice he saw picquets of soldiers guarding one of the narrow lanes. They had pounded through the area, their shouts echoing off the high walls, and had searched some houses, thrusting their long pikes under beds or into the dark corners of cellars and attics.

Night came. He was in torment because he had to escape, yet he was trapped. Mrs Swan would do what he had asked of her, but she could not smuggle him past the soldiers, so he waited. He prayed hopelessly, helplessly, and tortured himself by imagining Campion's fate.

It was past ten o'clock before the soldiers left and even then Toby had to move with infinite caution, seeking out each shadow before he crossed a street or moved down an alley. He went to the river, feeling naked under the flickering torch that illuminated the Temple Stairs, yet he knew this was the fastest way to find Scammell's house.

Few watermen worked at night; there was enough business to keep some afloat till midnight, but not many. Toby knew he must be patient, yet it was hard. He watched, frustrated, as bow lanterns appeared feeble to his right, grew brighter, then shot past towards the city. The boats carried the late traffic from Whitehall, yet none of their passengers seemed to want to alight at the Temple Stairs. Finally an empty boat appeared and Toby stepped into the stern. 'Do you know Scammell's yard?'

' 'Cos I know Scammell's yard. Where do you think the boats come from?' The oarsman spoke truculently, still leaning on his oar.

'I wish to go there.' Toby tried to contain his patience.

'At night, sir? At night!' The man laughed at him, then turned round to his fellow waterman. 'Hear that, Jake? Genn'l'man wants to go to Scammell's yard at night!'

The bow man grinned in the light of the torch. The first man looked back at Toby. 'Can't do it, lad, can I? It's dangerous down there at night. Damned great pilings in the river, rotten they are, they'll have the bottom out of this sooner than you can pay me. No, sir, not at night. I'll land you at the stairs, that's different. What do you want? Paul's or the Bridge?'

Neither would do. Toby had reasoned, hiding in Mrs Swan's parlour, that Scammell's yard would be closed up at night, the easiest ingress being from the river. He leaned forward, smiling. 'I wish to lighten your darkness.' Toby took out a gold coin that he had borrowed from Campion's hoard. 'I wish to be landed at Scammell's yard.'

The stroke oar looked at the coin, then at Toby. 'One each?'

'This is all I have.'

'Might be done. We can have a try.' He grinned. 'Very good, sir, we'll see how much light you can throw on our path.' He nodded, a signal to his companion, and at last the boat left the treacherous flame-light of the stairs.

The oars moved in to dark water and turned the boat, the current helping them downstream. Yet Toby knew he was late. The oars' rhythmic beat seemed to sound the endless message. Too late, too late, too late.

11

Thomas Grimmett waited for Scammell in the hall. He was grinning. 'Priest's out the back, sir. He'll be here in a minute.' He jerked his head towards the kitchen whence came the sound of someone being violently sick. Grimmett looked hopefully towards the shut study door. 'You want me to help look after her, sir?'

'No, no. She'll be out soon.' Scammell was shaking, his foot hurting. He wanted to marry Dorcas, yet he had never thought it would be like this. He did not like it, yet he was much too frightened of Cony's big henchman to protest. He waved towards his dining-room. 'I'll wait in there.'

'Yes, sir. You do.' Grimmett might call Scammell 'sir', but he made no attempt to hide his scorn for the plump, frightened man.

Scammell found that someone, Goodwife presumably, had prepared the dining-room for the wedding ceremony. The large table had been pushed aside, leaving the dusty floor clear, while a small table had been put under the window that looked towards the river. It had been covered with a white linen cloth and the whole room made bright with candles.

Scammell was unhappy. He was ashamed of himself, not just for being beaten by the girl, but because she had spoken the truth to him. He had gone to Werlatton first because of the money the marriage would bring him, expecting his bride to be as lumpish and unattractive as Matthew Slythe himself, and then he had seen Dorcas. To his greed was added lust. He knew she did not want the marriage, and he suspected that his wedded life would not be one of unalloyed bliss, yet he could in no way shake off his lust for her. He dreamed at night of the gratification that coupling with her would bring, and he was ashamed of his thoughts.

He had prayed about it. He had asked God to let him see his coming marriage as a partnership of Christian souls, procreating children who would be the next generation of Saints, yet that holy ideal was continually smirched in his head by his desire for her body in his hands.

He took his Bible from his coat pocket and turned to the seventh chapter of I Corinthians. 'It is good for a man not to touch a woman,' he read, and he had read the chapter so often in the days since he had met Campion that his eyes scarcely needed to pass over the words. 'But if they cannot contain, let them marry; for it is better to marry than to burn.' He could not contain himself, he could not! He moaned slightly, the sudden lust taking away the pain in his foot, and he knew St Paul was right. He should marry so he did not burn in the flames of hell, for his lust was already burning through him and he was ashamed of it.

It was better, he knew, that he should marry a woman who was as strong in the Lord as himself, yet the chapter in Corinthians offered him comfort for that predicament. '. . . the unbelieving wife is sanctified by the husband.' That was it, of course! That was the verse that justified this marriage, whatever Campion might think. By marrying her he was sanctifying her, he was saving her soul which he knew needed to be saved, and what greater love could he show her than that? This marriage, though she did not know it, was an act of grace, a work of the spirit, and whatever his reservations about their future or about her attitude to the wedding, he could console himself by knowing that he was saving her soul. One day, he thought, she will be grateful.

The door opened and Grimmett unceremoniously pushed a small, untidy man into the room. 'The Reverend Sobriety Bollsbie, sir. That's Mr Scammell, Sobriety.'

Scammell put his Bible away and smiled at the priest who was mopping his mouth with the hem of his cassock. 'Sir?'

Sobriety stared round the room, blinking in the sudden light. He let his cassock fall, hiccupped, then smiled brightly at Scammell. 'I preached to the Commons once, sir. Yes! To the Lords and Commons! For three hours, sir, and a great work was wrought there. Did you know that, sir?' He bobbed happily in front of Scammell.

'No.' Scammell was taken aback.

'Yes, sir! To the Lords and Commons. I took as my text the twenty-third verse of the twenty-sixth chapter of Proverbs. Do you know it, sir?'

'No.'

Sobriety raised an admonitory, shaking finger. ' "Burning lips and a wicked heart are like a potsherd covered with silver dross." Yes, sir. Two years ago it was, or maybe three, I don't exactly recall. It was well received.' He looked at Grimmett who had stayed in the doorway. 'It was well received, was it not?'

'They never forgot it, Sobriety.' Grimmett looked at Scammell and grinned. 'They only called the old bastard at the last minute and he was drunk as a judge. He vomited all over the pulpit. Now come on, Sobriety, get your damned book out!'

Sobriety sat down heavily, fishing under his cassock. 'I'm feeling poorly, Thomas, distinctly poorly. Do you have some of my physic?'

'When it's done, sir, when it's done.' Grimmett crossed to Scammell, his sword banging against the pushed back table. 'Here, sir. Sir Grenville thought you might not be prepared.' He handed Scammell a cheap ring. 'Don't worry, sir. He'll charge you, legal like.'

Sobriety Bollsbie, with the cunning of a drunkard, had produced a small tin flask from the recesses of his clothing. He sucked at it, emptied it, then smiled happily at the room. ' "Wine is a mockery," sir! "Strong drink is raging"!'

'Amen,' Scammell said, who knew when the Bible was quoted at him.

'For three hours, sir, to the Lords and Commons assembled! I spoke of the mockery of wine, sir.' He spoilt this declamation by hiccupping. 'Burning lips, sir, burning with the spirit, but not the spirit of God. Yes, sir.' He tried to stand up, suddenly filled with the power of his last, greatest, and unfinished sermon. Grimmett pushed him down.

'Wait there, Sobriety. Have your book ready.'

'I'm feeling poorly, Thomas. I want my physic.'

'When it's done, Sobriety. When they're married.'

'A wedding, is it?'

'A wedding.'

'Ah! A wedding.' Sobriety frowned as he fumbled with the pages of his prayer book. ' "Whoso findeth a wife," sir, "findeth a good thing, And obtaineth favour of the Lord." '

'Amen,' said Scammell.

Sobriety grinned at him. ' "It is better to dwell in a corner of the house-top, than with a brawling woman in a wide house." ' The priest seemed to be laughing at Scammell, who heard the text as a prisoner would hear a sentence.

Grimmett was bored. 'Get on with it, Sobriety. You need the names.' He watched the priest search for the page, then turned familiarly to Scammell. 'He's very good, sir.'

'Good?'

'When we need a wedding, sir. You'd be surprised how often we need a wedding in Chancery, mostly on deathbeds, of course, but Sobriety's your man. It's the responses, you see.'

'The responses?' Scammell was appalled by what was happening to his well-ordered life, but powerless to prevent it.

Grimmett smiled. 'The lady or gentleman, sir, does have to say "I will", and if they're reluctant then it helps to have Sobriety. He just keeps going, sir. Don't worry, it's quite legal.'

He fished in a pouch and took out a piece of paper. It was a marriage certificate, already filled in with a shaky signature at the bottom which read 'James Bollsbie, Clerk in Holy Orders'. Grimmett tucked the paper back into his pouch. 'Sir Grenville said he'd look after this for you, sir.' He looked at the priest, then back to Scammell. 'Shall I fetch the bride, sir?'

'Are we ready?'

'As we'll ever be.' Grimmett left the room.

Sobriety Bollsbie stood up successfully, showed surprise, then beamed seraphically at Scammell. 'Have we met, sir?'

'A minute ago, sir.'

'I preached to the Commons once, sir, did you know?'

Scammell was saved a repetition of the story by a scream from the hall, a slap that echoed through the empty house, the sound of heels dragging, a grunt from Grimmett followed by another scream. Sobriety was quite unmoved by the noise.

'For three hours, sir, three hours! But that, of course, was before my affliction.'

'Your affliction?' Scammell waited, horror-struck.

'I think it must be the falling sickness. Yes. God tries his servants, he does, he does.'

'Indeed and indeed.' Scammell's hands wound in apprehension, and then the door was filled with the struggling group. Grimmett dragged Campion by her arms, Goodwife slapped her, and Campion screamed and tried to kick at her tormentors. Sobriety was quite oblivious. He raised his voice. 'Your name, sir?'

'What?' Scammell was watching the bride's entrance.

'Your name, sir?' Sobriety asked with some asperity.

'Oh! Scammell. Samuel.'

'Good, good!' The priest had found a pen, some ink, and now he carefully wrote the name on the page of his prayer book. Scammell could see that the page was already thickly covered with other names. Sobriety looked at Campion, her bonnet hanging loose, her face red where it had been slapped and wet with tears.

'The bride's name, sir?'

'Dorcas Slythe.'

'A pretty name, yes, very pretty.' The pen scratched.

Campion screamed at them. Grimmett wrenched her arms back so that it hurt. 'Keep still, you bitch!' He dug his fingers harder into her upper arms. 'I'll tear your cursed arms out if you struggle!'

Sobriety draped his scapular about his shoulders, smiled at them both, then launched himself at breakneck speed into the wedding service. ' "Dearly beloved, we are gathered together here in the sight of God and in the face of this congregation to join together this Man and this Woman in Holy Matrimony." '

Campion shook her head, as if to clear it of a nightmare. Her arms hurt, the words clamoured at her, and she struggled against the brute strength of the man who held her. The priest stank of drink. She spat at him trying to stop the flow of words, and Grimmett yanked her backwards, pulling her back against his chest and then rammed his knee up into her skirts, forcing her feet apart with his boot. His breath rasped in her ear.

'Marriage', Sobriety was gabbling, 'should not be taken lightly in hand or wantonly, to satisfy men's carnal lusts and appetites, like brute beasts that have no understanding; but reverently, discreetly, advisedly, soberly, and in the fear of God." '

'No!' She screamed it, wrenching one arm free and clawing back at Grimmett who grabbed her wrist and twisted it, but had to lower his knee to regain his balance.

' "It was ordained for a remedy against sin, and to avoid fornication, that such persons as have not the gift of continency, might marry . . ." '

The candles burned high, throwing grotesque shadows on the dark panelled walls. Grimmett forced his knee between Campion's thighs again, pushing it higher.

Sobriety Bollsbie enquired if any present knew of any impediment why these two should not be lawfully joined in matrimony. Goodwife shook her head, Campion screamed, but it was all the same to Sobriety Bollsbie.

'Scammell Samuel, wilt thou have this woman to be thy wedded wife?'

Scammell nodded. 'I will.'

Sobriety looked at the girl who seemed to be leaning backwards with one leg cocked in the air. Her face was screwed up in hate, while Grimmett's face grinned over her shoulder. Sobriety knew better than to show surprise. ' "Dorcas Slythe. Wilt thou have this Man to be thy wedded husband, to live together after God's ordinance, in the holy estate of Matrimony? Wilt thou obey him, and serve him, love, honour, and keep him in sickness and in health; and forsaking all other, keep thee only unto him, so long as ye both shall live?" ' He did not wait for an answer, but simply read on faster and faster, wanting only to finish and collect his fee.

Grimmett was forced to bring his knee down when the moment came for the ring to be put on Campion's finger. He thrust her left arm towards Scammell and Goodwife came to help, unbending the fingers and holding them towards her master. Sobriety watched with relief as the ring was pushed on to her finger. 'Forasmuch as you and you,' he could not be bothered with names now, 'have consented together in Holy Wedlock, and have witnessed the same before God and this company . . .' he saw a flicker of light through the window to his left, but he was close to the end now, 'and thereto have given and pledged their troth either to other, and have declared the same . . .'

'Fire!' Scammell shouted.

Sobriety shouted louder. ' "I pronounce that they be Man and Wife together, in the Name of the Father, and of the Son, and of the Holy Ghost, Amen!" '

He dived for Grimmett's bag, ignoring the pandemonium, and grabbed the first bottle by the neck.

They were married.

Far ahead Toby could see the great shape of London Bridge, a dark mass dotted with yellow candlelight from hundreds of windows above the white tumbling where the river piled against the bridge's piers. He had just begun to hear the rush of water compressing itself through the narrow arches when his boat turned towards the city bank.

The watermen slowed their progress. There were old pilings in this stretch, left from decayed wharves, and they nosed the boat gingerly towards Scammell's landing stage. Water slapped on the boat. There was a brightly lit window just visible through the jumble of shadows and then the bow man reached out for the pier. Toby gave them the promised coin, climbed on to the jetty, then watched as the boatmen backpaddled silently into deeper and safer water.

He looked for the large, white-painted barge that had carried Campion away, but could see no sign of it. In the angle of the wharf and its pier, dimly lit by the light from the house window, he could see a small boat, its oars neatly stowed on its two thwarts, resting on the Thames mud. Dark water lapped a few yards beyond the boat's bows, while from beneath the pier, the wharf, and all around, he could hear the rustle and scratch of rats.

A voice startled him, making him crouch and turn, but it was only the watch in Thames Street. 'Eleven of the clock, and all's well!'

He moved slowly, holding his scabbard in his left hand so it should not knock against the stacks of timber which lay between wharf and yard. The shadows were deep here, disguising the yard's contents, but as he waited, looking and listening for any guard who might be left there at night, his eyes adjusted to the gloom. To his right was the house, brick built, with just one small lit window facing the yard. The large window, seen from the river, was invisible from where he waited. To his left were two tall sheds, one apparently stacked with uncut timber, the other filled with the mysterious shapes of half-built boats, racks of strakes and ribs, the everyday impedimenta of Scammell's business. Against the far wall, next to the wide gates that led into Thames Street, there was a strange, small hutch. It had an opening, facing Toby, and in the opening he could see the deep glow of fire. For a moment he had thought that the fire belonged to a night watchman, yet there was no movement, and then a smell registered. Pitch. Of course!

He smiled, the vestige of a plan coming to his mind. The boat-yard must consume quantities of pitch, the thick, evil-smelling substance being used to caulk the finished boats, and Scammell would not let the fire die overnight. The vat of pitch would take too long to heat each morning, and so, overnight, it was placed on a great fire of sea coal, the source of the light on the far wall.

He moved again, this time towards the lit window, and for a few seconds he almost let his anger take over. He could see Campion, grotesquely held in the grip of a huge, leather-jerkined man. There was a second man, dressed in Puritan black, to Campion's right, and a woman to her left. A third man, elderly and clothed shabbily in old vestments, faced Campion and the black-dressed man. A wedding.

Toby could see the book, he could see the priest's mouth moving, and for a second or two the urge was on him to smash the window, climb through, draw the sword at his side and hack blindly at Campion's captors.

Church bells struck in the city, the bells of Southwark answering with their hourly chimes, and the sudden cacophony distracted Toby and calmed his anger. He would gain nothing by blind fury. He would be cut down before he was half-way through the window, and he remembered the idea suggested to him by the pitch fire.

Two things, even more than war, gave fear to London. Fire and the plague. Plague was the worse of the two killers, but fire the more frequent. Much of London was still built of timber, the houses crowded together with thatched outhouses crammed into small yards. Fire often threatened the destruction of London, the sudden flames and smoke billowing above the rooftops. The citizens were practised in their response. Nearly every street corner was decorated with long hooks to haul down burning thatch or timbers and with axes to break into houses so that gunpowder charges could be laid. The powder would flatten a ring of houses about the fire, making a cordon over which the flames could not pass. Despite the new hand-driven pump that had just been invented, which could force water a full thirty feet into the air from its canvas hose, a fire was usually well alight before the parish could deploy it. London's gravest enemy was fire, yet tonight it would be Toby's ally.

Fire would bring the watch running. It would bring men with axes against the gates of Scammell's yard. It would fill the yard, the street outside, even the river, with people and confusion, and in that confusion Toby reckoned lay his best chance of rescuing Campion.

It was a terrible thing he planned, and he knew it, but he worked with a blind disregard of the damage he might do to the city. He was in love, and the distorting glass of love saw only one thing; that his loved one was in danger and he must split his enemy's forces and take her from them.

Toby moved between the two sheds, working quickly, though taking care to make little noise as he thrust bundles of unravelled rope and wood shavings into the space beneath the great timber stack. The space had been made by putting the bottom layer of timber on blocks to keep the wood from dampness, and it was there he planned his major fire. The rope strands, used for caulking, were dry. He glanced constantly at the small, lit window, but no one looked out.

When he was satisfied with the preparation, he picked up two long strakes, ready curved to become the ribs of a boat, and took them to the stone hutch that kept the pitch fire safe at night. He thrust them into the coals, feeling the wood grate on the lumps. An immense heat radiated from the glowing coals. The strakes caught immediately, the wood burning bright, and he drew them out. He carried them to the timber stack, the flames licking back towards his hands, the sudden light in the yard making him nervous. Yet no one shouted as he moved, nor as he knelt and pushed the two strakes deep into the tangle of rope and wood-shavings.

Perversely, for a few seconds, it seemed as if the flames would die. They burned low, threatening to flicker away, and then he saw the first strands of rope catch, curl and flare into yellow flame. Then the shavings caught. Suddenly there was a spread of flame and Toby backed away.

The moment had not quite come. He did not know how long it would take the fire to catch, but he could not wait here in fear. He lit two more strakes, putting one in a pile of shavings beneath a half-completed boat, the other beneath the rack of curved strakes, and then, afraid of being seen in the growing illumination, he went back to the shadows by the wharf.

The flames were lurid in the boat shed, licking up the boat on its trestles. Surely someone would see! He waited, apprehensive, knowing the enormity of his act. The first fire, in the timber stack, seemed dim. He wondered if it had gone out.

Deep in the great timber stack was a draught, coming in at the base, then funnelling up to stack's top at the roof of the shed. Unseen to Toby, the flames were being sucked into the natural chimney caused by the stack's construction. He was biting his lip, wondering whether he should re-cross the yard and feed the dim fire, when suddenly there was an explosion of flame, sparks and smoke. The stack had caught.

It caught spectacularly, the fire spreading through the interior by the chimney. One moment Toby could see a dull glow at the base, the next the whole roof of the shed was burning, there was a roar of flame, and Scammell's yard was lit like daylight. Sparks whirled crazily upwards, flames illuminating the base of the plume of smoke that rose above the city. Already there were shouts from the street: 'Fire!'

The blaze was roaring, feeding itself, spreading across the shed's roof and dropping burning fragments into the yard. Toby looked to his right and saw Scammell's face, appalled, at the window. He gripped the handle of his sword. The moment was coming!

Fists battered on the yard gate, voices shouted. The noise was huge now with the sound of flames and of panic, and Toby looked left to see the boat-shed tangled in fire. Scammell's business was gone, destroyed.

The watch raised the alarm. The church bell started tolling. All across the city people would look from their windows wondering if the fire would spread. Whole towns had been destroyed by fires that started as tiny, insignificant flames.

Timbers crashed in the stack, spreading the blaze to adjoining stacks, and then more light, feeble by comparison, was thrown into the yard. Scammell stood in his candle-lit doorway, his mouth slack, eyes staring at the churning red-grey smoke that billowed over his yard. He ran to the gates, shouting incomprehensibly and began to lift the bar to let the watch in. The heat was fearsome.

Toby was watching the window. He could see the big man,

his round, broken-nosed face frightening, staring at the flames. He still held Campion, one hand in her hair, forcing her head down. He turned and said something to the others in the room.

There were shouts at the gate; the watch bellowed orders; Scammell threw leather buckets at them as though pails of water might put out the furnace-like intensity of the fire. Now was Toby's moment. He ran, jumped the three steps into Scammell's house and began to shout: 'Fire! Out! Out!'

The priest was in the hall, a clinking bag of bottles in one hand, another bottle held to his lips. Toby cannoned into him, knocked him down, and then was in the candle-lit room. 'Fire! Out! Out!'

'We hear you!' the big man shouted at Toby. 'Go on, lad! We're coming!' He was dragging Campion by one arm.

Toby ignored him. He seized Campion's other arm and went on shouting as though he was an excited watchman. 'Hurry! Out!' He pulled Campion away from the man, trying to prise her loose.

'Leave her!'

Thomas Grimmett's shout seemed to wake Campion up. To Toby's eyes she had appeared dazed, almost half asleep, and her bonnet had come off in her struggles leaving her hair falling gold over her slapped, reddened face. Now she looked at her rescuer and recognition dawned. 'Toby!' She jerked away from Grimmett, clung to Toby, and the huge man bellowed in surprise. He heard her use the name, realized Toby was not of the watch and letting Campion go, he barred the door with his body and rasped his sword from its scabbard.

'Toby!'

'Stand back!' Toby drew his own sword, feeling the movement clumsy compared to the big man's ease. He had never fought for his life, he had never killed, and the elation of the rescue was evaporating in the face of the other man's evident confidence.

Grimmett half smiled. 'You came for her, did you? You're

not going to have her, lad. She's mine.' His sword suddenly lunged, a streak of silver light in the red glare of the fire, and Toby parried, trying to remember his fencing lessons, and felt a surge of relief as the blades rang, scraped, and Toby disengaged stepping back. Grimmett followed fast, threatening again. Again Toby parried and felt the fear rise in him. The big man was good, far better than Toby, and Toby tried to force the fear down by attacking. He tried to loop his sword beneath the other's guard, thought for a moment that he had succeeded, that he had tempted the other blade wide and that his own was poised at the big man's belly, but then he saw the sword coming fast at his head and ducked clumsily. His assailant laughed.

'You'll have to do better than that, son.'

Goodwife was screaming. Campion ran for the door, left unguarded by Grimmett's advance and the huge man stepped backwards to block her, but she changed direction. She leaped at Grimmett, teeth bared, hands clawing, and managed to catch his hair in her fingers. She screamed at him, her fingers hooked in filthy hair, pulling his head down. He shouted at Goodwife to get her off, swore, but Campion hung on and Toby jumped towards his enemy at the same time. He raised his sword, forgetting his teacher's constant adage that the point will always beat the edge, and hacked the blade down and sideways as if it were a pruning hook and his enemy a tangle of brambles.

Grimmett raised his own sword, but Campion was pulling at him, kicking and obstructing him, and Grimmett knew his parry would be too late. He bellowed in rage.

Toby had never killed. He had never known this killing rage, and he watched, almost detached as, in the light of the candles and the fire's glow, his blade hit Grimmett's bent neck.

Despite Campion, it seemed as if the head came upright as Toby's blade pierced tendon and muscle. Campion let go, and Grimmett came upright. He forced himself against the sword and Toby sawed the blade towards him. The big man's eyes shut. Toby staggered backwards, the blade free, and there was blood everywhere.

Grimmett fell slowly to his knees. His sword clattered on the floor and his hands came up, as if he wanted to pray, clawing at his own face and neck. Toby watched as his enemy fell forward, slumped like a sack of oats on the floor. Toby had killed for the first time and killed for love.

Goodwife screamed. She was standing in the doorway, staring at Toby. Campion stared too, her hands clutched in front of her mouth, and then she looked up at Toby. Suddenly he seemed to become aware again of the noise, of the fire, of the heat that was making the room unbearable. 'Come on!'

Goodwife cringed aside as Toby led Campion into the hall. The priest was in the corner, rescuing fallen bottles, sucking a second bottle dry. The heat through the open door was searing, the light brilliant.

'Come on!' Toby pulled Campion into the flame-light, his excitement overcoming the shock of his first kill, his vision of the bubbling throat and the astonished, shocked, fading eyes.

Scammell saw Campion come into the yard. He grabbed the captain of the watch. 'Stop them!'

'This way!' Toby turned, holding Campion's wrist, and whirled her round in the yard, blue cloak flying outwards. 'Come on!' They ran, hand in hand, towards the wharf, to the small boat Toby remembered drawn up on the mud.

'Stop them!' Scammell's first shout had been involuntary, startled from him by the sight of Campion with a strange man, but now the watch took up the shout. There was nothing they could do to save Scammell's yard, even his neighbours' property was doomed, but the shout convinced them that they had found the culprits. The shout was picked up, men started running, and the cries were for vengeance.

Toby and Campion jumped on to the mud. Campion fell forward into the stinking slime and Toby whirled his blood-stained sword and chopped down on the rope that tied the small boat. 'Push!'

Campion slipped in the mud again and Toby tossed his blade into the boat and heaved at it. His boots were inches deep in muck, the boat was firmly anchored in the mud, but his country breeding had given him strength and he felt the boat's keel release itself from the slimy suction and then slide down towards the lapping water.

'Push!'

'I'm trying!' Campion was laughing now, an inane laugh of relief and excitement. The flames lit the mud easily, throwing great wavering streaks of light on to the river. Timbers crashed behind them, sparks cascaded into the air, and Campion, black with mud, shook with laughter as she pushed at the boat.

'Stop!' The captain of the watch was on the wharf now, but the boat's stern was in the water and Toby ran it with huge strength clean into the river. He turned, picked Campion up and threw her unceremoniously into the boat. 'Go to the back!' He pushed again, wading deep into the water.

'Stop! In the name of the King!' The watch captain, in his excitement, forgot the rebellion. He dragged a long-barrelled pistol from this belt. 'Stop!'

Toby was half in the boat now, draped over its stern, and he kicked hard with his feet. Suddenly the current plucked at them, turned the boat, and Toby hauled himself over the side.

The watch captain swore, knowing the range was long, but ignored Scammell's frantic shouts, raised the pistol, and aimed at Toby. He could see easily, thanks to the fire, his stubby foresight settled on Toby's spine and he pulled the trigger.

Toby heard the bang, had a glimpse of the tiny explosion in the pan and the gout of red flame at the muzzle, and then the pistol ball smacked into the centre thwart, gouged a splinter and ricocheted up towards the bridge.

'Toby!'

'I'm not hurt. Sit still!'

The boat was picking up speed, circling towards the dangerous rapids where the river was compressed by the bridge's narrow arches. If the boat became caught in one of the miniature weirs it would be whirled down the white chute and destroyed. Toby fumbled with the oars, forced himself to be calm, and fitted them into the tholes that gave them leverage. Pistols banged and stabbed flame from the wharf, but the small boat was in shadow now. He leaned into his stroke, turned the boat, and headed upstream and away from the city bank. It was hard work, the oars bent at each stroke, but they were clear now, going into the darkness across the river.

'Toby?'

He grinned at her. Her face was a mask of mud, white-eyed where she had wiped it.

'You remember me?'

'He married me, Toby!'

'Do I call you Mrs Scammell?'

'Toby!' He was not sure whether she was crying or laughing.

They were pulling past the fire now, on the far bank, and Toby glanced over and saw the heart of the flames that fed the great plume of smoke. The firelight was reflected on houses, steeples and towers, even on the great, stone tower of St Paul's Cathedral itself.

Toby looked back at Campion. 'Hello, Campion.'

A huge crash sounded from over the river as the sheds finally collapsed. Campion looked in awe at the blaze, then at Toby. 'Toby.'

Scammell was shouting at a waterman, ordering him inshore so he could pursue his bride, but Campion and Toby were safe now. Toby paused for a second or two, leaned forward, and touched her mud-smeared hand.

'Everything will be all right. Mrs Swan's waiting for us in the Paris Garden. We're going to Lazen.'

'Lazen?' She shook her head.

'But your mother?'

'Don't worry about her!' He began to laugh. He could be executed for this night's work, and they still had to escape from the patrols about London. They would have a few hours' start over their pursuers. 'We're going to Lazen! We're going home!'

She seemed to be sobbing, but then Toby realized it was laughter. They were free.

12

The best way to approach Lazen Castle was from the north, across the humped hills that were grazed by Lazen sheep, dipping into the shallow valleys where willow and alder grew beside Lazen streams, and over the final crest that revealed the Lazen valley with the castle at its centre.

It was on this road that Toby brought Campion and Mrs Swan in the first week of September. Mildred Swan had insisted on making the whole journey, caught up in the excitement of the escape. 'There's no saying what you two will get up to if there isn't an older body with you,' she had declared, though Campion suspected that Mrs Swan simply enjoyed travelling. Mrs Swan had taken the truth of Campion's predicament well, abandoning her long-held worries about the supposedly ill mother with good grace. 'I suppose you couldn't trust anyone, dear, and you're quite right.'

The first two days had been the worst, escaping the tendrils of the London garrison, going west on minor tracks. Closer to Oxford their progress became faster. Toby had been given a Royalist passport, recognized by the first patrol that found them, and in Oxford Campion and Mrs Swan took once more to a stage wagon going west. Toby bought a horse, using Campion's money, and now, six days later, they stood and looked at Lazen from the north.

Mrs Swan sniffed. 'Not quite like Hampton Court is it, Mister Toby.'

'Not exactly, Mrs Swan,' Toby smiled. Mildred Swan was a Londoner and nothing could match anything in London for her. She had been invited to stay on with them at Lazen, but had trenchantly refused. She would travel gladly, but only so that she could return, her prejudices confirmed, to Bull Inn Court.

From Campion's view there were still signs that Lazen Castle had once been just that: a castle. To her left were the remains of a massive keep, square built on a small rise in the valley and used now, Toby said, as a storage place for Lazen's farms. Closer to Campion, and straddling the road just a hundred yards from the foot of the hill, was the old gatehouse, now quite separate from the main house but still habitable. An empty flagstaff awaited Sir George's return. There was a moat, too, that most proper decoration of a castle, but it now covered only the approaches from the south and west and, in truth, the water looked more like an ornamental lake than an instrument of defence.

Most of the ancient castle had disappeared. A brief length of battlemented wall joined the keep to the main house, but its chief purpose now was to provide support for the espaliered fruit trees in the kitchen garden. Another length of wall guarded the eastern approach, joining the keep to the huge stable-yard and sheltering the smithy, brewhouse, and a score of other buildings from the winter winds. The rest of the castle had gone, its stones used in the making of new buildings. Those buildings were beautiful.

Campion was in awe. She listened to Toby describing the castle, but the size of the place, its comfortable grandeur, reminded her that Lady Margaret Lazender waited within. She feared the confrontation and she knew, despite Toby's protestations to the opposite, that he was by no means confident that his mother would welcome her.

Closest to the gatehouse, some seventy yards further south,

was the Old House, built in the reign of Elizabeth and, despite its name, still less than a hundred years old. It was stone built, though its west front, that looked across formal gardens to the moat, had been faced with mock half-timber cladding. Its windows were high and wide, quite unsuited for defence, but marvellous for spilling evening light into the great hall.

Joined to the house, and so attached that the two buildings formed a large 'L', was the New House. This, Toby said, had been completed just ten years before and was his mother's pride. It faced south, was stone-built throughout, and Toby spoke of an interior that was splendid with marble and plasterwork, tiles and polished oak. He pointed, as they went slowly down the slope, to the new kitchens, inconveniently distant from the great hall when Lady Margaret decided to entertain the county, and he spoke with pride of the new bedrooms, each room separate, that had replaced the old ones which had been arranged like a corridor, each room leading to the next, and in which curtained beds had been a necessity of modesty. The bedrooms shared the upper floor of the New House with the long gallery, the throne room of Lady Margaret, and it was towards the gallery that Toby led them.

They made slow progress. At the gatehouse a child erupted from a doorway and shouted a welcome to Toby, offering to take his horse, and the child's shout brought more servants and retainers to see the cause of the commotion. Campion and Mrs Swan, walking, hung back as servitors and footmen, maids and cooks, the families who served Lazen came to greet him. They doffed hats, skimped bows or curtseys, and then stretched out to touch his hand and give what news they had. Mrs Swan shook her head. 'God knows how they feed all these mouths, dear.'

The closer she went to Lady Margaret, the greater was Campion's fear. Toby had spoken much of his mother, and though he spoke in terms of love and admiration, there was an unmistakable awe in his voice. She ruled Lazen: the castle, estate, village, church, the lives of tenants, servants, priest, family, and any other person who came within her wide purlieu. She was a formidable lady, a great lady even, and Lazen Castle was the setting for her considerable talents. She ran the estate, Toby said, far better than his father could have done, a fact recognized by Sir George, and within its bounds Lady Margaret's word was law.

It was not, Toby had hastened to assure Campion, a tyrannous law. It brooked little interference, knew great charity, and was subject to no known codification. Lady Margaret's whim was her desire, her desire was her law, and her strongest desire was to keep the estate happy for a happy estate was an efficient estate.

They climbed the wide staircase from the great hall, leaving the servants behind, and Toby plunged into a dark maze of old corridors, passage rooms, and odd, brief stairways. Their entrance into the New House was through a low, stone archway that opened into a magnificently light, high, decorated landing. A great tapestry took up one wall, a tapestry showing a chained and crowned unicorn that lay its head in the lap of a young girl. Above it the ceiling was a riot of intricate plasterwork, flowers and fruit spilling downwards and leaving, in the ceiling's centre, a great blank oval that Toby said awaited a suitable painter. He grinned at Campion and Mrs Swan. 'Wait here.'

Campion waited. Lazen Castle was less than a half day's ride from Werlatton, yet nothing in her life had prepared her for such a place. It crushed her with its size, its pretensions, and she felt gauche, awkward and out of place. How could she make an impression on Lady Margaret? She was dirty from travelling, unkempt, and though Mrs Swan brushed at her clothes and tweaked them straight, Campion could feel presentiments of failure. Voices and laughter sounded from the bottom of the vast, marble staircase that ended on this landing. What was she to these people? Why should they care for her?

She feared Lady Margaret. She could hear nothing from

within the long gallery into which Toby had gone, yet she knew that at this moment her fate was being decided. She knew nothing of Sir George's letter, delivered two days previously by the Earl of Fleet, and had she known then her melancholy would have been even more profound.

'Cheer up, dear.' Mrs Swan pulled Campion's collar straight. 'She'll like you. Can't help but like you.'

Toby had said, candidly enough, that Campion's best chance of acceptance lay in Lady Margaret adopting her as she adopted, at frequent intervals, new enthusiasms that made up in absorption what they lacked in duration. Toby had spoken laughingly of these enthusiasms and of the havoc they created in Lazen's life. Some were harmless enough, such as Lady Margaret's period of sonnet writing that had merely inflicted reams of poetry on the family and spattered a good inlaid table with ink. Her adoption of drama, Toby said, had even imported some excellent players and musicians to the castle.

Only once had Sir George firmly protested, and that had been when Lady Margaret had contracted an overpowering desire to be a taxidermist. She had written to a tradesman in Bristol, demanding the secrets of his trade, but Toby suspected that the man had kept his professional secrets and palmed Lady Margaret off with false instructions.

For a summer Lady Margaret had cut a swathe of death through the castle's chicken population, yet no matter how she practised, the stuffed chickens had become malodorous and alarmingly misshapen. The long gallery had become almost uninhabitable, so overpowering was the smell, yet still Lady Margaret scooped at hen cadavers and replaced their organs with her own mixture of sawdust and plaster. Every table in the gallery, Toby remembered, had been inhabited by strange, ghoulish chickens; creatures that resembled sagging, lumpen, be-feathered bladders with dangling heads. They had all, finally, been burnt, all except one prize specimen that Toby kept in a locked cupboard in the keep.

The gilded, panelled door of the long gallery opened. Toby

stood there, smiling, but his face gave no message of what had transpired in his half-hour talk with his mother. 'Mrs Swan? I'm going to settle you comfortably. We'll find some food.' He grinned at Campion. 'You're summoned to the presence.' He gestured her inside.

'Now?'

'This second. Don't be nervous.'

The order was impossible to obey. Her nervousness increased as she went past Toby, as he closed the door behind her and she found herself in a room of sumptuous magnificence. It ran the length of the New House, wide windows opening south on to the Lazen valley, with their white curtains billowing inwards in the slight breeze. Campion had an impression of rich tables and chairs, settles and chests, of a carpet laid the full length of the two hundred-foot room, of paintings on the white wall opposite the windows, and of more plasterwork on the ceiling. It was all a quick, overwhelming impression, for then she saw Toby's mother, half way down the room, watching her.

'Do I call you Miss Slythe, Mrs Scammell, Dorcas, or Campion? You seem to have a plethora of names for a simple girl. Come here.'

Campion walked along the rich carpet, feeling as she had imagined she might feel when, on the Day of Judgement, she would have to walk the crystal floor beneath the throne of thrones.

'Closer, girl, closer! I don't intend to eat you!'

Campion stopped close to Lady Margaret, bobbed an ungainly curtsey, and kept quiet. She looked once at Toby's mother, then avoided her eyes. She had a swift glimpse of a tall, grey haired lady with an imperious, commanding face.

Lady Margaret looked at her for a few seconds. 'So you're the girl my son burned down half of London for?'

An answer was required. 'Yes, ma'am.'

'My name is Lady Margaret. We have still not established what yours is, but doubtless we will agree on something.' Lady Margaret sniffed in evident disapproval. 'Three businesses destroyed, twelve houses burned to ashes and two men dead. Did you know that?'

'Yes, ma'am, Lady Margaret.' The news-sheets had overtaken Toby and Campion a day from Lazen. Lady Margaret sniffed again.

'It seems that in addition to the man my son killed, a priest also died. A strangely named man called Sobriety Bollsbie. I assume he officiated at your wedding?'

'Yes, Lady Margaret.'

'Let me look at you, child! If you stare at the floor you can't expect me to grovel to see your face. Chin up! Higher! And look at me. I'm not so old and ugly that you'll turn to stone.'

The clipped, authoritative voice matched the woman Campion now saw in front of her. Margaret was tall, with an aquiline nose, and blue eyes that looked on the world with an expression of inquisitive challenge. Toby had inherited his mother's firm line of jaw and mouth, and taken from her too, a tall, upright body. She was, indeed, far from old and ugly. Campion knew that Lady Margaret lacked two years of fifty, yet, apart from the full, grey hair, she could have been ten years younger.

'Take off the cloak, child. Let me see you.'

Campion felt shabby. Lady Margaret was dressed in a gown of pale yellow, embroidered with gillyflowers. There were strange specks of paint on the bodice, paint that was also on the right hand which raised Campion's chin higher. 'Take the bonnet off, child.' Mrs Swan had brought Campion's clothes with her, including her last, black, Puritan bonnet.

'You're not ugly, are you, child? I can see why Toby went to such inordinate lengths for you. He said that killing a man was unpleasant. Did you find it unpleasant?'

Campion nodded. 'Yes, Lady Margaret.'

'I'm not sure I would find it unpleasant. Turn round.'

Campion obeyed.

'All the way round, child, I don't want to talk to your

back.' Campion faced Lady Margaret again, who sniffed. 'I see the Slythes did raise a rose among their unprepossessing thorns. Did you think my son was justified in his slaughter and destruction on your behalf?'

Campion swallowed and thought quickly. 'I would have done it for him, Lady Margaret.'

To Campion's surprise, Lady Margaret laughed. 'He can be precipitate, Toby. I don't understand where his enthusiasms come from. Certainly not from us. I don't understand, either, where his red hair came from. It's tasteless. I assume it was because he was conceived at the full moon. I made a note of it in my journal. George kept his boots on.' This was all said in a matter-of-fact tone, as if Lady Margaret was talking of everyday household things. She went on in the same manner. 'Are you a virgin, child?'

Campion gaped, then recovered herself. 'Yes.'

'You're sure?'

'Yes.'

'You're twenty?'

Campion nodded. 'Yes, Lady Margaret.'

'You're certainly clinging to it for a long time. I suppose those are the clothes your family provided?'

'Yes, Lady Margaret.'

'Quite horrible. I met your father once in Shaftesbury. He was a disagreeable man. I remember he had scurf on his shoulders. I asked him if it had been snowing.' She elaborated no further, but turned to a small table, covered with her work, and picked up a letter. She read it aloud. ' "The girl is, bye Tobie's owne Account, quite Unlettered except in the Scriptures." Is that true?'

Campion nodded miserably. 'Yes, Lady Margaret.'

Lady Margaret looked at her with what seemed to be distaste. 'Which is your favourite reading in the scriptures?'

Campion wondered what book of the Bible would most impress Lady Margaret, but settled on the truth lest she pause too long before her reply. 'The Song of Solomon, Lady Margaret.'

'Ha! You have some taste then. George is quite wrong, of course, in implying that birth and breeding are the only begetters of elegance and taste. You haven't met my son-in-law, Fleet. He's an earl, but in his armour he rather resembles a pig in a leather jerkin. If that's what birth and breeding does, then perhaps we're better off without them. You're small in the bust, child.'

'I am?' Campion, to her surprise, was beginning to enjoy Lady Margaret. There was an excitement in never knowing what would be said next.

'A few children will fill you out. Love-making does too. Fortunately my eldest daughter was generously endowed before she met Fleet, otherwise there'd have been small hope for her.'

Lady Margaret suddenly pointed to the ceiling. 'Tell me what you think?'

Campion looked up. The cornice of the long gallery, like the landing outside, was heavily decorated with elaborate plasterwork. Yet unlike the landing, which had been an orthodox representation of harvest's bounty, the long gallery was decorated with a shameless array of half-clothed gods, goddesses and grotesques. Half-clothed was an exaggeration. Most of the heavenly beings were almost totally naked, chasing each other in permanent riot about the long room. Above the huge, marble fireplace and a painting of Lazen Castle from the north, was the dominant figure of the plaster extravaganza. A naked woman, erect in a chariot, held a spear in her right hand. The woman's face was uncannily like Lady Margaret's.

'Do you like it, child?'

'Yes.'

'Why?' The question was a challenge.

Campion did not know what to say. She was not educated in such things, had never before seen such mouldings. She thought, briefly, of the great picture in Sir Grenville Cony's room, of the naked boy stooping over the pool, yet these plasters were quite different. There had been something sinister in Sir Grenville's picture. These naked romps were altogether more innocent and joyful.

'Well?'

Campion pointed to the woman in the chariot. 'Is that you?'

Again Lady Margaret was pleased. 'Of course it's me. The Italian master-plasterer did it as a compliment. He guessed my figure, and guessed remarkably well.' Lady Margaret was paying herself a compliment. The figure in the chariot was splendid. 'Do you know who it represents?'

'No, Lady Margaret.'

'Diana the huntress.'

Campion smiled. 'She was worshipped in Ephesus.'

'Of course.' Lady Margaret sounded sour. 'I forget that you know your scriptures. Does the nakedness not shock you?'

'No, Lady Margaret.'

'Good. Prudery is not an attribution of the godhead.' Lady Margaret spoke as if she was privy to the deity's secrets. 'So, you know nothing, you dress badly, yet you are in love with my son. Are you in love?'

Campion nodded, embarrassed. 'Yes, Lady Margaret.'

'And George tells me that there's some nonsense about ten thousand pounds a year. Is it nonsense?'

'I don't know.'

'Well tell me.'

Campion told the story of the seal, of her meeting with Sir Grenville Cony, of the letter she had found in the secret compartment of her father's chest. At first she was hesitant, but soon she forgot her nervousness and discovered in Lady Margaret a surprisingly sympathetic listener. The older woman snorted when Sir Grenville's name was mentioned. 'The frog-king? Little Grenville! I know him. His father was a boot-maker in Shoreditch.'

She demanded to see the seal and was impatient as Campion took it from about her neck. 'Let me have it! Ah! Venetian.'

'Venetian?'

'It's obvious, isn't it? Look at the workmanship. No London clodpole could have made this. It unscrews, you say?' She was fascinated by the small crucifix. 'A recusant's cross!'

'A what, Lady Margaret?'

'A secret crucifix, child. The Catholics wore them once their religion was decreed unlawful, the crucifix disguised as jewellery. How very fascinating. Did Sir Grenville's have the same?'

'No.' Campion described the silver naked lady and Lady Margaret burst into loud laughter.

'A naked woman!'

'Yes, Lady Margaret.'

Lady Margaret still smiled. 'How singularly inappropriate. Sir Grenville wouldn't know what to do with a naked lady if he rolled on one in his bed. No child, Sir Grenville's tastes go the other way. He likes his naked flesh to be male.' She looked up at Campion and frowned. 'You haven't the first idea of what I'm speaking about, have you?'

'No.'

'Such innocence. I thought it disappeared with the Fall. You know about Sodom and Gomorrah, child?'

'Yes.'

'Well Sir Grenville would have been happy as the frog-king of Sodom, dear. I'll explain it all to you when you're ready.' She rejoined the two halves of the seal and gave it to Campion. 'There. Keep it safe. George didn't believe you, but then he can be very foolish at times. I've no doubt his principles will fall along with the tiles of the old roof.'

Campion, by now, was scenting success. It was not just the ten thousand pounds, each of them an excellent reason for her birth and breeding to be overlooked; she was enjoying Lady Margaret's company and felt the enjoyment to be reciprocated. She had noticed when Lady Margaret suddenly addressed her as 'dear', though Lady Margaret had seemed oblivious.

The older woman frowned at her. 'You have no means of knowing if this money is to be yours?'

'No.'

'Well that's truthful of you. You say you're a virgin?'

'Yes.'

'Promise me?'

Campion smiled. 'Yes.'

'It's important, child. Good Lord, don't you realize how important?'

Campion shrugged. 'For marriage?'

'For marriage!' Lady Margaret scoffed. 'George deflowered me in a hayrick weeks before the marriage. He was noisy and clumsy, though I'm glad to say he's improved over the years. No, you foolish child, not for marriage, but for the law courts.'

'The law courts?'

'I assume you do not wish to stay married to Mr Scammell?'

Campion shook her head. 'No.'

'Then the marriage may have to be annulled. To achieve that you will have to prove that he never consummated the marriage. Do I have to explain what that means?'

Campion smiled. 'No.'

'Thank God for that. The priest doesn't marry you, child. When George and I married, the bishop was quite splendid and very impressive, but God didn't take a blind bit of notice till George had taken me to bed. Not that he hadn't anticipated a little, but what happens between the sheets, child, is just as important as the priest's ministrations. I shall send Toby away.'

Campion dared not protest.

Lady Margaret nodded to herself. 'He can go to Oxford and fight for the King. It will do him good, though whether the King will be grateful is another matter. That way I will remove him from temptation and we shall keep you in one piece, so to speak.' She looked sternly at Campion. 'I'm not saying you should keep yourself in the hope of marrying

Toby. He's bound to meet far more suitable girls than you in Oxford, and some of them not without prospects. No. But I think I like you, and I need a companion. You know what a companion does?'

'No, Lady Margaret.'

'A companion amuses me, serves me, reads to me, obeys my whims, anticipates my desires and never, child, never bores me. Can you manage?'

'I shall try.' Campion was rising on wings to a heaven of happiness, even if it meant being apart from Toby. She had found her refuge, a place of safety, and she liked this tall, abrupt woman in whom she could see a wealth of hidden kindness.

Lady Margaret, for her part, had seen things she liked in Campion. She recognized the girl's transcendant beauty, a beauty that was remarkable, and she understood that Toby was captivated by it. So, she thought, he ought to be. Any man ought to be. Yet a few months apart would do them no harm.

Whether her son would, or should marry Campion was not in her thoughts. As long as the girl was legally married to another then the occasion did not arise, and as long as her virginity must be preserved, so long would Toby be tested. He could go to Oxford and there, Lady Margaret guessed, he might meet someone else. Yet if he did not, if his love endured the absence, then the girl's inheritance, if it came to her, would be more than an acceptable dowry.

Yet above all, Lady Margaret had found her new enthusiasm. She liked this girl. She had found in her an innocent slate, a virgin page, and Lady Margaret would write what she willed on that page. She would educate Campion, she would open her mind, fill it with beauty, and she would turn a Puritan maid into a lady of elegance. Sir George would protest, of course, but Sir George had never seen her. One sight of this beauty and Lady Margaret knew her husband would be as docile as a lamb. She smiled.

'Come here, child. What are you called?'

'Toby calls me Campion.'

'So he says. A fanciful name, but it suits. Very well. Come here, Campion.'

She pointed to her work table. In the centre of it, amongst a litter of paints, brushes and smeared papers, was a tiny, tiny portrait. It was Lady Margaret's current passion; the painting of miniatures. This one, done from memory because the servants had learned to make themselves scarce when Lady Margaret prowled for sitters, was of Sir George. Campion did not know that. She saw what seemed to be a picture of a doleful egg, eyes crooked and mouth lopsided, with what seemed to be a speck of bird-dropping on its bald pate. Toby, when his mother had asked his opinion, had said just that; that it was bird dropping. Lady Margaret thought it was one of her husband's distinguished, greying temples. 'What do you think, Campion?'

'It's lovely. It's beautiful.'

'So you've learned to lie, as well?'

Campion laughed, a lovely sound, rare in her life. 'I think it's beautiful.'

Lady Margaret smiled. 'I think we shall get along splendidly. We shall clean you up, child, then pack Toby off to Oxford. Come along.'

She led an imperious path through the furniture of the long gallery, beneath the naked romps of the deities who paid homage to the erect, slim Diana in her chariot.

'I think it's very clever of Toby to have killed for you. George never killed for me. I shall demand that he does so as soon as he returns. I shall expect slaughtered suitors to pave the road between Lazen and Shaftesbury. Come along, child, don't dawdle. And put your shoulders back, you're in Lazen now, not grovelling in Werlatton. You'll sleep in there, next to my room. That's Caroline's room, Toby's younger sister. She's sixteen now and time she was married. What are you wearing on your feet? You sound like a carthorse. Good Lord, child, do you call those shoes? Take them off instantly,

I shall have them burnt. And why are you smiling. You think you're here to enjoy yourself?'

She did, she had come to Lazen, and Campion, again, was happy.

Sir Grenville Cony had still not forgotten the horror of hearing of his faithful Grimmett's death. Dead! And the girl fled, rescued by some man who had cut down Sir Grenville's servant. The lawyer had howled with anger at the news, howled like a hurt animal, and within hours he had been assailed by a pain in his vast belly. The pain felt like a great snake that heaved and coiled inside him, rending him with poisonous fangs, and the diet of goat's milk and pigeon-flesh that Dr Chandler had prescribed had done nothing to relieve the pain.

Now there was more bad news. He had been summoned from a debate in the Commons, a turgid session in which the members debated changes to the present arrangements for the disposal of captured Royalist property. Sir Grenville knew there would be no changes—he had made sure of that—but it was necessary to give the canting fools the impression that their self-important maunderings carried some weight in the councils of the state. His secretary waited at the door of Westminster Hall. 'Sir Grenville?'

'What is it?'

'This, sir. From Cottjens.'

Sir Grenville seized the letter. His secretary had already opened it, read it, and judged it necessary to bring it immediately to Westminster. Sir Grenville read it through once, twice, and then seemed to growl. The growl turned into audible words. 'The bastard. The Jewish bastard. The filthy, Jewish bastard!'

Julius Cottjens was a merchant on the Amsterdam Exchange, a dealer in cloth and fine spices who also dealt with a select clientele for another commodity; information. Cottjens charged highly for his privately gathered news, and men met his prices, for he was accurate and trustworthy in a world subject to strange rumours. Julius Cottjens was a listener of genius, a man of unbounded curiosity and seeming discretion, and endowed with a prodigious memory, yet the news he had just despatched to Sir Grenville Cony had required none of those qualities. Sir Grenville had long been a client of Cottjens's, and there was a standing instruction that the Dutchman was to send to Sir Grenville any information, however trivial, concerning Mordecai Lopez. For two years there had been nothing, and now this. Lopez had returned to Amsterdam. The Jew had opened up his old, opulent house, while his ship, the *Wanderer*, was tied to an Amsterdam wharf. He had brought, Cottjens said, ten crates of belongings from Venice, and there was no evidence that he planned to move on for some while. The *Wanderer* had been stripped of her masts and was undergoing a thorough repair.

Sir Grenville Cony led his secretary towards a quiet space by the old Jewel Tower. 'Why? Why? Why does that Jewish bastard come now?' Sir Grenville turned his back on a beggar who was hauling his crippled legs over the grass. The man claimed he had been wounded in Parliament's service.

Dear God! Sir Grenville did not need this news now. First the girl disappears into a burning London night, Grimmett, faithful Grimmett, is killed, and now this! To add insult to injury, that fat fool Scammell had not even bedded the bitch before she fled. At least the wedding certificate, valid till proved otherwise, had survived in Scammell's unburned, brick house. The only joy Sir Grenville had taken in the whole affair was to watch Scammell cringe as he was tongue-lashed.

Now this! Lopez had come north to Amsterdam. Sir Grenville kicked the beggar who had pulled at the lawyer's coat, then kicked him again. 'He knows, John! He knows!'

The secretary shrugged. 'You think so, Sir Grenville?'

'Of course! Why the hell else does he come? The girl must have got a message to him. Christ and damnation! God! She has the seal, John. She has the seal!' He had been pacing up and down the patch of grass, but on these final words the small, fat, man whirled round and pointed a finger accusingly at his secretary, as though John Morse was responsible.

The secretary kept his voice mild. 'We don't know that, sir.'

'We don't know that there'll be a Second Coming! Of course he knows! Why else would he be here?' Cony shut his bulging eyes as if in pain. 'God damn, God damn, God damn! She had it all along! She had it! She tricked me! God damn!' He snarled, then seemed to freeze.

When he moved again, eyes opening slowly, he was quite calm. Morse was used to this metamorphosis. The anger was over, now would come the calm, efficient plan that would attempt to retrieve the damage. 'Which of our people would recognize the girl?'

Morse thought. 'Myself, sir. The boat crew.'

Sir Grenville snapped his fingers. 'The boat crew. Who's the best man?'

'Taylor, Sir Grenville.'

'Send Taylor to Amsterdam. Two of our guards to go with him. If the girl is seen going to the Jew's house, seize her. One hundred pounds apiece if they're successful.'

The secretary raised his eyebrows, but said nothing. Sir Grenville frowned for a second. 'She's got to be found, John, she's got to be. Who's at Werlatton?'

'Davis, sir.'

Sir Grenville had sent one of his guards to Werlatton, to make sure that the chastened Samuel Scammell pulled the house apart in his efforts to find the seal. 'Send a message to Davis; can he read?'

'No, Sir Grenville.'

'Damn. Send a messenger. Twenty pounds if anyone spots the girl.'

'At Werlatton, sir?' Morse was surprised.

'Don't be a bigger fool than God made you. She only knows Werlatton, where the hell else would she have made friends to rescue her?' Sir Grenville was thinking swiftly. 'Lopez may send men to her, rather than expect her to make

the journey. I want her found. I'll pay twenty pounds for a sighting, understand? Get Scammell's servants out looking, but find her! Find her!'

It was not much, Sir Grenville knew, but it was all he could do at this time. He had always known this moment would come, the gathering of the seals, and he did not intend to lose the battle that was imminent.

There were four seals: Matthew, Mark, Luke and John. Sir Grenville's enemies were seeking to assemble any three of the seals. It did not matter which three. Three seals controlled the Covenant and victory would go to the man who gathered them first.

He thought about it as he walked back to the Commons. He had thought these thoughts for years, since the Covenant had first been made and the permutations surrounding the seals were old in his mind.

Lopez would never succeed in laying his hands on the Seal of St Mark. That was in Cony's keeping, and Sir Grenville guarded it well. St Mark was safe.

On the other hand Sir Grenville knew that he would never gain possession of the Seal of St Luke. That was in Lopez's keeping and the Jew guarded it as carefully as Sir Grenville guarded St Mark.

That left two seals. St Matthew, he was now sure, was in Dorcas Slythe's hands. If it reached Lopez, then the game was almost certainly lost, the battle won by the enemy. The thought hurt.

The problem was the Seal of St John. That had belonged to Christopher Aretine, the begetter of the Covenant and a man whom Sir Grenville hated more than he had believed it possible to hate. Damned Kit Aretine, failed poet, wit, soldier, and the holder of St John. Aretine was dead. Sir Grenville would have liked to be utterly certain of Aretine's death. He would like to dance on the rotting remains of his enemy's body, but failing that he had to believe the sea captain who had sailed back from the American settlement of Maryland and swore on a Bible to Sir Grenville that he had seen the headstone of Aretine's grave. Aretine, then, was dead. But where was his seal?

The thought haunted Sir Grenville as he edged his awkward bulk along the benches of the Commons. Where was the Seal of St John? Was it lurking somewhere, ready to take away his control of the Covenant?

He sat down and stared into the dust that drifted in the sunlight above the Speaker's chair. He thought suddenly of Ebenezer Slythe, and the thought brought some comfort to the lawyer. Sir Grenville had told Ebenezer almost everything, all the details of the Covenant except for the amount of the income, and he had watched the greed work on the bitter mind inside the crippled body. A bitter mind, Sir Grenville thought, but a clever one. Ebenezer was intelligent, ambitious, and utterly without scruples. He would have made, Sir Grenville thought, an excellent lawyer, but Sir Grenville had another profession in mind for Ebenezer, a profession that would link his piety with his talent for cruelty. Sir Grenville would keep Ebenezer content until he needed his help to secure the Covenant.

He listened for a moment to some doddering fool who suggested that captured Royalist land should be distributed among the poor of the nearest parishes. The poor! What would they do with it? Except to manure it with their own dung and fill it with their sour whining! Sir Grenville dutifully applauded as the member sat down.

Sir Grenville would not allow himself to think of defeat. The escape of the girl had been a setback, a dreadful setback, but he would find her, and he would destroy her with Ebenezer's help. He could yet win, and no damned Jew, no dead poet, and no foul bitch of an empty-headed girl would thwart him. Sir Grenville growled on his bench. He would win.

13

Campion thought sometimes of the stream where she had first met Toby, beside which she had sat in the days after her father's death, and she remembered her desire, in those unhappy days, to go with the stream's current away from Werlatton and discover where the waters would take her. It seemed to her now that she had done just that. The death of Matthew Slythe had pushed her into a great, dark stream, its current fast between banks she could dimly discern, and her visit to London had whirled her into a raging, dangerous rapid that had done its best to drown her. Now, at Lazen, the stream had carried her into a calm, sunlit stretch of water. She had prayed so often and so hard for happiness, and now, at last, it seemed the prayers were answered.

The autumn and winter of 1643 were happy months for Campion, shadowed only by Toby's absence and by the unanswered mysteries surrounding the seal.

Toby was now what he had long wished to be; a soldier of King Charles. His father's eminence had assured him an immediate captaincy, yet even so his first letters home were cheerful confessions of ignorance. He had to learn his trade, and he was determined to be worthy of the name 'Cavalier'. The nickname had been given to the King's soldiers by the Puritans and was intended to be a deadly insult. The *caballeros* of Spain were the notorious enemies of true Protestantism, and the English adaptation, 'Cavalier', was supposed to tarnish the Royalists with Roman Catholic foulness. Yet the Cavaliers, like the Roundheads, had enthusiastically adopted their enemy's insult and invested it with pride. Toby would be a Cavalier.

Campion missed Toby, yet his letters, funny and affectionate, kept alive the promise of the future they had so intemperately planned in London. At the same time the Seal of St Matthew, constantly about her neck, was a reminder of the threat to that future. Lady Margaret had been for immediate action. Sir Grenville Cony must be bearded, must be forced to divulge his secrets, but Sir George Lazender, home at last, forbade any such foolishness.

'Sir Grenville is not a man we can force! What means do we have of forcing him? Force, indeed!'

Lady Margaret frowned. 'Then what do we do?'

'Nothing, of course. There's nothing to be done.'

Inaction was like gall to Lady Margaret. 'Nothing! Something must be done. What about Lopez? Why do we not make enquiries of Lopez?'

Sir George had sighed. 'In the first place, my dear, we do not know which Lopez the letter refers to. Suppose we did? So what then? For all we know he's just as unscrupulous as Cony. If Campion falls into his hands she might suffer quite as much, if not more. No. Let the waters settle and we shall see what we shall see.'

Sir George's prudence, natural to him, was reinforced by a desire not to become deeply involved in Campion's affairs. He had been surprised, irritated and disappointed to find, on his return, that Lady Margaret had so wholeheartedly embraced Campion.

'She's unsuitable, Margaret. Quite unsuitable.'

'You haven't met her, George.'

Most of his objections to her presence in the castle evaporated when she was introduced. She had curtseyed prettily and Lady Margaret had watched, amused, as her husband responded to the girl's extraordinary beauty.

As the days passed Lady Margaret noticed Sir George enjoying Campion's company more and more. Sir George, for his part, was happy now that she should be in his household. He accepted her as his wife's companion, yet he still had reservations about her as a possible daughter-in-law. The seal, the strange Covenant, these were not certainties. It was best, Sir George thought, to give the girl time and see whether Toby's passion would abate with the passing of the months.

Lady Margaret acquiesced. Nothing could be done, but

that did not stop her constantly speculating on the Covenant. She brought to bear on Campion's few facts her vast knowledge of England's families. 'Aretine, dear. How very extraordinary.'

Campion put down her needlework. 'Sir George says he only knows one Aretine.'

'George would, dear. He was thinking of Kit, I suppose?'

'Yes.'

'Sweet Lord, no. England's positively awash with Aretines. Let me think now. There was an archdeacon at Lincoln. Percy. He preached a very dull sermon and he married a most unsuitable woman. Her parents must have been very pleased. They had eight children who were all quite unbearable. Then there was an Aretine in Salisbury, a lawyer. He went mad, dear, and thought he was the Holy Ghost.'

'And Kit Aretine, Lady Margaret?'

'That's different. He was an exceptionally handsome being. Poor man.'

'Poor man?'

'Kit must be dead. It's always the best that go, child.'

Lady Margaret was frustrated in the autumn. She had abandoned the painting of miniatures to take up the art of warfare, convinced that her husband's almost imperceptible change of allegiance would result in the storming of Lazen Castle by Parliamentary hordes. Work on the estate suffered as she insisted on labourers digging new defences that connected the gatehouse to the Old House on one side, and to the northern tip of the moat on the other. Behind the ditches she made earthen banks and then compared her achievements with the diagrams in her book of military fortifications. Somehow her own ramparts looked more like untidy farm ditches and she fretted over it.

She had more success at the east of the castle, where a new stone wall spanned the short gap between the stable-yard and moat, and on the completion of the wall she grandly declared Lazen Castle ready for any attack by the enemy. Sir George, lured out of his library to inspect the wall, prayed inwardly and fervently that the enemy would refrain from testing his wife's work.

The war seemed far from Lazen. The King had survived the summer, though he had failed to capture London, yet the autumn brought grim news to the Royalists. The Scots, fervent Presbyterians, had declared war on Parliament's side. Now King Charles must face the rebel armies in the south, and the Scots to the north, and Sir George, reflecting on these things among his books, sensed that the fighting would become worse. Lazen, he knew, might well be attacked.

The castle was in the centre of a wide tract of country that had mixed allegiances. One village, following the lead of its lord, would support Parliament, while the next would follow their own lord into the King's camp. Most people wanted no part on either side, desiring only to be left to farm their land in peace, but the war was forcing itself on the county.

Three large houses had been fortified for Parliament, one castle and another house for the King, and the garrisons of all five strongholds raided indiscriminately for food. Neither side touched Sir George's land; the Parliamentarians may still have thought him one of their own, while the Royalists hoped he would side openly with them.

Sir George could not sit eternally on the fence. His son-in-law, the Earl of Fleet, visited in November, together with his wife, and taxed Sir George on his allegiance. Sir George intimated that he had none, but Lady Margaret, sitting at her end of the great dining table, frankly declared that Lazen Castle was for the King.

Her daughter, Anne, was shocked. 'You can't be, mother!'

'Can't, child! Can't! You wish me to rebel against my King? The Fleets may do that, but the Lazenders no.'

The Earl of Fleet frowned at the table. 'This is unhappy. Unhappy.'

'Certainly it is unhappy, Fleet. I have no wish to see my daughter's husband lose his head, yet I probably shall. Tower Hill is a bad place to die.

Sir George hurried to say that it was doubtful whether

anyone would be executed on Tower Hill, that times had changed, that men of moderation would doubtless find a compromise to the struggle, but Lady Margaret would have none of it.

'Rebels are rebels, and rebels should be executed.'

Anne, the Countess of Fleet, stared at her mother. 'I am a rebel, Mother?'

'I just hope the axe is sharp. Pass the butter, Campion. George, your sleeve is in the gravy.'

The subject had been dropped, the Fleets leaving next day with an unhappy promise to return for Christmas. The war was souring the family.

Yet war or no war, these were happy days for Campion and days of change. For the first time in her life she dressed in clothes that were intended to be pretty instead of acting as shrouds to hide the shame of being a woman. Lady Margaret had once been a passionate dressmaker, a job now sensibly left to the castle's two seamstresses, but old chests were opened and Campion was clothed in satin, muslin, lace and silk. Her new dresses had soft, flowing lines and were tight-waisted with their skirts split to reveal the petticoats beneath. The necklines were low, trimmed with satin or lace, and even though they were worn with shawls about her shoulders, the dresses seemed so immodest that, at first, Campion was ashamed to wear them. Lady Margaret would have none of it.

'What's the matter?'

Campion pointed to the expanse of skin revealed above the dress. 'It feels strange.'

'Strange? You've got nothing there that's big enough to be strange!' She twitched the diamond-shaped velvet stomacher that was tight at Campion's waist. 'You're thin, dear. Now show me the blue.'

The blue dress was Campion's favourite, perhaps because the powder-blue satin was the same colour as the cloak Toby had bought her. She had waited impatiently as the dress was stitched, yet the waiting had been worthwhile.

The blue dress was shockingly low, the square neckline hemmed in white silk that was cold on her breasts when she first put the dress on. The sleeves, too, were of white silk, but covered in blue ribbons that were sewn at wrist and shoulder so that, when she moved, her sleeves seemed a coruscation of white and blue above the triple cuffs of lace. The skirt was split in the centre, pinned back to show the full-length white satin petticoat, and even Lady Margaret, curmudgeonly with compliments, shook her head in admiration. 'You look lovely, child. Quite lovely.'

Her hair was long and golden, a pale gold like wheat two weeks before the harvest, and her mother had made her scrape it severely back and then coil the tresses in a tight bun that could be hidden by a Puritan bonnet. Once a month at Werlatton, Campion and the maids would sit in the kitchen and Goodwife would shear the ends of their hair, chopping one straight line with long scissors, and that was the extent of Campion's knowledge of hair. Caroline Lazender, Toby's younger sister and the third of Lady Margaret's seven children to survive infancy, repaired the damage. Caroline herself had long, dark hair, and Campion had the impression that the sixteen-year-old could happily spend half of eternity doing nothing but curling and decorating it. Caroline was delighted to have another head to play with. 'It's got to be ringlets.'

'Ringlets?' Campion sounded dubious. Caroline had appeared with a tray heaped with scissors, tongs, strange implements that had to be heated, and a pile of pale blue ribbons.

'Everyone's in ringlets. Absolutely everyone.' The words were said with finality. Ringlets it would be.

So ringlets she had, and for a few days Campion would catch an unexpected glimpse of herself in a mirror or darkened window, and she would stop in amazement at her own reflection. Instead of the demure, modest Puritan, dressed to cover the shame of woman's sin, she saw a creature of golden softness, bare shouldered, long necked, her skin

just tickled by the long curls that hung from the silver fillet in her hair. The seal hung at her breasts, and on her fingers were rings lent by Lady Margaret. Sir George, on the first night that she appeared in all her finery, pretended surprise and asked to be introduced. She laughed, curtseyed and wished that Toby could see her.

She spent her days with Lady Margaret, sharing her energy and enthusiasms, and each evening before dinner she read aloud to her patroness. She had a good voice and read well, though at first she was sometimes shocked by the things Lady Margaret wished to hear. She was introduced to books she had never heard of, could never have imagined had been written, nor did she suspect that Lady Margaret was choosing the books deliberately. Lady Margaret was especially fond of poetry and, one night, Campion stopped reading and blushed. Lady Margaret frowned.

'What on earth is the matter, child?'

'It's rude.'

'Sweet Lord above! Jack Donne was in holy orders, the Dean of St Paul's Cathedral. We knew him well when we were young.' Lady Margaret forebore to mention that John Donne, when young and before he became a priest, had been a rare and boisterous companion.

'Is he dead?'

'Alas, yes. Read on!'

Campion read, despite her embarrassment:

Licence my roving hands, and let them go
Before, behind, between, above, below.
O my America! My new found land,
My kingdom, safeliest when with one man manned . . .

She blushed again when she reached the final couplet:

To teach thee, I am naked first, why then
What needest thou have more covering than a man?

Lady Margaret smiled through the window. 'Very nice, dear. You read it tolerably well.' She sighed. 'Dear Jack. He was the kind of man who kept his boots on.'

'He what, Lady Margaret?'

'Never mind, dear, some things should not be told to the young.'

Yet Lady Margaret knew this girl was not so young. Campion was twenty-one now, well past the age when most girls were married, and she was still innocent. Yet she learned. Lady Margaret taught her, opening the mind, filling it, and Lady Margaret enjoyed the occupation.

There was laughter in the castle, conversation and endless excitements. Campion was forced to help Lady Margaret with her warlike preparations, which, after the completion of her 'fortifications', took the form of musketoon practice across the moat. One November morning, after Campion had erected the target and walked back across the rickety plank bridge, Lady Margaret waved a paper at her. 'A new letter from Toby. Don't worry, there's one for you.' Campion could see the carrier being given ale in the castle yard. Letters arrived when the carriers came, though some letters took weeks if the carrier decided that business demanded a long detour. Lady Margaret looked down her Roman nose at the letter. 'Ha! He's killed a man. Good!'

'Killed?'

'He says he went on a *chevauchée*, whatever that is. Ah, I see, a raid. Why doesn't he call it a raid in the first place? They met some lobsters in a village and he shot one with his pistol. Good for him!' Campion knew enough now to know that a 'lobster' was a heavily armoured Roundhead cavalryman.

'Is he well?' She asked anxiously.

'No, dear, he's dead. Toby killed him.'

'I mean Toby.'

'Of course he's well! He couldn't have written otherwise! There are times, Campion, when I fear you might be quite as stupid as my own girls. Ah! Good Lord!'

'Lady Margaret?'

'Be patient, child. I'm reading.' She finished the letter,

then handed it, with its enclosure, to Campion. The news that had provoked the surprise from Lady Margaret was ominous. The fight in the village where Toby had shot his lobster had resulted in the capture of a Roundhead messenger and, among the papers found in his pouch, was a Commission of Array addressed to 'Oure Loyal Servant Samuel Scammell'. Scammell was ordered to raise a troop of men, raising it presumably with money that came from the Covenant. Toby went on to say that it was thought that Parliament wished to scour the Royalists from Dorset, releasing the next year's rich harvest for their own armies. Campion looked at Lady Margaret. 'They'll be very close to us.'

'I should like to see your husband come, dear.' Lady Margaret liked referring to Scammell as Campion's husband. She put a wealth of scorn into the word. She sniffed, and raised the musketoon to her shoulder. 'Let him come!' The target, a man-sized piece of sacking suspended from a pole, stirred in the small breeze. Lady Margaret squinted down the barrel, only half charged with powder, flinched, then pulled the trigger. The gun coughed, belched filthy smoke, and the ball went far wide of the untouched sacking. Lady Margaret frowned. 'There's something wrong with this gun. It's most perverse.'

Campion was still worried. 'Do you think they'll come here?'

'No, child. They're more troops for Corfe, I expect. Stop worrying. They'll never come here.' Lady Margaret dismissed Werlatton and Scammell from her mind. The two houses were just twelve miles apart, but Puritan Werlatton looked south while Lazen went north for its supplies and market days. There were deep woods between the houses, of interest only to pig keepers and hunters of deer, and Toby's incursion into Matthew Slythe's land had been a rare occurrence.

The first frosts of winter came with the long nights. The labourers on the estate swathed themselves with sacking as they brought in the animals. Some were kept alive for the following year, but most were slaughtered and their meat salted down in the store rooms. Barns, paddocks, stables, and home pastures were filled with animals who all needed winter feeding, the great ricks being sliced open like giant loaves, and even the bees in their hives in the kitchen garden needed food. Lady Margaret and Campion put small bowls of water, honey and rosemary into each hive. The castle was closing down for winter's siege, stocking up on timber and food, looking towards Christmas.

There was still some warlike activity. The hides of the slaughtered cattle were taken to the lime-pits where they were soaked till most of the hair was gone. Then the skins were scraped, tanned with oak-bark and steeped in farmyard dung. The finest leather was treated with dog dung, but this year's leather did not have to command a high price in the market. This year Lazen made leather for defence, boiling the hides to toughen them, fashioning them into heavy jerkins that could stop a sword cut or a half-spent bullet. Sir George expected war.

He had finally declared his new allegiance. The King, wintering in Oxford, had issued a summons for a parliament to meet in the university town and Sir George had replied with an acceptance. He had asked, in the same letter, that the King should provide a small force to protect and fortify Lazen, and he had warned the tenants and servants that they, too, might have to bear arms beneath the banner of Lazender. The flag now flying on the gatehouse showed a bloodied lance across a green field.

The weather was cold and dirty now, the grey clouds sometimes so low that they obscured the flag and hid the topmost stones of the keep. The trees beside the Lazen stream were bare and black, and there were days when Campion sat in the long gallery and stared at a valley swamped by slanting rain, a grey and dark landscape, and she was glad of the three great fires that warmed the gallery and made mysterious shadows among the prancing deities of Lady Margaret's heathen ceiling.

Her plasterwork might be pagan, but Lady Margaret was

shocked to discover that Campion had not been confirmed into the Church of England. It was hardly likely that she should have been. Her father had despised bishops, and so the confirmation at the hands of the bishop had been dropped in Werlatton parish as had the other services of the church which Matthew Slythe disliked. The Reverend Faithful Unto Death Hervey (and it was with a strange, small shock that Campion sometimes recalled such people from her past) had even abandoned the service of Holy Communion, replacing it with what he chose to call the 'Lord's Supper'. Lady Margaret was outraged. 'The Lord's Supper! Quite ridiculous! You might as well have the Lord's Breakfast, or the Lord's Midday Rabbit-pie!'

She took it upon herself to prepare Campion for confirmation, declaring she could do the task quite as well as Mr Perilly, Lazen's vicar, and, inevitably, the lessons led to talk of God and religion. 'You make it entirely too complicated, child.' Lady Margaret's grey head shook in disapproval. 'God is good, and anything He provides is good. That's all there is to it.'

'All?'

'Of course! Do you truly think He put us on the earth to be unhappy? If you enjoy something then it's a good thing, it comes from God.'

'But what if it hurts somebody?'

'Don't be impertinent, I am instructing you. If it hurts somebody then it's bad and comes from the devil.' Lady Margaret sniffed. 'Sir Grenville Cony obviously comes from the devil, but think of all the good things God has given us. A good meal, a gallop to hounds, a kind deed, marriage, pretty dresses,' she rattled off the ineffable blessings of Almighty God in a confident tone, 'good books, music, fishing, mulled wine, friends, killing rebels, and a warm house. They're all God's gift, child, and we have to be thankful.'

Campion tried to explain her own fears, fears that sprang from her education that had depicted life as a constant struggle against sin, and taught her that sin pervaded every corner of everyday life. Lady Margaret would have none of it.

'You're being quite tedious, child. You make my Creator sound an extremely unpleasant man, and I won't have it.'

It was a new kind of Christianity to Campion, an acceptance of religion that did not demand tortuous struggle and endless self-flagellation. Lady Margaret's Christianity saw the world as God's gift, filled with His love, available to be enjoyed. It was a simple faith, but Campion liked it for that, for she was tired of the endless Puritan wrangles about the triune nature of God, about the doctrine of predestination, about redemption and faith, the splitting of countless hairs in the vicious endeavour to prove that one man was 'saved' while another was not. Lady Margaret's faith was rooted in her conviction that Lazen Castle was a microcosm of God's world, and that the Almighty was a grandly omnipotent type of manorial lord, a kind of heavenly Sir George Lazender. 'My dear Campion, I don't expect the tenants to stand around adoring George! No work would get done! They have to be respectful, of course, if they meet him, and we expect them to come to us when they're in trouble and we do our best to patch things up, but we'd all be in a fine kettle if they spent half their lives worrying what he's thinking and shouting his praises to the sky. They expect things of us, of course, like feasts on Plough-Monday, May Day, harvest and Christmas, but we enjoy those, too! Our tenants are happy and that makes us happy. Why on earth should man be gloomy to make God happy?'

It was an unanswerable question, and so, through the autumn and winter, the fear of God leeched itself from Campion's soul, to be replaced by a more robust and self-reliant faith. She was changing, inwardly and outwardly, and though she knew that she was being changed, it was an incident shortly before Christmas that threw before her a grim reminder of her old life, and made her see herself as she was now compared to the person she had been, and filled her, temporarily, with stark fear.

Sir George had declared for the King, but the declaration was by no means public. The Parliamentary leaders of the county still had hopes of his support and, in an attempt to discover his loyalties, they sent the County's Committee for Assessment to Lazen.

The Committee for Assessment visited each property within Parliamentary lands and levied, according to the property's size, a tax that helped pay the costs of the war. Sir George, the Roundheads decided, would pay the tax if he was still of their persuasion while, if he refused, they would take that as a declaration of enmity.

The Committee for Assessment, delayed by rain, arrived late one afternoon. Sir George, polite as ever, invited them into the hallway of the Old House where they stood, cloaks and scabbards dripping. He offered them ale. They were mostly known to him, men who were neighbours, but might soon be enemies. One or two he did not know, and he needed an introduction. One name interested him. 'Sir George? This is the vicar of Werlatton, the Reverend Faithful Unto Death Hervey.'

Hervey bobbed his head, smiling ingratiatingly at the evidently wealthy owner of Lazen Castle. Faithful Unto Death had still not achieved the fame and fortune he so much desired, though he was pleased to be on the Committee for Assessment, a position he owed to Sir Grenville Cony who had been prompted by Ebenezer Slythe. Faithful Unto Death spoke his usual greeting when visiting houses he hoped to tax, 'May the Lord be in this house.'

'Quite so,' Sir George said.

At that moment Campion came into the hallway, laughing with Caroline. Both girls were dressed for early dinner, Campion brilliant in red silk draped with dyed muslin. She dropped a polite, shallow curtsey in the direction of the visitors.

Sir George did not falter for one second. 'My daughter, Caroline, and my niece, Lady Henrietta Creed.'

The lie alerted Campion. She kept her smile, looked at the

visitors, and saw, half lit by the hall lanterns, the lean, sallow face from her past. The Reverend Faithful Unto Death Hervey stared back, his Adam's apple bobbing up and down like a rat trapped in a barley sack. His mouth opened to speak, but Sir George anticipated him. He gestured the girls towards the private parlour. 'I'll join you, ladies, in a moment.'

Campion leaned against the linenfold panelling in the parlour. She had gone pale, and her hand clutched the seal on its chain. 'He recognized me! He recognized me!'

'Who?'

'That priest out there.'

Sir George dismissed her fears. 'My dear! It's impossible! Your hair, your clothes, everything about you is different. Everything! He asked me. I told him you were my niece from Leicestershire and he merely said you reminded him of someone he once knew. Calm yourself!'

Campion would not be calmed. 'He recognized me!'

'He did not. And what if he did? It doesn't matter. Now, I challenge you to a turn at cribbage before you read to Margaret.'

And it seemed Sir George was right. There were no rumours from Werlatton that Matthew Slythe's missing daughter had been seen in Lazen and, as the days passed, Campion forgot her conviction that Faithful Unto Death had spotted her, and even laughed at it.

And, indeed, there was much laughter at Lazen, something there had never been at Werlatton, and it seemed to reach its peak at Christmas when Sir George, lured from his books, supervised the dragging of the yule log to the great hall. The heartbeat of Lazen, that had slowed for winter, quickened in anticipation of the feast that would be held on Christmas Eve. Christmas Day was reserved for the church, though the celebrations were resumed the next day and would last through to Twelfth Night. Christmas was an occasion of grand style at Lazen Castle.

Guests came on Christmas Eve. The Earl and Countess of

Fleet, their differences with the Lazenders forgotten for the festival, arrived with Sir Simon and Lady Perrott, Lazen Castle's closest neighbours to the north. A dozen more of the local gentry were present with their families, and the villagers, tenants and servants were invited so that the great hall would be full. It was a night for everyone to enjoy, a night of feasting, laughter, old jokes, drink, and a night that always ended with Sir George singing in the servants' hall.

Campion was excited at the prospect. She wished Toby could have been at the castle, but even without him she was determined to enjoy this Christmas Eve. She chose the blue dress, her favourite, and Lady Margaret came into her room late in the afternoon as Enid, Lady Margaret's own maid, dressed Campion's hair. Lady Margaret looked critically at the dress, then smiled.

'You're looking very lovely, Campion.'

'Thank you, Lady Margaret.'

'Don't thank me, child. Thank your parents.' Lady Margaret watched as Campion's hair was drawn back and the candlelight showed the line of her jaw. It was remarkable, she thought, that such clods as Matthew and Martha Slythe should produce this beauty, for Campion was truly exquisite. Lady Margaret had seen the heads turn. She frowned, unable to let a compliment pass without an attendant criticism. 'Your bust is still too small.'

'You won't let me do anything to remedy that.' Campion smiled at Lady Margaret in the mirror.

'It's your own predicament, child. You shouldn't have married that dreadful man. Don't be shocked tonight.'

'Shocked?'

'George always gets drunk at Christmas. It's a family tradition. He then goes to the servants' hall and sings extremely dubious songs. I can't think where he learned them, they're certainly not in any of his books.'

Enid, her lips holding pins, muttered something about Sir George's father having handed the songs down to his sons.

'I can believe that, Enid.' Lady Margaret sniffed. 'Men

always get drunk at Christmas. I've no doubt that Joseph was extremely tiresome when our Lord was born.' On that imperious note she left the room, summoned by loud shouts that announced the arrival of more guests.

Enid put lamp-black cream on Campion's eyelids, a faint touch of rouge on her cheeks, then stood back. 'You do look nice, Miss Campion.'

'It's your work, Enid.' Campion looked at herself in the mirror, a fine piece of silvered glass from Venice, and she was astonished at what she saw. She smiled when she thought what Ebenezer, Scammell or Goodwife might say if they could see her now, her hair hanging in golden rings from her head decorated with silver and ribbons, her shoulders mostly bare above the silken neckline. She wore something new this day, too, a pair of sapphire ear-rings that Sir George had insisted on her having. Lady Margaret had pierced her ears, freezing them first with ice and then stabbing with a sharpened leather-worker's awl. 'Don't make a fuss, child. A little pain for a lifetime of pleasure. Keep still.'

Campion now hung the seal about her neck, letting it fall on her dress. She frowned at the mirror. 'Are my breasts too small, Enid?'

'You don't want to listen to what she says, miss. It's what Mister Toby thinks what matters.'

'I wish he was here. I thought he was coming.' There was a touch of sadness in her voice. She had not seen Toby since September.

'You'll enjoy it just the same, miss. Everyone does. Now you go downstairs, miss, and don't you drink too much of that wassail bowl. Half a ladle of that and a horse would fall down.'

Music echoed in the passageways of the New House as Campion walked towards the Old. The musicians were in the gallery, their playing still unaffected by the drink that would eventually silence them. Campion walked through the Old House towards the brilliantly lit great hall and stopped at the head of the stairs to look at the splendour.

The hall was lit by scores of candles; in sconces, on tables, and in the two ancient iron-ring chandeliers that had been hoisted to the yellow ceiling. Two great fires burned, warming the throng that laughed, chattered, and manoeuvred friends and neighbours beneath the enormous sprig of mistletoe hanging between the chandeliers. The tables were already set with pewter and earthenware, the gleam of silver at the top table where the gentry would sit.

She looked for Sir George or Lady Margaret, needing allies to help her deal with all these strangers, and she saw them with their special guests at the largest of the two hearths. She started down the wide, polished staircase, then stopped.

Toby had come home.

He stood by the fire, still in travelling clothes with his long boots muddied to the knees, and he paused himself as he put a tankard of mulled wine to his lips. He stared, unbelieving, at the woman who came down the stairs, a woman who seemed to gleam and sparkle in the flame-light, a woman of deep beauty who stared at him, whose face was suddenly suffused with joy, and he knew he was smiling uncontrollably when his mother tapped his shoulder. 'Don't stare, Toby, it's rude.'

'Yes, mother.'

He went on looking at Campion. Lady Margaret, who had engineered this surprise, looked too. A small smile showed on her face. 'I've done rather well with her, don't you think?'

'Yes, mother.' Toby felt a catch in his throat, a shiver of the blood in his body. She was magnificent, her beauty almost frightening.

Sir George looked from Campion to his son, back to Campion, then to his wife. He gave a small, secret shrug and he saw the flicker of amusement on Lady Margaret's face. She knew, they both knew, that there was nothing now to be done. These months in Oxford had not cured Toby, any more than they had cured Campion. Sir George knew he would have to surrender. Only the fires of hell would keep those two apart.

14

London was not a happy city that Christmas. The King's possession of Newcastle meant that coal was desperately short, and though Parliament's allies, the Scots, sent what coal they could, its price was way beyond the means of most citizens. Even when the trees in the royal parks about London had been chopped and cut for firewood and the logs distributed in the city's streets, most of London's quarter of a million inhabitants were still bitterly cold. There was never enough coal and timber to go round, and so the people muffled themselves in what clothes they could, wrapped their faces against the east wind, and watched as the Thames slowly froze above London Bridge. It would be a long, cruel winter.

Christmas should have been a bright spark in that cheerless, bleak winter, but Parliament, in its immemorial wisdom, abolished Christmas.

The Scots were to blame. Parliament's new allies, fervent men from Edinburgh and the draughty houses of the north, declared Christmas to be a heathen abomination, a pagan feast artificially grafted on to Christianity, and the Scots, good Presbyterians all, declared that in a world made perfect by saintly rule there could be no Christmas. The House of Commons, eager to appease their new allies whose armies, though they had achieved nothing yet, might well usher in the glorious Day of the Lord, knuckled their foreheads to the Scottish divines and, in a vote of Parliament, declared Christmas to be no more. To be joyful at Christmas was now not only a sin but also a crime. Truly the Day of the Lord was at hand.

London, a city sympathetic to Parliament, filled with Puritans of all descriptions, seemed ungrateful for this decision. Parliament declared that on Christmas Day businesses were to be open as usual, shops selling what little there was to be sold, watermen plying for hire where the encroaching ice allowed. Parliament ordered in vain. Christmas could not be abolished so easily, not even with the passionate pleading of the Scottish ministers who had brought the light of truth from their cold homeland. London insisted on its Christmas, pagan or not, but the celebration was half-hearted, the gaiety subdued. The Presbyterians stolidly ignored the lawbreaking and consoled themselves that godliness would come in time.

Sir Grenville Cony, in public, espoused the Presbyterian faith. Most members of the House of Commons now did, but Sir Grenville would not allow political Presbyterianism to affect his celebration of Christmas. On Christmas Day itself, once he had made an obligatory appearance at Westminster, and scowled at the evidence of shuttered shops and open ale-houses, Sir Grenville went back to his house on the Strand where a huge fire roared in the great marble fireplace beneath the unshuttered picture of the naked Narcissus. Sir Grenville had secured a swan, that was even now being roasted, but he began his Christmas feast with goose and pork. He gorged himself throughout the afternoon, washing the delicacies down with his favourite claret, and not once did his stomach protest. Even when he was forced to loosen the top of his breeches, fumbling with the laces that joined them to his coat, his stomach was free of pain. He could feel great bubbles of air moving upwards, erupting in his throat, but that was usual and there was no pain. He rubbed his hands with glee as the roasted swan, filled with a forcemeat stuffing, was brought to his fireside table. 'My dear Ebenezer, let me carve for you. Pour yourself wine! Please! More!'

Life was good for Sir Grenville again. He had weathered the storms of autumn, and now he could see the end of the struggle. The Covenant would be his. He lifted slices of swan breast on to Ebenezer's plate. 'There are turnips on your left, dear boy, and giblet gravy. Do cut the new loaf. A wing? You're sure?'

They ate for a moment in companionable silence.

Ebenezer, nineteen now, would have been as unrecognizable to his sister as she would have been to him. He had aged for a start, his darkly shadowed face seeming to possess a bitter wisdom far beyond his few years. His hair was longer too, swept back in a great wave to fall at the nape of his neck. It gave him a predatory look, a look enhanced by eyes that seemed to glitter with an inner fire.

He was crippled still and would always be so, yet now he had found the power that was within him, a power that gave him mastery over the whole-bodied. He was dressed, not in black, but in ecclesiastical purple, and he would have liked the thought that his clothes were the colour of religious vestments. He, like his sister, was happy, though where his sister had found happiness in love and generosity, Ebenezer had found it in darker, bloodier pathways. He had harnessed his religion to pain and he had discovered, thanks to Sir Grenville Cony's influence, a vocation.

In the name of God, and in the service and employ of Parliaments's Committee of Safety, Ebenezer tortured the truth from those suspected of disloyalty. The screams of women torn on the rack, the moans of those who fainted as the iron boot was screwed tight on their feet, crushing all the bones, those sounds were joy to Ebenezer. He used the blade, the fire, the pulley, the hooks, the needles, the pincers of his profession, and in the infliction of pain he had discovered a freedom. He was above the law, man's law or God's law, and he knew himself to be a special person, unfettered by the moral constraints he would impose on others. He was different, he had always been different, but now Ebenezer knew himself to be superior. Yet he still acknowledged one master: Sir Grenville Cony.

Sir Grenville sucked on a bone, then tossed it into the fire. 'Barnegat was right,' he chuckled. Barnegat was Sir Grenville's astrologer and he had forecast good news at Christmas. Sir Grenville ladled more gravy on to his plate. 'You were right about that priest. I'm glad we helped him. What's he like?'

Ebenezer had finished his meal. He leaned back, his dark eyes giving no hint of his thoughts. 'Ambitious. He feels cheated.'

Sir Grenville grunted. 'You're describing half of Parliament. Can he be trusted?'

'Yes.'

There had been a strange pair of visitors to Sir Grenville's house that Christmas morning. The Reverend Faithful Unto Death Hervey and Goodwife Baggerlie had stood, cold and tired, in the alley porchway. Sir Grenville had been at Westminster, but Ebenezer had received them, listened to their tale, and then sent them to lodgings in St Giles. Ebenezer had then greeted Sir Grenville with the glad tidings of great joy.

Sir Grenville had savoured the news all afternoon. It had wiped out his pain, it had given him comfort. He still savoured it. 'Why did the woman come?'

Ebenezer shrugged, sipped his wine. 'She hates Dorcas. Hervey wanted her to show him where you lived.'

'Does she want twenty pounds as well?'

'No.' Ebenezer put his wine glass carefully on the table. He was precise in all his movements. 'I suspect Goodwife knows there's small future with Samuel Scammell.'

Sir Grenville laughed. 'Sensible Goodwife. Mind you, she'd have saved us all a deal of trouble if she'd been able to tell us who that bastard was who took the girl. Still, it's no matter now.' He smiled.

Sir Grenville knew he had been fortunate. Just four months before, he had known real fear. Lopez was in Amsterdam, the girl vanished, but his fears had been groundless. The Jew, it seemed, was in Amsterdam merely to be closer to the war in England. Doubtless, Sir Grenville reflected, Mordecai Lopez had money with both sides, though Sir Grenville had only heard of money lent to the King. Lopez had done nothing that suggested he knew of Matthew Slythe's death, and the girl, evidently, had not attempted to reach Lopez. Sir Grenville would call his watchdogs back from Holland the next day.

He pushed his plate away, belched quietly and smiled at Ebenezer. 'Shall we move to the window?'

They sat staring at the Thames. It was almost dark. A single boat, a lantern at its prow, was rowed upstream. It was hard work for the oarsman because the current was compressed by the ice on both banks. Soon, Cony knew, there would be no boats on the river till the ice loosened its grip. He would have to put more guards into the garden, for the frozen Thames would give easy access to his property.

There were grapes on the low table between them and almonds from Jordan wrapped in sweet French marzipan. Sir Grenville's office had been transformed into a room fit for this feast, and the day's news had made the feast perfect. Sir Grenville bit an almond in half and smiled. 'We have been lucky, Ebenezer, we have indeed been lucky.'

'We have.' The unsmiling, thin face nodded gravely.

The girl was at Lazen Castle. The priest, Ebenezer said, had been utterly certain, certain enough to brave the winter roads to London. Sir Grenville chuckled, his bulging, frog-like eyes surrounded by happy crinkles. 'And she was wearing the seal!'

'She was wearing a golden cylinder on a chain of gold,' Ebenezer corrected his master pedantically.

Sir Grenville's spirits were rising higher. He seemed to giggle in his pleasure, a strange sound, and then he poured more wine for himself. Ebenezer's glass rarely needed filling. Sir Grenville drank.

'Lazen Castle. Lazen Castle. We have been luckier than you know, Ebenezer.'

Ebenezer said nothing, just watched the small, grossly fat man. The flap of Sir Grenville's breeches lay on his thighs, the cloth greasy from fat dripped from the roast meats. Sir Grenville looked at Ebenezer. 'They're going to fortify Lazen, so my man in Oxford tells me.'

Ebenezer frowned. 'Shouldn't we take her before they do?'

'No, Ebenezer, no!' Sir Grenville seemed filled with delight. 'It would be difficult at the best of times to snatch her from that house, but I think a word from Sir Grenville Cony would send troops against it. We shall besiege it, we shall take it, and we shall take her. And much more besides.' He laughed, pouring more wine. 'Do you know the castle?'

'No.'

'It's very fine, very fine.' Sir Grenville nodded happily. 'Half of it goes back to Elizabeth, and there's a splendid modern wing designed by Lyminge. I'm told the plasterwork in the long gallery is quite exquisite. There's a good acreage of forest, over a thousand in plough and twice that in sheep.' He laughed silently, his shoulders heaving. When he spoke his voice was curiously gleeful, like that of a small, naughty boy. 'I think the County Committee for Sequestration would look happily on awarding the property to me, don't you think?'

Ebenezer gave one of his rare smiles. He knew that Sir Grenville, using his position on the Parliamentary Committee that oversaw the fate of captured enemy property, was amassing land for himself throughout southern England. 'Who owns it now?'

'Sir George Lazender. A painfully honest man. He has a formidable wife. Sir George has seen fit to join our enemies, Ebenezer, so I think we can punish him with a clean conscience.'

'Amen.'

'And amen. And he has a son, I can't remember the boy's name. I presume that is why your dear sister is there?'

Ebenezer shrugged. 'I don't know.'

'Not that it matters, so long as she is there.'

He laughed as he heaved himself out of his chair, holding his unlaced breeches with one hand while, with the other, he unlocked and opened a great iron chest. He took from it a piece of paper which he presented, with a flourish, to Ebenezer. 'Do the needful, dear boy.'

Ebenezer took the paper, holding it in his fastidious way as if it might infect him. It was the marriage certificate of Samuel Scammell and Dorcas Slythe, signed by James

Bollsbie, Clerk in Holy Orders. Ebenezer looked at Sir Grenville. 'You're sure?'

'I am sure, dear boy, I am certain, I am filled with certainty and with sureness. Proceed!'

Ebenezer shrugged, then held the brittle, browned paper into the flame of the closest candle. The certificate flared up, curled, burned, and Ebenezer dropped it on to a silver plate where the flames died. Sir Grenville, chuckling, leaned over and pounded the ash into unrecognizable powder.

'Your sister has just been given her divorce.' He sat down again.

'Will you tell her?'

'Dear me, no. Nor him! Nor the world! They must think themselves married to the end of time itself, till eternity is old. Just you and I know, Ebenezer, just you and I. So!' He pointed with a blackened finger to the ash. 'Your sister is no longer married to Brother Scammell, so who now is the guardian of the seal?'

Ebenezer smiled again, but said nothing.

'You are, Ebenezer, you are. Congratulations, you have become rich.'

Ebenezer raised his glass and sipped. He drank little, preferring to face the world sober.

Sir Grenville moulded marzipans and almonds into a ball. 'And your father's will, moreover, says that if your sister should be so unfortunate as to die before she is twenty-five and without children, then the monies of the Covenant must be used for the spreading of the gospel. I think we could spread the gospel most effectively, don't you, Ebenezer?'

Ebenezer Slythe smiled, nodded. 'What about Scammell?'

'You tell me, dear boy.' The lawyer's bulging eyes watched Ebenezer closely.

Ebenezer steepled his fingers. 'He serves no purpose for you any more, if he ever did. He's an inconvenient witness to a marriage you don't now want. I think it is time Brother Scammell crossed the River Jordan.'

Sir Grenville laughed. 'Indeed. Let him await the resurrection in the peace of his grave.'

In the last of the daylight a great raft of yellow-grey ice lurched in the river, lodged against more ice, then came to rest. The unfrozen stream, black in the near darkness, foamed briefly white, then settled. Far off Sir Grenville could see dim splinters of light from the miserable hamlet at Lambeth. 'So, Brother Scammell must die, but at whose hand?'

The dark eyes showed no emotion. 'Mine?'

'It would be a kindness to me, dear boy. There is, unfortunately, another witness to this now inconvenient marriage.'

Ebenezer shrugged. 'Goodwife will say nothing.'

'I do not mean Goodwife.'

'Ah.' There was a flicker of a smile on Ebenezer's face. 'Dear Dorcas.'

'Dear Dorcas, who will be most inconvenient should she live to be twenty-five.'

Ebenezer stretched out his legs, the one long and thin, the other twisted and bent inwards beneath his full-length purple robe. 'It would also be inconvenient, surely, if your name or mine were connected with her death. You tell me Lopez could still be a nuisance.'

'So?'

Ebenezer again smiled, a smile of satisfaction, of cleverness. 'We never spoke of the priest's reward.'

'The Reverend Faithful Unto Death Hervey? He wants more than his twenty pounds?'

'Maybe he's deserved it. He did not, after all, tell Scammell. He told no one, except Goodwife, and he needed her to reach you quickly.'

'What does he want?'

'Fame.'

Sir Grenville gave a short, braying laugh. 'Is that all? That's easy. I'll have him in St Paul's Preaching House this Sabbath, and every Sabbath if he wants.'

'No.' Ebenezer contradicted Sir Grenville without

embarrassment. His self-assurance, since he had come to this house, was extraordinary. 'He has his own ideas about fame.' He told Sir Grenville quickly, concisely, seeing the pleasure on the older man's face.

Sir Grenville thought about it, staring at the dark window in which the room's candles were now reflected. He smiled. 'So the courts will finish her off?'

'Yes. And there'll be no blame attached to us.'

'You could even plead for her, Ebenezer.'

The thin, ascetic face nodded. 'I will.'

'While Faithful Unto Death—what an apposite name—will make sure she dances on a rope.'

'Or worse.'

'How very fitting it all is.' Sir Grenville rubbed plump hands together. 'You'll have to go to Lazen, Ebenezer. I'll make sure the Committee of Safety releases you from your services.' Ebenezer acknowledged the order with a grave nod. Sir Grenville, despite the drink in him, was thinking clearly. 'Take the priest, and I'll make sure Scammell is there. Let me know when it's about to fall, I'll come down.'

'You want to be there?'

'There is a seal to collect, remember?'

Ebenezer did not move, did not say anything.

Sir Grenville chuckled. 'And a large estate. I'll take possession quickly.'

'When?'

'As soon as we can march.' Sir Grenville shrugged. 'It will be early spring, but we can keep an eye on the place till then.' He smiled broadly. 'I shall make you my heir, Ebenezer.'

Ebenezer gave a tiny bow, then smiled. 'I hope your astrologer was wrong about the other thing.'

Sir Grenville wished the words had not been said. Despite the heat of the fire, despite the warmth in the room, he felt a chill go through him. Barnegat, poring over Sir Grenville's charts, had said an enemy would come from beyond the seas. He thought of Kit Aretine, but Aretine was dead! Sir Grenville shivered. If Kit Aretine had heard one hundredth part of what had been spoken in this room this Christmas night, then Cony could fear a death that would make the dying of Ebenezer Slythe's victims seem merciful.

'Put some logs on the fire, Ebenezer. Aretine's dead. He's in his American grave, and I hope the American worms vomit on his corpse. No. Barnegat meant Lopez, and if the Jew dares show his face in England we'll have him behind bars.'

Ebenezer limped to the fire, fed it with logs, and watched as the flames leaped bright. He leaned on the mantel, curiously elegant in his fur-edged, purple gown. His eyes were like twin points of white light. 'Do you want entertaining this evening?'

Sir Grenville twisted his head round. 'Do sit down, dear boy, my neck is hurting.' He watched Ebenezer limp back to the chair. 'What do you have?'

'A girl. She wants clemency for her father.'

'Who is?'

Ebenezer shrugged. 'A tallow-chandler. We think he was sending messages to Oxford. He says not.'

'Will you release him?'

Ebenezer shrugged. 'That rather depends on his daughter now.'

'What's she like?'

'Seventeen, a virgin, pretty enough.'

Sir Grenville laughed. 'She has no idea whose house this is?'

Ebenezer gave his master a pitying look. 'What do you think?'

'Forgive me, Ebenezer, forgive me.' He chuckled. 'Lead on, dear boy, lead on.' He heaved himself upright. He liked to watch Ebenezer taking his revenge on a world that had for so long not recognized the cripple's talents. Sir Grenville could watch from a darkened room through the window into Ebenezer's bed-chamber. Even without the instruments of torture which the government supplied for his work, Ebenezer was skilled at humiliating, hurting and befouling the innocent whose wholeness he hated. Sir Grenville followed him eagerly.

Rain started to fall outside the house, a freezing rain that fell in utter blackness, falling softly on the darkness of the marsh, on the river and on the congealing ice that slowly and imperceptibly spread towards the calm, western country hidden by night.

'Do you always wear it?'

'Yes.' Campion firmly pushed Toby's fingers away from the seal and away from the white silk that covered her breasts.

He smiled. 'Mother says you've been reading John Donne.'

'And Spenser, and Drayton, and Ford, and Greene, and Shakespeare, and Sir Philip Sidney, and Royden, and even someone called Thomas Campion.'

Toby ignored her list. He shut his eyes. ' "Full nakedness, all joys are due to thee." '

'Not here, and not now, Toby Lazender.'

'Yes, ma'am.'

Campion sat on a fur-covered chest that was in front of one of the great fires in the hall. The remains of yesterday's feast had still not been entirely cleared. The huge logs burned above a mound of glowing, shifting embers. Most of the castle was asleep.

They had sat up late the night before, after Toby had helped his father from the servants' hall and steered him to his bedroom. They would sit up late again this Christmas night, sharing words and silences into the small hours.

Toby, sitting at her feet, slid his hand up her be-ribboned arm, cupped her shoulder, pulled her gently towards him. He kissed her, feeling her respond, and then he opened his eyes to see if hers were closed. He found himself looking into two very open, very blue eyes. He leaned back. 'You're not taking me seriously.'

'Oh.' She mocked him with gentle pity.

She could see little change in him, though she wondered if there was a new toughness about him, put there by days in the saddle and the slowly accrued knowledge that he could survive in a fight. He had killed four times now to his certain knowledge, five if he included Thomas Grimmett in Scammell's house, and all four men had been killed at close range with pistol or sword. He had had time to see the fear in their eyes, to smell it even, and he had learned to conquer his own. He was, she thought, tougher, but that had not stopped him from being very gentle with her.

He smiled at her. 'The Reverend Perilly says you're not married. He says you're not married till . . .'

'I know what he says. Your mother says the same. He's right. I'm not married.'

'So are you going to marry me?'

She traced a finger down his nose, pretending to think. 'Yes.'

'When?'

'In three days' time.'

'I go back to Oxford in two!'

'I know.' She smiled.

They would marry. Even Sir George had given his consent, frowning after the Christmas morning service. He still thought her not the most suitable bride, would have preferred some girl with more certain prospects of a dowry rich enough to replace the roof of the Old House, but he would not stand in his son's way. 'You can't marry her yet, Toby.'

'I know, father.'

The Reverend Perilly, consulted after matins, had outlined the difficulties. Campion's marriage to Scammell, he had said, could be declared invalid by a properly convened church court and, even if Scammell dared attend the hearing, he could not fight the evidence of Campion's virginity. But that, Perilly said, must be attested by good witnesses; doctors beyond reproach, trusted midwives, and the process would cost money and time. The church courts no longer sat in

London, the whole process must take place in Oxford, and he suggested it would be an ordeal for Campion. He had shaken his head. 'Are you sure Mr Scammell won't go to Chancery? There must have been a settlement.'

Sir George, hungover, had been gloomy. 'I'm sure of nothing, Perilly, except that Toby won't see sense.'

'You can hardly blame him, Sir George.'

Sir George smiled. 'No. So it seems.'

Campion would go through the ordeal, though not till later in the year when the roads were fit for travelling. She smiled now, looking at the two dogs that slept fitfully before the fire, their paws twitching as they chased imaginary rabbits. Her cat, Mildred, slept on Campion's lap. She had named the kitten, now almost full grown, after Mrs Swan. 'I wonder if she'll get our letter.'

'Mrs Swan?'

'Yes.'

'I don't know.'

She still smiled. 'Next Christmas we'll be married.'

'I know. You'll have to promise to obey me.'

'Like your mother obeys your father?'

Toby smiled. 'Just the same.'

Campion frowned. 'Do you think the Fleets are happy?'

'Mm,' Toby yawned. 'Anne likes the fact that John's boring. It makes her feel safe.'

'Will they really be enemies of ours?'

'No. Lots of families are divided. There's not much hatred.' He twisted his head round to look at her. 'I think the mistletoe needs us.'

'I think you've exhausted the mistletoe. I think I'm going to bed.'

'I'll take you.'

'Toby Lazender, I am quite capable of climbing stairs on my own.'

'Someone might jump out at you.'

'Not if you stay here, dear.' She laughed. 'That dreadful Ferraby boy might. Who is he?'

Toby smiled. There were times, he thought, when Campion began to sound like his mother. 'Mother wants him to marry Caroline.'

'All he did was stare at me with ox-eyes. Like a great, sad ox. I spoke to him once, and he dribbled.'

'Like this?' Toby made a grotesque face, drooling at the same time.

'Stop it. You'll frighten Mildred.'

He laughed. 'Ferraby's nervous of you.'

'I can't think why. Is he really to marry Caroline? He's so young!'

'He probably is.' He grinned at her. 'Money.'

'I didn't think it was for his looks.'

Toby gave her a slow smile. 'I shall marry you for your looks.'

'Will you now?'

'Yes.' He twisted around so he was kneeling in front of her. 'For your hair, your eyes, your mouth, and for the big, brown mole that you have,' he paused, his finger hovering just above her navel. He stabbed it down on to her stomacher. 'There.'

'Toby!'

He laughed. 'I'm right, there's no use in denying it.'

He was right. She was blushing. 'Toby?'

'My love?' He spoke in pure innocence.

'How do you know?' She spoke loudly enough to disturb the dogs who opened their eyes, saw it was not time for breakfast, and slumped back into growly comfort. The kitten stretched its claws.

Toby was grinning. 'When you catch trout with your bare hands, you must move very, very slowly, and very, very quietly.'

'You saw me?' He nodded. She could feel her face redden. 'You should have made a noise!'

'I'd have frightened the fish!' he said indignantly. He laughed. 'I just looked through the reeds and there you were. The nymph of the stream.'

'Then, I suppose, your feet got stuck and you couldn't move?'

'That's exactly what happened.' He smiled. 'And when I'd seen all there was to see I went back downstream, splashed about a bit, and came back. And you said you hadn't been swimming.'

'And you pretended you hadn't seen anything!'

'You didn't ask me!' He pretended to be as indignant as Campion.

'Toby! You're dreadful!'

'I know, but you'll still marry me?'

She looked at him, loving his smile, but one thing worried her. 'When you were in the stream, Toby . . .'

'Yes?'

She was hesitant. 'Your mother says . . .' She stopped and waved a hand over her breasts. 'She says . . .'

He laughed at her confusion. 'Mother doesn't know tits from trout.'

'Toby!' The dogs stirred again.

He laughed. 'I'll tell you, then. They're beautiful.'

'You're sure?'

'You want me to make certain?' He smiled. 'Will you marry me?'

'If you promise me one thing.'

'What's that?'

She leaned forward, kissed him swiftly on the forehead and stood up, clutching Mildred in her arms. 'That sometimes you'll leave your boots on.'

'Whatever does that mean?'

She walked away from him, imitating Lady Margaret's voice. 'Nothing. There are some things that should not be told to the young.'

He caught up with her under the mistletoe, but she did eventually climb the stairs, regretting that she had to leave him, wishing she could wake next to him in the morning.

Yet, as she undressed in her room, it seemed to her that their future was once more a seamless blue sky of happiness, that her past was a fading, irrelevant memory of unhappy people who blamed their God for their own inadequacies. She had a whole life ahead of her, a life she would share with love, and she smiled when she thought that not once in three months had she given any thought to the Recording Angel with his massive, accusing book. He had been replaced by a guardian angel, shining and happy, and, as she knelt beside the bed in which the warming pan had long gone cold, she prayed in the chill bedroom, giving thanks to her God for a life that had become happy, as He wanted lives to be, and she prayed for the turn of the year, for the spring, when she could seal that seamless, happy, innocent future.

PART III
The Seal of St Luke

15

25 March 1644, New Year's Day, was bright and cold, one of the good March days that promise spring. Lady Margaret Lazender, with typical perversity, refused to recognize it as New Year's Day, preferring the continental and Scottish 1 January. Sir George, who liked tradition, scoffed at the January date, and made sure that he sent lavish greetings to his wife from Oxford. Yet, New Year's Day or not, it promised well. The corn had been seeded, there were calves in the steadings and Lazen Castle's dairy was busy after the winter's scarcity; the milk made sweet by the parsnip leaves on which the cows had been fed while they waited for the spring grass.

Great fires still burned in the castle, but now some windows were opened to let cold air scour the halls. There had been the usual rash of new babies, hastily christened, all owing their lives to last year's May Day. Lazen's church, oddly, was built within the circle of wall and moat and thus was in the castle's gardens. Each mother returned to the village bearing a small silver cup, of which Lady Margaret seemed to have an inexhaustible supply.

Most of the castle's treasures had disappeared. Colonel Andrew Washington, the commander of Lazen's garrison, had suggested that Sir George hide his most valuable pieces. They had been taken to the cellars, only a handful of old servants privy to what was happening, and there they had been walled up. The new wall had been smeared with a diluted mixture of cow-dung, to make it look old and encourage the growth of lichen to disguise the hiding place. The household now ate off pewter and the gold and silver had disappeared from halls and rooms.

Colonel Washington, sent from Oxford, was a short, tubby man who did not look, at first sight, like an experienced soldier. The first impression was wrong. He was efficient, authoritative and he proved his reputation for bravery on his first meeting with Lady Margaret. He had been standing by his horse, staring thoughtfully at the ditches she had dug either side of the gatehouse, ditches that had suffered from the snow and rain of the winter. Lady Margaret had beamed at him. 'You see, Colonel! I have begun your work!'

Washington gave her a respectful look. 'What are they, your Ladyship?'

'What are they?' Lady Margaret looked astonished. She drew herself up to her full height, towering over the small colonel. 'They are fortifications, Colonel Washington, defences!'

'Your Ladyship's expecting an attack from a church choir, perhaps? They'll be soldiers, ma'am, soldiers! Fortifications!' And he had walked away, leaving Lady Margaret speechless, and the castle trembling as to which would win the battle of wills.

Yet Colonel Washington was not a successful soldier for nothing. He knew which battles to fight, and when to call for a truce, and once he had surveyed the defences, and once his one hundred and fifty men were settled into the keep, gatehouse and Old House, he made his peace with Lady Margaret. He skilfully sought her advice and, just as skilfully, planted his own ideas into her head so she would think them her own. Thus the last months of the old year had been peaceable enough. The colonel and his twelve officers ate with the family and, after two months, the officers even gave up their siege of Campion.

Yet the first day of 1644 brought a new excitement to the

castle. The murderers came. Murderers and sakers.

They had been expected since early February, but the snow of the hard winter had kept them in Oxford, and even now the roads were so deep in mud that Colonel Washington had been surprised that they had arrived safely.

Caroline brought the news to the long gallery. 'They're here! They're here! They've arrived!'

Lady Margaret looked up from the half-bound book that somehow would not come right. 'Who's here? You sound as if it's the Second Coming! I heard no trump.'

'The murderers, mother! They're here!'

The book was instantly forgotten. 'Campion! My cloak. Your own too, child. Do hurry! I need boots. Caroline, find me boots. Come along! Come along!'

The murderers were at the front of the Old House, brought in wagons and escorted by thirty men who would be valuable additions to the garrison. Colonel Washington beamed at the wagons. 'Aren't they just splendid, Lady Margaret? Just splendid!'

'I wish to try one, instantly!'

Washington suppressed a smile. He had known that as soon as the cannons arrived Lady Margaret would want to play with one of them. He half bowed. 'I thought the honour of the first shot should belong to your Ladyship.'

'How very kind, Colonel.'

Oxford had been generous. They had sent four sakers, big guns, and six of the smaller murderers, though only the latter had been promised. The murderers were mounted on swivels and got their name because the recoil could swing the iron barrels round and kill the men who served the guns. The sakers fired round shot, while the smaller guns blasted out a dreadful fan of bullets and scrap metal that Colonel Washington said could scour a great swathe in an attacking enemy.

Campion watched as one of the big saker barrels was winched slowly on to a wooden carriage. It frightened her. She thought of Toby and she imagined his body caught by one of the great balls, mangled to pulp, and the sight of the assembled guns reminded her that the clouds of war, that had seemed so far away last year, were now closing in on Lazen. Colonel Washington, who was kind to her, thought that she worried needlessly. 'They've bigger fish to catch than us, Miss Campion. They'll try to capture Corfe Castle first. Besides, I'm keeping them on their toes.' The Colonel had started a vigorous campaign of patrols and raids, encouraging the enemy to stay away from Lazen.

Lady Margaret could scarce contain her impatience. She wanted to fire a murderer, the name appealing to her, but Washington tactfully pointed out that the saker was a bigger gun and would make a bigger bang. Lady Margaret agreed to fire a saker. She watched closely as powder was thrust into the hooped barrel, as the wadding was pushed down and finally as the iron ball was rolled into the muzzle and rammed down. A gunner sprinkled fine powder on the touch-hole and then Colonel Washington ordered everyone to stand clear. The gun faced west, across the moat towards the water meadows that had flooded in the winter.

Colonel Washington lit a linstock from the bowl of his pipe and handed the fire-tipped wand to Lady Margaret. 'Stand well clear of the wheels, Lady Margaret.'

She made a caustic comment to the effect that her father had been firing cannons when Colonel Washington was sucking milk, and then she walked with confidence to the ornate, square-breeched gun. She looked about her, at the soldiers, at Campion and Caroline and at her household servants. The linstock smoked. She poised it dramatically above the touch-hole. 'For King Charles!' She lowered the fire.

Lady Margaret squealed in alarm, a squeal that, luckily for her, was drowned by the saker's bellow. It hammered back on its heavy trail, its wheels bucking off the gravel, and Campion watched, appalled, as a cloud of filthy smoke billowed and rolled across the lily pads on the moat. The round shot landed in a water meadow, bounced in a silver haze of spray, bounced again, then slammed into a pollarded willow far down the valley.

'Magnificent!' Lady Margaret held the linstock like a sceptre. 'Let them come!'

'Give me more guns if they do.' Colonel Washington said the words quietly, but Campion heard him.

Lady Margaret stalked towards the colonel. 'Is my technique right, Colonel? Another attempt, perhaps?'

Colonel Washington hastened to assure her Ladyship that her gunnery was magnificent, as fine as any he had seen, and that much as he would like to see her demonstrate her prowess again, he had to confess that powder and shot were both scarce and expensive. Lady Margaret gracefully accepted the title of Honorary Gunner to Lazen Castle, as she was already an Honorary Musketeer and Honorary Engineer. It had been only with the greatest difficulty that Colonel Washington had dissuaded her from hacking with a sword at the butts he had erected in the Glebe Field.

Two weeks later in April the war did come to Lazen, though in a manner surprising to Campion. It was all so different from her expectations.

Colonel Washington had led most of his men north, tempted by a convoy of powder wagons that was rumoured to be going westward, and in his absence the Roundhead troops raided the Lazen valley. Lady Margaret, despite a parting admonition from Colonel Washington that she was to do nothing rash in his absence, rammed a ball into her musketoon.

Campion watched beside Lady Margaret from the long gallery. 'They're not doing very much.'

'They're cowards, dear.'

The enemy, wary perhaps of the soldiers left behind by Colonel Washington, had come no closer to the castle than the outskirts of Lazen village. The villagers, possessions on their backs and household animals led by ropes, trooped miserably towards the safety of the castle.

For a long time it seemed as though the Roundheads would

do nothing. They waited around the watermill, staring at the castle, and then, after a half hour of so, some of them cantered westward into the valley fields. They were dressed just like the Royalists: leather jerkins, some with a breastplate strapped on top and tall boots that were turned over above the knee. Their helmets had a flap at the back to protect their necks, and bars in front beneath the peak to stop a sword-cut to the eyes. The only difference Campion could see was that these men, the enemy, wore red or orange sashes about their waists, denoting their allegiance, while Lazen's defenders wore sashes of white or blue. Captain Tugwell, left in command for the day, lined his musketeers along the moat, each man thrusting a forked musket-rest into the soft lawn on which they could support the heavy musket barrels.

The Roundheads were not interested in the castle, only in its cattle. They herded what cows they could find, driving them back to the mill, and Lady Margaret frowned because no enemy trooper had come within range of the shrunken garrison's firearms. After watching for an hour she was resigned to the raid. 'We'll just have to take some of theirs. Oh, good! They've taken that very ill-tempered brindle cow. I don't understand why we kept it alive over the winter.'

An hour later the Roundheads began to withdraw and there followed what, to Campion, was an extraordinary incident. A single man rode slowly towards the castle moat, his hands spread wide to show he meant no harm. He was dressed superbly. Instead of a helmet he wore a wide, velvet hat from which flowed an extravagant plume. His breastplate, shining as if it was silver, was strapped over a scarlet jacket. His tall boots were an improbable white, stained with mud, but impressively impractical. Captain Tugwell ordered his men not to shoot, and Lady Margaret, peering from one of the long gallery's windows, suddenly smiled. 'Sweet Lord! It's Harry! Come, child!'

As she hurried Campion downstairs and into the garden, Lady Margaret explained who 'Harry' was. 'Lord Atheldene, dear. A very charming man. I always thought he'd be quite perfect for Anne, but she had to marry that bore Fleet.' She stopped at the edge of the moat. 'Harry!'

Lord Atheldene swept his hat from his head. 'Dear Lady Margaret.'

'How are you, Harry?'

'Busy. I do apologize for all this.'

'Don't be foolish, Harry. We shall simply take them back from you. I suppose my son-in-law ordered it?'

Atheldene smiled. He was a handsome man, Campion guessed in his early thirties, who wore his blond hair long and curled. 'He did, Lady Margaret. I fear he dare not show favouritism to you.'

'I notice he didn't dare come himself. How's that girl you married?'

'Very pregnant.' Atheldene smiled. 'Sir George? Is he well?'

'So far as he tells me. He's in Oxford. You can tell my son-in-law that he's attacking defenceless women.'

Atheldene glanced at Lazen's soldiers, smiled, but did not give Lady Margaret a rejoinder. She sniffed. 'I'm sorry to see you fighting against your King, Harry.'

'Only against his advisers, Lady Margaret.'

'You're cavilling, Harry!'

Again he did not accept the challenge. He turned his charm on to Campion. 'I don't believe we've been introduced.'

Lady Margaret answered, 'Nor will you be. She's much too young to meet traitors.'

They exchanged family news, local gossip, and then Atheldene bowed low from his saddle and turned his horse. He waved a hand in salute of Captain Tugwell's courtesy in not firing and then spurred his horse towards the village.

The incident puzzled Campion. She had an idea of the King's enemies as men like her father, stern Puritans, dull-dressed and crop-haired, and it was difficult to imagine how a charming, elegant, polished nobleman like Lord Atheldene should be in their ranks. Lady Margaret explained. 'The King's an extremely foolish man, dear. He's quite charming on two days of the year, but the rest of the time he's exceedingly dull and pig-headed beyond belief. Every time he wanted money he invented a new reason. It wouldn't do. He almost bled us dry, and he certainly wrung a fortune out of Harry. There were taxes here, taxes there, and when the taxes wouldn't do he demanded loans that will never be repaid. Then he tried to do without Parliament and the English don't like that. They like Parliament. It gives men like George something to do. I'm not at all surprised that so many good men rebelled.'

Campion was amused by this sudden reversion of Lady Margaret's normally belligerent partisanship. 'Then why did you choose the King's side?'

'Me, dear? None of my family has ever been a rebel, and I do not intend to be the first.' They were back in the long gallery and Lady Margaret stared ruefully at a book in a frame that was supposed to help her sew its pages together. She was not having great success with book-binding. 'Besides, the King is the King, even if he is a fool. It's not just that.' She frowned. 'Ever since this rebellion started horrible things have been crawling out from every dark corner. I do not wish to be ruled by Baptists, Anabaptists, or anyone else! They'll demand I take a bath and call it religion!' She shook her head. 'In truth, dear, I wish this war had never come. If Queen Elizabeth had been sensible and bred a son, we wouldn't have these wretched Scots on our throne. We have to have a King, but why he has to be Scottish is beyond me.' She picked up her unfired musketoon and looked at it wistfully. 'Perhaps I can shoot a rabbit.'

It was all so complicated. Some of the nobles had sided with Parliament, while some of the Commons had sided with the King. The King was Scottish, yet the Scottish nation, that acknowledged Charles as their King just as he was King of England, had sent an army against their monarch. Some said the war was fought against the King's illegal taxation, others said it was fought to stop Parliament taking power that was properly the King's, while many believed it to be truly a war about what kind of religion should be imposed on England. Neighbour fought neighbour, father fought son, and soldiers captured in battle cheerfully changed sides to avoid imprisonment.

Colonel Washington, with whom Campion spoke that evening and who had fought in the religious wars of northern Europe, was sanguine about the fighting. 'It's not a bad war, Miss Campion. There's no real nastiness.'

'Nastiness?' Campion asked.

He looked sideways at her, stroking his small moustache. 'There's not a lot of hatred in it. Oh, we're fighting, and men are dying, but we're not seeing what we saw in Germany.' He shook his head. 'I've seen them slaughter whole towns. Not pretty, not pretty!' He stared into his tankard of ale. 'Mind you, if it goes on too long then it could turn very bloody. Very bloody indeed.' He swallowed his ale. 'I'm to bed, my dear, and I suppose you're not going to make an old man happy tonight?'

She laughed. It was becoming an old, familiar joke. Colonel Washington, in some ways, had replaced Sir George in the life of the castle.

Sir George Lazender was at Oxford where the King had summoned his Parliament. Its members, meeting in the hall of Christ Church, were all members of the old Parliament who had stayed loyal to the King, and Sir George had gone even though he knew that this Oxford 'Parliament' had no power and was merely a device to give the King's decrees an appearance of legality. He had gone too, Lady Margaret suspected, because he wanted to haunt the libraries of the university, and because he missed the political gossip denied him by his banishment from Westminster.

Sir George wrote early in April suggesting that, if Colonel Washington could spare an escort, Campion should visit Oxford in May. There were doctors and lawyers available, a church court convened, and Campion could annul her marriage to Samuel Scammell. She was embarrassed at the need to prove her virginity, but she would do it.

April, apart from Atheldene's raid, was a good month. The rain was soft, the land green and the air was warming. Campion taught herself to ride side-saddle, though Colonel Washington refused to allow her out of sight of the castle, insisting that officers escort her, and she explored the lower valley or rode on to the nearer hills where the lambs were already growing fat. There were days when the sky was almost clear, when only a few white clouds were piled high in the blue and a fresh breeze promised to clear them away and bring her the seamless blue sky of which she dreamed. The river of her life was keeping her in this calm pool, like the one in which she had swum at Werlatton, where Toby had wached her through the rushes, and sometimes she would think of that and laugh. Sometimes she would look at the seal about her neck, a jewel now so familiar that she often forgot that it was also a mystery. When the war was over, Lady Margaret said, when the King returned in triumph to London and Sir Grenville Cony was among the defeated, then, and only then Lady Margaret said, would they force the secret from him.

The end of the war seemed a long way off. The Scots were stirring in the north, turning the King's eyes from London and Campion accepted that she must wait for the unravelling of the seal's meaning.

Then, as a quiet stream can be disturbed by the melting of winter's snows, by a torrent of cold, harsh water that floods the banks, scours the pools and muddies the tranquility, so the war came with appalling suddenness.

It was presaged, on 20 April, the day before Easter, by a great clatter of hooves in the castle yard, by shouts, and by boots echoing on the stairs of the New House. The long gallery door was flung open.

Campion and Lady Margaret turned. A tall figure stood in the doorway, a figure in leather and armour. Campion spoke first. 'Toby!'

There would be no doctors, midwives and lawyer in Oxford. There would be no marriage for the moment. The

King had dissolved his Parliament and his army had gone to face the Scots, but that was not the news that had brought Sir George and Toby hastening back to Dorset. Parliament, the London Parliament, had decreed that the great food-bearing counties were to be scoured of Royalists, that London must be supplied with wheat this year, with beef, mutton, fruit and ale, and they had sent orders for their armies to concentrate and clear the west. One of the spies who swarmed on either side had sent word to the King, and his news was hard on Sir George. Lazen Castle was to be taken, the siege to begin at Easter, and Sir George and Toby had ridden desperately, bringing what reinforcements they could, so they could reach the castle before their enemies closed the ring.

Sir George had followed Toby into the gallery, Colonel Washington coming after. Lady Margaret stood, dominating the room. 'Campion, you must go!'

'No!'

'Yes! George! She can stay with Tallis in Oxford?'

Sir George nodded. 'She can. She might be safer even further away.'

Campion shook her head. 'No!'

'You'll not be going anywhere, Miss Campion.' Colonel Washington was looking through one of the wide windows. His face was grim. 'Those laddies moved fast. Damned lobsters if you'll excuse me, your Ladyship.'

The villagers were streaming from Lazen, hurrying towards the castle, while beyond them, beyond the mill and the cottages, Campion saw the Roundhead troopers in Lazen's fields. Lobsters, horsemen whose jointed armour, curiously resembling a lobster's shell, covered their bodies, thighs and arms, followed their standard-bearer on the far side of Lazen's stream. Sir George frowned at Colonel Washington.

'You didn't know they were close?'

'I did not, Sir George. I've patrolled each day, but my belief is they've come from the forest land to the south. You could hide an army in there.'

'From Werlatton?' Campion asked.

'That direction, Miss Campion.' Washington smiled. He was a small man, yet now he seemed to grow in stature and confidence. He walked to the fireplace and stood beneath the proud, naked Diana. 'They'll find us a tougher nut to crack than they think. The lads are shaped well.' He spoke of the tenants and labourers of Lazen who had been drilled with musket and pike, swelling the garrison to a formidable size. 'Aye. I think we can make them regret their temerity.'

'We'll make them regret more than that.' Lady Margaret stared with hatred at the growing mass of Parliamentary troops. 'You'll excuse me, Colonel.' She pushed open a window and shouted one word across the moat, startling two sentries. 'Bastards!'

'Margaret!' Sir George sounded shocked.

Colonel Washington smiled, one finger brushing at his moustache. 'I think they'll be surprised. We'll see the back of them by the end of May!'

Toby moved to Campion's side, his eyes gentle on her nervousness. 'You heard the Colonel, my love. They'll be gone by the end of May.'

She held his arm, feeling the leather stiff and cold beneath her right hand. With her left she touched the seal and wondered if it was this talisman of gold that had brought the armoured men to Lazen.

War had come to Lazen. Her enemies had come. They were surrounding her, threatening her, and she sensed, even as she listened to the garrison preparing their defence, that the river of her days was gathering her again, plucking her from the calm waters and carrying her to unknown land. She held Toby's arm as if it was her anchor.

Lazen Castle was under siege.

16

The Roundheads were not gone by the end of May, but nor did they seem any nearer to capturing the castle. Their efforts, even to Campion's untutored eye, seemed amateur and ineffective.

The enemy concentrated their siege works to the north, building a great battery of earth and timber in which their main guns were placed and from which, one morning, they had opened fire with a guttural thunder that startled the rooks and sent them flapping and cawing in alarm. The round shot, that seemed to crash horrendously against the north wall, did remarkably little damage. Colonel Washington was far more concerned by the enemy's mortar, a gun he described to Campion as a 'vicious cooking pot', which threw its missiles high into the air to crash down within the defences. The mortar claimed the first victim in Lazen, crushing the skull of a kitchen-maid within the scullery. Colonel Washington sent a letter to the enemy, carried out of the castle under a flag of truce, that mockingly congratulated them on the death of the maid. He told them of the hour of her funeral and requested a cessation of the guns during the service. The truce was observed and the Roundhead guns did not fire again that day.

The Roundheads were either camped to the north or else living in the deserted houses of the village, though their guardposts and patrols encircled the whole castle. They outnumbered the garrison by at least three to one, but it seemed to Campion that Colonel Washington treated his enemies with contempt, not caring about the odds. In the first week of May he led a sally against the main battery, his men debouching from the new walls by the gatehouse at dusk, charging the guns and throwing themselves into the Parliamentary works. Campion watched with Lady Margaret from the keep and she saw the Lazender banner planted on the enemy battery, heard the cheer of the Royalists, and even, clear in the twilight, the hammering as Washington's men drove nails into the touch-holes of the enemy cannon. She saw the sparkle of musket fire in the falling darkness, watched the spread of smoke like winter fog, and listened to the war shout of the castle's defenders: 'King Charles! King Charles!'

'Back! Back!' Colonel Washington, mounted on his horse, waved at his men. A last musket volley splintered light towards the enemy who tried to counter-attack, and then the Royalists were leaping over the remains of the timber palisade that they had pulled down and were streaming back towards the castle. Campion could see Toby, his sword drawn, shepherding his own men away from the battery, and then it seemed that the whole northern sky was filled with sheet lightning, a great spread of red flame that lit the horizon, boiled smoke over the battery, and was followed, seconds later, by the huge thunder of the enemy's powder magazine exploding. 'King Charles! King Charles!'

The enemy did not fire their guns again for ten days, their battery was rebuilt further back, and in the meantime they suffered a further reverse, this entirely of their own making. The moat at Lazen was fed by a spring that rose north-east of the castle, and the enemy damned the spring despite the fire from the sakers that Colonel Washington poured among the labouring soldiers who shovelled earth and carried stones to divert the water. Their success seemed to presage a parliamentary victory, for the water sank swiftly in the next three days. The moat drained at the south-western corner and, by the fourth day, the northern branch of the moat that was normally thick with lily pads was nothing more than a ditch of stinking slime. It was still a formidable obstacle, but the thick mud would dry and Colonel Washington was forced to take defenders from the northern and western walls to guard the moat-banks. On the fifth day the fish in the main stretch of moat were flapping frantically, their water reduced to a shallow strip in the centre of the littered mud, and that night the defenders dug pits in the lawn from which they could fire at an attack across the drained moat.

Yet the water, diverted from its normal course, had seeped into the low ground at the foot of the northern hills where the enemy were building their new battery. Their own earthworks became waterlogged, the mortar sank through its plank base into sodden slime and the ready powder was ruined by damp. The new battery was a quagmire, useless for guns, and in desperation Lord Atheldene ordered the dam removed so that the water again flowed fast and clear through its underground conduit to the moat. The fish were freed from their shrinking death, the defenders breathed relief, and the ditch of slime was again filled with fresh water.

Lord Atheldene was a courteous opponent. Informed by Colonel Washington that the women and children of the castle were concentrated in the New House, he ordered his gunners to avoid it. A second battery, with just two guns, had been placed to the south, firing over the water meadows from the edge of the village, and denied the New House as a target they concentrated on the stable-yard. Horses were wounded and had to be put out of their misery. For two days the stench of blood hung about Lazen.

The northern guns eventually broke down the old wall that connected the keep to the Old House and, two nights later, the Roundheads attacked the breach. Their shouts startled the air just before dawn, and Campion awoke to hear the sakers and murderers coughing their death. She pulled a robe over her nightgown and ran to the Old House to watch. Smoke shrouded the buildings and the kitchen garden into which the enemy came. She dimly saw the flash of swords and pike blades, listened to the cheers of the enemy as they swarmed through the breach, and then she understood why Colonel Washington had not been worried. He had expected the attack, wanted it even, because the enemy was now trapped in the walled enclosure of the garden. The defenders, receiving the signal they had waited for, attacked from the keep and the old kitchens. For the first time, Campion heard the clatter of pikemen fighting pikemen, and in the first grey light of dawn she saw the huge spiked poles being carried forward against the enemy. The cheers of triumph turned to alarm, to screams, and she bit her lip as she watched the leather-jacketed defenders going grimly forward, pikes levelled, their wickedly long spikes already reddened by blood. Muskets sparked, making a continuous crackling, and then the Roundheads were pushed back and scrambling for safety. Campion saw the prisoners being taken, some horribly wounded, and she breathed relief. She was safe again.

The wounded were treated in the New House and Campion became used to the horrid mutilations, to helping the doctor amputate legs or arms, to sitting beside the dying as they tried to endure the pain bravely. She sat with defenders who died, with the captured enemy, and she would read psalms to the Puritans and pray with them in the cruel, small hours when dawn seemed an eternity away.

The fighting was not constant. Some days seemed calm, punctuated only by fitful gunfire, and there were constant courtesies in the middle of battle. Prisoners were exchanged, the wounded restored to their comrades, and Lord Atheldene sent weekly news to Sir George and Lady Margaret. The news-sheets were all parliamentarian, and thus unlikely to print news that might cheer the defenders, but Sir George was ready to believe much of what they said. They spoke of the King being harried in the north, of the Scots coming slowly south, and they trumpeted the tidings when an isolated house or castle, much like Lazen, was taken by the rebel forces. Yet not even the parliamentarian news-sheets could demonstrate a pattern of victory. The war seemed hesitant, patchy, and neither side had won the great victory that could tip the balance. Lord Atheldene sent more than news. Once he sent a great ham studded with cloves, a barrel of wine and a letter regretting that he should be fighting old friends and neighbours. He offered safe conduct to the women trapped in Lazen, even suggesting that Lady Margaret and her retinue would be welcomed by his own wife, but Lady Margaret refused the offer. 'This is my house. I have no intention of going to Harry's house. It's draughty and there are young children screaming everywhere.' She had already composed her epitaph to be carved on a plaque to be erected in Lazen's shot-battered church. 'She Dyed in the Defence of Her Owne House, Foullie Besieged bye Traitors.' She looked at Campion. 'You must leave, child.'

Campion shook her head. 'Not without you, Lady Margaret.'

Campion's fear of her enemies had grown less. So long as Lord Atheldene commanded the besiegers, she did not fear. He was a man, as Sir George said, of honour and decency who would ensure that the women of Lazen Castle would be spared the horrors of war. Even when Samuel Scammell joined the enemy, Campion being made aware of his presence by a wounded prisoner, she did not fear. Scammell could have no power over Lord Atheldene.

She looked for Scammell, searching the enemy lines with a clumsy telescope that Lady Margaret had mounted on the roof of the keep. Toby was with her, his red hair stirred by the wind. 'Perhaps he's not here.'

'I can't imagine him as a soldier.' She turned the great tube on its iron tripod to face the village. The image wavered. She could see the earthwork that the enemy had dug across the track that led to the castle, she could see soldiers sitting in the sunlight, their helmets off, eating bread and cheese. A chicken pecked in the village street. 'Ah!' She began to laugh. 'I've found him!'

'Let me see. Let me see.'

'Wait!'

She had half thought that the sight of Scammell would make her afraid, but instead she found him laughable. He had appeared at a house door, blinking in the spring sunlight, and he was scratching his bottom beneath an ill-fitting leather jerkin. He looked lost, out of his depth, and it was impossible to see him as an enemy to be feared.

Toby who had hardly glimpsed Scammell on the night of

the fire in London, stared at his enemy. 'What's the matter with him? Has he got the pox?'

'He's always scratching himself.'

Toby grinned. 'Captain Scammell, Warrior of the Lord. How could you possibly marry him instead of me?'

She punched him on the arm, moving the telescope, and she waited as Toby re-aligned the tube. He steadied the image. 'My God! He's got his own bodyguard.'

'Let me see.'

Campion squinted through the eyepiece, stooping slightly, and Toby heard a hiss of breath from her. 'What is it?'

'It can't be!' Her amusement had gone. 'It can't be!'

'What?'

'It's Ebenezer! He looks so different. And the Reverend Hervey.'

Toby took over the glass. 'Which one's Ebenezer?'

'Black hair.'

Toby saw a slight, tallish young man who stood just apart from Scammell. He was dressed entirely in black, even his elegant high boots were of black leather, and Toby could see a breastplate that had been lacquered the same colour. He limped as he moved, but there was a strange dignity to his movements. The third man, the Reverend Hervey, his sandy hair falling over his thin face, talked urgently to Scammell.

'I'm frightened, Toby.'

'Why?'

'They've come for me.'

'Nonsense.' He straightened up. 'Atheldene's in command.' He smiled at her. 'They probably don't even know you're here.' He laughed, trying to cheer her up. 'It's natural that they've come. This is the closest Royalist house to Werlatton. Don't worry. James and I will look after you.'

He spoke confidently. James was Toby's servant, a huge young man who was the son of Lazen's blacksmith and had inherited his father's great muscles and easy strength. James Wright had grown up with Toby. They had learned to hunt game in the woods together and to poach neighbour's fish together, and now they fought in the war together. Toby had often spoken of James's prowess with a woodman's axe carried against the Roundheads.

Yet she did worry and, to calm her, Toby offered a purse of five pounds to any man who could kill Samuel Scammell. The target was pointed out to gunners and musketeers, so that Brother Scammell, every time he appeared in the enemy lines, was pursued by musket balls as though they were hornets. Men fell to his left, to his right, yet somehow he survived. He took comfort from Psalm 91: 'A thousand shall fall at thy side, and ten thousand at thy right hand: but it shall not come nigh thee,' yet even so, he was fearful of his hours of duty and he wondered whether Campion was somehow directing the storm of musket fire that hummed and whirred about his head.

On 11 June the gatehouse fell. Its old stones were undermined by the enemy gunfire and it collapsed, sliding in dust and noise to make a heap of stone under which ten defenders were buried. The ring became tighter, the morale of the defenders lower, for though they were resisting the enemy's fumbling attacks, the enemy would not give up and go away. There was food within the castle still and plenty of water, but thirty men had died, as many were lying in stinking, suppurating pain, and boredom gnawed at the people trapped by the siege. The guns still fired, making inroads now on the Old House, opening its northern rooms to the spring rain and the fire of the enemy.

Sir George, seeing the path by which the enemy would come into the castle and understanding that the simmering war in the north would mean no relief from the King's army, wrote to Atheldene. He wrote despite the protest of his wife, and his letter requested the safe conduct that had been offered in May for the ladies of Lazen Castle. They would go, Sir George said, with Lord Atheldene's permission and protection, to Oxford.

The guns stopped as the messenger rode from the castle, a white pennon attached to his sword blade. The letter seemed an admission of defeat to the garrison, a defeat brought about not by the enemy's superior fighting ability, but by the gnawing, endless attrition of the big guns. Campion, unhappily collecting clothes to be packed in a great leather travelling trunk, listened to the horses being harnessed to the coaches that would carry her, Lady Margaret, Caroline and their maids away. Colonel Washington agreed with Sir George that Lord Atheldene's permission would be readily forthcoming.

The reply came in two hours. Lord Atheldene, it said, had left that morning, summoned to London, there to face charges that he had 'delivered comforte to oure enemies in Lazen Castle'. The Parliamentarian forces were now under the command of Colonel Fuller, the author of the letter, who claimed to have no knowledge of any safe conduct being offered by Lord Atheldene.

'Fuller!' Colonel Washington frowned. 'I know of Fuller.'

'Who is he?' Sir George asked.

'One of these new men, Sir George.' Colonel Washington stroked his moustache. 'A ranting Puritan, if you'll forgive me. He was a cobbler in Bedford and now he's called a colonel.'

'Is he honourable?'

'I don't suppose he can spell the word.' Colonel Washington shrugged. 'But he's not a bad soldier.'

Sir George went back to the letter, reading it aloud. Fuller was not impolite. He offered safe conduct, even promising an armed guard, for Lady Margaret, her daughter, 'and those other females of the household who wish to depart', yet the letter singled out an exception.

'You have inn your midst one Dorcas Scammell, Wife to one of Mine Officers, and she wee cannot release. Her marriage was Witnessed before Almightie God, in Whose Cause wee fight, and this Warrant of Safe-Conduct depends Upon her Restorral to her Rightful Husband.'

Lady Margaret had one word for him. 'Bastard!'

There was an unhappy silence in the long gallery. Campion

felt the horrid weight of her past coming on her, as if the river of her life had carried her back to the mud of Werlatton. She saw the worry in Toby's eyes, and she felt responsible for the carnage that was being wreaked on Lazen Castle. She turned to Lady Margaret. 'You must go. You must.'

'You've lost your wits, child. I might be persuaded out by Lord Atheldene, but not by some cobbler from Bedford. Colonel Fuller, indeed! If you think such a man can frighten me from my home, you are very much mistaken.'

Sir George rubbed his eyes. In the new silence Campion again felt that this siege was her fault, that the seal about her neck had drawn the Roundhead forces to Lazen and had turned its peaceful acres into a place over which the gunsmoke drifted and in which men were daily buried. She sat down, her face troubled, but Sir George smiled at her. 'It's not your fault, Campion. They would have come anyway.' A crackle of musketry sounded from outside. He looked at Washington. 'Can we hold them, Colonel?'

Colonel Washington nodded. 'I think so, Sir George, I think so.' His fingers tugged at his grey moustache. 'We've deepened the trench between the Old House and the moat and I think we can flood it tomorrow. I think we can hold them.'

'Of course we can hold them!' Lady Margaret looked imperiously on the group. She needed only a chariot and spear and she would have personally scoured her enemies from about her house. 'Two more deserted yesterday! They'd hardly be deserting if they thought their own side was winning!'

Colonel Washington nodded. 'That's true, your Ladyship, very true.' Two Roundhead gunners had come to the castle at night, as other deserters had come before, risking the sentries' musketry, to come safely into the defences. Very few men had deserted the other way, a sure sign that the soldiers themselves believed Lazen could resist siege. The two new deserters were, so Colonel Washington said, scoundrels both, but experienced gunners were always welcome and the two men manned one of the murderers that threatened their erstwhile colleagues.

Sir George tamped tobacco into his pipe. He, like the rest of the garrison, was rationed to two bowlfuls a day. 'I think Campion should leave.' He waved down his son and his wife who had both begun to talk. 'Campion's enemies are here and we no longer have Harry's protection.' He turned his mild eyes to Colonel Washington. 'I think she might get through their cordon by night?'

It was Campion's turn to protest, but she was quietened. Sir George smiled ruefully. 'If they capture you, my dear, then I suspect you may no longer have grounds for annulling your marriage.'

The thought was horrible. It chilled her. She saw the anger come on Toby's face. He looked at Washington. 'You say we can hold them, sir?'

Washington nodded. 'There's no guarantee, not in war. They might stay here for ever! They've been at Corfe since God knows when. If Miss Campion can get out, then she should.' He paused because the Roundhead guns to the south had fired. He waited for the echo to die then looked at Toby. 'Would you take her?'

Toby shook his head, unhappy with the course of the discussion. 'I must stay here. I can't leave my men.' Toby, as a Captain, commanded one quarter of the garrison. He shrugged, hating the moment. 'James could take her. If they can get into the woods above the road, they'll be safe.'

James Wright, the son of Lazen's blacksmith, knew the country about the castle as well as any man. If any man could take Campion through the enemy lines, it was he.

Sir George smiled at her. 'I don't want you to leave, my dear.'

'She must,' Lady Margaret announced decisively.

Colonel Washington looked out of the window. 'It won't be tonight.'

Somehow the sentence shocked Campion. She did not

want to leave, she did not want to be thrown out into the world, yet if she had to go then she had not realized it would be so soon.

Toby grunted. 'No cloud?'

Washington nodded. 'It'll need a dark night. There's too much moon. Will Wright agree?'

Toby nodded. 'He'll be happy to do it.' He smiled at Campion. 'Jamie will get you to Oxford.'

She would become a fugitive, driven from this haven by the seal she wore about her neck. She could not escape it, her life was inextricably bound with the golden jewel, yet she wondered how long she would have to run from her enemies. They had followed her to Lazen, they were about to drive her forth, and she pondered whether there would ever be safety while she wore the broad axe of St Matthew about her neck.

She sat with Toby at dusk, holding his hand as the sun sank in dazzling splendour above the water meadows, touching the looping Lazen stream with scarlet. There was no cloud. He smiled at her. 'You won't go tonight.'

'I don't want to go.'

In the village a trumpet announced the evening duty. Soon, Campion knew, she would see the patrols in the water meadows, the new guards going to the sentry posts that surrounded the castle. Tomorrow night, if there was cloud, she would have to be smuggled past those sentries by James Wright. She leaned her head on Toby's shoulder. 'I don't want to leave.'

His hand stroked her cheek. 'I don't want you to.'

The rooks were loud across the stream. She stared at their ragged flight. 'Perhaps we should never have met.'

Toby laughed. His face was deeply lined, his eyes tired. He took little sleep now. 'Do you wish that?'

She was silent a moment. Her cheek rubbed against the leather of his jerkin. 'Perhaps we're not meant to be together.'

He pushed her away from him, turning her face so she was

looking at him. He smiled. 'We'll be married before the year's out.'

She leaned against him again. She was unhappy. The river of her life was gathering speed, she could sense it sweeping her away from Toby and carrying her into a new darkness, a clouded darkness, and she was afraid. 'Hold me.'

Her right hand clutched the golden seal, clutched it as if she wanted to crush it out of existence and thus release her life from its thralldom. With a last, triumphant blaze of red light, the sun died in the west.

' "Clouds and darkness are round about him: Righteousness and judgement are the habitation of his throne. A fire goeth before him, and burneth up his enemies round about." '

The voices of young men were strong in the dusk, chanting the psalm. The preacher, Faithful Unto Death Hervey, stood on the wagon-loading platform of Lazen's mill and raised his hands at the troops in the mill field. 'Louder! Let the enemy hear you! Louder!'

The voices surged. The men grinned. They were happy, united by the metrical beat of the psalm, confident that the Lord was with them.

Ebenezer Slythe, standing where the great water-wheel clanked and dripped, its blades weed-grown and dank, listened to the noise. It uplifted him, exalted him, made him know that God was truly with Parliament. He liked being with the army, liked the smell of leather and horses, the sight of strong men. He was feared, as a man who worked for Parliament should be feared, and no man mocked him for his shrunken, twisted leg.

He limped into the miller's house, the sound of the psalm still filling his head with glory and righteousness. The girl, a miserable wretch who had been found in the woods, smiled at him.

'Get out!' He scowled. He needed her at night, but her fawning wish for approval annoyed him at other times. She was a sin, of course, but Faithful Unto Death had assured

him that some men were so burdened by God's responsibilities that they were granted special privileges by heaven; did David not have Bathsheba? Within days he would discard her, because in days this siege would be over.

He sat at his table and reflected on the coming success. He had sent two men into the castle, gunners who were ostensibly deserters, but who were in fact sworn to him. They would fire the castle's magazine at their first chance. They were ordered to do it when the morning trumpets sounded in the Roundhead lines and Ebenezer prayed that they would do it soon. Let it be tomorrow! He had waited with excitement this very morning, praying that the great flame would explode over his enemies, but the dawn had come as usual. Colonel Fuller, the man sent by Grenville Cony to take over the siege from Lord Atheldene, had given his opinion that perhaps the two men had been detected and imprisoned. Ebenezer had given Fuller his coldest smile. 'Is the Lord not on their side?'

It was the clinching argument. Colonel Fuller had not been able to reply.

Ebenezer had discovered power, and the knowledge of it filled him with the same glorious excitement as the chanting of the psalm. Even Colonel Fuller, a hard, grim soldier who fought with a sword in his right hand and a Bible in his left, treated him with deference. Fuller had let Ebenezer reply to the letter of truce from the castle, had acquiesced humbly when Ebenezer had dictated how the castle was to be taken. Ebenezer spoke with Sir Grenville's authority, and his demands that the new part of the castle was not to be damaged, and that Fuller's men were not to interfere with his activities in the fallen castle, had not been questioned.

Ebenezer had power.

Tomorrow, if God willed it, he would have the Seal of St Matthew.

And tomorrow, when Samuel Scammell was dead, Ebenezer would be the legal holder of St Matthew's Seal, receiver of the monies passed from Sir Grenville, and the thought of the income filled him with excitement.

He would use the Covenant. He stared at the millpond through the window, watching ducklings trail busily behind their mother, and thought of his plans. A third force was rising in England, a force that threatened to defeat both King and Parliament. Ebenezer could hear that force now, hear it in the strong, virile voices of the young men who prayed as hard as they fought. They hated the King, they hated the Royalists, but they hated the Presbyterians of Parliament almost as much. They fought for Parliament, but Ebenezer knew they would never consent, after victory, to be ruled by Parliament. Presbyterianism made heaven into a lottery, and it was not to the taste of these Independent Puritans.

Sir Grenville had sided with the Presbyterians. Ebenezer would not. He would bide his time, and in time he would give a strong, harsh voice to the demands of the common soldier. It was the common soldier who carried the sword and the gun, and it was the sword and the gun that would make England holy. And it was the Covenant that would give Ebenezer the power to make his voice heard.

All was prepared for the morning, whichever morning it was to be. The men Ebenezer had hired as his own troop knew what was to be done. Samuel Scammell, in whom Ebenezer detected reluctance, was nevertheless obedient. Most of all, Faithful Unto Death Hervey and his new housekeeper, Goodwife Baggerlie, knew what was expected of them. They were rehearsed, ready, and their actions would bring the day of the Lord closer.

Sir Grenville Cony did not expect the castle to fall till the end of the month. That was good. Tomorrow, beneath the smoke from his explosion, Ebenezer needed just a few moments with the seal that was rightfully his. He did not know where those moments would lead, he knew only that he must prepare himself for the time when he would have to destroy Sir Grenville, as he planned to destroy his sister, and as he would destroy anyone who threatened the Kingdom of God he saw flowering in England.

He raised his voice. 'Girl!'

She came in, her face pathetically eager to please.

Ebenezer limped to the bed and lay down. 'Lock the doors.'

He closed his eyes. He would not open them or speak till she was done. His brain was filled with the emblazoning splendour of his vision as the darkness fell softly on the Lazen valley.

17

Campion's cat, Mildred, usually woke her before dawn, pacing to and fro on the covers, licking her exposed face with its rough tongue, purring loudly in her ear or forcing its warm, soft fur against her neck. 'Go away, Mildred.'

The cat interpreted any words as affection, redoubling its efforts to rouse Campion. 'Go away, Mildred. It's too early.'

Yet, coming into wakefulness, Campion knew that it was not the middle of the night. She could hear the sound of boots on the castle yard and knew that the garrison, as it did each morning, was standing to arms. Every soldier was on the ramparts at least an hour before dawn, and it was a time when Campion liked to be up. She stroked the cat's reddish fur and then hugged her. 'I might not see you again. No! I must go away, Mildred.' The cat purred louder than ever. 'You don't care, do you?'

She dressed quickly, putting a bonnet over her drawn-up hair. She would not dress properly or set her hair until the morning was half over. Mildred went to and fro between her ankles, rubbing her body against Campion, demanding to be fed. 'You're supposed to catch mice, Mildred, that's what you're supposed to do.'

She dressed in a plain grey dress. She could hear Lady Margaret next door ordering Enid to open the curtains and the sound made Campion pull back her own. The sky was still dark and she could not see if there were any new clouds. Mildred protested and Campion stooped to stroke the cat. 'You really don't care, do you?'

She opened her bedroom door, releasing the cat which sped away down the corridor, heading for the kitchens downstairs where, along with a dozen other cats, she would be fed and watered. There was not enough milk for the cats now. Campion followed more slowly.

She liked the dawn. She liked to walk on the dew-wet lawns and greet the soldiers who peered into the darkness across the moat. She would sometimes go into the church and kneel in the Lazender pew, saying a morning prayer for the safety of the garrison, adding a special prayer for Toby beneath the stone memorials of his ancestors. It was a quiet period of the day, a time before the big guns would begin to spread their dirty smoke across the meadows, a time when there was a semblance of peace at Lazen.

'Miss Campion?' It was Captain Tugwell looming in the darkness.

'Captain.'

'And a pleasant sight you are this morning, Miss Campion.' Tugwell, a small man, forced jollity into his voice. 'Did you have a quiet night?'

'I did. You?'

'There's not a lot happening. They were quiet all night.' Tugwell's silhouette nodded towards the lights of the village. 'They were moving early this morning, but that's probably their new man, Fuller. A new broom, Miss Campion.'

'I expect so.'

Tugwell hitched his sword belt higher and thrust his brass-hilted pistol further into its holster. 'Captain Lazender's at the gatehouse ruins, Miss Campion.'

'I know. Thank you. I'm going to the church.'

'Say one for me!'

She smiled. 'I will.'

She saw the faintest strip of pearl-grey light limning the eastern horizon. The trees of the great woods were outlined by the first appearance of dawn. She hesitated by the church porch, unwilling to exchange this first token of day for the gloom of the chancel.

'You're up early!' It was Mr Perilly, Lazen's vicar.

'Mr Perilly!'

He was coming from the church. A candle was lit inside, revealing him as he came to stand beside her. He sounded downhearted. 'Another window gone.'

'That's sad.'

The Roundheads had been trying, with increasing success, to shoot out the stained windows with their musket fire. Anything that was beautiful and dedicated to God gave them offence. Each depredation of his church made Mr Perilly more gloomy. 'I've swept it up as best I can, but there's still a lot on the floor.' He sighed. 'The rain gets in, you know.'

'I know.'

He stood beside her, staring unhappily at the sheen of light on the moat. 'I hear you're leaving us, Campion.'

'I'm afraid so. James is taking me, if it's dark enough.'

Mr Perilly shook his head. 'It's dark enough. Darkness throughout the land, Campion. I don't understand it, I truly don't. God tests his servants, but I sometimes wish we could be more certain of the outcome.'

A cock crowed in the stable-yard. The sound seemed to shake Mr Perilly from his depression. He smiled. 'I'll see you at matins?'

'Of course.'

'Be careful on the south aisle! It was the window of the raising of Lazarus. Quite destroyed! Quite destroyed! And there's no one who can do work like that nowadays! We can only destroy, it seems, only destroy.' His gloom was returning.

The explosion came.

At first Campion did not know what was happening. It seemed as if the ground shook, a small quiver that startled her, and she saw the moat, that had been silver and quiet, suddenly ripple with small, urgent flickerings of pre-dawn light.

Then there was thunder, the growling of rocks, the sound of ancient, massive stones moving and splintering, and then the great keep, whose stones had dominated Lazen for four hundred years, was lit by a spike of fire, a sheet of flame following, and then the noise came properly. It shattered the air, it fled outwards across the valley. It hammered at the defenders.

'Mr Perilly!' She seized his arm.

The keep was boiling flame and smoke now, a cauldron of fire that spewed its foul cloud over the valley. It reminded her of Samuel Scammell's burning yard, only this smoke seemed to erupt at far greater speed. There were new explosions now, smaller, but each one sent another flash of light to illumine the stones that toppled from the keep.

'To the house!' The Reverend Perilly took her arm, pulled her over the lawn.

'Watch your front!' Captain Tugwell shouted, and then a musket fired from across the moat, there were shouts and all the defenders on the castle lawn rested muskets on the spiked forks, pulled triggers, and at the same moment Campion became aware of a great, growling cheer from the north. She was running now, panic giving her speed, and in the light of the burning, destroyed keep, she saw where the stones, flung by the explosion, had shattered windows of the Old and New House.

The two gunners who had deserted from the Roundhead lines, and who had been promised twenty pounds apiece by Ebenezer Slythe, had done their work well. They had gone for powder, waited until the other gunners had collected their small kegs and then laid a simple powder trail. An old sergeant in charge of the magazine had found them, but he was dead in seconds, his throat cut, and then they had lit the powder trail and sprinted for the safety of the stable-yard. The explosion, coming sooner than they expected, had flung both men down, but they were unharmed. They went on towards the stable, laughing at the sound of destruction and burning behind them, intent only on hiding for the next few minutes until the castle was taken.

Toby, by the gatehouse ruins, saw the great spike of flame, saw the sheet of fire that followed which outlined the tall chimneys of the Old House. His men stared, aghast, and then there was a thunder of hooves mixed with the noise of the exploding powder, and Toby turned. 'Your front! Take aim!'

The Lobsters stormed out of the darkness, wheeled their horses and fired pistols at the defenders. More men came from the west, their muskets spitting fire over the moat, but then, in the light of the fire, Toby saw a mass of the enemy moving towards the keep and the kitchen garden.

Most of the defenders in that area, he knew, would be dead or dazed. 'Sergeant!'

'Sir?'

'Hold here with your men. The rest of you! Follow me!'

Ebenezer Slythe felt an exultation as he saw the enemy magazine destroy the keep. This he had prayed for! Lord Atheldene, when there had been a suggestion that a mine might be dug beneath some part of the castle's defences, had refused the suggestion. It was not an honourable way to fight, he said, not unless the garrison was given warning of the explosion and time to remove their men from the immediate area. Ebenezer had no such scruples. This was the vengeance of the Lord, the mighty hand of the Almighty come to earth, and he felt a sudden, unexpected excitement as the killing fragments of the disintegrating keep scythed outwards and took death to Lazen Castle. Truly God was great!

The banners of the Parliamentarians surged forward. A cheer went up. The fire was bright on swords, pikes and helmets. The flags, bearing texts of scripture, forged ahead of the throng. Ebenezer smiled at Samuel Scammell and raised his voice: ' "The Lord is mighty in battle!" '

'Indeed and indeed.' Scammell swallowed, hardly believing

the thunderous pit which belched flame and smoke into the sky. 'Amen.'

The first Roundhead standards were going through the old breach into the kitchen garden, turning right to assault the Old House, and Ebenezer urged his horse forward. 'Come along, Brother Scammell. We take possession of your bride!'

Scammell stumbled forward, his feet clumsy in the darkness. His sword almost tripped him. They went onwards towards the shouts and the steel-ring of battle.

Colonel Washington was blinded, stone scraps taking his eyes and leaving him helpless. He sat, his face a mask of blood, and listened to the rush of enemy feet in the yard.

Toby, cutting through the Old House, met the first enemy in the washroom. Toby felt about Lazen as his mother did. This was home, the seat of the Lazenders, and his fury gave him a massive strength. One man, then another, was slashed by his sword, tipped bloodily into the low stone trough where the castle's linen was scrubbed. James Wright, beside him, hewed with an axe, saying nothing as he slaughtered two men with horrid efficiency.

'Lazender! Lazender!' Toby bellowed his war cry, leading his men out into the lurid yard. He caught a fragmentary glimpse of the carnage wrought by the explosion, of the house savaged by masonry blocks, and then he was all but overwhelmed by a rush of Roundheads. A flag was close to him, its legend from the second book of Kings: 'Smite them with the edge of the sword'. Toby did the smiting. He was sobbing in anger and hatred as he chopped down the standard-bearer and thrust his sword into the belly of an officer who tried to defend the falling flag. James Wright was beside him, axe whirling in the flame-light, driving their enemy back.

'Lazender! Lazender!'

Pike blades came for them, the fifteen-foot weapons offering safety to the Roundheads, and Toby swept in impotence at the steel-spiked poles. As soon as a blade was pushed aside, another pike would take its place, jabbing forward.

'Come back, Toby!' James Wright forgot about rank, remembering only his boyhood companion of stream and forest. 'Come back.'

'Damn them!' He hammered with the sword, hearing it ring on a pike blade, seeing another come forward, and then Toby saw the flash of a musket from the enemy ranks.

He seemed to be on fire, such was the pain, and the echo of the ringing blade rose to a screeching pitch in his ears. His sword fell. The pain was slamming back and forth and the pikes were coming over him. He fell. James Wright tried to pick him up, to pull him backwards, but the Roundheads were charging now and the huge man went back before the pikes, seeking safety in the warren of rooms in the Old House.

Toby moaned, rolled over, tried to rise, but a sword blade slashed light in the early dawn, came down, and there was a terrible pain in his left hand. He screamed, fell back and the boots of the enemy went over his unconscious body. Lazen Castle had fallen, as so many houses fell, to treachery.

'Be brave!' Lady Margaret ordered the group of women in the gallery. 'Be brave!' She put the musketoon on the table beside her, but Campion could see it was not loaded.

Muskets sounded in the gardens below. Enid screamed, making Lady Margaret turn furiously round. 'Be quiet!'

The shouts of the victors echoed through the castle. The slaughter was nearly over. The garrison was being taken prisoner, stripped of its valuables and herded towards the stable-yard where the two traitors greeted their rescuers warmly. One man, from Captain Tugwell's company, tore off his leather jacket and tried to swim the moat. Campion, standing at a window of the long gallery, saw the Roundheads run to the bank. They pulled pistols from their belts and used the bobbing head for target practice. A red stain appeared on the grey water. Others of the enemy were pushing into the church. She knew they would tear out the altar rails, thinking them Popish, and then wrestle the great, heavy altar into the centre of the church. Once that was done and the decorations had been destroyed or defaced, it would be thought to be a house worthy of God.

'Campion! You will stand by me!' Lady Margaret beckoned peremptorily. 'Enid! Be quiet! I do not wish to tell your mother that you were weak. Stand there, Campion.' Caroline, still in a night-gown over which she had put a cloak, stood on her mother's right, Campion to Lady Margaret's left. Lady Margaret put an arm about Campion's shoulder. 'They won't touch you, child. I shall see to that. The name of Lazender will carry some weight, even with these scum.'

More shouts, closer now, and another rattle of musketry. Dogs barked in the castle. Men laughed. There was a scream from the kitchens. The smoke of the explosion smelt acrid in the long gallery. In the Old House the victors tore down curtains, ripped bed linen, fired muskets into furniture and pictures.

Campion was terrified, yet she dared not show it. She wondered, grasping for any straw, if Ebenezer would be kind. He was, after all, her brother.

Mildred, hair standing on her back, erupted through the door of the long gallery and ran straight to Campion. She stooped, picked the cat up and held it close to her breasts. She felt the seal. She fumbled with her left hand, pulling the seal up and over her bonnet, and then there seemed no place to hide it. She dropped it inside her dress, feeling it lodge where her white linen stomacher was tight at her waist. The seal. It had brought this horror to Lazen. She wondered where Toby was. She had not had time to say a prayer for him that morning.

Footsteps sounded loud on the great marble staircase, a single man running, and Campion desperately wanted it to be Toby. She wondered if she ought to run, to hide, maybe to try and make her own escape in the confusion, but she wanted it to be with Toby.

Captain Tugwell, his right arm bloody, came into the long gallery. He stopped, staring at the group of women, and his sword, red like his arm, dropped. 'You're safe. Thank God!'

'We do thank him, Captain. What happened?'

Captain Tugwell had no time to answer Lady Margaret's query. There was the sound of more boots on the stairs, a group of men this time, and Campion saw the Captain turn to the open door. She saw his sword come up, waver, then go slowly down. There was a look of resignation on his face. The moment she feared had come.

Four men came into the long gallery. They wore leather jerkins beneath breastplates, barred helmets over their faces, and at their waists were the bright orange sashes of Parliament. The steel-barred faces, anonymous in the gloom, turned towards the women, then, seemingly as one, back to Captain Tugwell. He was disarmed, pushed out of the long gallery, and then the four faces looked back. One man walked towards them, his sword drawn. His boots were loud on the chequered tiles until he reached the long central rug. 'Lady Margaret Lazender?'

'I am she.' Campion felt Lady Margaret stiffen.

The man stopped. He pushed his helmet up by the steel peak, dragging it backwards off his head. His dark hair showed the imprint of the leather helmet-liner. It was a man Campion had never seen before.

'My name is Colonel Fuller. I assume you are yielding the castle to me?'

'That is for my husband. I would not be so presumptuous.'

Colonel Fuller frowned. He had not expected the answer. 'The castle's taken.'

'So you tell me. I trust that even a rebel will ensure the safety of women's lives?'

Fuller frowned again. 'I do not fight women.'

'Then I do not understand why you see fit to approach me with a drawn sword, Colonel. If you wish to kill me, do so now. Otherwise please put it away. Where is my husband?'

More footsteps at the door. Campion felt Lady Margaret tighten her arm on her shoulders. The sky was lightening, filling the Lazen valley with dawn. The birds sang as if this day was any other.

Six men came into the room. At first Campion thought them all to be soldiers, but then she saw the black clothes, the lacquered breastplate of her brother. Next to Ebenezer, easily recognizable despite his barred helmet, was Scammell.

Ebenezer's voice was low, yet it carried easily to Campion. 'I thought it plain, Colonel, that only Sir Grenville's men were to be allowed in this part of the house?'

Colonel Fuller turned, his sword halfway into his scabbard. Campion almost expected him to draw the sword, to punish Ebenezer for his insolence, but to her surprise the Colonel nodded. 'We're leaving.'

'Do so.'

Campion had changed in these last nine months, yet she was astonished to see that her brother too had become such a different person. The awkwardness was gone, the sullen face had become hard and lean. The long gallery seemed filled with his quiet menace.

The door closed behind Colonel Fuller. Ebenezer limped towards the women. 'Which of you is Margaret Lazender?'

Campion felt Lady Margaret's body draw upright. 'My name, boy, is Lady Margaret Lazender.'

'Your name, woman, is Margaret Lazender.' Ebenezer's limp made his slow progress along the carpet seem sinister. 'The book of Job, Margaret Lazender, chapter thirty-two, and the twenty-first verse, ". . . neither let me give flattering titles unto man." On the last day, Margaret Lazender, you will have no flattering title. You may as well accustom yourself to the loss.' He looked casually at Campion. 'Hello, sister.'

Lady Margaret tightened her arm on Campion's shoulder. 'This girl is under my protection.'

Ebenezer laughed, a sour sound. 'You have no protection

to offer, woman. This house is now the property of Parliament, of the people of England.' His voice was rising, whiplashing across the room. 'You may stay here, woman, as the law says, until its disposal is agreed, but in that time you have no protection to offer. You have nothing.'

Lady Margaret was astonished, taken aback by the confidence of Ebenezer's voice. She played an unlikely card, recognizing, perhaps, that in defeat she must seek the help of the victors for the vanquished were powerless. 'The Earl of Fleet, young man, may curb your insolence.'

Ebenezer had stopped a few feet from the women. 'The Earl of Fleet, Margaret Lazender, will be a voice in the wilderness. The day of your kind is over. There will be no more Lords, no more gentry, no more King.' He turned, raising his voice, 'Brother Scammell? Come!'

Lady Margaret grasped at another straw. 'Where is my husband? I demand my husband is brought here.'

Ebenezer whipped back, pointing a long, white finger. 'You have no demands. None.'

'Ebenezer!' Campion took a pace forward, her voice pleading. 'Ebenezer?'

'Quiet.' His face mocked her, his voice was filled with hatred. 'You are nothing, sister, nothing. You were given gifts that any person could dream of. Yours is a wealth beyond the blessings of God, and what did you do? You came here, to this den of thieves, to this Papist household, to our enemies! Do not plead with me, sister.'

Samuel Scammell walked uneasily towards them, his plump body heavy among the fine furniture. He looked nervous, uncertain whether to smile or scowl, his helmet awkward in his left hand. His scabbard knocked against a chair.

Ebenezer smiled. 'Your bride awaits, brother.'

Lady Margaret pulled Campion back to her side, she opened her mouth to speak, but at that moment the door to the gallery was thrown open and a white-faced, frantic Mr Perilly shouted down the gallery, 'Lady Margaret!'

'Hold him!' Ebenezer shouted.

'My lady!' Mr Perilly dodged one soldier, but was held by the next. Scammell had stopped, made more nervous by the interruption.

Lady Margaret frowned. 'Mr Perilly? What is it?'

Ebenezer did not let the priest answer. 'Who are you?'

Mr Perilly seemed to notice Ebenezer for the first time. He shook off the hand of the soldier and straightened his black, soiled coat. 'My name, sir, is Perilly. I have the honour to be vicar of this parish.'

Ebenezer laughed. 'You have the honour to be sucking the teat of the scarlet whore of Babylon. What do you want?'

Mr Perilly looked at Lady Margaret, his hands clenched as if in prayer. 'Sir George, Lady Margaret!' He stopped.

Lady Margaret took her arms from the girl's shoulders. She was suddenly very calm, very erect. 'Go on, Simon. Tell me.'

'He's dead, your Ladyship. And your son's wounded, but Sir George is dead. A musket ball, your Ladyship. Dead!'

Caroline cried out, the maids sobbed, but Lady Margaret called for quiet. Campion seemed frozen, the news clamouring in her head. Toby wounded? She remembered she had not prayed for him that morning and she cried out.

'Quiet, Campion.' Lady Margaret looked scornfully at Ebenezer. 'I am going, young man, to my husband and my son. If you wish to stop me, you will have to kill me. I have no doubt you are capable of any such filthiness. Come!'

With that she began walking. Ebenezer stepped aside, half smiling, as if Lady Margaret had paid him a compliment. He watched the women go past, but, as Campion followed Caroline, he reached out a claw-like hand and took her elbow. 'Not you, sister.'

She wanted to pull away, she wanted to cry out, but this was no time to call on Lady Margaret for help. Lazen Castle had been overtaken by a tragedy far greater than Campion's fate. She hardly felt her brother's hand gripping her arm. She could only watch Lady Margaret follow Mr Perilly from the room, and she cried out inside for Toby. It was her fault, her fault, and she wondered if Lady Margaret would ever forgive her for bringing this vengeance on Lazen because it had sheltered her and the Seal of St Matthew. The cat stirred in her right arm and she stroked it. It was the only scrap of love left in her destroyed world.

A soldier shut the long gallery door behind the women. Scammell, who had watched them go, turned to Campion and gave her a nervous smile. She did not see it.

Another soldier, who had been searching the rooms of the New House, came into the gallery through its western door. 'Sir?'

Ebenezer looked at the man. 'Yes?'

'I found somewhere, sir.'

'Good.' Ebenezer looked at Scammell. 'Come along, brother.'

He took Campion with him, the soldiers coming behind, and she hardly knew what was happening. Toby wounded was all she could comprehend.

The soldier had found the bedroom that opened off the western end of the long gallery. It was rarely used for sleeping because, in the evening, it was filled with a delicate, fading light and Lady Margaret liked to sit there before dinner. Campion had often read aloud in the room.

Ebenezer glanced inside. A second door opened on to the corridor. 'Is it locked?'

'Just locked it, sir.' The soldier held out the key.

'Good.' Ebenezer smiled. 'In you go, sister. I trust the bed is comfortable.' He laughed. The soldiers, all men in Sir Grenville Cony's debt, laughed with him. She was pushed inside.

Ebenezer smiled at Samuel Scammell. 'Do your duty, brother.' He took the key from the door that opened on to the long gallery, gestured Scammell inside, and then shut the door on both of them.

Campion was delivered to her enemies.

18

This was the moment she had feared, yet somehow it was impossible to be scared of Samuel Scammell. He shambled into the room behind her, blinked as the door was closed on them, and then stood helplessly as Campion went into the recess of the bow window. She clutched the cat to her. 'You're not going to touch me.'

He moved to a chair. That morning, in fear of the assault and remembering how the musket bullets had flayed around him, Samuel Scammell had dressed in full lobster armour, his arms and thighs protected by the overlapping plates which Campion could hear scraping on each other as he moved. He sat heavily in Lady Margaret's chair. 'I won't touch you.' He sounded miserable. He put his head back, staring at the plaster pattern that criss-crossed the ceiling. He wiped his fleshy lips, blinked again, then shook his head.

'I didn't want this. Your father didn't tell me about this.'

There were shouts from the garden behind Campion. The Roundheads were dragging away one of the big sakers, but she took no notice. She still held Mildred tight. She was confused. 'You came after me! You forced that wedding on me!'

He shook his head, leaning forward now, his cavernous, dark nostrils repelling her even as his eyes pleaded with her. 'You don't understand. Sir Grenville Cony. Your brother.'

'My brother!'

'He forced this!' Scammell was strangely indignant. 'He does what he wants now. It's the seal. Always the seal. I hope you haven't got the seal!' he added petulantly.

'Why?' She shook her head. 'Why?'

'Don't you understand? They don't care about you, they don't care about me, they only care about the Covenant! If we'd married, if we'd lived at Werlatton, we'd have been left in peace. But you had to run away!'

She ignored the complaint. She had run because she had no wish to marry this weak man, a man who she saw now was in the same state as herself. He was beaten, victimized, manipulated into this room that looked on to the morning light in the Lazen valley. She felt an anger in herself. 'You wanted the money!'

He nodded heavily. 'But it was always for you. It has to be for you. That's what the Covenant says. The money must be spent on you. Your father bought Werlatton with the money, but it was a house for you to live in.' He looked wearily at her. 'Do you have the seal?'

She did not answer. He saw the scorn in her face. He seemed almost on the point of tears. 'I don't care, Dorcas, I don't care any more. Give him the seal. Give it to him! I'll say we're married properly. That's what they want, and you can go. Truly! In God's name I promise it. You can go.. Sir Grenville will go on stealing half the money, more than half, and you can have the rest. I just want peace.'

'Dear God! And what do you think I've been wanting?' She thought of Toby, wondering if he was alive, or whether he was bleeding to death in the smoke-stenched yard. 'You did this to me! You wanted the money!'

'I want peace.'

'Now you want peace! Because you're frightened! You should have thought of that before. Damn you, Samuel Scammell. Damn you and your weakness!'

He looked at her, seeing her beauty outlined in the window, and he shook his head. There was no fight in him, there was nothing left. He had been dragged into turbulent water and he wanted nothing now but to save himself from drowning. Even his lust for Campion was far off, forgotten. He put his head in his hands as if to obliterate her voice.

She did not give him peace. 'You want none of this? Is that what you want?' She saw him nod, almost imperceptibly. 'Then get us out of here. You've got a sword, haven't you? A pistol? Then fight, Samuel Scammell. Fight, damn you! I don't care about the money, I don't care about the seal, but I do care about my life. You help me, for a change. Is that sword just decoration?'

He shook his head and she turned, exasperated, and saw the armed men in the garden who stared up at the window. She turned away from them.

The door opened.

Ebenezer came in, shut the door behind him, then leaned against its painted panels. He looked from Scammell to Campion, then back to Scammell. 'I thought I would find you in your marriage bed! I brought you a candle.'

In his left hand he held a tray on which Campion could see paper and a lit candle. He carried it carefully to a small table and set it down. Scammell had not looked up.

Ebenezer smiled at him. 'Brother-in-law. What is it?'

Scammell's voice was muffled by his hands. 'We must do what is right in the eyes of the Lord.'

'Oh! Indeed and indeed!' Ebenezer mocked him, then kicked Scammell's shin with his lame foot. 'Are you married to this woman?'

Scammell looked up. He turned to Campion and shook his head. 'No.'

'Then in the eyes of the Lord, brother, you are not the rightful owner of the seal. I am.' Ebenezer came towards Campion, his eyes bright. 'Do you have the seal, sister?'

'Ebenezer?' She tried to put a sister's love into her voice.

'I have no sister. I have no family. Don't think that you can wheedle me, Dorcas, I asked if you had the seal.' He had stopped a pace away from her. Scammell, behind him, seemed oblivious, sunk in his misery. Ebenezer smiled at her. His hair was sleek and black, as shiny as his lacquered breastplate. He lifted his right hand slowly, his eyes glittering, and Campion shrank back.

His hand moved fast, gripping the high neck of her grey dress. He pulled hard, easily overcoming her resistance, and she felt the hook at the back of the dress break. He stared at her neck. 'You're not wearing it, sister. Where is it?'

'I don't have it.'

He raised his eyebrows in mock surprise. 'You mean this was all in vain?' His right hand was behind his back now. 'We went through this siege for nothing? Those men died for nothing?' His right hand moved again, once more with snake-like speed, and Campion saw the flash of light on a long, thin dagger, and then there was the chill of steel against her cheek. 'Where is it, sister?'

She dared not move. She could feel the point of the knife on her skin. Ebenezer smiled. 'Where is it, sister?'

Still she said nothing. She was terrified of him. The cruelty of Matthew Slythe had been handed to his son, but mixed with a cold-blooded detachment. She knew of no way to appeal to him.

His left hand moved, startling her. She gasped because the knife had gone from her cheek and she felt the cat in her arms, suddenly protest. Ebenezer had grasped the cat by the neck, had put the knife on her fur.

'Tell me, sister.'

'No!' She tried to pull Mildred away from him. 'No!'

The knife sliced at the base of her thumb, a quick surprise of pain. She gasped, blood dripped, and then Ebenezer was holding the cat by the scruff of her neck and the knife point was at the cat's throat. He held it at her face. 'Where is it, sister?'

'Ebenezer! No!'

The cat squealed, twisted, tried to claw the man who held the knife point at her throat. Campion grasped at Ebenezer's wrist, blood running from her cut hand, but Ebenezer jerked the knife. 'You want the cat to die?'

'Ebenezer!' She shook her head. 'Please!'

'I'll kill it, Dorcas. You've seen me do it before. I'll kill it. And then I'll start on you, sister dear.' He laughed. 'If Brother Scammell's not willing, then I've a dozen men who'd like to have you, sister. One by one, one after the other. Do you want that, sister? Do you?'

'Ebenezer!'

Scammell watched, appalled. He did not move.

Ebenezer smiled. He ignored the cat that twisted frantically to avoid the dagger's point. 'Where is the seal, sister?'

'I have it! I have it! I don't want it.'

A look of triumph twisted on Ebenezer's face, and then he screwed with his right hand, glee in his eyes, forcing Mildred on to the knife and twisting the body so that the cat's dying spurt of blood sprayed on to Campion's face. He jerked the blood-matted body off the knife point and laughed at her. 'So you do have it. Where?'

The dagger was coming towards her face again.

She fumbled inside her dress, but the seal had slipped down to her waist and she could not reach it. She watched the knife, smelling the blood of the cat on her face. 'I'll get it for you!'

He took the neckline in his left hand, pulled and sawed down with the knife. The point drew blood from the skin over her breastbone, ripped on through the dress, and she shrank back, screaming, the dress falling away where he had cut it down close to her waist. The seal's chain fell out and Ebenezer reached for it, pulled, and held the jewel up to the growing light. He glanced uninterestedly at her breasts, smiled as she pulled the dress up to cover her nakedness, then stepped away from her.

'The seal.'

It hung from his left hand. The gold looked rich, the bands of precious stones sparkled as the jewel twisted on its chain. The Seal of St Matthew. Ebenezer took it, almost reverently, to the table. He put it down.

Scammell stared at it as if, until this moment, he had doubted its existence.

Campion was half crouching, her back against the window-sill. She held her dress with both hands. At her feet was Mildred's bloody fur.

Ebenezer stepped away from the table. The chain of the seal hung over the edge, swinging slightly. He smiled. 'Who does it belong to?'

No one answered him. Behind Campion, below in the

garden, a file of prisoners was marched towards the ruins of the gatehouse. The smoke of the explosion still lingered above the valley.

Ebenezer reached for the bed-hangings. The cords that had tied them had long been cut up for the matchlock musket fuses. He wiped his knife blade clean on the embroidered silk, sheathed the knife, then wiped his hands as if the bed-curtains were a towel. 'I asked who it belonged to?'

Scammell's armour scraped harshly as he turned to look at Ebenezer.

Ebenezer rubbed his hands together fastidiously. 'Is it yours, Brother Scammell? Or is it mine? I thought we were brothers-in-law.'

Scammell said nothing.

'Come, Brother Scammell!' Ebenezer made his voice hearty. 'She's your wife, is she not? Do you not want her? She's pretty enough. She may not be a virgin, of course, but she's still your wife. Don't you want to beget heirs? Shall not the tribe of Scammell inherit the earth?'

Scammell licked his lips. Frowned.

Ebenezer put his hand on the collar of Scammell's leather jerkin. It seemed to rest there in a friendly manner. 'If she's your wife, brother, then the seal is yours. Don't you want it? The bitch has burned your business down, at the very least you can take her money. Go on! Take her!' He pulled at the collar, yanking upwards. 'Go on! Move!'

The harshness of the command rather than the pull on his collar made Scammell jerk upright. He seemed to have no volition of his own. He was terrified of Ebenezer, as he was terrified of the soldiers sent by Sir Grenville who waited outside the door. He looked at Campion, crouched by the window, and he licked his lips.

Ebenezer pushed him. 'Go on, brother. Claim your bride! Claim the seal! Think what I do for you? I could take it myself, but those whom the Lord hath joined together, let no man part asunder.'

Scammell's lips parted in a silent, automatic 'amen'. He

was breathing heavily, fear on his face, but he stumbled towards Campion in the window, Ebenezer's hand still on the collar that protruded above his backplate. He walked clumsily, the flanges on his thighs scraping.

Ebenezer smiled. 'You do want her, brother, don't you?'

'Brother Slythe?' Scammell found his tongue and turned nervously to his tormentor.

'Look! Look!' Ebenezer lashed out with his right foot, holding his balance by gripping on Scammell's collar. 'Look!' His foot lashed into Campion's face, bruising her, forcing her to cover her face with her hands. The dress fell open, showing her naked breasts and Ebenezer pushed down with his hand. 'Look at her! Don't you want her?'

She tried to pull the dress up. She was shrinking back into the corner of the bay window, and again the foot lashed at her. She was screaming, one hand protecting her face, the other fumbling at the torn dress.

'Don't you want her, brother? Look at the breasts. Touch them! Touch them! Go on, take her!' Ebenezer forced Scammell's head down. 'Touch her!'

Scammell tried to straighten up, but Ebenezer had drawn his knife again and he pricked the blade into Scammell's neck. 'Touch her, brother. Touch her.'

'You're mad!'

'I said, touch her!' He shouted it, forcing the heavier man down.

'I'll touch her!' Scammell put out his right hand. Touched Campion's hair. She was screaming, trying to bury herself into the corner of the window, and then she heard Ebenezer laughing above her.

'But you're not married, brother. Your wedding certificate was burned six months ago! And now I find you molesting my sister! I'm surprised at you, brother! I am shocked! I had thought you a man of God, and you are nothing but lust!'

Scammell was trying to straighten up, trying to protest, but the knife was already at his throat, piercing through skin, fat and into the blood vessels. Samuel Scammell tried to throw

Ebenezer off. He pulled back and raised his arm, but Ebenezer laughed and hooked the blade. Blood poured on to Campion. It soaked the curtain, the window, the polished floorboards. With a despairing, choking breath of air and blood, Scammell fell dead on top of Campion.

She screamed. She was choking in blood, crushed by the weight of man and armour. She thought she was drowning in it, that the sky itself ran with ribbons of the thick, warm liquid. She screamed again, knowing it was a dream and her scream faded away.

Ebenezer looked at her. She would regain consciousness soon. He had seen it happen before. She would be calmer when she came round, but not if the body was still slumped over her. He stooped, grunting with the effort, and rolled Scammell's body off her legs.

Ebenezer wiped the blade clean again, doing it meticulously, and then returned the knife to its sheath. He wiped his hands, spitting on them to remove the last of the blood that he found offensive. He glanced at his sister. She was moaning, the moans hinting at hysterical sobs.

He went to the table. Sir Grenville Cony, he knew, would want the seal delivered to him, and Ebenezer had thought long and hard about how that could be avoided. Ebenezer was young, too new to the world of power and men to have garnered the support he would need to fight Sir Grenville yet, but he would not easily surrender the Seal of St Matthew. He knew too though, that if he did not give the jewel to his patron, then his patron would destroy him as easily as he had made Ebenezer destroy Scammell.

He smoothed a piece of paper on the table. He took the candle and held its flame on to a stick of red sealing-wax. The wax turned blackish, dripped, and Ebenezer swiftly put the candle down, picked up the seal and pressed the broad axe head into the hot wax. He smiled at the result.

He worked swiftly, single-mindedly, ignoring his sister's sobs. He made twelve impressions, spaced equally on the paper and then he blew the candle out, tossed the truncated wax stick into the fireplace, and laid a second sheet of creamy, stiff paper over the first. He folded the two sheets carefully, making sure that the creases were in the spaces he had left for them and then he put the thick, stiff square of papers into his leather pouch.

He glanced at Campion. She was sobbing hysterically, her eyes open. He knew she was not seeing anything. He had seen his victims like this before, at the times when he would rest from his labours and walk up the stone steps to stare across the River Thames as he flexed the stiffness from his lamed body.

He picked up the seal. He unscrewed it and stared, without expression, at the crucifix. He had not known what to expect, half thinking it might contain a naked woman like that inside the Seal of St Mark. The small, silver statue was very still in his fingers.

He glanced at her again. He was thinking.

He screwed the two halves of the seal together, stood up, and crossed gently towards her. Her eyes moved as he came close, but he knew she was still not recognizing him. He made soft, crooning noises of reassurance as he stooped over her. She did not move away from him. She seemed aware that someone was present, she seemed to want comfort, and, indeed, his hands were surprisingly gentle as he tipped her head forward and slipped the seal round her neck.

Then, still making the quiet, comforting noises, he backed away from her. He opened the door to the long gallery, slipped through, then locked it behind him. He nodded at those who waited outside, expectancy on their faces, and put a finger to his lips. 'A few more minutes, I think.' One of his men offered him wine, looted from the castle cellars, but the offer made Ebenezer scowl. 'Water! Bring me water! But make sure it's clean!'

He leaned against the door, shut his eyes, and reflected on the satisfaction of a job well done.

For what seemed hours, yet were only minutes, Campion did

not move. She shrank into the window corner like a trapped, scared animal, fearing everything, not daring to move in case the motion should invite new horrors. The blood on her smelled thick and nauseating, and she heard her great, lung-emptying sobs, and only slowly did she realize that she was listening to herself. She touched a finger to her face, feeling the stickiness, and she thought she was in the realm of madness, or else falling through some wild, shrieking hole towards hell itself. She wailed like a child in pain and the sound, or else the thought of hell, made her strength rebel against her predicament.

She moved. She shook her head. She made herself see where she was and the first object before her eyes was the great, dark hole in Scammell's throat. She felt her stomach heaving, heard the retching mingled with sobs and threw herself sideways, away from the body. She was gasping for air, panting, but she forced herself into one action at a time. First to reach the bed, next to wipe her hands, her face, and then to suck at the wound on the base of her thumb that still bled. She wiped with the corner of the sheet at her breasts which were sticky with blood. The seal hung there.

She held it in her right hand, staring at it as if she had never seen it before, seeing where the bright gold had been smeared with congealing blood. She loathed it, knowing it trapped her and the sudden, surprising discovery of it about her neck threatened to drive her once more into the abyss of madness from which she was so painfully climbing. She shut her eyes, leaning back against the high bed and clutched the seal in her hand as if to hide it.

Toby. Sir George. The cat. Scammell. The smell of blood. Vomit rose in her throat. She moaned, but again a part of her forced her to move, to do one thing at a time, and she pulled herself up on the bed, sitting on it, and dragged the runner that was draped over the pillows towards her. She put it on like a shawl, covering her nakedness, and only then did she start to breathe more shallowly, to take stock of herself.

The room was smothered in blood. Scammell's body,

grotesque in its layered armour, was sprawled crooked by the window, one plump hand outstretched in helpless appeal. Mildred, her fur matted with blood that looked black, seemed tiny in death. The light was full outside now. Through the small leads of the window she saw the piling clouds that would have meant her salvation this coming night. James Wright, Toby, Lady Margaret. They all seemed so distant now. Her old life had flooded back in a horror that still threatened to overwhelm her. Now, just as she had endured the wrath and punishment of God at Werlatton as a child, she must simply survive. She shut her eyes, crooning to herself and heard the dread sound of the key turning in the lock.

She opened her eyes, clutching the shawl at her neck.

Ebenezer smiled at her. He spread his hands as if in welcome. 'Sister Dorcas! My dear sister!' He seemed to glance casually about the room and took a dramatic backward pace when he saw Scammell's body. He gasped.

Goodwife Baggerlie was next into the room. She pushed past Ebenezer and stared at the body of Samuel Scammell. She took a deep breath. 'Murder! Murder!'

'No, no! My sister!' Ebenezer came into the room properly. 'No! No!'

Campion was shaking her head, rocking back and forth on the bed. 'Go away! Go away!'

'Murder!' Goodwife's shrill voice filled the room. 'She killed him!'

'No!' Campion moaned.

'Don't go near her! Don't touch her!' A new voice cut over the clamour, a voice that touched a memory in Campion. She opened her eyes, looked around dully, and there was the Reverend Faithful Unto Death Hervey, one hand raised, the other clutching a Bible to his black jacket.

'Harlot! Murderer! Witch!' Goodwife shouted.

Ebenezer had knelt beside Scammell's body. 'How could she have killed him? She's only a girl! He was an armed man! She can't have killed him!'

There was a slight pause before Goodwife remembered her cue. She stepped forward, her voice like the breath of the pit, and she raised a raw, bony finger which she stabbed towards Campion.

'She's a witch! I saw the devil rescue her in Mister Scammell's house. Flaming hair, he had! From hell itself. The devil! She's a witch!'

'No!' Ebenezer protested.

'Quiet!' The Reverend Faithful Unto Death moved into the centre of the room. He had studied witchcraft these last few months, seeing in demonology a ladder that would take him to the vast pinnacle of his ambitions. This was the thing he had suggested to Ebenezer on Christmas morning; that Dorcas Slythe was a witch and that he, Faithful Unto Death Hervey, would unmask her. He had not been selfish with the thought, admitting that Goodwife Baggerlie had always maintained the girl to be possessed of a devil, but now, at last, he was ready to pit his strength against the Prince of Darkness who was Dorcas Slythe's ally. He also still wanted this girl, but now he wished to abase her, to humiliate her, to use her for his fame. He looked grandly about the room, remembering what Ebenezer had said. 'Ah! A cat! Her familiar!'

Goodwife gasped, recoiled in horror.

Faithful Unto Death stepped resolutely closer to Campion. He put his Bible on the table, and his Adam's apple bobbed up and down his long, pale throat. 'There is a sure way to find out. A sure way!'

'Brother Hervey?' Ebenezer sounded awed.

Faithful Unto Death took another pace towards the staring, gasping girl. 'I will need your help, both of you. Fear not! God is with us!' He did not need to tell them what was expected. 'Now!'

Campion screamed, but the three had her on the bed, Goodwife forcing her head back, Ebenezer swinging her legs on to the mattress. Campion screamed again, fought against the hands that groped at her, but she was powerless. Faithful

Unto Death tore the dress apart, pulled the shawl away and Goodwife seized Campion's hands.

'Hold her!' Faithful Unto Death bent over her breasts, his breath warm on her skin. She struggled, but Goodwife had an arm over her throat while Ebenezer weighed down her legs.

Faithful Unto Death's hands were dry, almost scaly. They stroked her breasts, touching her nipples. His voice, like his hands, was dry. He might have been explaining the doctrine of the Trinity. 'These, Brother Slythe, are the teats for giving suck to children. A witch will not use those when she feeds the devil, for those teats come of God.' His fingers rubbed her nipples. His hands slid down towards her belly, kneading her ribs. 'We are looking for another mark, the witch mark. Ah!' He probed the mole above her navel, the mole that Toby had teased her about on Christmas Day. 'Here it is! The witch mark!' His hands, even though they had found the mole, moved back to her breasts.

'Sir! Look!' Goodwife had the seal. 'Is this what you looked for?'

'It is! It is!'

Faithful Unto Death was forced to help Goodwife remove the seal. Released from their grip, Campion turned away from them, curled herself up, and sobbed into the bed's cover. She felt as if filth had been smeared on her, irrevocably smeared.

'Look!' Ebenezer had unscrewed the seal, was showing the crucifix to Faithful Unto Death.

'A Papist witch!'

Campion was past caring. She wept. She was sliding into the abyss again. She dimly heard Faithful Unto Death intoning the 23rd psalm, heard her brother call for the guards, and then, mercifully she fainted. They wrapped her in a blanket, unwilling that Colonel Fuller's soldiers should know what they had been doing, and Campion was carried down to the travelling coach which had been prepared.

Ebenezer smiled at the Reverend Faithful Unto Death Hervey. 'You were right, brother.'

'God has been good to us.'

'He has, he has.'

Faithful Unto Death shook his head solemnly. 'She must be tried, brother.'

'She must, she must.' Ebenezer smiled. He walked to the window and stared down to where Goodwife followed Campion into the coach. From now on, Ebenezer reflected, they could deal respectably with his sister. The law would be relentless, properly conducting her to either fire or scaffold. He looked at Faithful Unto Death.

'She must be a witch.'

'She is.'

Ebenezer shrugged and limped back into the long gallery. He waved a hand at the decorated pagan plasterwork, at the curtains, the rugs, the paintings and the fine, inlaid furniture. 'She must have used witchcraft to come here. Why else would they welcome her?'

He did not listen to Faithful Unto Death Hervey's reply. He stared instead at the richness of the room and he hated it. It was beautiful and that was an anathema to him. It had belonged to privileged people and that was a further cause for hatred. Ebenezer had always hated the privileged.

He was now one of them. He was, since Scammell's death, the legal holder of the Seal of St Matthew. He would now receive the monies of the Covenant. He would be rich. Yet, he decided as he fingered a lace tablecloth, he would use his riches towards a better end than they had been used here. He would work for an England that was disciplined under God, devout under the law, and he knew that such a country would need harsh, far-seeing masters. God's Kingdom would come and he would be one of its regents. He had discovered, in this last year, that he had the gift of leadership, though he still feared the older men of more power and experience. Those he was careful to flatter and copy.

He turned back to Faithful Unto Death, seeing in his erstwhile minister a future follower. Ebenezer's voice was grating and harsh, befitting a conqueror. 'I believe a word of thanks might be in season, brother?'

'Indeed.'

They knelt beneath the pagan plasterwork and thanked Almighty God for his mercies, for this signal providence that had brought them to this great victory.

'Amen,' said Faithful Unto Death, 'and amen'.

19

' "Man, that is born of a woman, hath but a short time to live, and is full of misery." ' Lady Margaret, listening to the Reverend Perilly's words, thought it had not been true. Sir George had not been full of misery. He had been full of worry, yet he had known much happiness.

' "He cometh up, and is cut down, like a flower." ' That, she thought was true, if a flower had ever been blasted in the face by a musketeer.

She stood on the flagstones of Lazen church's aisle. Fittingly it was a grey day, threatening rain, and the light which came through the windows which had been stripped of their fine, stained glass was gloomy. The escutcheons of Lazen and Lazender had been hacked with pikes, while the stone effigies of Sir George's ancestors, beneath whose gaze he was laid to rest, had been hammered with musket fire and then daubed with limewash. They looked leprous.

Lady Margaret looked through her veil into the hole that had been made by lifting four flagstones. The vault of the church was damp. She could see the rotted end of an old coffin that abutted on to Sir George's new coffin, just lowered into place. One day, she thought, she would lie in that hole, her eyes staring endlessly towards the worshippers above. Then, with the sudden realization that the world was turned upside down, she knew she might never lie beside Sir George. Even as the Reverend Simon Perilly read the obsequies, so was the County Committee for Sequestration meeting in Lazen's great hall. Lazen was to be taken from her, from Sir Toby, the rightful heir.

It was wicked, it was unfair, yet she could do nothing. The Committee, gleeful in their victory, had picked the hour of the funeral so that the family could not be represented. John, Earl of Fleet, newly back from the Earl of Essex's army that marched through the west, had nevertheless attended the committee. Lady Margaret doubted if he would achieve anything. On her right stood Anne, the Countess of Fleet, and on her left was Caroline. Toby was in his bedroom, and whether he would not be next beneath the earth was still in doubt.

Perilly's voice rose. ' "The grace of our Lord Jesus Christ, and the love of God, and the fellowship of the Holy Ghost, be with us all evermore. Amen." '

Lady Margaret stood for two seconds, staring at the clean, planed wood of her husband's coffin, then turned about. 'Come.'

She stood outside, close to the charred patch of grass where the victorious Puritans had burned the altar rails, and there she thanked the villagers, tenants and servants who had crowded the church. She could give them thanks, but she could offer no hope for the future. She looked at Mr Perilly. 'Thank you, Simon. You did it well.'

The Reverend Perilly, whose theology was not to the taste of the victors, faced a future as uncertain as Lady Margaret's. He folded his scapular on his prayer book. 'He will be resurrected, Lady Margaret.'

She nodded. 'I trust God will give time for revenge on the day of resurrection, Mr Perilly.' She turned away, leading her daughters across the ravaged gardens towards the New House.

Upstairs, in Toby's bedroom, Lady Margaret found the doctor bleeding her son. 'Again?'

'It is the best course, Lady Margaret.' Dr Sillery had taken a cupful of blood from Toby's arm and now he pulled blankets over the patient. 'The sweating will help.'

Lady Margaret suppressed a retort that nothing had helped so far. She sat beside her son and put a hand on his forehead. It was hot. He had a fever and she knew that most fevers led to the grave. She looked at Sillery. 'The wounds?'

'The hand is healing well, extremely well.' He shrugged. 'The shoulder . . .' He did not finish.

Lady Margaret looked back to Toby's sweating, unshaven face. He had been struck in the left shoulder by a musket ball that had mangled the joint and torn itself raggedly free from his armpit. That wound had thrown him to the ground. Then a sword had chopped down and taken two fingers from his left hand. The finger stumps were healing well, the skin pink and free of smell, but the shoulder seemed to fester. Each day Sillery would sniff the wound, frown, and then draw blood to equalize Toby's bodily humours. Each day, too, Mr Perilly said prayers for the sick, and Lady Margaret feared they would become prayers for the dying. In another room of the New House Colonel Washington sat up in bed, his face bandaged where once he had eyes.

'Mother?' Anne looked round the door.

'I'm coming.'

In the long gallery, a room untouched by the victorious troops, the Earl of Fleet waited with a drawn, anxious face. His allegiance was torn between his convictions that looked forward to a Parliamentary victory and his duties towards his wife's family. He nodded heavily, 'Lady Margaret.'

'John? I assume from your face that the news is not good?'

'No.' He spread his hands in a quick gesture of futility. 'I did my best, but we could not offer enough money. Indeed not.'

Lady Margaret's face was as calm and stern as it had been throughout her husband's burial service. 'May I ask who did offer the most money?'

The Earl of Fleet frowned, twisted his body uncomfortably and then walked towards the nearest window. 'Money was not offered.' He held up a hand to ward off a question. 'It seems that the estate will be awarded as compensation in repayment for a loan to Parliament. The amount was unstated.'

'To whom is my house compensation?'

The Earl of Fleet faced her. His hands rubbed uneasily together. 'Sir Grenville Cony.'

'Ah.' Lady Margaret stiffened her back. 'I trust that unspeakable piece of slime is not in the castle now?'

'No.'

'And I assume, too, that the property is confiscated? Not sold?'

Fleet nodded unhappily. 'Confiscated.'

'So I am penniless?'

'No, mother!' Anne protested.

The Earl of Fleet paced uneasily back towards the fireplace. 'Sir George's other properties were not discussed. The Shropshire land.' He stopped, knowing he was giving no comfort.

Lady Margaret sniffed. 'The Shropshire land will have to be sold, and I've no doubt at a laughable price. I suppose I can have no hopes of selling the London house?'

He shook his head. 'The London Committee will doubtless award that.'

'Doubtless. And to Cony, no doubt.'

The Earl put his hands behind his back. 'There is the plate, Lady Margaret. I notice it is all gone, yet I assume Sir George took pains to make it safe?'

Lady Margaret shook her head. The treasures of Lazen were still within the castle, walled up in the cellars, and it had been a small satisfaction to her that the victors had neither found it, nor had they been told where it was by one of the few servants who knew of the treasure's existence. She looked at her son-in-law. 'There is no plate.'

'No plate!' The Earl looked shocked.

'John!' Anne looked at her mother. 'What did father do with it?'

'That is no business of the King's enemies.'

There was an awkward silence, broken by the Earl of Fleet.

'It will be some time before the transaction is completed. You won't have to leave immediately.' He smiled. 'You are, of course, welcome to use our house. We shall be honoured.'

'Thank you, John.' Lady Margaret smiled at her daughter. 'And thank you, Anne. There is one other thing you can do for me.'

'Yes?' The Earl sounded eager, glad to be moving on from the bad news he had delivered.

'There was a girl here, a Dorcas Slythe, who has disappeared. I want to know where she is.'

'Mother!' Anne, who had been longer in the castle since its fall than her husband, frowned. It was Anne's belief that Campion's presence had brought this ruin on her parents, and she had tried to persuade Lady Margaret, from the evidence of the blood in the bedroom, that the girl was wounded and probably dead by now.

Lady Margaret quietened her daughter. 'I want news of the girl. The soldiers say she was taken to London. Can I rely on you, John?'

He nodded. 'Yes, of course,' then he glanced at his wife. 'I think Anne is right, Lady Margaret. The girl has caused endless trouble.'

Lady Margaret's voice was cold. 'Would you like to explain that to Sir Toby when he recovers?'

The Countess of Fleet frowned. 'Toby will get over it, mother.'

Lady Margaret sniffed. 'I hope not. If Lazen's downfall was brought about so that my enemies could destroy that girl, then I wish to save her. I wish to deny them that victory.'

The Earl of Fleet stood beside his wife. 'Even if we find her, Lady Margaret, I doubt if there is a thing we can do now.'

'You mean your influence in the councils of my enemies is declining?'

Fleet frowned. 'It was never great.'

Lady Margaret turned back towards her son's sick-room. She feared, if he should come out of the fever, telling him of

Campion's unknown fate. 'Find her, John! Let me know, and then we shall see how helpless we are. I want the girl found!'

Campion was in the place of the ravens; the Tower.

The river swept its southern wall, while a moat, as filthy and stinking as the sewer it was, guarded its other three sides. On the hill to the north-west London's crowds gathered for public executions.

The Tower of London was a royal palace, an armoury, a garrison, a zoo, and the strongest prison in the city. In its cells were priests and noblemen, soldiers and civilians, all of them deemed to be enemies of the Lord's anointed. The prisoners here were not the common prisoners, not the murderers and thieves, but the enemies of the revolution. William Laud, Archbishop of Canterbury, upholder of the Divine Right of Kings, was the most notorious.

At nightfall, when Campion came beneath the outer gates for the first time, the Tower's Parliamentary governor had been puzzled, even irate. 'Who is she?'

'Dorcas Slythe.'

'So?' He reluctantly took the warrant given him by a trooper. He grunted when he saw the seal of the Committee of Safety. 'Charge?'

'Witchcraft and murder.'

The governor sneered. 'Put her in the clink.'

The Reverend Faithful Unto Death Hervey was not overawed by the Tower's governor. 'She may be a Papist spy.'

'Ah.' The governor frowned at the warrant. 'It says nothing about that here.'

'You may argue with the Committee of Safety. If you prefer, I can ask Sir Grenville Cony to explain.'

The governor glanced up. 'Sir Grenville? That's different.' He climbed on to the step of the coach and looked inside. 'Is she to have privileges?'

'None.'

The Governor, who was annoyed at being summoned from his quarters by the captain of the guard to deal with the unexpected prisoner, bawled at the captain to do the paperwork. Campion was taken from the coach, the hooves of the horses were loud as they turned the cumbersome vehicle about and then the gates clashed shut. She was a prisoner.

There was no window in Campion's cell. The only light, feeble at best, came from the tallow candles that lit the tunnel beyond the door's grille.

The cell floor was stone. In one corner was a heap of old, stale straw. There was no furniture. She was given one blanket, ridden with lice, but it was hopeless against the cold. As there was no day or night in this place, so there was no season but winter.

She shivered. She moaned to herself, and sometimes she sang in a small voice that was thin in the dank gloom. She rocked herself in the straw corner, huddled with the blanket, and the cell reeked with the stench of sewage. Rats scuttled about, their claws loud on the stone.

She lost count of time, lost count of the number of pots of thin gruel that were pushed through the door. The bread was rock hard. She stank. Her hair was matted, her body bitten by lice, and her sleep was broken by the clanging of doors and the scraping of bolts that told her other prisoners were somewhere in these cells.

Sometimes the grille of her door would darken and she would look up to see a face pressed against the small opening. Eyes looked white at her. Sometimes there would be laughter; sometimes the hiss of hatred: 'Witch! Papist! Whore!'

She did not descend into the abyss of madness. Two things saved her. She did not know if Toby was alive or dead, yet she imagined him alive. She forced herself to imagine him alive, and she would rock in her corner, arms clutching her knees, and imagine the life they would one day have. She saw Toby avenging her on her enemies, she saw him strike down Sir Grenville, the sword blade opening up that world of which they had dared dream. She imagined the Reverend Faithful Unto Death Hervey whining for mercy. She saw her brother on his knees, and she imagined the sweetness of offering him a sister's forgiveness, more terrible than the sword's swift revenge.

When she was not in her dream world, living among the fields of eternal summer beside cool streams, she forced herself to recite aloud. She tried to remember the whole of the Song of Solomon, and she would weep sometimes as the words sounded in her head: 'His banner over me was love.' She recited psalms, remembered from the long hours of childhood, but most of all she spoke aloud the words of a poem she had read so often in Lazen Castle. She could only remember the first verse, and of that she was not certain that her memory was correct, but she loved the words. Lady Margaret had said that the poem mocked love's intensity, but Donne's words were like music in her stinking, cold, rat-running cell:

> Go, and catch a falling star,
> Get with child a mandrake root,
> Tell me, where all past years are,
> Or who cleft the Devil's foot,
> Teach me to hear mermaids singing,
> Or to keep off envy's stinging,
>   And find
>   What wind
> Serves to advance an honest mind.

She had never seen the sea, the closest she had been was when she had met Mrs Swan in the inn yard at Southampton, but she imagined it as full of mermaids' singing, and she saw herself and Toby listening to the songs and knowing peace.

At other times she came close to despair. She remembered the week of travel from Lazen Castle, a week in which Goodwife had spat out a vituperative stream at her, dredging from the past every small sin, every disobedience, and flaying

Campion with her envy and malice. In her cell, day after indistinguishable day, Campion was determined to live, yet there were moments when it seemed so futile. When the water ran on her cell walls, when her mouth and throat were sour with the stink of urine, when the rats woke her in the darkness, when she shivered uncontrollably and could not even be bothered to pick off the lice that she could see on her skin, then, at those moments, she sometimes wished she was no more. At those moments she was sure Toby was dead and she wished only to be with him. Perhaps, she thought, the mermaids only sang to the dead.

'Magnificent! Magnificent! Your men will clear the gardens?' It was posed as a question, but Colonel Fuller knew better than to treat it as anything but an order.

'Of course, Sir Grenville.'

'With haste, Colonel, with haste. Ah! A loggia! A pity the guns damaged it. See if you have masons.'

'Yes, Sir Grenville.'

Sir Grenville climbed the single step into the loggia's arcaded shadow. He looked at the vine, trailing where round shot had smashed its supports. 'You say, Colonel, that the plate wasn't found?'

'No, Sir Grenville. I believe it was sold for the enemy's cause.'

'No doubt, no doubt. Or melted down. A pity, a pity.' He did not sound disappointed, nor, he reflected, should he be. Sir Grenville's cup flowed over with success. True, the castle had fallen earlier than he had expected, but Ebenezer Slythe had not done anything so foolish as to run away with the seal. It had been delivered to Sir Grenville in Winchester when he had met Ebenezer returning with his sister to London. Sir Grenville now had two seals. No one, but no one, could now assemble three of the four except for him. The Covenant was safe.

Dorcas Slythe, of course, would die. At Winchester, in the tavern in Jewry Street where Sir Grenville had spoken with

Ebenezer, he had given the younger man the warrant charging her with witchcraft and murder. Ebenezer, quietly pleased with himself, had read the words. 'We could add heresy.'

'Heresy, dear boy? Do you not think the pie has enough plums already?'

Ebenezer gave his secret, slow smile. 'The seal has a crucifix inside.'

'Indeed?'

Ebenezer showed the small, silver figure to Sir Grenville. 'I don't think Parliament will like that.'

'I'm sure they will not.' Sir Grenville smiled and poured himself wine. 'But I would like it even less, Ebenezer, if we were to draw attention to the seals. No, dear boy. But by all means spread the rumour that she's Romish. It will only whip up London against her.' He put the Seal of St Matthew into his pocket. 'You know what to do?'

Ebenezer nodded. 'The Presentment first, then the Grand Jury.'

'Exactly.' Sir Grenville pushed a piece of paper over the table. 'See this man, Caleb Higbed. He's a good lawyer, he'll do it all. Good! Good!'

The affable mood had lasted. Victory was Sir Grenville's, and now Lazen Castle was his too. He had acquired much land in the last year, yet nothing to compare with this estate. The guns had knocked it about more than he cared, but the New House was splendidly undamaged. Soon, he thought, he might retire, and he could think of few places more fitting for him than this.

Retirement was a possibility, but only after his cause was victorious. That victory had come suddenly, splendidly nearer. News had arrived from the north of England, and the news was of a great victory by Parliament and the Scots over the Royalist forces. If the wind was turning against the King, then nowhere did it blow more cruel and cold than over bleak Marston Moor. A great victory which had loosed the north from the King, would lead soon, Sir Grenville knew, to the fall of York, and meant that the kingdom of Charles was shrinking fast.

Victory, rest, and then the Covenant to support him in his old age. Sir Grenville smiled as he walked into the house, looking with satisfaction at the great marble staircase. He was a rich man now, as he had been since the Covenant's founding, yet he still needed the Covenant's money. The income was so huge, so unimaginably large, that no amount of English land could replace it with rents. Two seals had given him the safety of the Covenant, and though he must share the monies with Ebenezer, he would, as he ever had, make sure that Ebenezer never knew the full income. He looked at Colonel Fuller. 'Is the family gone?'

'No, Sir Grenville. I don't think they expected you this soon.'

Sir Grenville chuckled. He hauled on the marble banisters, pulling his grotesque body up the stairs. His cherubically curled white hair was tipped backwards so he could look at the plasterwork. 'Italian, Colonel!'

'Sir Grenville?'

'Italian work, the plaster. Very fine, very fine!'

'Yes, sir.' Colonel Fuller would happily have let his men destroy the plasterwork with their firearms, but Sir Grenville had given him careful orders.

Sir Grenville Cony paused on the landing halfway up the stairs. He was in an excellent mood. He glanced down to where his secretary and his personal guard followed. 'I should marry, John! Lazen Castle needs a mistress, yes?' He laughed.

John Morse, who knew his master's views on women better than most, stopped in surprise. 'Marry?'

'That worries you, eh?' Sir Grenville laughed. 'There's an unmarried daughter to the house, isn't there, Colonel?'

'Yes, sir. Caroline.'

'Do you think she'd have me?' Sir Grenville barked with laughter. His men had never seen him in such high spirits. 'Never mind! Never mind! Who needs a penniless wife?'

The men on the staircase laughed.

Sir Grenville waved upwards, 'On, on! *Veni, vidi, vici!*'

Colonel Fuller who, more than Sir Grenville, had come, seen, and conquered Lazen Castle, went ahead of his patron and opened the long gallery door.

'Sir Grenville?'

'Ah! The gallery. I have heard so much of it.' He walked in. 'Who are you?'

Lady Margaret, sewing in a window seat, frowned at the interruption. 'Cony?'

Sir Grenville chuckled. 'You recognize me. The price of fame. I suppose you are Lady Margaret Lazender? Is it not customary to rise when the master of the house enters a room?'

Lady Margaret, who had seen the frog-like face of Sir Grenville in the garden, and who had made herself sit calmly in the window with her work, did not reply. She put a careful stitch into the laurel wreath she was embroidering about the crown that decorated the curtain square.

'Sir Grenville?' The Earl of Fleet, waiting further down the room, came forward.

'My Lord! I am surprised to find you here.'

'This is my wife's childhood home, Sir Grenville.'

'Of course! Of course!' Sir Grenville peered up at the plasterwork. 'Oh, very good! Most excellent.' He turned suddenly back to Fleet. 'My Lord! You must be overjoyed with the news from the north? A most excellent providence of God?'

Lady Margaret sniffed. The Earl of Fleet nodded. 'Indeed, sir.'

Sir Grenville laughed. He strutted into the room, looking at the decorations. 'God is indeed blessing our cause, my Lord. Blessing it richly!' He stopped in front of the fireplace, turning to face the room. 'I was delayed in my arrival. I thought it expedient to visit Essex. He misses you, my Lord.'

The Earl of Fleet had been forced to turn round as Cony passed him. 'I will return to my duties soon, Sir Grenville.'

'I never doubted it, my Lord, I never doubted it. May I ask what happy accident finds you in my house?'

The Earl of Fleet frowned. He hardly knew Sir Grenville Cony, though the name was familiar to him. He knew Sir Grenville was now on the Committee of Both Kingdoms, the committee of English and Scots that effectively ruled wherever the King did not. The Earl was in some awe of this small, gross man. Sir Grenville represented power, and a power that was conquering the land. 'I came, sir, for my mother-in-law.'

'You came for her? Why is she still here?'

Lady Margaret had her back to Cony. She did not turn round.

The Earl frowned again. 'Her son is ill, Sir Grenville.'

'Ill?'

'Wounded.'

'Ah! You mean the whelp was fighting against us, my Lord!' Sir Grenville shook his head. 'He is a prisoner, I suppose?'

Colonel Fuller spoke from the door. 'He's too ill, sir, to be a prisoner.'

Sir Grenville Cony smiled. He had looked forward to this moment. He had delayed it some days, going first to see the Earl of Essex who led an army that was trying to clear the west of Royalist troops. Now, that chore done, Sir Grenville was prepared to enjoy himself. A week at Lazen was a pleasant prospect, time to raise the rents and tally up the wealth of this new property. His frog-like eyes were wide on the Earl of Fleet. 'Is this a hospice, my Lord? Am I to tender charity to my enemies?'

The Earl looked astonished. 'This was his house, Sir Grenville. He cannot be moved.'

'Cannot? Cannot? There were those who said the King's tyranny could not be moved, but they were wrong.' He waved a careless hand. 'Move him! This afternoon. Now! I want the whole family out, you understand? Out!'

Lady Margaret, at last, moved. She put her sewing down, stood, and walked calmly towards Sir Grenville. She stopped opposite him, forcing him to look up at her. 'My son, Sir

Grenville, will die if he is moved. That is the physician's opinion.'

He smiled. 'I have never found physicians reliable in these matters.'

'My son will die.'

'That will teach him not to fight Parliament.' He smiled again. 'He was wanted, I believe, for treachery in London. His death, Lady Margaret, will only save the hangman effort.'

'You cannot force us to leave. My son will die.'

'I cannot! I cannot!' Sir Grenville laughed. 'Lady Margaret, this is my house now, not yours. You may stay as a scullery maid or as a seamstress, but your son will go. He will go now.'

'He will die.'

'Then let him die!'

She slapped him. A swift, open-palmed crack that echoed about the long gallery like a pistol shot. Sir Grenville raised his own arm, fury contorting his face, but the Earl of Fleet stepped forward, his sword already inches out of its scabbard. 'Sir Grenville!'

Cony's bodyguard, taken by surprise, looked on appalled. Sir Grenville, slowly, lowered his arm. 'You will get out of this house, Lady Margaret, you and your family, and you will take nothing, you hear? Nothing but your clothes. Nothing!' He turned to Fuller. 'They have one hour!'

'Yes, sir.'

Sir Grenville wheeled back. His eyes, angry now, looked at the Earl of Fleet. 'And you, my Lord, in this house of the enemy. I hear you wished to know the fate of Dorcas Slythe?'

The Earl of Fleet, surprised that his message should be so widely known, nodded.

Sir Grenville laughed. 'She'll be dead soon, if not yet. Either hung as a witch, or burned as a husband murderer.' He smiled. 'She was my enemy, my Lord, which I think you are now, too. Get out.'

Lady Margaret did not look back. She, Caroline and Anne

shared the Earl of Fleet's travelling coach with Toby. He lay on one bench, groaning. Colonel Washington, his eyes still bandaged, rode on the groom's seat outside. The servants whom Lady Margaret had asked to come walked behind. They skirted the ruins of the gatehouse and climbed into the humped northern hills which were grazed by Sir Grenville's sheep.

Lady Margaret held her son's hand and she knew, with a terrible sickness inside, that her enemies were winning. She had lost everything. Husband and house. Her son's life was flickering, her daughters were silent beside her. The Reverend Perilly caught up with the coach, riding his old nag. She smiled out of the window at him, knowing that he, like she, had nowhere to go.

Caroline sniffed. Lady Margaret frowned at her. 'Quiet, child! There's no need for tears.'

'But, mother . . .'

'Don't "but mother" me.' Lady Margaret heard James Wright's voice chivvying the horses up one of the slopes that led from the alder-bordered streams. 'We shall be back, Caroline. You can be sure of that. We shall be back.' She gripped her son's hand as if she would pour into Toby all her own formidable strength. 'We shall dance on that man's grave. We shall be back.'

20

Sunlight almost blinded Campion. She cried out, dazzled by the glare, tripped, and one of the two soldiers who had fetched her kicked her. 'Get up! Come on!'

They took her to a small, stone chamber. The July sun warmed these rooms, but she was still cold. Her hair was matted and filthy, some of Scammell's blood still clotted in it. She was cruelly thin. Her skin was scabrous and filthy, her body a thing of fleas and lice.

The soldiers had come for her, but had not told her why. She leaned on the stone wall and saw the ring of filth about her wrists. She rubbed at the dirt, spitting on it, but somehow the hopelessness of the effort made her cry. A soldier growled.

'Quiet, woman.'

She could hear voices, the murmuring of many voices like a church before the service began. The soldiers talked quietly to each other. One of them held a looped rope in his hands.

A door opened, the soldiers stiffened and a voice called out. Campion's elbow was taken, she was pushed forward, and she had an impression of a room crammed with people. There was a gasp as she appeared.

They took her to a single chair in the room's centre, forced her down, and then one soldier wrenched her arms behind the chair. She resisted, but was powerless as he tied her hands to the woodwork. Her breath was gulping now, the aftermath of crying.

'Dorcas Scammell?'

Her eyes were shut. She tried to control her breathing. The crowd behind her buzzed excitedly.

'Quiet!' The noise faded. 'Dorcas Scammell?'

The voice made her look up. Five men faced her, sitting behind a long table draped with a green cloth, their faces shadowed by the light from the window behind them. She blinked.

The man in the centre of the five spoke again. His voice was kind. 'Is your name Dorcas Scammell? I think that it is.' He was a pleasant-faced, middle-aged man.

Still she did not reply. The man looked to Campion's right. 'Is this Dorcas Scammell?'

'It is, sir.' The Reverend Faithful Unto Death, sharing a small table with another minister, rose halfway from his chair as he acknowledged the question.

The man behind the long table looked the other way. 'Record her answer as "yes".'

Two clerks, their hands stained with ink, sat behind a table on Campion's left. Their pens scratched.

The man looked back to Campion. 'I have the task of explaining to you what is happening. My name is Caleb Higbed and I am a lawyer. My companions are also lawyers.' He indicated the men who shared the long table with him. 'This is not your trial, Mrs Scammell, indeed there may not even be a trial!' He said this as if he was offering a child a piece of sugared fruit. 'Today, Mrs Scammell, we will ask you questions. We are a tribunal and the purpose of a tribunal is to draw up a presentment that we will give to the Grand Jury, and it will be the Grand Jury which decides if you are to stand trial. Do you understand?' He said it in such a kindly manner, leaning forward solicitously, that Campion nodded. Higbed leaned back, still smiling.

'Good! Good! Now I see you're accused of witchcraft, and that's why you will be questioned by ministers. That's what we always do with witchcraft.' He smiled again, somewhat apologetically. 'And that is why we have tied your hands. We don't want you flying away on a broomstick!' He raised his eyebrows at her impishly. 'Good! Good! Now I know that all of us are busy men, busy indeed, so I do not think we shall dally in this.' He pulled papers towards him. 'Are we agreed to take the two charges at once? Witchcraft and murder? They are combined, it seems?'

There were nods from the lawyers. Two of them put spectacles on their noses to examine papers. The crowd behind Campion murmured.

Caleb Higbed looked back at her, gave her his kindly smile. 'We'll begin, Mrs Scammell. Can you hear me clearly?'

She nodded.

'Will you speak, Mrs Scammell? It's important that the clerks can hear you.' He said this as if he was apologizing for troubling Campion with such an irrelevant manner.

She nodded. 'Yes.' It came out as a croak, so she cleared her throat, swallowed, and tried again. 'I can hear you.'

'Good! Good!' Caleb Higbed looked towards the

ministers. 'Mr Palley? I believe you wished to begin. Please do. And speak up, please!'

The Reverend Palley, a scowling, bald man, stood up and walked to the empty space before Campion. His hands clenched together. His voice, when he spoke, was deep and forceful. 'Shall we seek the Lord's guidance?'

Palley hammered God for ten minutes, praying that the truth would be exposed, that evil would be defeated and the tribunal echoed with amens and praises. When Palley finished he bawled out his own 'amen' and then, without drawing breath, turned his heavy face on Campion and shouted at her, 'When did you first practise witchcraft?'

She stared at him in fear and astonishment. She could feel tears coming. The question had been bellowed at her, Palley leaning forward with a face distorted by rage. The spittle from his lips specked her face. He waited ten seconds then flung an arm towards the clerks. 'Record that the witch refused to answer.'

He stared at her, his arms folded now, and he rocked back and forth on his big black shoes. 'Woman!' his voice was like something from the depths of the earth, 'it will go better with you if you confess now! Are you a witch?'

'No!' She shouted it defiantly. 'No!'

'Ha!' He span round to face the lawyers, his face triumphant. 'The devil ever protects his own, gentlemen! You see! She denied it, which is the devil speaking in her!' There were appreciative murmurs from the audience behind Campion at this irrefutable logic. The clerks scratched on their curling paper.

It seemed that the Reverend Palley's duty was to extract a confession which would spare the tribunal the bother of longer proceedings. He threatened her with the torture chamber, ranted at her, bullied her, but she repeated her simple denial. Each denial, Palley was careful to point out, was further proof of her guilt, and though Caleb Higbed professed himself sympathetic to that point of view, he nevertheless thought it sensible to adduce further proof. The

Reverend Palley, defeated, went back to the table he shared with the silent, watchful Faithful Unto Death Hervey.

Caleb Higbed shook his head ruefully. 'We have no simple denial, do we?' The lawyers agreed they did not and Higbed looked at Campion. 'We must hope for a clear truth, Mrs Scammell, you do understand that? Otherwise we must seek the truth through pain. I hope that will not be necessary. I'm sure it won't. Now,' he went back to his papers, 'perhaps we can establish some facts? I think so. Is Goodwife Baggerlie in the tribunal?'

Goodwife was, and a chair was brought forward by one of the soldiers. As Goodwife was not herself accused of witchcraft it was thought safe for the lawyers to address her with questions. Higbed smiled at her. 'You've known Mrs Scammell many years, Goodwife?'

'I have, sir. Since she was barely walking.'

'That long? Well, well! Perhaps you can tell us about her?'

Goodwife's litany of malice, honed by much repetition, was repeated to the tribunal. The pens scratched busily. Campion's childish wilfulness, her temper and all her small disobediences were now shown to be of devilish origin. Caleb Higbed prompted her, the pens duplicated the work of the Recording Angel and then the story was brought forward to the time of her marriage to Samuel Scammell. 'Did she consent to the marriage?'

Goodwife, her red face almost hidden by a new bonnet, looked at Campion, then back to the lawyers. 'Oh, yes, sir. She was fortunate. A good man, he was, better than she deserved. She said she agreed, sir, but she didn't. Oh, no!'

'What happened?'

'She ran away, sir! Ran away! Dressed as a harlot, sir! To London. And that when she should have been in mourning for her poor father, sir, God rest his soul.'

Yet all this was but an overture to Goodwife's grand theme, a theme she embellished wonderfully as she told of the marriage itself. She had been well coached, saying that the wedding had taken place in the legal hours between sunrise and noon, but claiming that Samuel Scammell was holding a service of celebration in his house by the Thames. 'Shrieking and crying she was, sir, calling out to the devil! Calling out to the devil, as my name's Goodwife! And he came, sir! He came!' She paused to let the horror sink in. 'A head of flame, sir, fire all around, sir, and a sword in his hand. And he took her, sir, right through the flames and she was unscathed. Unscathed!'

Caleb Higbed shook his head in wonder. 'You say the house was locked?'

'Tight, sir. Yet he came! The smell, sir! Oh, the smell. So long as I'll live, sir, I won't forget it. Brimstone and sulphur, just like the good book says, sir, and the next thing the Prince of Darkness was in the room, sir, right in the room! Killing, sir, burning, and her laughing.' A finger jabbed towards Campion. 'Laughing. And that poor Reverend Boolsbie, sir, you should have seen the poor old gentleman, sir . . .'

Caleb Higbed held up a hand. He guessed that 'Boolsbie' was Sobriety Bollsbie, a name that would not add much lustre to the prosecution. 'It must have been terrible for you, Goodwife, quite terrible. A cup of water?'

'Please, sir.'

The audience murmured as a cup of water was brought to Goodwife. One of the lawyers took off his spectacles and stared at Campion, shaking his head slowly.

The questioning was carried to the day of Scammell's death. Goodwife spoke of the body soaking in blood, of Campion alone with it, and she shook her head sadly. 'A big man he was, sir, and a kind man!' She sniffed. 'A man of God, sir. Only that morning he prayed with us, yes, sir! He girded on his armour, sir, and he went to do battle. And in the moment of victory, sir, he was cut down! Cut down! I found them, sir, him and her, and I looked at her and I thought she was scrawny and I couldn't see how a scrawny girl could kill a soldier of the Lord, sir, in all his armour, not unless, sir, there was a greater power in her. I thought that, sir, and then I remembered the devil coming for her, his head on fire, and I knew! I knew! I remembered all the spoiled hams, the curdled milk, and I thought of her poor dear mother's death and the sudden death of her father and I thought of her poor dear brother's twisted leg and I knew, sir! I fell on my knees right there, I did, and I thanked God that he had spared me. She's a witch!'

The crowd murmured. The lawyers were silent for a moment. Only the pens scratched.

'Did you see the witch mark?'

'Oh, yes, sir. Plain as the nose on her face! I saw it, sir. God is my witness.'

It was not necessary to call on God so long as the Reverend Faithful Unto Death Hervey was at hand. This was his moment. Goodwife was helped back to her place in the audience and Higbed silently signalled Hervey to stand. The tribunal was hushed now, shocked by the story they had heard, and in the quietness Faithful Unto Death Hervey slid from behind the table and walked slowly up and down in front of the lawyers. For a few seconds it seemed he would not speak, but then he jerked his head up, stopped walking, and looked at the audience over Campion's head.

'This is a sadness to us, a great and manifold sadness, that this girl, whom I numbered among my flock, should now be seen as a servant of the enemy. And no earthly enemy! No! She is the devil's spawn! Yes! He is among us as a raging lion! The devil! Lucifer! Apollyon! Beelzebub! Satan!' He stopped, eyes glaring at the audience. He dropped his voice, becoming almost confidential. The two clerks had stopped writing. 'He was in the Garden of Eden, brothers and sisters, and as we in this country try to plant a new garden, a kingdom of heaven, he is back! Yes! The devil!' He pointed a dramatic finger at Campion. 'Dorcas. Did you have a familiar?'

She said nothing. Faithful Unto Death's Adam's apple slid down his throat as he shook his head. 'She is reduced to silence, brethren, for the truth is not in her.' He shook his head again sadly, turned a pace or two up the room, and stopped again. 'In the room where we found her good husband's body, in that room, brethren, there was a cat. A dead cat. It is my belief, and it can be no more unless Almighty God wrings from this wretched woman a confession of her evil, that the cat, the dead cat, was Dorcas Scammell's familiar.' He sighed.

'You heard, all of you!' Here he swept his finger round to encompass the lawyers at their table. 'You heard Goodwife puzzle how a slim girl, of no strength, could overcome an armed man in the prime of his life. She did not, brethren, she did not!' He leaned towards the audience, in full flow now. 'The devil did it! The devil! For he had given her a familiar! It is my belief, my prayerful belief, that the cat, at her command, tore the throat from our dear departed brother. Oh, brethren! Strange are the workings of evil. Brother Scammell, calling upon the Lord, killed his assailant, thus rendering the witch powerless, but in winning this battle over the cat he lost his own life too.' He paused for effect and in the pause Caleb Higbed cleared his throat and spoke in his mild, friendly voice.

'Reverend Hervey? It is our duty to provide a full presentment to the Grand Jury, men not as conversant with demonology as yourself. Would you be good enough to describe a "familiar"?'

'Indeed.' Faithful Unto Death resumed his pacing, frowning now so as to give his lecture the full weight of academic authority. 'A witch, gentlemen, is a servant of the devil, yet the devil cannot be always with each of his servants. He is not omnipresent. In his place he furnishes each witch with a familiar. Customarily this will be either a cat or a toad. I have known it to be a goat, but normally, as I said, a cat or a toad.' He turned at the end of the room, paced back. 'The familiar, gentlemen, whispers the instructions of the devil, its master, into the ear of the witch. It can also, as in this case, act on her behalf. There is more!' He turned again. 'The familiar, though disguised as an earthly animal, cannot endure earthly sustenance for all good things come from

Almighty God and thus, to provide an example, a cat-familiar, eating an earthly mouse, would be sickened by the food.' He stopped and faced the audience. 'Instead, brethren, the witch herself provides sustenance. The devil provides her with a third teat, disguised as a bodily blemish, and from this teat she will give her familiar suck of the vileness within her. That, gentlemen!' and here he whipped round to face the lawyers, 'that is the true test of a witch. The third teat!'

One of Higbed's companions, who had not yet spoken, leaned forward. 'You are an expert, Brother Hervey?'

'Alas, sir, yes. It is a miserable field for study, strewn with thorns, serpents, and constantly threatened by the evil one, yet there are those of us, a few, who labour in that foul vineyard for the better protection of the people of God.'

The lawyer took off his spectacles. 'You saw this witch mark?'

'I did, sir!'

The lawyer smiled. 'How can you tell, brother, what is a witch mark, and what is a normal bodily blemish?'

Hervey smiled. 'The Good Lord has provided proof, sir, and I will show you that proof.' His Adam's apple was going up and down. He turned again to the audience, walking past Campion towards them. 'The third teat, brethren, is a protuberance, as you might expect, for how else will the familiar take hold!' His voice was close behind her now. He paused. 'Your assistance, soldier.'

She screamed, she fought with the man, but she was hopelessly weak. The soldier had one foot on her feet, his hands on her right shoulder, while Faithful Unto Death leaned over her and slit her filthy dress open. It had been sewn up during the journey to London, but now he ripped it open, helping with a small, pointed knife in his hand.

Faithful Unto Death could feel the excitement thick within him. He had wanted this girl, thinking she was unattainable, but it had come to him, as if in a blaze of light, that the study of witchcraft could be the way to many womens' bodies. This

girl was filthy now, stained and stinking, her ribs showing, but even so he felt the heavy thrill of this act. He pulled the tattered edges of the dress apart.

'There!' The lawyers stared.

She jerked, twisted, hearing the soldier's breath loud in her ear as he leaned over to look at her breasts. Only the Reverend Palley did not look, staring instead at his clasped hands on the table.

'There!' The Reverend Faithful Unto Death Hervey slid his left hand down her skin until his index finger pointed close to the mole above her navel. 'A protuberance, gentlemen!'

The clerks had stopped writing and stared instead. Two soldiers sidled down the wall for a better view.

Campion screamed again, the scream turning into sobs. She pulled at her bonds, hurting her wrists, but she was unable to move, unable to hide herself from this humiliation. She felt the Reverend Hervey's left hand spread itself on her stomach, pushing into her skin, and then she saw, in his right hand, the knife going past her eyes.

'No! No!'

His voice whispered in her ear. 'Stay still, Dorcas, quite still. You won't be hurt if you're still. Quiet now!'

She was frightened. Her breath heaved in great gasps. She looked at Hervey, his face close to her left shoulder, and he smiled. The knife in the right hand went lower. He looked away from her eyes, down to the mole, and suddenly she felt the cold tip of the knife on her belly. It stayed there, quite sharp, and she heard him grunt and it seemed to her that he had pretended to force the knife into her belly. She felt no pressure, only the cold, needle-sharp tip of the blade on her skin.

Suddenly he leaped away from her, holding the knife in the air. 'See? No pain! You saw me, gentlemen, you saw me! You saw the knife on the witch mark, you saw me dig it in! Yet did she cry out? Did she struggle? No! And that, gentlemen, is the way to distinguish a witch mark from a natural blemish. The first will not feel pain, the second will!

The devil frees the teat from pain, for it might be clamped by a cat's teeth or clawed by a toad! Yes!' He sheathed his small knife.

Campion's head was bowed now, the tears running down her cheeks and falling on to her naked breasts. Hervey came back to her, stood behind her, and his hands came over her shoulders and clamped on to her breasts. They were cold and dry. His fingers kneaded her, holding her still, and he groped and pressed, rubbed and squeezed as he talked over her filthy hair. 'See, gentlemen! The mark of the devil!' He tilted the chair back, began turning it, and she wrenched her body uselessly. He swung her round, staying always behind her, until she faced the benches on which the audience sat. He took her right nipple in his fingers. 'See, brethren? A teat, a woman's teat, provided by God for the sustenance of the young. And here!' The hand slid to her belly again. 'The devil's mark!' He took his right hand away, leaving his left hand to stroke her left breast. The audience stared. They were mostly men, mostly friends of the lawyers or of the officers in the Tower's garrison, and it was for this that they had come. A witch was not uncovered at a trial, only at the tribunal that gathered the facts for the Grand Jury. They stared. Those at the rear stood up. Faithful Unto Death put his dry, cold hands on her breasts again and rubbed his palms down her body, either side of the mole, until his fingers were probing at her pelvic bones. 'Look well, brethren! The body of a witch!' He brought his hands up again, right to her shoulders, and then tipped the chair once more, swung her, and she again faced the lawyers. Hervey stepped away.

She was filthy, defiled, broken. She could not even cover her nakedness. She felt a revulsion of men, of their traffic with women, and she was once more smeared with the horrid filth that obscured the innocence she had once felt beside a summer stream. She sobbed.

'Can she not be covered?' the Reverend Palley's strong, indignant voice demanded.

Cloth was found, a piece of sacking that was stuffed under

the door in winter to keep out draughts. Her shame galled her. She was defiled.

Faithful Unto Death Hervey stared at her. Her head was bowed, her upper body draped with the sacking. He slowly raised a finger that pointed at her, 'A witch revealed!'

They were reluctant now to let her go. Caleb Higbed peered hopefully at Faithful Unto Death. 'Are there other tests?'

'There are, sir.' Hervey began his pacing again. 'A woman suspected of witchcraft can be thrown, bound hand and foot, into a pool. If she sinks, gentlemen, then she is innocent. If she floats, then the devil is holding her up.'

Higbed chuckled. 'Then every dead dog in the Tower moat must be an angel of hell.' He seemed to consider for a moment taking Campion to the moat or river, but evidently decided it was impractical. 'Another test?'

Hervey nodded. 'There is one, sir.'

'Pray proceed, Brother Hervey.'

Faithful Unto Death reached into a pocket and brought out a black-bound Bible. 'The Lord's Prayer, gentlemen, the Lord's Prayer.' He turned the pages. 'It is a fact that no witch can repeat the words of the Lord's Prayer. They are words of such power, of such holiness, that the devil will not allow his own to utter them! Oh! She might say the words, but at some point she will choke, or cry out, for the filthiness inside her will revolt against the purity of the words.'

It was not the kind of test that the lawyers had in mind, preferring some other examination of her body, but they were tempted. The simplicity of the test worried one man who muttered that where would they be if she succeeded, but Caleb Higbed waved the Reverend Faithful Unto Death closer to Campion. 'We must be sure, Brother Hervey, we must be sure! This is a tribunal of law and we must be fair to the prisoner!'

The Bible, open at the sixth chapter of Matthew, was put on her lap. The pages, tightly bound, immediately fanned upwards, obscuring the text, but Campion had no need to read the words. She knew them. She sobbed still, but quietly now, as the Reverend Faithful Unto Death went behind her. 'You see, gentlemen? She cannot even begin! She is dumb!'

' "Our Father!" ' Campion silenced him with a sudden, strong voice, a voice that came from an inner strength and a determination to fight back against this persecution. She had prayed, quickly and silently, for this strength, and now her voice rang hard and clear in the stone room. ' "Which art in heaven, hallowed be thy name. Thy Kingdom come. Thy will be done in earth, as it is in heaven." ' She poured her soul into the words, giving them the breath of meaning, intelligence and love. Her eyes were closed, but her head was up, and she spoke the words, not to this tribunal, but to the Christ of love who had also faced enemies who were priests and lawyers. ' "Give us this day our daily bread. And forgive us our debts, as we forgive our debtors." ' None of the lawyers moved, even the clerks stared, wondering if she could finish. Her voice was strong. ' "And lead us not into temptation, but deliver us from evil." ' And Faithful Unto Death Hervey, close behind her, jabbed the knife through the bars of the chair, digging the point into the skin over her ribs, twisting, and she cried out with the sudden pain, her eyes opening.

'You see!' Faithful Unto Death was fumbling the knife into his pocket. 'She cannot say the words! She cannot! See how she twists? See the agony of the fiend within her?' He took the Bible from her lap. 'She is a witch!'

'No!'

Faithful Unto Death was backing away from her, his finger pointing at her. 'A witch!'

' "Our Father, which art in heaven, hallowed be thy name. Thy Kingdom come. Thy will be done in earth as it is in heaven." ' She was shouting the words defiantly, but Faithful Unto Death stepped close to her, slapped her once, twice, and then a third time.

'Blasphemer!' Faithful Unto Death bellowed.

The audience were roused now, growling at her,

applauding Faithful Unto Death. Campion's face hurt. The
noise behind her was threatening and Caleb Higbed, fearing
that these decorous, legal proceedings were getting out of
hand, thumped his right hand on the table top. 'Silence!
Silence!' He waited for the excitement to die, then smiled. 'I
think we've heard enough. Yes?' The lawyers nodded. Caleb
Higbed shuffled the papers in front of him. 'The hour of
lunch approaches and I know we must be hungry.' He
chuckled good-naturedly. 'I have to thank the Reverend
Faithful Unto Death Hervey, and of course the Reverend
Palley.' The two divines gave him small bows. Caleb Higbed
looked at Campion. 'An interesting morning. We shall
present our findings, our presentment, to the Grand Jury and
they will decide whether you are to stand trial.' He smiled at
her, then nodded to the soldiers. 'You may take her away,
and thank you for your help!'

They took her to her foetid cell, threw her in and the door
clanged on her unchanging winter night. She sat in the straw,
glad almost to be alone in her own place, and she scrubbed
her breasts with the sacking, scrubbed till the skin was chafed
and her nipples sore, but nothing could remove the sense of
defiling filth. She leaned her head against the cold, wet stone,
and cried. She was doomed.

Ebenezer Slythe had watched his sister's humiliation. He had
sat at the end of the last row of benches and he knew she had
not seen him. She had been in no state to see anyone, and he
smiled as he remembered her former confidence. As a child,
oppressed by Matthew and Martha Slythe, she had always
retained a hopeful air, a sense that life would be better, and
Ebenezer had resented her ebullient, vivid personality. He
had resented that she could run, skip, laugh, while he was
imprisoned in a twisted, lamed body. Now he had seen the
life wrung from her soul.

He waited until the room cleared, then followed the
lawyers out on to the small patch of grass before the Tower's
chapel. Caleb Higbed saw him, made excuses to the men he

talked with, and came across. 'Mr Slythe. You're content?'

'And grateful to you, sir.' Ebenezer did not want to offend
Caleb Higbed, a successful and influential lawyer. 'I assume
there will be no problems?'

'Problems, ah!' Caleb Higbed stretched his back, turning
his rubicund, kindly face to the sun. 'What a lovely day! You
know there's a field of poppies at Houndsditch? I passed it
yesterday in the sunlight and it was quite wonderful! I've
often pondered how many wild flowers grow in our city. We
have some scarlet pimpernel in Gray's Inn, and very good
they look too.' He smiled around him, looking at sunlight on
grey walls. 'Now then, problems. Shall we walk? Or are you
enhorsed?'

'I'm riding back.'

'Ah! You see so much more on foot, Mr Slythe, you truly
do.' He looked at Ebenezer's limp. 'Still, I do understand.
Problems.' He had stopped again. 'I do wonder, Mr Slythe, I
truly do, whether you would not have been wiser to restrict
the prosecution to simple murder. I suppose there's no doubt
but that she did slay her husband?'

'There's no doubt, sir.'

'A soul will go to hell for murder as surely as for
witchcraft. Still, it's too late to change the charge, I
suppose?' He looked hopefully at Ebenezer.

'Sir Grenville, sir, was insistent on witchcraft.'

'Ah! Sir Grenville! Good Sir Grenville!' Caleb Higbed
laughed. 'A Chancery man, but we can teach him no law, eh,
Mr Slythe? Indeed not. So witchcraft it will be, with an added
touch of murder.' He turned to watch a file of soldiers march
towards the main gate. The sun flashed on pikes and
breastplates. 'Such a fine sight I always think.' He looked
back to Ebenezer, smiling. 'I've no doubt the Grand Jury will
find for us, no doubt at all, but I have one small worry.
Small, Mr Slythe, but a worry nonetheless.'

'Sir?'

'It is a question, Mr Slythe, of *maleficio*.' He nodded, as if
he had made a good point.

Ebenezer, respectful and grave, smiled. '*Maleficio*, sir?'

'Ah! The lawyer's disease! Expecting those who are not lawyers to understand us. *Maleficio*, Mr Slythe, is demanded by the Witchcraft Act of '04. In brief, the act says that no person can be convicted of witchcraft, teats or no teats, unless the prosecution establishes that they were motivated by *maleficio*. That they had previously stated, clearly stated, that they wished to destroy the victim of their malevolence. In your sister's case, Mr Slythe, we must have proof that she intended to kill her husband by witchcraft, and that she had publicly said as much. Do you follow me?'

Ebenezer shook his head in astonishment. 'But that's nonsense! No witch will announce her intentions!'

'Ah, nonsense! How often our laws seem nonsense to the young! And how right you doubtless are, but the law is the law, Mr Slythe, and we are, so to speak, mired in it. I think what we need is either a witness who will testify that she heard your sister expressing malice and an intention to kill, or we need a confession.' He shook his head. 'I had great hopes of Palley, but he failed.'

'A confession?'

'Freely given, if possible.' Higbed nodded. 'Which raises another point, Mr Slythe.'

'Sir?'

Caleb Higbed squinted up at the great White Tower. 'Kestrels nested there last year, I haven't seen them this year. A colleague told me they had been shot, which is a pity. Yes, Mr Slythe, another small problem. You can, I am sure, torture a confession from her, and most valuable that would be, but if she is to be tortured then I think she may end up looking even more wretched than she does now. Am I right?'

Ebenezer nodded to the lawyer's eager, friendly face. 'True, sir.'

Caleb Higbed smiled. 'We'll convict, fear not, Mr Slythe, but we must take all precautions. I thought I discerned beneath the layers of filth on your sister the lineaments of beauty. Indeed so. Is she a pretty girl?'

Ebenezer frowned. 'She is.'

'You are puzzled!' Higbed laughed. 'I think you will find twenty years in the law have not addled my head, Mr Slythe. Think of this. Your sister will be taken before a judge and jury. We will tell them, we will prove to them, that she is a witch, a murderer and a Royalist! And what do they see? They see a wretched girl, thin and pale, crying helplessly, and who can blame them if they feel some pity?' He raised a hand. 'Oh, I'm sure they will convict, but there is a chance, a tiny chance, that they will see in her fragility a helplessness that arouses their pity. I know two things of men and women, Mr Slythe. The first is that if a man pities a woman, he will try to help her. We don't want to risk that.'

Ebenezer shifted his weight, dipping on to his maimed left leg and straightening again. 'The second thing, sir?'

'Ah, the second thing. If men see a woman in the pride of her beauty, dressed in the finery of her gender, they will often resent it. Why should one man be allowed to possess such a woman while they are condemned to share a bed with a shrewish, sickly, ugly old wife?' He laughed. 'I speak not from personal experience! And when, Mr Slythe, our jury of freeholders see such a beautiful, proud woman they have but one thought in mind. If they cannot possess her, they will destroy her! Have you noticed, Mr Slythe, how men like to destroy beautiful things? So give them something to destroy! Besides, she's supposed to be a witch! A Royalist! Make them hate her!'

'I should clean her up?'

'How acute you are. More than that! For a small sum, a paltry sum, ten pounds only, you can have her housed well here, with matrons to attend her. She must be washed, clothed, and she must be fed! Buy her a pretty dress, something that will show her off! Make her look like a harlot, as Goodwife described her! And get a confession!'

Ebenezer frowned. He could think of no way of getting a confession except by pain.

Higbed laughed. 'Sir Grenville says you're a rising young

man, Mr Slythe, and not bereft of intelligence. Think of a way! You'll find one! And have her cleaned up! That way we'll be sure!'

Caleb Higbed bade Ebenezer farewell, and walked back through the city, beaming greetings at old acquaintances. It was none of his business why a brother should want a sister destroyed, nor were such family quarrels so unusual. He doubted, personally, whether witchcraft existed, but lawyers were not paid for their beliefs, only their skill in making other people believe. He would prosecute, and he had no doubt that he would win, and it would be a small favour to Sir Grenville Cony who was a fount of patronage and success. He nodded cheerfully to the guards at Ludgate. 'A fine day, my men, a fine day!'

God was in his heaven, the King had lost at Marston Moor and all was well in a Protestant world.

In her cell, rocking in seeming madness, Campion sang a line over and over, her voice wavering in the chill dankness. ' "Teach me to hear mermaids singing, teach me to hear mermaids singing." ' She was doomed.

21

All was not well with Faithful Unto Death Hervey. Ambition is a hard master, not satisfied with small gains, wanting only complete success, and that complete success eluded Faithful Unto Death. He could not complain too loudly, for Ebenezer had provided him with an ample house in Seething Lane, a house that was magnificently kept by Goodwife, yet comfort in London was not enough. Fame still eluded him.

He could console himself with the first small signs of fame. Three ministers had called on him, two to learn from him the art of detecting witches. He had sent them away to pray that God would armour them against the devil. He had received one invitation to preach, but that Sunday it had rained torrentially and few parishioners turned up at St Mary's Overie. Besides, St Mary's was across the river in Southwark, and Faithful Unto Death dreamed of filling the preaching house that was once St Paul's with his impassioned oratory.

The case of Dorcas Scammell had attracted attention, but the news of war, of the success in the north, gave London a greater subject for talk. A Royalist witch, locked in the Tower, was not so fascinating as tales of a beaten army and stories of good Protestants slaying the King's troops. Dorcas Scammell's execution would be popular, drawing the crowds to Tower Hill, but Faithful Unto Death knew too that a Roman Catholic priest had been discovered in Bedford and tried, and his execution would come first. Nothing cheered London so much as the sight of a burning Papist. It even made the shortages in the shops seem momentarily worthwhile.

Fame was eluding Faithful Unto Death. He fretted over the problem, prayed about it, and paced long hours in his comfortable, upper chamber. The answer to his prayers, when it came, was astonishingly simple. It was late one night, the candles bright on his desk, when he was reading the newest *Mercurius Britanicus* London's chief news-sheet, and he scanned the latest account of Parliament's siege of York. It was going well, the commanders of the army winning the renown denied to Faithful Unto Death, when suddenly his hands shook with excitement. Of course! His melancholy torpor was over, he seized paper and ink and sharpened a goose-quill with fervent expectation. For two hours he wrote. He corrected, amended, and it was well past three in the morning when he leaned back, tired but happy, sure that he was at last to be rewarded.

He was not mistaken. The editor of the *Mercurius* had been given small news to print since the glorious victory of the Saints at Marston Moor. The fall of York was daily expected, indeed he had already set the story in type and waited only for the messengers, but in the meantime there

was not much to inflame London's passions. Then, into his dusty, crowded office, came Faithful Unto Death with his account of Dorcas Scammell. The editor liked it.

The story was printed at great length. It told of the devil appearing in London and burning down part of Thames Street. It described the murder of Captain Samuel Scammell, 'a doughtie warrior of ye Lord', and the editor commissioned a woodcut that showed Dorcas Scammell's cat tearing the throat from an armed man whose sword was being restrained by a leering Satan. Campion, nails held out like claws, urged the cat on. The artist gave her black hair, a sharp nose, and missing teeth.

The story then paid tribute to Ebenezer Slythe who had 'putte familie love aside, preferring the Love of Almightie God, and in Sorrow and Pain broughte His Sister from Lazen', yet that brief acknowledgement of his patron was as nothing compared to the glory given to himself by the Reverend Faithful Unto Death Hervey. He had written his account in the third person, and it dwelt lovingly on his discovery of her witchcraft, of the devil's mark, and how he had pinioned her to the floor 'strengthened by the strength of Him who is Mightier than the Devil'. In his account, the Reverend Faithful Unto Death described the subduing of the witch as a titanic battle, a mighty foretaste of the clash between good and evil at Armageddon, but one which, strengthened by the Lord, he had won. Then, with a stroke of genius, he condemned Campion properly.

The Reverend Faithful Unto Death Hervey had been puzzled when Ebenezer insisted on forgetting the presence of the crucifix in the jewel about Campion's neck. He had asked Ebenezer and the young man had smiled. 'Don't you think there are enough plums in the pie, Brother Hervey?' Brother Hervey did not. Catholicism was the matter which scared Londoners. Witchcraft was not common in the capital, happening more in the country areas, but if Faithful Unto Death could give London a witch who was also a Roman Catholic then he knew he could arouse the interest and fanaticism of the mob. That groundswell of public hate and indignation would carry Faithful Unto Death to fame.

Mercurius Britanicus revealed that Dorcas Scammell was a Roman Catholic. She bore, about her neck, a crucifix. 'Itt was a strange Crucificks, that emblem of the Devil, that the Witch wore. She was att pains to Conceal it, to which end it had beene cunningly hidden within a jewelled Seale so that noe man might Perceive its proper nature. Yet Almightie God in His goodnesse Revealed it to His Servant Faithful Unto Death Hervey and thus Defeated the Wiles of the Evil One as Wee praye He will continue so to doe.'

The Reverend Faithful Unto Death Hervey was pleased with his work. He had tied witchcraft to Catholicism and both to the Royalists, and in so doing he had ensured himself the lion's share of the credit. The editor of *Mercurius*, sensing that the tale would prove popular with his readers, wrote his own comments on the story. He praised Faithful Unto Death and warned Protestant England that the Devil was indeed in the land, and then he spoke of Faithful Unto Death's determination to grub out all witches who would destroy the purity of the kingdom of God. At Faithful Unto Death's urging he added a further paragraph. Faithful Unto Death, he said, did not want women to live in fear. Any woman, be she poor or rich, could visit the Reverend Faithful Unto Death Hervey in Seething Lane, and there he would prayerfully examine her and issue, for a trifling sum, a certificate that bore witness to the absence of the devil. Thus armed, no woman needed to fear.

It was a stroke of genius. Within days of the *Mercurius* being distributed, Faithful Unto Death Hervey was besieged by women who sought his certificates. Fame was his overnight. He was asked to preach in the city, in Westminster, in parishes far from London, yet he could not accept all the invitations. He was busy, toiling day and night with the women who came to consult him; whose bodies he searched minutely for devilish protuberances. He worked faithfully in God's vineyard, a happy man at last.

'Christ on his cross! Who did it? For God's sake who?' Sir Grenville Cony, newly returned to London, was furious, more furious than Ebenezer had ever seen him. The small man thumped a fist down on the *Mercurius*. 'Are there nothing but fools in this city? I go for two weeks, no more! And when I come back! This!' He sat, hands clutching his great belly. 'For God's sake! How, Ebenezer?'

Ebenezer shrugged. He stood staring across the river at the Lambeth marshes. 'Hervey, I suppose.'

'Hervey! Damned Hervey. Wasn't he warned?'

'Not in so many words.'

'Christ! Are words so damned expensive? Why wasn't he warned?'

Ebenezer turned his expressionless gaze on Sir Grenville. 'It was my fault.'

The confession of guilt seemed to mollify Sir Grenville. He picked up the *Mercurius* and stared at the crude woodcut. 'You must always, always, know what your people are doing. God! Men are such fools! If you didn't point it at the ground for them they'd piss up their nostrils. God's bowels, Ebenezer!'

Ebenezer well understood Sir Grenville's anger. The *Mercurius Britanicus*, as the most important news-sheet of the rebels, was distributed far from London. Copies went, fresh from the press, to the cities of Europe where money had been lent to the warring sides. The bankers of Florence, of the Low Countries, of Venice were desperately interested in the war's progress. One battle could mean their loan was safe, a defeat could mean ruin. As Sir Grenville had shouted earlier, the *Mercurius* was available in Amsterdam before it reached the Parliamentary army in the north. He had shrieked a question at Ebenezer: 'And who's in Amsterdam?'

'Lopez.'

'Lopez! That damned, filthy Jew. Lopez!'

Now Sir Grenville shook his head. His voice seemed to be a moan of pain. 'That bastard priest described the seal! For God's sake! The seal!'

'You think Lopez will come?'

Sir Grenville nodded grimly. 'He'll come, Ebenezer. He'll come!'

'What can he do? He can't take her from the Tower? You have two seals.'

Sir Grenville leaned back, his gaze sour on the younger man. He remembered his astrologer, Barnegat, saying an enemy would come across the seas and Sir Grenville was inflicted with a sharp stab of pain in his belly. Aretine! That damned Aretine! He feared Kit Aretine. But Aretine was dead, his grave halfway across the world in the American wilderness. Sir Grenville shook his head. 'There's nothing he can do, Ebenezer, but he might try. I don't want complications. Do you understand? I want that damned girl dead and then we will have nothing to fear.' He rubbed his white, round face with both hands. 'We must bring the trial forward. Look after that! See Higbed. Tell him we'll pay whatever's necessary. But bring the trial forward!'

'Yes.'

'And double the guard on this house! Triple it!' The bulging eyes still had anger in them.

'You're certain you want me to do that?'

'I am certain. God! I am certain!' Sir Grenville remembered the handsome face of his enemy, he remembered the reckless daring that had eventually put Kit Aretine into the Tower. His voice was gloomy. 'Lopez got a man out of the Tower before.'

'Not this time.' Ebenezer smiled.

'Get that trial forward, Ebenezer! Get it forward!'

Ebenezer shrugged. He raised his eyebrows as he drew his hand across his neck. Sir Grenville shook his head, though he was tempted simply to have the girl killed.

'No. Aretine's dead, Ebenezer, but the bastard had friends. If the girl dies, there'll be a vengeance. But they can't take vengeance on a whole country. No. Let the law kill her, and then no one can accuse us.' Sir Grenville looked at the sentence in *Mercurius*: 'Ebenezer Slythe putte familie love aside, preferring the Love of Almightie God, and in Sorrow and Pain broughte His Sister from Lazen'. Sir Grenville began to laugh, his fat shoulders heaving up and down, and the laugh grew louder. It was a strange contrast to his previous anger. He held a shaking finger out to his protégé whose face, pale and cold, was not amused. 'You'd better get yourself a bodyguard, Ebenezer! A bodyguard. You're rich enough!' He put his frog-face back and bellowed with laughter. 'And watch your back, Ebenezer! Always watch your back!'

On the day after the tribunal they fetched Campion again, dragging her from the horrid cell and forcing her up winding stairs and down long passageways. She thought that she must face another ordeal, and she whimpered at the horrors she imagined, but to her surprise the guards took her into a pleasant, well-lit building and pushed her into a sunlit, warm room. The floor was carpeted. The windows, though barred, were large and velvet-curtained. Two women waited for her. They were kind, in their matter-of-fact way, and they stripped her, bathed her, washed her hair, and then put her in a great, warmed bed. One of them brought a tray of food, hot food, and sat by her and helped her eat. 'We're feeding you up, dear.'

It seemed to Campion that every thought, every action, took minutes for her. She ate clumsily, still not understanding what was happening, though the feel of clean skin, of freedom from lice, of hair that was washed fine, was wonderful to her. It seemed heavenly. She cried, and the woman patted her.

'That's all right, dear, you cry. It's good for you.'

'Why are you doing this?'

The woman smiled. 'You've got friends now, dear. Friends. We all need friends. Now eat up all the pastry! That's it! That's a good girl.'

They let her sleep. When she woke it was evening. A fire burned in the small parlour and one of the women waited with a jug of wine and yet more food. Campion wore a great wool robe, and her hair was tied in a ribbon. The woman smiled. 'Warm enough, dear?'

'Yes.'

'You sit by the fire.'

It was marvellous to be clean, to be warm, but she still felt filthy inside. She shrank from the memory of Faithful Unto Death touching her, sliding his dry hands over her skin. Nothing, she thought, could ever be the same again. She had been mired in Hervey's filth, and it could not be removed. Yet what did it matter? She had no future. Someone had paid for this comfort—she assumed it was Lady Margaret for she could think of no one else, and she knew it to be a kindness that her last days on this earth should not be spent in filth. She looked at the woman. 'How's Toby?'

'Toby? I don't know any Tobys, dear. We've got a syllabub in the kitchen. Would you like some?'

The next day, standing at the barred window of the bedroom, she looked down on a small, greying man who walked up and down in the tiny courtyard beneath her window. He walked the same course every day so that his shoes had made scars on the grass. One of her new gaolers nodded down at him. 'That's the Archbishop, dear.'

'William Laud?'

'That's right, dear. He's been cut down to size.' She laughed. 'He'll be cut down some more soon, I shouldn't wonder.'

Campion watched the Archbishop of Canterbury as he walked, up and down, up and down, his head bowed over a book. He was a prisoner like her. Like her he faced the services of the executioner. He looked up once, saw her, and gave a slight inclination of his head. She raised a hand and he smiled. Thereafter she looked for him each day, and he for her, and they would smile through the window bars.

Then, as if her blessings could only increase, a lawyer came to see her. He was called Francis Lapthorne and he exuded certainty that she could win her trial. The Grand Jury had committed her to judge and jury. She asked Mr Lapthorne who had sent him, but he just smiled and winked. 'Now that would be dangerous, Miss Slythe, most dangerous. Even stone walls have ears! But be glad I'm here.'

She was. 'How's Toby?'

He smiled. 'You have nothing to worry about. Nothing! Do you understand?'

A smile spread on her face, a smile of such delight and love that Mr Lapthorne was touched. He was a youngish man, in his thirties, with a fine face and a deep, expressive voice. He laughed at her happiness. 'You're crying! Let me give you a handkerchief.'

He laughed too at the evidence of the presentment. 'You a witch, my dear? It's nonsense! Nonsense! Now that Goodwife could be, oh yes! A secret, black and midnight hag if ever there was!' He was full of plans. He would summon witnesses from the London watch who had fought the fire at Scammell's yard and he would take statements from them that none had seen the devil that night. He scoffed at the thought of a cat killing an armed man, or of Campion murdering Samuel Scammell. Campion's spirits began to rise. On his second visit he made her recite the Lord's Prayer and he applauded her when she had finished. 'Wonderful! Wonderful! You'll do it in court?'

'If no one sticks a knife in my back.'

'They tried that, did they? I wondered. Dear, oh dear!' Mr Lapthorne shook his head. 'If only I had been there. Still! I'm here now!' He pulled a leather bag on to the table and took from it a quill, an inkpot, and a great sheaf of papers. He unclipped the lid of the ink and pushed it, with the pen, towards her. 'You've got to work now, Dorcas.'

'Call me Campion.' She smiled shyly.

'Campion! What a lovely name. What a lovely name. Your middle name?'

She nodded, not wishing to explain.

'Campion! Splendid. You must sign papers, Campion. So many papers! I sometimes think we lawyers will choke ourselves with paper. Let's start here.'

He had written out her own story, telling the truth, and she skimmed through it, admiring the style, and signed her name. Then followed a batch of receipts, acknowledging favours received in the Tower. He smiled when she queried those. 'We want your gaolers to be happy, don't we? It makes a good impression in court if they smile at you, help you. The jury knows you can't be such a bad girl after all. Don't worry. We'll pay a little money here and there as well.'

Then he put a pile of letters on the table. They were requests for witnesses to come forward. Twenty-four alone were to members of the watch, another forty-five were for soldiers who had served at the siege of Lazen Castle. Francis Lapthorne said he had taken their names from the Parliamentary muster rolls, and he rubbed his hands with glee. 'We'll make them regret this trial, my dear! Oh yes! We'll make them look the fools they are!' He laughed at her suggestion that the Roundhead soldiers would be afraid to give testimony. 'The law is the law, my dear. You've seen a harsh side of it, but you'll find it can be a tender preserver of the truth too. They'll come if they are ordered. Now, you read the letters and then you sign them.'

She laughed at the great pile. 'Read all of them?'

'Always read what you sign, my dear.' He laughingly allowed that the letters were all duplicates of each other, but made her read through the top copy. Then he fanned them out on the table. He watched her write her signature again and again and, as she did so, explained that he had thought it far too dangerous to invite Lady Margaret or the Reverend Perilly to give evidence as she had suggested. 'This is not the time for avowed Royalists to be in London. You do understand?'

'I do.'

'But worry not! We will win, indeed we will!' Francis Lapthorne sanded her signatures, tipped the sand off and packed the papers away.

'Is that all?'

'You want more?' He laughed. 'That's all, my dear.'

He promised to return the next morning and Campion, cheered by his visits, watched him walk away across the footprints left by Archbishop Laud. He paused in the small archway, turned, smiled and gave her a bow. She waved.

An hour later, in a private room of the Bear Inn at the city end of London Bridge, Francis Lapthorne took the papers from the leather case. He burned all of them, except for two which bore Campion's signature on otherwise blank sheets. Those two, with a flourish, he put before Ebenezer Slythe. 'A deal of work, sir.'

'But well paid.'

'Indeed! Better than the theatre!' Since the Puritans had closed the playhouses, actors like Francis Lapthorne had been short of work. 'It's always a pleasure doing business for Sir Grenville.'

Ebenezer looked at him sourly. 'And doubtless a business when you provide him with pleasure.'

Lapthorne shrugged. 'It's an honour to be a friend of Sir Grenville,' he said defensively.

Ebenezer was not listening. He was staring at the signed sheets. 'God in his heaven!'

'What?'

'Look!' Ebenezer pushed the sheets across the table. 'Fool!'

'What?' Lapthorne did not understand. 'You asked me to get two signatures, I got two signatures! What more did you want?'

Ebenezer turned one of the sheets round and read it aloud in a sarcastic voice, 'Dorcas Campion Scammell. What the hell is that supposed to be?'

'Her name!'

'Campion? Her name's not Campion!'

Lapthorne shrugged. 'She told me it was. She said it was her middle name.'

'You're a fool.'

The actor assumed an air of hurt dignity. 'A person may

assume whatever name they like, it's not illegal. If she says that is her name, then that is her name. It will be quite sufficient for her confession.'

'Pray you never have to make a confession to me, fool.' Ebenezer took the two sheets. 'And pray you're right.' He put two coins on the table.

Lapthorne looked at them. Four had been promised, and even that was hardly a great amount for the deal of writing he had done, yet he did not care to argue with the intense, dangerous young man whose eyes were dark and fanatical. He smiled. 'Pray give Sir Grenville my regards.'

Ebenezer ignored him. He limped from the room, gesturing for his men to close behind him. He walked slowly, using a cane to assist his limp. He crossed the street and went slowly down the steps to the wharf. People parted for him, awed by his face and by the armed guards. His own boat waited, its oars held upright so that the black blades were outlined against the myriad points of light upon the river. Ebenezer settled in the stern and nodded to the oarsmen. He felt good. He guessed the signatures would do for the confessions, one for witchcraft and one for murder. His sister was doomed and not even the Jew in Amsterdam could save her. Ebenezer smiled. Even the news from Europe was showing that Hervey's foolish ambition had caused no harm.

Julius Cottjens, the man who provided his clients with privileged news from the financial capital of the north, walked to the wharves again that evening. He had done it every evening since Sir Grenville's faintly hysterical letter had reached him and Cottjens was content with this duty. He liked to walk, his pipe drawing sweetly and his dog running happily about him, but to be paid for his evening constitution was a piece of beneficent luck. Amsterdam looked rich and peaceful in the evening light, its people plump and prosperous. Cottjens felt a great contentment.

He stopped in his usual place and sat on a bollard while his dog sniffed excitedly at bales of cloth. Cottjens's pipesmoke drifted over the placid canal waters in the evening, summer air.

The *Wanderer*, the object of these evening strolls, was still tied up. It was high out of the water, its cargohold empty as it had been for weeks. The mainmast had been stepped up again, but the spars were still lashed to the ship's deck. It was a beautiful ship, Cottjens reflected, but it was days from being ready for sea.

A sailor came over the gangplank carrying a wooden box of wedges. Cottjens waved his pipe stem at the ship and raised his voice. 'Ships don't make money tied to wharves, my friend?'

'*Mijnheer*?'

Cottjens repeated himself and the sailor shrugged. 'She's made plenty of money in her lifetime, *Mijnheer*.'

Cottjens looked impressed. He nodded at the name, elegantly carved beneath the windows of the stern gallery. 'An English ship, yes?'

'Lord no, *Mijnheer*! Mordecai Lopez owns it. It was built here! I think he likes an English name.'

'My friend Mordecai? He's back in Amsterdam?'

The sailor hefted his box. 'He's here, but he's ill. May the good Lord preserve him if He watches over pagans.'

'Amen to that.' Cottjens knocked his pipe out on the bollard. 'Badly ill?'

'So they say, *Mijnheer*, so they say. You'll excuse me?'

Cottjens called his dog, then started back, a happy man. He could write with more news to Sir Grenville, news that would undoubtedly make that fat, subtle Englishman also a happy man.

Cottjens made a short detour to look at Lopez's house. The windows of the two lower floors, as ever, were barred and shuttered, but higher up he could see lamplight through windows. A shadow moved across a curtain.

Cottjens whistled for his dog. Like Ebenezer Slythe in London, he was a happy man; a little richer, a little older, and a little wiser. He would write to Sir Grenville with his news, his good news, that Mordecai Lopez was sick in Amsterdam, unable to interfere in Sir Grenville's affairs.

22

The day before Campion's execution dawned grey and wet, rain slamming down from the west and beating the river into a surface of pewter-grey misery.

The bakers were worried. A fine day meant a fine profit. Even if it poured with rain there would still be a vast crowd on Tower Hill to watch the execution, but few of them would want to buy soggy pies. The bakers prayed for a break in the clouds, for God to send fine weather to London. By midmorning it seemed their prayers were answered. A great hole was tearing itself in the western clouds, the first shafts of sunlight falling on Whitehall and Westminster, and the weather-wise proclaimed that the morrow would be a good July day.

There was still the small matter of the trial to be completed, but that had not stopped the bakeries working late for days before the execution. There was no doubt about the verdict, merely what sentence Sir John Henge, the judge, would pass down. Most of London favoured hanging. The time had passed when witches were burned, and the city believed that Dorcas Scammell should be convicted of witchcraft and hanged, high and slowly above their heads. Others preferred a longer death, saying that her crimes were so heinous that a signal punishment was needed to deter others. They favoured that she should be hung, drawn and quartered. It had the added advantage, as well as persuading other witches not to loose their familiars on armed men, that the victim would have to be stripped naked before her entrails were cut out and burned in front of her face. The body of a naked young girl would double the price that could be charged by those whose upper windows, fortuitously, overlooked Tower Hill. The builders of London, who customarily made small, laddered platforms from which spectators could watch executions, were similarly in favour of the severer punishment.

Yet others, mindful perhaps that the revolution was releasing strange ideas on England, preferred that she should be burned. If a man killed his wife the punishment was death by hanging, but if a wife murdered her husband, then the punishment was worse because the crime was worse. Women must be restrained, and there was a goodly body of London opinion that believed the sight of a burning, screaming woman would remind wives that the revolution did not encourage husband-murder.

Yet on one thing all were agreed. In church after church, in parishes a good half-day's walk from London, the preachers roused the faithful in preparation for the great event. Perhaps never in living memory had so many Puritan preachers simultaneously taken the same words of scripture as their text: Exodus 22, verse 18, 'Thou shalt not suffer a witch to live.' The *Mercurius* had done its work well. Faithful Unto Death Hervey was a hero to the city, the witch would die and already an enterprising publisher had put on sale a lurid and lengthy pamphlet that told the sorry tale of the witch Dorcas Scammell. Mothers subdued troublesome children by threatening them with Dorcas.

On the day before the execution there was already a fair crowd that gathered solely to watch the preparations, despite the rain that intermittently swept like smoke over Tower Hill. Many of the crowd were connoisseurs of this place, remembering the deaths of noblemen who had the privilege of sword or axe, the death swift so long as they had given a fat purse to the executioner. There was general agreement that they would have preferred Dorcas Scammell to die at Tyburn; the facilities for spectators were better there, though they were sympathetic to the authorities who thought it unlikely that they could safely escort the witch that far. She was bound to be lynched somewhere on the journey across London.

Carpenters came and constructed a scaffold. The crowd jeered them good-naturedly, yelling at them to build the platform higher. Later, as the rope was fixed to the crossbar, a portion of the crowd began to shout that the witch should be burned, as witches used to be burned, but the anger died when one of the workmen mimed a dancing, hanging death on the raw planks. Laughter sounded on the rainswept hill.

Someone, seeing the completed gibbet, asked if the sentence had been passed, but it seemed that the authorities were merely anticipating Sir John Henge's final decision. Rumour swept the crowd, but nothing was certain.

Some of the chief actors in the drama were cheered by the people. The weather improved, a weak sun shining on the hill when the hangman came to inspect the work. He waved at his public, exchanging jokes with them, delighting the crowd when he pretended to measure up a fat, loud-mouthed woman who screamed for the workmen to build the gibbet even higher.

Faithful Unto Death Hervey visited the hill three times from the courtroom within the Tower. At his third visit there was still no sentence, but he climbed on to the scaffold and calmed the crowd by waving his hands.

'It will soon be over, good people! Soon! Tomorrow you will see a witch die! Tomorrow this city will be a safer place for us all!' They cheered him again. He prayed with them, asking God to give him strength to fight the evil of witchcraft, and then he promised the crowd that he would deny himself all comfort, all rest, until the last witch had been extirpated from among the Saints. The Saints clapped and shouted for him.

Far off, in the Strand, Sir Grenville Cony was in his house. He expected four eminent visitors, members of the Commons who were devout Puritans, and so the naked Narcissus was hidden behind its closed shutters. A Bible, that his secretary had lavishly inked with marginal notations, was prominent on his desk. The four visitors were waiting and would continue to wait until Sir Grenville had finished with his present visitor.

Septimus Barnegat was perhaps the only man who did not fear Sir Grenville Cony. Barnegat could have no fear, for as an astrologer he sheltered behind the destiny of stars and planets, and the truth he told could not be swayed by fear or favour. Barnegat was an expensive astrologer, as highly thought of as any seer in Europe, and he charged high fees to those merchants who sought his advice about insurance, or as to whether a ship should set sail on a particular tide. Barnegat was a busy man, in demand by politicians, lawyers, merchants and nobility. He was also irascible, jealous of his science and easily annoyed by questions that were beyond that science's competence. Sir Grenville had just asked such a question and Barnegat's small, fierce face scowled as he replied.

'How can I tell, Sir Grenville? Give me the girl's natal date and I will answer, but it will take time! Indeed time! The charts, the influences.' He shrugged. 'All of us must die, nothing else is so certain, but whether it will be tomorrow I cannot tell.'

Sir Grenville rocked back and forth in his chair, hands clasped on his great belly. 'There's nothing in my chart?'

'Of course there is! But no feminine influences. You might assume the lack of them to be the affirmation you want.' Barnegat allowed himself a smirk. 'I cannot imagine Sir John Henge showing mercy to Dorcas Scammell.'

'No. And the other matter?'

Barnegat sighed. 'There are a thousand other matters. Which one?'

'An enemy across the sea.' Sir Grenville sounded positively humble in the presence of the famous astrologer. Septimus Barnegat was not an easy man to approach; he turned down the majority of applicants. Now he frowned, stared at the beautifully drawn planetary chart and nodded slowly. 'You have an enemy across the sea, yes. Matters fall into alignment, indeed they do.' He pursed his lips. 'He is to the east.'

'You're sure?' Sir Grenville leaned forward eagerly. The east was Holland, and Holland was Lopez; he did not fear the Jew as much as the enemy to the west.

Barnegat shook his head wearily. 'If I am not sure, I say so. If I do not know, I say so. You have no need to ask me if I am sure.'

'Of course, of course.' Sir Grenville took no notice of the reproof. 'Will he be coming to England?'

The science of astrology was not easily mastered. No King, no statesman, no banker, no merchant in Europe would dream of taking action without first consulting the heavens, but not one of them truly understood the intricacies of the astrologer's work. It was a mystery, confined to those practitioners who had given their days and nights to the study of the delicate and beautiful movements of stars and planets. There were some, a few, who scoffed, but as Septimus Barnegat was fond of saying, if the science did not work, why did the astrologers not starve in the streets? Yet sometimes, and this was one of the most closely guarded secrets of the science, it was easier to seek answers of an earthly origin than go through the painstaking, time-consuming endeavour of plotting the harmonious spheres.

Septimus Barnegat, as befitted a man of his wealth and reputation, took some earthly help. He paid his monthly retainer to Julius Cottjens, as did all the better London astrologers, and he paid for any news concerning his clients.

Barnegat knew about Sir Grenville's fear of Lopez. He knew too that Lopez was ill. He traced a tobacco-stained finger along an elliptical line. 'I detect sickness. Yes.' He glanced up at Sir Grenville. 'I think there will be no voyage across the sea.'

Sir Grenville smiled. Cottjens's news was safely confirmed. 'And from the west?'

'Nothing. A void, Sir Grenville.'

'Excellent, excellent!'

Sir Grenville truly was happy. For months now, Barnegat had reported a tangle of influences, but now the truth emerged. Sir Grenville was safe. No enemies across the sea, and, though the astrologer had not confirmed it, the certainty of the death of Dorcas Slythe. The two men talked as Barnegat rolled up his charts and put almanacs into his case. The astrologer believed, as Sir Grenville was beginning to believe, that the Presbyterians were losing ground. The Independents, the radicals of the revolution like Ebenezer Slythe, were in the ascendant. Barnegat, who was consulted by some of the Independent leaders, offered Sir Grenville the news that soon they would be seeking money.

'A lot of money?'

'They wish to raise their own forces,' Barnegat sneered. 'A fervent army of rabid Puritans, doubtless chanting psalms as they lop heads. They could be formidable, Sir Grenville.'

'And victorious.'

'If they raise the money. At present they feel the Low Countries might be more friendly towards them.'

Sir Grenville knew he was being sounded out. He nodded slowly. 'They might save themselves a journey, Barnegat. I will be happy to talk.'

'Many of them want no king.'

Sir Grenville smiled. 'At present we have no king. The sky does not seem to have fallen in.' He did not bother to ensure Barnegat's silence. The astrologer was not a man to betray his own clients, and Sir Grenville's slow defection from the Presbyterians, who would keep a figurehead king, to the Independents who thought the ship of state would sail quite well without one, was safe in Barnegat's memory. Nevertheless, Sir Grenville knew, he had put out a secret hand of friendship to the turbulent Puritans of the revolution. 'We'll meet next week?'

'Indeed, Sir Grenville. The same time?'

'Of course!'

Sir Grenville waited for his next visitors, men with whom

he would talk politics, and stared at the river which went past to the Tower. He smiled. The girl would die tomorrow, and he, Sir Grenville Cony, would continue to take the income of the Covenant. Some he would pass to Ebenezer, as he had passed some to Ebenezer's father, but not even Ebenezer Slythe, a subtle young man, would ever know just how much was never passed on.

Sir Grenville had two seals, and no one could take them from him. His enemy across the sea, the one man who could rescue Dorcas Slythe, was ill. As Septimus Barnegat had said, all was indeed well in Sir Grenville's heaven.

All was not well in the heaven of the Reverend Simon Perilly. Lady Margaret had asked him to travel to London, a dangerous business, and there find a lawyer who would defend Campion.

Sir George's old London lawyer, on hearing the request, developed a sudden and inconvenient illness. Another man, whom Perilly had thought a friend, threatened to report Perilly's presence to the authorities. He could be arrested as a spy. The Reverend Perilly had failed miserably. Now it was too late and he could see no way to save the girl.

He must travel back to Oxford, taking a circuitous route, to tell Lady Margaret that he had failed. She had moved to the King's capital, preferring other Royalists about her to refuge in the Parliamentary house of her son-in-law, and Simon Perilly knew how desperately she wanted Campion's freedom. To Lady Margaret, Campion's survival would be a blow against her enemies. Yet she would be disappointed.

He called on one last friend in London, a man he had known since Cambridge, and a man he knew would not betray him. Luke Condign was a lawyer, but of no use to Perilly, for he worked to the Commons. His office was in Westminster itself and it was there, in the very heart of the enemy stronghold, that Perilly found Condign. The lawyer was gloomy. 'There's nothing to be done, Simon, nothing.'

'It's so unfair. So unfair.'

Condign shrugged. He doubted there could be smoke without fire, but he did not wish to disappoint his friend. 'I'm sorry.'

'There is one thing you can do for me.'

Condign was wary. 'Tell me.'

'Can I send a message to her? I suppose it's hopeless trying to see her.'

'Not unless you want to take her place, my friend.' Condign smiled. 'Yes, I can get a message to her.' Each evening an official bag of papers went to the Tower. Some were letters to embassies abroad, sent from the Tower wharf, while others were orders for the movement of armaments from the Tower's armoury. A few were letters to prisoners. 'You know they'll read it? They won't give her anything which they see as unfriendly to Parliament.'

'I know.' Simon Perilly took the offered paper and ink. He sighed, thought, then wrote swiftly, 'Toby is well, recovering the use of his arm. He is in Oxford at Lord Tallis's house. All there pray for you.' He wondered briefly whether he should put down that they would meet in heaven, but decided it might be inappropriate. 'Be strong in the Lord.' He signed it, sanded the ink, then pushed it to his friend.

Condign nodded. 'They should allow that. You know that my Lords Fleet and Atheldene pleaded for her?'

'I know.' Lady Margaret had written to her friends and acquaintances, begging help.

Luke Condign sighed. 'Strange days, my friend, strange days. There was a time when the Commons beseeched the help of these Lords, but now?' He shrugged again. 'You'll sup with us tonight? Grace will be delighted to see you.'

'Of course.' The Reverend Simon Perilly had done his duty. He had done all he could, and the rest was up to Sir John Henge.

Judge Sir John Henge, tyrant of lawyers, groaned with the pain of the stone that he refused to let the doctors cut out.

The trial, he reflected, had been more tiresome than he expected. Caleb Higbed, forever smiling ingratiatingly and bobbing up and down like a pigeon, had been overlong. At least the prisoner had not had a lawyer, but that had not stopped her making protests at the proceedings. He had growled her into silence.

The jury now had the girl's fate in their hands. Sir John had no doubt what that fate should be. He had known from the moment she had entered the courtroom, flaunting herself in a scarlet dress cut so low that he half expected her breasts to ride over the neckline with every breath she drew. She had tried to pull the dress up, but the jury, all Protestant men of property, had frowned at the harlot costume.

Sir John's troubles had begun at the opening of the trial. That fool Higbed had assured him there was a confession, but Sir John, who prided himself on his thoroughness and his meticulous application of the law, had found an anomaly. 'It says here her name is Dorcas Campion Scammell. That's not the name on the charge.'

Higbed had half stood, half bowed and smiled. 'As your Lordship observes, it is the name she chose to sign herself.'

'But is it her name?'

'No, my Lord.'

'If this isn't her name, then this isn't her confession. I would have thought the rawest lad in the law would have known that, Mr Higbed.'

'As your Lordship pleases.'

It had not pleased Sir John, but the law was the law, and Sir John embodied the law, and so he had demanded evidence.

So the witnesses were called, the evidence laid damningly before the jury. Goodwife Baggerlie, coached by Caleb Higbed who had thought the confessions too pat to convince Sir John, swore that she had heard Campion declare she would murder her husband by witchcraft. *Maleficio* was established.

Ebenezer Slythe, his face pale, pleaded for his sister's life.

Sir John interrupted him. 'I thought this witness was here to give evidence.'

Caleb Higbed smiled at Sir John. 'We thought your Lordship might listen to a brother's plea.'

Sir John groaned, shifting because of the pain in his guts. 'The time for a plea, Mr Higbed, is after the verdict, not before. Have you lost your wits? Or do you think I'm a fool?'

'Nothing is further from my mind, your Lordship.'

Ebenezer was dismissed. He stepped down with a smile. His plea for mercy was no more than a gesture to public taste, what the simpletons would expect of a brother. Higbed had assured him that Sir John Henge did not know the meaning of the word mercy.

Now, as the evening light dimmed the courtroom and shadowed the great royal coat-of-arms above Sir John's head, an escutcheon that kept up the pretence that Parliament fought not the King but his advisers, the jury whispered together on their benches.

Sir John did not like his juries to take a long time, especially after he had more or less dictated their decision to them. He growled, 'Well?'

The foreman stood up. 'We are agreed, my Lord.'

'All of you?'

'Yes, my Lord.'

'Well?' Sir John Henge wanted this over.

'On the charge of witchcraft, my Lord. Guilty.'

A buzz went round the spectators, quelled by an angry glance from Sir John. Caleb Higbed looked with relief at the darkening beams. Sir John had already written both verdicts in his book, but he pretended to make a note.

'And the charge of murder?'

'Guilty.'

Sir John half expected the girl to cry out, but she kept her composure as she had throughout the trial. Sir John looked at her. A pretty thing, he thought, but the devil often chose the best. He looked sardonically at Caleb Higbed. 'You had a plea, Mr Higbed?'

Caleb Higbed shook his head, smiled. 'The substance of the plea is already before your Lordship, unless you wish it repeated?'

'No, no!' Sir John closed his great book. He picked up his black cap and stared at the scarlet-dressed prisoner. A few seconds before she had been on trial, now she was a witch and a murderess. Sir John's mouth curved in malevolent dislike.

'Dorcas Scammell, you have been found guilty of offences so vile that they defy Christian comprehension. You willingly entered into a pact with the devil and you thereafter used the sorcerous powers he gave you to murder your husband, Samuel Scammell.

'The penalty for witchcraft is hanging. Parliament, in its wisdom, decreed that should be so, but you have also been found guilty of your husband's murder for which the penalty is death by burning.' He shifted heavily in the uncomfortable chair. He hated trials in the Tower, a draughty, cold, inconvenient place.

'I would bring it to the court's attention, and for the edification of those lawyers here who will one day bear my responsibilities, that there was a hallowed belief in this land that witches should be burned. The purpose was not to give pain, but to prevent the spirit of evil from passing away from the body of the witch into her family. This seems to me to be a precaution worthy of this court. Therefore, using the discretion given me by your conviction of murder, I sentence you, Dorcas Scammell, to be taken tomorrow forenoon to a place of execution, and there burned to your deserved death. May God have mercy on your soul.'

There was a second's silence in the courtroom, every eye on Campion, and then a great explosion of exalted applause.

Campion, her face pale, her hands tied behind her back, did not move a muscle. She showed no shock, no distress, nothing. Then the guards turned her and led her away.

The next day dawned as fine as any man could wish. There was a feeling of cleanness to the city, as if the rain had

scoured it and the night wind aired it, and in the morning the burgeoning crowd on Tower Hill saw the last, high, ragged clouds fleeing eastwards.

The crowd was huge, as big, some said, as that which had collected for the Earl of Strafford's death. They were in good mood, cheering as the gibbet was taken down and the wagonloads of faggots brought to the stake which had been hammered between the cobbles. The crowd shouted at the workmen, 'Build it high!'

'Remember the people at the back!'

The workmen piled it eight feet high and only the shortness of the stake prevented them building it higher. They provoked laughs by pretending to warm their hands at the unlit pile, but stood respectfully back when the executioner came to inspect their work.

He climbed to the top of the faggots, jumping up and down to test them, and then his assistant nailed two chains to the stake that would bind Campion's neck and waist. Back at the foot of the great pyre the executioner ordered two holes forced in the piled faggots, holes where he would place the fire, and only then was he satisfied.

Those closest to the fire would see best, though the cordon of soldiers who held them forty feet from the piled timber were constantly being asked to remove their helmets and crouch a little. Small children were pushed between the troops to wait expectant in the warming sun for this spectacle they had stayed up all night to see. The next best vantage points were on the houses to the west of Tower Hill where the rich had rented rooms. Some householders offered refreshments as part of the price, while others set up spyglasses in windows and on roof-leads; every space was crammed. To the east, on the ramparts of the Tower itself, the privileged guests of soldiers and officials stared down at the huge throng. The morning passed slowly.

The preachers had been active the night before, whipping the faithful into a new hysteria, and now those same ministers moved among the crowd and held extemporary meetings. The air was loud with psalms and prayers.

The children fretted, wanting the entertainment to begin, while some toddlers cried, thinking their parents would not lift them up soon enough to see the fire. The pie-sellers forced their way through the throng, shouting their cries, while water-sellers carried their heavy barrels on their backs.

It was a holiday, a true holiday, a holy-day, because today the wishes of God, the preachers said, were being fulfilled by the children of God. Today a woman would die in exquisite, horrid agony to protect the kingdom of God, and it was no wonder, the preachers said, that He had sent fine weather.

They had told Campion, the previous day, that the scarlet dress was the only dress available. Now it had been taken away and in its place she was dressed in a light, cotton shift. It was shapeless, loose and she suspected it would flare up at the first touch of flame to scorch her body.

She seemed, to her gaolers, to be in a daze. Ever since Francis Lapthorne had disappeared and she had realized, too late, that he had been yet another of her enemies, she had given up all hope.

Only once in the time since had she shown emotion. The Reverend Perilly's letter had reached her and she had cried terribly. Partly she cried for joy, that Toby lived, yet she cried for herself that there would be no green meadows beside a stream with him. She would die.

The gaolers let her cry her heart out. They were embarrassed.

The Reverend Faithful Unto Death Hervey was not embarrassed. He would accompany her to the scaffold, and he had prayed that, on this her last journey, she might repent. That would make a fine story! He could preach how the witch had begged forgiveness, had thrown herself on God's mercies, and how he, Faithful Unto Death, had led her to the throne of grace. He came into Campion's room with the soldiers who would take her to the stake and he started immediately, preaching the word in her dumb, dazed face.

The soldiers were not embarrassed. One tied her hands, pulling the knots behind her back so tight that she cried out. Another soldier laughed. 'Watch it, Jimmy! She'll put a spell on you!'

Their captain snapped at them to be quiet. He felt uneasy performing this duty, even troubled by it. He had believed the law to be sacred, yet only the night before he had taken dinner with his parents at Caleb Higbed's house and the lawyer had laughed when asked about the trial. 'Of course it's all nonsense! There are no witches! That girl's no witch! But the law says there are witches, so there are! This is very fine pork.'

At least, the captain thought, the girl was quiet. She seemed drained of life and emotion. The only remnant of her last, troubled night was the drawn look on her face, her red eyes, and one quick glance she gave him that seemed, somehow, to reek of the terror he guessed she must feel. The captain, wishing he had thought before her hands were tied, stepped forward with a leather bag in his hands. It seemed heavy and had a long, looped thong hanging from its neck. He smiled nervously. This was not part of his duty, but his father had suggested it and the captain was glad. 'Mrs Scammell?'

The eyes looked at him. She said nothing. She could, he thought, have been miles away.

He hefted the bag in his hands, smiled, 'Gunpowder, Mrs Scammell. If it can be hung about your neck, under your shift, it will give you a swift end.'

'Gunpowder!' Faithful Unto Death frowned. 'Gunpowder? On whose orders, Captain?'

'No one's, sir. It's customary.'

'I doubt that.' Faithful Unto Death Hervey smiled. 'The witch's victims did not have a swift end, so why should she? No, Captain, no. Take it away. She must suffer the rigours of the law!' He turned back to Campion, and his onion-smelling breath hissed on her face. ' "Ye have ploughed wickedness," woman, "and ye have reaped iniquity". Repent! It is not too late! Repent!'

She said nothing, not even when the soldiers pushed her towards the door and one of them fondled her breasts through the cotton shift.

'Stop it!' the captain shouted.

The girl seemed oblivious.

A bell sounded the single, flat note that told the world it was a quarter past the hour. The captain looked at the beautiful, pale face. 'We must go.'

She walked as if in a trance, hearing nothing, seeing nothing, crossing the Archbishop's footprints in the grassed courtyard. Behind her and above her, at a barred window, the Archbishop made the sign of the cross towards her. One day, he knew, he would tread the same path and walk towards a death that the Puritans would applaud. He watched her disappear beneath the archway, then turned back into his quiet room.

Some of the crowd were calling out, impatient for the witch to be brought, while others waited more good-naturedly and pointed out there were still fifteen minutes to go. A great pathway had been cleared by soldiers from the Tower's gateway to the heaped faggots, a road that was kept clear by levelled pikes and by hard pushing. Some vendors were allowed into the roadway to sell pies, ale, or the rotted fruit that always sold well at executions and was hurled at the victim.

In the cleared space beside the pyre the executioner's assistant used bellows to heat up a coal brazier. The air shimmered above the glowing coals while, on the ground beside them, two pitch-smeared torches waited to carry the flames from the brazier to the faggots. Someone called out to the executioner for a farthing's worth of chestnuts. The big, leather-jacketed man smiled tiredly. He was used to all the old jokes. Dying had no surprises for him.

A cheer started low down the hill, hard by the Tower gate,

a cheer that turned into a spreading, growing roar. She was coming! Small children were hoisted on to their father's shoulders, people stood on tiptoes and stretched their necks. The preachers shouted praises.

God's will was about to be done on earth.

The cheer had started because the Tower gates had opened. Those closest in the crowd could see the horse and cart waiting that would draw Campion on her short, last journey. She could have walked, but that would have cheated the crowd of their sight of her, and so the soldiers had commandeered one of the Tower's dung carts to carry her to her death.

Campion walked towards the cart. She could see through the open archway and she sensed the presence of the vast crowd. The noise was appalling. A roar, a growl, the sound of a crowd baying and howling their hatred, egged on by God's ministers. The noise was like a furious animal, assaulting her, and for the first time that day she flinched from her ordeal.

Imagination was her curse now. She was afraid. She shrivelled inside at the thought of the first touch of flame, the heat on an ankle perhaps, and then the searing agony of light about her, the shift burning, her skin bubbling, her screams winging out to feed the crowd's hatred. She imagined her hair burning and she knew the pain would be terrible, far worse than her imaginings, a hell on earth that would be followed, at last, by peace in heaven. She would meet Sir George, she thought, and she imagined his shy smile greeting her in heaven, and she wondered whether there was such happiness in heaven that earthly sadness was forgotten. She did not want to forget Toby.

Faithful Unto Death Hervey hissed in her ear, ' "Hath I any pleasure at all that the wicked should die? Saith the Lord God: and not that he should return from his ways." That's the scripture woman, the scripture! Repent!'

She ignored him. She could not climb unaided into the

cart, but the captain of her guard lifted her himself, then held her elbow as he walked across the foul, slippery boards. He tied her by the neck to the high upright poles that protected the driver from his normal loads. The captain wanted to say something to her, but he could think of nothing that could have any meaning to her now. He smiled instead.

The Reverend Faithful Unto Death Hervey pushed through the jostling soldiers to the cart's edge. He had been warned to walk behind, rather than on the cart, because of the missiles that would be hurled. He shouted up at her, his voice hardly audible over the crowd, over the laughter of the troops, 'Repent, woman! Your death is at hand! Repent!'

Campion had her back to the Tower gateway. She heard hooves behind her, but did not see the four horsemen who crowded the archway. Their boots, jackets, and orange sashes were spattered with mud as though they had ridden a long way. The presence of the four strange horses made the carthorse jerk to one side, restless because of the noise, and Campion mistook the lurch of the cart for the beginning of her journey. She spoke at last. Her eyes were shut, but her voice rang out loud and clear in the small courtyard, ' "Our Father which art in heaven." ' She had planned to shout this from the stake, but the clawing noise of the mob warned her she would not be heard. Nevertheless she wanted these men to know that they burned an innocent woman. ' "Give us this day our daily bread." '

'Stop!'

The voice was huge and harsh, deep and cruel. She would not stop. She could hear Faithful Unto Death screaming blasphemy, but she went on with the prayer. ' "And forgive us our debts, as we forgive our debtors." ' She steeled herself for the cart to move, for the wash of hatred from the crowd. The captain was still beside her. ' "And lead us not into temptation, but deliver us from evil: For thine is the kingdom, and the power, and the glory, for ever. Amen." '

'Amen'. The harsh voice mocked her.

She opened her eyes to see a mounted soldier who had forced his way beside the cart. He was in leather and steel, one gloved hand restraining his big horse, the other holding one of the cart's upright poles. He looked at her with a face more terrible than any she had ever seen. He had a steel-grey beard that framed a cruel, wide mouth. One eye, surrounded by the lines of middle age, seemed to mock her, while the other eye, his right, was covered with a leather patch, but a patch unlike any she had ever seen. It covered not just his sightless eye, but also most of his cheek and forehead, and it disappeared under his steel helmet. There was something utterly terrible and savage about the man, as if he was the kind of human beast unleashed by warfare. He easily dominated the gateway's courtyard. 'Is this the witch?'

The captain was still in the cart. 'Yes, sir.'

The bearded, scarred man felt in his pouch and handed a scroll to the captain. 'This is a warrant for her.' The captain took it, unrolled it, and Campion saw a great red seal hanging from a short ribbon. The captain frowned.

'You're Colonel Harries, sir?'

'No, I'm the King of Spain. Who in God's holy name do you think I am?'

The captain stepped back from the blast of savagery. He looked at the warrant again. 'It seems to be in order, sir.'

'Seems? You bastard! Seems? Are you doubting it?' Colonel Harries put a leather-gloved hand on a battered sword handle. 'Is it all right, you filth, or is it not?'

'Yes, sir! Yes!' The captain was horrified by the anger that bellowed at him.

'Then cut the bitch down and give her to me.' Harries twisted in his saddle. 'Mason!'

'Sir!' One of Harries's three men spurred his horse forward.

'See if the damned boat's here.' He looked back to the captain who, astonished, had not moved. Harries smiled, not prettily, and his voice dropped, 'What's your name, boy?'

'Wellings, sir. Captain Robert Wellings.'

'Cut her down, Wellings, or I'll cut your bloody entrails apart. Move!'

Wellings still held the warrant. He shifted it from hand to hand, obviously confused. He had no knife so, nervously, he half drew his sword. Harries exploded in wrath.

'Bastard! Has she put a spell on you?'

There was a scraping noise, a movement so fast that Wellings blinked, and Harries held his long sword. He looked at Campion. 'Lean forward, witch. I said, lean forward!'

She strained ahead, stretching the thong that tied her to the cart. She heard the swish of the sword, she shut her eyes, and felt the passing of the blade at the back of her hair. She cried out, felt a jerk, and then Captain Wellings was steadying her. Harries had severed the thong without touching her and now he pushed the blade back into its straight scabbard.

'What is this? Who are you?' Wellings's own colonel pushed through the soldiers. He was red-faced, sweating, angry at the delay. The crowd was chanting now, chanting for the witch to burn.

Harries held a hand out to Wellings. 'The warrant.'

'Sir.'

Colonel Harries turned his single eye on the newcomer. 'Who out of hell are you?'

The red-faced colonel frowned. 'Prior.'

Harries looked round at the soldiers. 'This is a warrant requiring the Papist witch to appear before the Committee of Safety. This,' he touched the seal, 'is the seal of Parliament, put there this morning by the Speaker of the House of Commons. If any of you wish to dispute the warrant, tell me now!'

No one seemed likely to dispute anything with Colonel Harries, but Prior tried a feeble protest. 'She's to be burned this morning!'

'She can burn another morning.'

'But the crowd!' Colonel Prior waved a hand at the archway beyond which the baying and chanting was rising to frenzied pitch. The soldiers, guarding the roadway, were struggling against the mob's impatience.

'Good God Almighty.' Harries leaned forward in his saddle. 'In 1629, you worm, I held a fortress for nine months against the armies of the Holy Roman Empire. Are you telling me you can't hold the Tower of London against a rabble of women and apprentices?' He looked at Captain Wellings. 'Don't stand there, filth! Take her off the cart!'

The soldiers, crowding the space between the outer walls of the Tower, muttered protests. As Wellings helped Campion forward the mutterings became louder and Harries stood in his stirrups. 'Silence!' He looked about him, waiting for quiet. 'You're not damned children! You'll see her burn, but not today!'

'Why not?' a voice shouted from the back.

'Why not? Because, you bastards,' Harries was angry again, 'she was tried for witchcraft and murder, but no one thought to ask about the damned crucifix she was carrying. Suppose it came from Rome or Spain. Do you want to be fighting the Pope's armies as well as the damned King?' The soldiers listened reluctantly. Harries tried to placate them. 'She'll be back for her warming, but first we want to ask some questions. We'll help her answers out with a little torture.' He twisted about. 'Shut those gates!'

Harries's promise of torture and the undoubted veracity of the seal of the House of Commons which had been passed to Colonel Prior, seemed to mollify the troops. They grumbled, but Harries promised she would be back within the week, and that would mean a second holiday for them. Faithful Unto Death Hervey demanded to see the warrant, but when Harries scowled at him he swiftly backed down.

'Sir! Boat's here, sir!' Harries's trooper had returned.

'Bring the girl, Mason,' Harries swung easily off his horse. 'You two! Take the horses and meet us at Westminster.'

'Sir!'

Suddenly all was activity. Two of Harries's men turned their mounts, took the other horses by the reins and spurred towards the closing Tower gates. The crowd's fury was filling the air. Wellings lifted Campion down, trying to be gentle, and his solicitude earned a sneer from Colonel Harries. 'You fancy the witch, Wellings?'

'Her hands are tied, sir.'

'She can jump, can't she? Christ! You new soldiers couldn't fight a damned elf. Come on, girl.' He took her shoulder, pulled, then looked at Colonel Prior. 'Is Ebenezer Slythe here?'

Colonel Prior frowned, but Faithful Unto Death knew the answer. 'He's on the ramparts.'

'Making sure of the best view, eh?' Harries laughed. 'I can't wait. Move, witch!'

Harries and Mason took her under the Bell Tower and down to the slopping, smelly Water Gate. The Traitor's Gate. A large boat was floating amid the rubbish that was trapped inside the tunnel leading to the steps. Six oarsmen waited in the boat, their faces nervous, for these steps led only to the axe, noose or fire. Harries pushed her down the stone steps. It was low water and the bottom of the stairs was treacherously slippery. 'Get in.'

Colonel Prior had followed them. He frowned. 'You'll not clear the bridge, Colonel.'

'Of course I'll not clear the bridge!' Harries snapped. London Bridge's narrow archways could only be passed by boats at high water, and even then the passage was dangerous. 'We've got a damned coach waiting at Bear Wharf. Do you think I was going to take her through that bloody mob?'

Mason, the trooper, sat her in the stern thwart. Colonel Harries dropped beside her, his scabbard rasping on the boat's planks. He nodded at the oarsmen: 'Go!'

They shoved off, using their oars to pole the boat through the dark, dripping tunnel of stone and beneath the great portcullis that could slam down to bar the gate. Campion saw the bow go into the sunlight, then the warmth was on her face and the oarsmen were turning the craft upstream. They leaned forward into their stroke, pulled, and the boat left the Tower wall behind.

'Look, witch!' Harries pointed to his right. He seemed to be laughing beneath the steel bars of the helmet.

Campion saw the crowd on the hill, a great mass of people through which the road was carved which should have led her to the piled timber and stake that was clearly visible at the hill's low summit. The noise lashed at the boat, a growl that seemed to spread across the city. The sight made her shiver.

Harries plucked at her cotton shift. 'I see you're dressed for a warm day.' He barked out a laugh. The oarsmen grinned as they leaned forward in unison.

The Customs House hid Tower Hill from her view, though still the baying of the mob came after her. She was shivering uncontrollably now. She had escaped the fire, but for what? What irons and spikes and flames would rend her now?

The oarsmen bent towards her, pulled, and their eyes never seemed to leave her. She was crying, though whether with relief or whether because her ordeal was not to be ended in swift horror but prolonged, she could not tell. Sun glittered on the water. The high houses built on London Bridge loomed ahead.

'Bear Wharf!' Harries growled.

The starboard oarsmen backed water for one stroke, the boat turned, then headed towards a decrepit timber pier on the city bank. A sailor, pouring slops from a Dutch sloop, stared down at the small boat that went beneath his ship's stern.

'Come on, witch!' Harries hauled her on to the pier, tossed a purse to the stroke oarsman and led her swiftly to a waiting coach. The leather curtains had been nailed shut. A man waited on the driver's seat and Mason climbed up beside him while Harries pushed Campion into the dark interior. They lurched forward.

She could not tell how long they travelled. It did not seem long. She heard the driver shout at obstructions, felt the swaying turns as the coach negotiated the narrow city streets, and sometimes, as the coach went into the sunlight, she would see the narrow strips of brightness thrown from the slits at the curtains' nailed edges. She did not know if they went north or south, east or west, she only knew that she was being carried to new torments.

Then a gate slammed on the sounds of the street, she could hear the hooves of the horses loud on stone echoing from walls, and Harries pushed open the door. The coach stopped, swaying on its leather springs. 'Out.'

She was in a courtyard of stone. The walls were windowless. A single arched doorway led into a dark interior.

'Inside, witch.'

Campion thought of the book of martyrology she had been given as a child. She knew she would not have the bravery to endure the pincers, fires, claws and racks of truth. She cried.

Harries pushed her down a long, chill passageway. His boots echoed from the stone walls. Campion shrank from the pain that awaited her.

Colonel Harries stopped at a doorway. He took out a knife and cut the bonds that still bit into her wrists. She heard him grunt as he sawed with his knife. The leather gloves were rough where they touched her skin. He pushed the door open. 'Inside.'

A fire burned. It waited for her.

A bed waited. There were new clothes, food and wine. She expected rough hands to seize her, but it was a motherly woman who came forward and cradled her in comforting arms. The woman soothed her, stroked her hair, held her tight against the horrors. 'You're safe, child, safe! You've been rescued!'

But Campion was past understanding. She wept, collapsed, and her head was filled with the fire that had reached up to burn her, and which, though she had not yet comprehended it, had been cheated of her. She was safe.

23

Colonel Joshua Harries was an aide to the Earl of Manchester, the general who commanded the army of Parliament's Eastern Association, the army that had done most to win the battle of Marston Moor. Thus, when Colonel Harries had requested a warrant from the Speaker so that the fighting men could discover whether the Dorcas Scammell mentioned in *Mercurius* was part of a Catholic conspiracy to bring fresh enemies against Parliament, the Speaker had small option but to agree. The army that was winning the war had to be indulged, and the Speaker reflected with relief that it was not he who would have to explain to the howling mob on Tower Hill why their entertainment was delayed.

Yet the Speaker might have been a good deal less complacent had he known that on the day fixed for Campion's execution Colonel Joshua Harries was in the great Minster of York, giving thanks for the Roundheads' successful siege of that city.

The man who called himself Colonel Harries should also have been in York. He too was a colonel in Parliament's army, but, unlike the real Colonel Harries, he would not have been giving thanks to God for the Roundhead victory. Colonel Vavasour Devorax was a King's man serving with the enemy; in short, a spy.

Vavasour Devorax had discarded the thin, leather half-mask by the time he returned to Campion's room, yet, even without the patch, his face was frightening. His eyes were grey and cold, his skin tanned and lined, while on the right side of his face, running from the steel-grey beard to his hairline, was a jagged, ridged scar that narrowly missed his eye. Vavasour Devorax had a hard, bitter face, a face suggesting he had seen everything and that there was nothing left in this world to surprise him.

He stood beside the girl's bed. 'What did you give her?'

'Laudanum.' The woman had a strong foreign accent.

He looked at Campion in silence, staring at her. One hand fidgeted with the hem of his greasy, filthy leather jerkin. He stared a long time, then looked at the woman. 'I want you to cut my beard off.'

'Your beard?' She sounded surprised.

'Christ, woman! Half the army's searching for a man with one eye and a beard.' He looked at Campion, eyes shut in sleep. 'And all because of her.'

'You think she's not worth it?'

'Who knows?' He left the room.

The woman looked at the shut door. 'Get drunk, Devorax.' The dislike was strong in her accent.

Vavasour Devorax would get drunk, too. His face had been ravaged by war, and further by alcohol. He was sober most mornings, sober through most days, but it was a rare night when Vavasour Devorax was not drunk. In company he could be boisterously drunk, but most nights he was morosely alone, savage in his drinking.

He was not without friends. The men who followed him, the men who had ridden desperately for London after Devorax had read the *Mercurius*, were all soldiers who were proud of him and, in their way, friends. They too were adventurers, mercenaries from the European wars of religion, and their allegiance was to neither King nor Parliament, only to Vavasour Devorax. When he ordered, they obeyed.

Devorax in turn had a master whose orders he obeyed. He was the Jew's man, though none knew why. It was rumoured that Mordecai Lopez had bought the Englishman out of a Moorish slave galley. Others, more fanciful perhaps, said that Vavasour Devorax was the Jew's bastard son, whelped on a gentile woman, but no one had ever dared ask Devorax if that were true. Only one thing was certain; Devorax obeyed Mordecai Lopez's wishes.

Marta Renselinck, the motherly woman who nursed Campion out of her terrors, did not like Vavasour Devorax. She resented his influence on her master, hated his savage moods, and feared his careless, biting tongue. Marta was Lopez's housekeeper, devoted to him, and the only servant who had crossed the North Sea with him to London. The other servants in Amsterdam had been instructed to say that their master was dangerously ill, and in the meantime Lopez had taken the first available boat that sailed to England. He carried papers that identified him as an agent of the Bank of Amsterdam, come to negotiate one of that bank's loans to Parliament, and the false papers had taken them swiftly past the soldiers who guarded London's docks against Royalist agents. The two, master and servant, had come straight to this house and here, for the first time since Lopez had read the *Mercurius*, he seemed to relax. 'Vavasour is here, Marta, he's here. Everything will be good now!' Lopez had been pleased, confident that the girl would be freed, and Marta, to please her master, hid her dislike of the big, crude, English soldier.

It took three days for Campion to recover. She was slow to trust her rescuers, slower still to persuade herself that she was truly safe, and in those three days only Marta tended her. It was not until the third evening that Marta finally persuaded Campion to meet the man who had sailed from Amsterdam on her behalf, the Jew, Mordecai Lopez.

Campion was nervous as she dressed, hardly aware of what clothes she put on, thinking only of the distrust she had for all the seal-bearers. Marta Renselinck laughed at her fears. 'He's a good man, child, a kind man. Now, sit down while I arrange your hair.'

The room into which Marta showed her and left her was magnificent. It faced the river and, for the first time, Campion realized she was on the south bank of the Thames. To the right she could see the Tower of London, its highest ramparts touched with the sun's dying light, and to her left was the great bridge, rearing high above the water. The room itself was dark-panelled, its floor covered with eastern rugs, while one wall was covered with bookshelves, the gold-blocked spines of the packed volumes glinting from the light of the few lit candles. She moved nervously towards the wall of windows, towards the magnificent view, and then started, cried out, for a shadow moved in an alcove among the books.

'Don't be frightened! Come, Dorcas! It is my pleasure to meet you.' The man smiled. 'At last.'

An old man moved towards her. He was thin and upright, his face made distinguished by white hair brushed back from a tanned, wrinkled skin. He had a small, neatly pointed white beard, and his clothes were of black velvet trimmed discreetly with white lace.

'My name is Mordecai Lopez. I own this house, and all that is in it is yours.' He smiled at his own flowery courtesy, then bowed to her with solemn grace. 'Will you sit with me in the window? The sunset over the bridge is the best sight in London, truly magnificent. I don't think Venice can offer anything as good. Please?'

His manner was gentle, his courtesy exquisite. He moved slowly, as if any sudden gesture might frighten her, and for some minutes he spoke of the house in which they sat. 'My people are not welcome in England. I used to live in London, but we were expelled, so I closed up my fine mansion in the city, but kept this house in secret.' He smiled. 'I can come here by boat and leave quickly by boat too.' The house was right on the river, the sound of the water slapping at piles easily audible to Campion. Mordecai Lopez offered her wine. 'Vavasour uses the house now. He hides his Royalist friends in it. I suppose one day it will be discovered and I'll come here to find nothing but destruction.' He handed her a beautifully cut crystal goblet. 'Did you like Vavasour?'

Marta had told Campion that 'Colonel Harries' was truly Vavasour Devorax. Campion was still nervous. She looked at the shrewd, kindly Jew. 'He seemed very frightening.'

Lopez laughed. 'He is, my dear, he is. Very frightening!'

'Who's frightening?' The voice was harsh, unexpected, coming from the door of the room. Campion turned, startled, and she saw the tall, grey-haired colonel. She would not have recognized him except for the voice. Devorax's beard was gone, the patch was gone, but his face was still brutally ugly, a merciless face. He looked at her as he approached. 'A sunset you never expected to see, Miss Slythe? Or should it be Mrs Scammell?'

She stammered her reply, 'Miss Slythe.' She felt threatened by Devorax.

'She speaks! A miracle.' He flourished a bottle at her, as if in a toast. 'You'd better thank me, Miss Slythe. I saved you from a scorching.'

Her heart was beating on her rib-cage. 'I thank you, sir.'

'And so you damn well should.' Vavasour Devorax slumped into a chair, his legs in filthy boots sprawled out on one of the rugs. He grinned at Lopez. 'I've been walking the streets of this once fair city. They say the devil rescued her! The devil!' He laughed, rubbing his chin that was paler than the rest of his face.

Lopez's voice was patient, even affectionate. 'Are you getting drunk, Vavasour?'

'Very drunk.' He said it savagely, then looked at Campion. 'If you ever wish a bottle emptied, Miss Slythe, a maiden rescued, or a cause betrayed, I am your most excellent servant.' He tipped the bottle. Two thin trickles of wine dripped on to his leather jerkin. The bottle went down and his hard, cold eyes looked at her. 'Do you think I make a good devil, Miss Slythe?'

'I don't know, sir.'

' "Sir", she calls me "sir"! What it is to be old, Mordecai.' He shook his head, then suddenly looked accusingly at Campion. 'That priest with you at the Tower—stringy man with the twitch—that was Faithful Unto Death Hervey?'

She nodded. 'Yes.'

'I wish I'd known then. God! I saw the bastard today, preaching at Paul's Cross, calling me the devil! Me! I should have dragged the bastard back here when I rescued you and gelded him with a rusty knife. If there's anything to geld, which I doubt.'

'Vavasour!' Lopez chided him. 'You're offending our guest.'

Devorax laughed silently. The cynical eyes looked at Campion. 'You see? I'm not frightening at all. I can be reprimanded by my master. No one who can be reprimanded can be frightening.' He looked at Lopez. 'I need money, master mine.'

'Of course. For food?'

'And wine, and women.'

Lopez smiled. 'You can eat with us, Vavasour.'

Campion hoped silently that the big soldier would refuse. To her relief, he shook his head. 'No, Mordecai. Tonight I buy my men pork. You never serve pork because of your weird religion. I need pork, drink and flesh, and a place where women are not offended by my common soldier's tongue.' He stood up. 'Money?'

Lopez stood, looked at Campion. 'I shall be one minute.'

She was left alone. She felt a wave of relief that Vavasour Devorax was gone. He might have rescued her, yet she felt unsafe in his presence. She calmed herself and stared out of the wide windows.

The sun setting behind the bridge was, as Lopez had said, magnificent. The eastern reach of the Thames was dark beneath the great bridge that was silhouetted against the crimson, dying light. The tide was ebbing so that the river water was forcing itself through the narrow arches, and the mixture of falling foam and slickness was gilded by the hidden sun so that it seemed as if the whole, great bridge was afloat upon a mass of molten gold that poured itself into the dark water. It seemed unreal that she was here, watching the magnificence, and she wished she could see Toby or Lady Margaret. She needed friends, not strangers.

'He frightens you a lot, doesn't he?'

She turned to see Mordecai Lopez in the doorway. He closed the door and walked towards her. 'You don't have to be frightened of him. He's my man, sworn to me, and I

promise he will protect you.' He sat opposite her and looked at her with grave eyes. 'You think he's not kind? I think maybe he is, but he's very unhappy. He's close to fifty now and he's never found happiness. He's growing old, and he buys his contentment out of bottles and whores.'

Lopez smiled. 'Vavasour's a soldier, perhaps one of the best in Europe, but what does a soldier do when he's too old? Vavasour's like an old, experienced wolfhound who fears he can't keep up with the pack any more.' Campion liked that thought and she smiled. Lopez saw the smile and was pleased. 'Remember that once he was young and he had hopes and dreams and plans, but not any more.' He shook his head. 'He can be vilely rude, noisy and frightening, but that's because he doesn't want anyone to see what's inside him. So don't be frightened of him. Even an old wolfhound deserves a bone or two. Now!' He changed the subject abruptly. 'Marta's going to light more candles, we'll have a fire, and we shall eat supper.'

Campion wondered if she could feel sympathy for a man like Devorax, whatever Lopez said, but over the supper she forgot the soldier and warmed to the elegant, gentle old man who proved a wondrously sympathetic listener. He coaxed from her the story of her life, all of it, and she even told him, shyly, of Toby's name for her. He liked it.

'May I call you Campion?'

She nodded.

'Then I will. Thank you.' He gestured at her plate. 'The duck is from Holland, Campion. You must try it.'

When the supper was over, her story told, he took her back to the chairs by the window. It was black night beyond the panes, a darkness sparked by candlelit windows on the great bridge and by the poop lanterns of moored ships that streaked their yellow reflections on the water which slid like dark oil beneath them. Mordecai Lopez closed the curtains, shutting off the sound of water. 'You'd like Toby to know you're safe?'

She nodded. 'Please.'

'I'll have one of Vavasour's men go to Oxford. Lord Tallis, you said?'

She nodded again, remembering the note from the Reverend Perilly.

Lopez smiled at her. 'Of course he's Sir Toby now.'

She had never once thought of that. She laughed, an uncertain sound for it was unpractised. 'I suppose he is.'

'And you'll be Lady Lazender.'

'No!' The thought was ridiculous, not of marrying, but of a title.

'Oh yes! And rich.'

The word made her alert. Not once had Mordecai Lopez spoken to her of the seals, though he had listened closely as she talked of the efforts Sir Grenville Cony and her brother had made to obtain the Seal of St Matthew. Now, Campion knew, the moment had come, that moment she had innocently sought once in Sir Grenville Cony's house. She had gone there in search of the secret of the seals, and had been trapped instead by the greed they engendered. Lopez had stood, had crossed to a bag he had placed on a table and she felt, as he returned to the windows, that she was on the brink of a great discovery. It frightened her.

Mordecai Lopez did not speak. Instead he put his hand down on the table beside her, glanced at her, then went back to his chair. He left something on the table.

She knew what it was without looking.

He smiled. 'It's yours to keep.'

The gold seemed to have an added lustre in the candlelight. She saw in the gold, jewel-banded cylinder the cause of all her misery. She hardly dared touch it. Samuel Scammell's throat had been cut for one of these, and she had been brought very close to the hideous flames, Lazen Castle had fallen, Sir George had been killed, and all for these seals.

She picked it up, almost holding her breath as she did so. Again she was surprised by the weight of the precious gold.

St Matthew had shown an axe, the instrument of that martyr's death, while St Mark had the proud symbol of the winged lion. This seal, St Luke, was similar. It showed a winged ox, head high and burly, the symbol of the third Evangelist.

She unscrewed the two halves and the small, silver statue inside made her smile. St Matthew had contained a crucifix, St Mark a naked woman arching in pleasure, while in St Luke was a little, silver pig.

'Each of the seals, Campion, contains a symbol of the thing the seal-bearer most fears.' Lopez's voice was quiet in the room. The moment seemed almost unnatural to Campion; the mystery unravelling. 'To Matthew Slythe went a crucifix. To Sir Grenville Cony went a naked woman, and I received a pig.' He smiled. 'I don't count that as much of an insult.'

She put the halves together and looked at the white-bearded old man. 'What's in the fourth seal?'

'I don't know. The man who had those seals made is the holder of St John. I would like very much to know what it is that he fears.'

She frowned, almost afraid to know what, for a year, she had longed to know. 'Is Christopher Aretine the man who has St John?'

'Yes.' Lopez was staring intently at her, his voice still quiet and gentle. 'It's time, Campion that you knew it all.' He sipped some wine, listening to the damp river wood spit at the screen in front of the hearth. Every second seemed heavy to Campion. Lopez put his wine glass down, the movement delicate, then looked at her again.

'We shall begin with Christopher Aretine. My friend.' He stared at the seal in Campion's hands as if it was something strange, something forgotten. 'It was said that Kit Aretine was the handsomest man in Europe, and I think he truly was. He was also a scoundrel, a wit, a poet, a fighter, and the best company I ever knew.' Lopez smiled wistfully, then stood again. He talked as he crossed to the bookshelves. 'He was a great lover of women, Campion, though I think he was a dangerous man for women to love.' He reached to the topmost shelf, grunted, and brought down a book. 'There was a fine madness in Kit, I'm not sure even now I can describe it. I don't think he knew fear, and he had too much pride, too much anger, and he refused ever to bow the knee. I sometimes wonder if he was driven by hatred in search of love.' Lopez smiled at the thought as he sat again, the book on his knees.

'Kit Aretine could have had everything, Campion, everything. He could have been an earl! The old King offered him an earldom, and Kit threw it all away.'

He paused, sipped more wine, and Campion leaned forward. 'Threw it away?'

Lopez smiled. 'You have to understand, my dear, that King James was like Sir Grenville Cony. He preferred his lovers to be men. I think he fell in love with Kit, but Kit would have none of it. None. The King offered him everything, and in return Kit gave him a poem.' Lopez smiled. 'It was printed anonymously, but everyone knew Kit Aretine was the author. He even boasted about it! He described the King in the poem as "that Scottish thistle of ungendered prick".' Lopez laughed, pleased to see the same from Campion. The old man shook his head ruefully. 'It was a bad poem, a bad idea, and it could only have one result. Kit ended up where you were, in the Tower. Everyone said he'd die, that the insult was too great and too public to go unavenged, but I managed to get him out.'

'You did?'

Lopez smiled. 'I owed Kit a great debt, and the King of England owed me a small one. I forgave the King his debt, and in return he gave me Kit Aretine. There was a condition. Kit Aretine was banished, never again to set foot in England.' Lopez picked the book up from his lap. 'He stopped being a poet then, if he ever had been one, and became a soldier instead. Here,' he held the book out, 'that's him.'

The book felt odd, as if the leather covers were too big for the pages. Campion understood when she opened it. Someone had ripped the pages from the spine, leaving only

two behind. One was the title page. 'Poems, &c. Upon Severall Themes. By Mr Christopher Aretine.' On the opposite page was a woodcut, framed in a complex design, that showed the poet. It was a small, lifeless drawing, yet the artist had conveyed arrogant good looks. It was an imperious face, staring at a world it would conquer.

She turned the title page to find the empty space where the binding threads hung ragged. Something was written here in a bold, dashing hand. 'To my friend, Mordecai, this much Improved Booke. Kit.' Campion looked at Lopez.

'He tore the poems out?'

'Yes. And burned them. In that very fireplace.' Lopez chuckled at the memory, then shook his head sadly. 'I think he knew he could never be a great poet, so he decided to be no poet at all. Yet I don't think he ever knew what an extraordinary man he really was. Kit Aretine, my dear, was a terrible waste of enormous talent.' Mordecai Lopez sipped his wine. He was looking at the seal, but as he put the wine down he lifted his eyes to Campion and said the words which, somehow, were no surprise, yet which turned her soul inside out. 'He was also your father.'

24

The bells of St Mary's rang eleven. From across the water, from the city that climbed to the great cathedral, dozens of other bells echoed the hour. The gates of London were being shut, its thousands of inhabitants were mostly already asleep, and in the morning they would awake to another day not much different to the one on which they had closed their eyes. Yet not Campion. She would never again have a day like the ones before this night, for suddenly she had been wrenched as few people are wrenched. Matthew Slythe, the grim Puritan who had burdened her with God's wrath, had not been her father. Her father was a failed poet, a wit, a lover, and an exile. Kit Aretine. She turned the page of the ruined book back to the portrait. She tried to see a likeness to herself in the arrogant, imperious portrait, but she could not. 'My father?'

'Yes.' Lopez's voice was gentle.

She felt as if she had fallen into a chasm of immeasurable darkness, as if within its bleakness, she struggled to make great wings beat that could take her once more into the light. 'Poems, &c. Upon Severall Themes.' But what? What themes had motivated her real father?

'It's a story that begins long ago, Campion, in Italy.' Lopez had rested his head against the high back of his chair. 'There was a riot against my people. I don't even remember why, but I suppose some Christian child had fallen into a river and drowned and the mob thought we Jews had kidnapped it and sacrificed it in our synagogue.' He smiled. 'They often thought that. So they attacked us. Your father was there, a very young man, and I think it simply struck him that it would be more amusing to fight the mob than join it. He saved my life, and that of my wife and my daughter. He fought for us, rescued us, and was offended when I suggested payment. I paid him in the end, though. I heard he was in the Tower and I had lent money to the King of England. So I cancelled King James's debt for your father's life.

'He was penniless when I took him back to Holland. I offered him money and he refused it, then he made a bargain with me. He would take the money and return it, with interest, in one year. Anything he made in addition would be his.'

Lopez smiled at the memory. 'That was 1623. He bought a ship, a splendid vessel, and he recruited men and bought guns and sailed of against Spain. He was a pirate, nothing else, though the Dutch gave him letters of commission that wouldn't have stopped the Dons putting him to a slow death. They never did. When fortune smiled on your father, she really smiled well.' Lopez sipped wine. 'You should have seen his return. Two more ships with him, both captured and both full of Spanish gold.' He shook his head. 'I've never seen money like it, ever! Only two men have ever taken more off the Spanish, and no man ever cared less about it than your father. He paid me his debt, took some for himself, and he charged me with a new commission. I was to make the rest of the money available to you. It was a fortune, Campion, a true fortune.'

The fire was dying behind its screen, the room becoming chill, but neither moved to put more wood on the feeble flames. Campion listened, her wine forgotten, listened to a stranger tell her who she was.

Lopez stroked his beard. 'Before all that happened, before Kit wrote his poem about King James, he fell in love. Dear God! He was smitten. He wrote to me that he had found his "Angel", and he would marry her. By then I'd known him six years and I doubted he'd ever marry, but he wrote to me again, six months later, and he was still in love. He said she was innocent, gentle and very strong. He also said she was very, very beautiful.' Lopez smiled at her. 'I think she must have been, for she was your mother.'

Campion smiled at the compliment. 'What was her name?'

'Agatha Prescott. An ugly name.'

'Prescott?' Campion frowned.

'Yes. She was the younger sister of Martha Slythe.' Lopez shook his head in wonderment. 'I don't know how Kit Aretine met a Puritan girl, but he did, and he fell in love, and she with him, and they never had time to marry. He was arrested, taken to the Tower, and he left her pregnant.'

Mordecai Lopez sipped his wine. 'She was alone. I suppose she asked Kit's friends for help, but he ran with a swift pack in those days and the help never came. Who needed a pregnant angel?' He shrugged. 'I didn't know her, she didn't know me. I wish I could have helped, but she did the fatal, perhaps the only thing. She crawled home in disgrace.'

Campion tried to imagine how Matthew Slythe would have behaved if she had come home pregnant. It was a fearful thought. She felt a pang for the girl who had been forced back to the Prescotts.

Lopez clasped his hands on his knees. 'They hid her. They were ashamed, and sometimes I think they may have been glad at what happened. She died of the childbirth fever just days after you were born. Perhaps they hoped you'd die, too.'

Campion had to blink back tears, swept by a terrible pity for a girl who had tried to break the same bonds that she had tried to break. Her mother, like the daughter she left behind, had wanted to be free, yet in the end the Puritans had snatched her back to a lonely, vindictive death.

'So there you were,' Lopez smiled, 'a little bastard, the shame of the Prescott family. They called you Dorcas. Doesn't that mean "full of good works"?'

'Yes.'

'That's what they wanted you to be, yet the works were to be their works. They would bring you up as a good Puritan.' Lopez shook his head. 'When Kit was released from the Tower he wrote to the Prescotts, asking for news, and he offered to take you from them. They refused.'

She frowned. 'Why?'

'Because they'd solved their problem by then. Agatha had an older sister. I'm told Martha was not as beautiful.'

Campion smiled. 'No.'

'Yet the Prescotts were rich, they could afford a large dowry, and they attached more than a bride to the dowry. They attached you. Matthew Slythe agreed to marry Martha, to take you, and to bring you up as his natural daughter. Matthew and Martha promised never, ever, to reveal the shame of Agatha. You had to be hidden.'

Campion thought of Matthew and Martha Slythe. No wonder, she thought, they had leaned the wrath of God heavily on her, fearing that every smile and every small act of joy might be Agatha Prescott's shameful personality breaking through the Puritan bonds.

'Then,' Lopez went on, 'Kit Aretine made his fortune and wanted you to have it.' He laughed softly. 'You'd think that to give a child a fortune would be easy! But, no. The Puritans wouldn't take the money. It came from the devil, they said, and it would seduce you from the true faith. Then Matthew Slythe's business began to fail.' Lopez poured more wine. 'Suddenly Kit Aretine's offer became less devilish, even began to smack of Godliness!' He laughed. 'So they asked a young lawyer to negotiate for them.'

'Sir Grenville Cony?' Campion asked.

'Just plain Grenville Cony then, but a subtle little toad all the same.' Lopez smiled. 'And like all lawyers he loved subtlety. Subtlety makes a lawyer rich. Things, my dear, began to get difficult.'

The clocks chimed a ragged cacophony of the quarter hour. From the river came the mournful sound of halyards slapping against masts.

'We couldn't give you the money as an outright gift. The law made that difficult and we simply did not trust Grenville Cony. He came to Amsterdam to see us and that proved a disaster.'

'A disaster?'

Lopez's face showed a wistful amusement. 'Cony had to fall in love with your father. I suppose that wasn't difficult if you loved men instead of women, but Cony managed to offend Kit. He pursued him like a slave.' Lopez chuckled. 'I told your father to encourage it, that we should use Cony's devotion to our advantage, but Kit was never kind to that sort of man. He ended by stripping Cony naked, thumping his arse with a scabbard, and throwing him into a canal. All in public.'

Campion laughed. 'I wish I'd seen it. I wish I'd done it!'

Lopez smiled. 'Cony took his revenge, of a sort. He bought a painting, a naked Narcissus, and he paid to have your father's face painted over the original. He wanted people to think that Aretine had been his lover. An odd sort of revenge, I suppose, but it seemed to please Grenville Cony.'

Campion had stopped listening. She was remembering. She was seeing in her mind's eye that splendid, savage, pagan, arrogant face that had transfixed her in Cony's house. Her father! That man, that face of unbelievable handsomeness, that creature she had thought too good-looking to be true, and it was her father! Now she understood why so many spoke with such awe of Kit Aretine as the handsomest man in Europe. Her mother would never have stood a chance, the Puritan seeing the god and falling in love. Campion remembered the golden hair, the strength of the face, the sheer beauty of it.

Lopez half smiled. 'You saw the painting?'

She nodded. 'Yes.'

'I never did, but I often wondered how good a likeness it was. Cony hired a Dutch painter to sketch your father in an ale-house.'

'He made him look like a god.'

'Then it sounds a good likeness. Strange it should come out of hatred.' Lopez shrugged. 'Mind you, it didn't make our task any easier.' He left the subject of the painting and went back to the Covenant. 'You see, I'd already bought a great deal of property with the money. You own land in Italy, Holland, France, England, and Spain.' He smiled. 'You're very, very rich. All that land, Campion, produces money, some in rent, some in crops, but a very, very great deal of money. I doubt if there are twenty people in England richer than you. We proposed, quite simply, that we kept control of the land, but passed the profits of the land to Matthew Slythe. When you were twenty-one you would take the profits for yourself. But that wouldn't do.

'Master Cony said that if we controlled the land then one day we might simply dam the golden stream. That it gave Matthew Slythe, indeed yourself, an uncertain future.' Lopez shook his head ruefully. 'You have no idea, Campion, how hard we tried to give that money to you, and how difficult it was. So, we drew up a different scheme, a little more subtle. We agreed to give up control of the properties on the condition that it all went to you when you were twenty-one. You would take control of the land, the profits, everything, but Matthew Slythe wouldn't accept that. He believed that if you became rich too quickly then you would slide back into the pagan ways of your real parents. He wanted more years to save your soul, so we agreed, in the end, that you would inherit at twenty-five.

'We'd agreed, remember, to give up the control of the properties, but not to Grenville Cony and Matthew Slythe. Instead we all decided that the Bank of Amsterdam would administer all the land. Even Grenville Cony agreed to that, because it's the one bank everyone trusts. It doesn't belong to one family, but to the whole nation, and it hardly ever cheats anyone. To this day, Campion, they administer your wealth.'

Lopez's references to 'her' wealth seemed strange. She did not feel wealthy, or even fortunate. She was a Puritan girl, struggling for freedom, far from the man she loved.

Lopez looked at the ceiling. 'The bank administers your property. They receive the profits from all the agents throughout Europe. The agents, of course, deduct their fees and I've no doubt that every single one is cheating you. The bank takes its own fee for its trouble, and I'm sure they sometimes add the sums wrong in their own favour, and then the money goes each month by draft of hand to Sir Grenville Cony. And he, my dear, undoubtedly takes an enormous fee. The remainder of the money was sent to your father, and the Covenant, which is the agreement between the four of us and the bank, says that the money must be used for your comfort, education, and happiness.'

She laughed at the thought of Matthew Slythe caring for her happiness.

Lopez smiled.

'Truly it was not very subtle, it might even have worked, but there was one terrible mistake. Your father, Kit Aretine, had to interfere. We'd made a provision in the Covenant for changes to be made. Suppose that England went to war with Holland and the money could not be paid? In that case we'd need to transfer the control of the property somewhere else, and we'd decided, quite simply, that any three signatures from the four of us should be sufficient to change the arrangements. That seemed safe, after all neither I nor your father were ever likely to agree with Grenville Cony or Matthew Slythe, but then Kit had to complicate matters. What happens, he asked, if one of the four men dies? Wouldn't it be simpler, he said, if every man had a seal and each man can hand the seal on to whomever he likes. The seal gives its owner one quarter of the authority over the Covenant and it authenticates the signature of anyone who writes to the Bank of Amsterdam about the Covenant. I said it was a dreadful idea, but I think Kit had already hatched the idea of sending Matthew Slythe a crucifix and Grenville Cony a woman, and so it was done.

'But now, you see,' Lopez leaned forward, 'it was not three signatures that were needed, but three seals. Any man who could gather three seals would control the whole fortune. All of it. They could end the Covenant. If Sir Grenville, whom I very much suspect at this moment has two seals, can take a third, then he will simply go to the Bank and he will take all the property for ever. All of it. You'll have nothing.'

Campion frowned. 'And if Sir Grenville has two seals then no one else can change the Covenant.'

'Exactly. And if he had succeeded in having you killed then you could not have taken the Covenant when you were twenty-five.'

Lopez lifted his wine and smiled at her over the rim of the glass. 'What you have to do, young lady, is to collect those seals of Sir Grenville's and take them, with the Seal of St Luke to the Bank of Amsterdam. That's what your father wanted, and that's what I will help you do.'

Campion picked up the seal on the table. She understood now why Sir Grenville had hunted her and tried to kill her,

she understood why Samuel Scammell had died so that
Ebenezer could inherit control of one seal, she even
understood why Matthew Slythe had lied to her when she had
asked about the seal. She understood so much, though her
mind would still have to go over and over the information,
yet there was one thing she did not understand. She looked at
Mordecai Lopez.

'Where's the fourth seal?'

'I don't know.' He sounded sad.

'Is my father alive?'

'I don't know.'

She had solved so much of the mystery, and now a new
mystery presented itself, a mystery that now seemed even
more important than the four golden seals.

'Why didn't my father come and take me from the
Slythes?'

'Would you have wanted that?'

'Yes, oh, yes!'

Lopez shrugged uncomfortably. 'He didn't know that.'

'Did he try and find out?'

Lopez gave her an unhappy smile. 'I don't think he did. I
don't know.'

She knew that there was much unsaid. 'Tell me what you
know.'

Lopez sighed. He had known these questions would come,
yet he had hoped they would not. 'I think Kit always thought
the time would come when he would fetch you, but the time
was never right. Once the Covenant was made and the seals
distributed, he took himself to Sweden. He fought for the
Swedes and he became close to the King.'

Campion knew that Lopez spoke of Gustavus Adolphus,
the great warrior king who had driven the sword of
Protestantism deep into the Catholic Holy Roman Empire.
'Your father was with the King when he was killed and after
that he left the Swedish army. He came to see me in
Amsterdam. He'd changed, Campion. Something happened
to him in that war, and he'd changed.'

'How?'

'I don't know.' Lopez shrugged. 'He was in his late thirties. I think he knew that he'd failed, that he would never be the great man that his youth had promised. You were eleven. I know he thought of going to see you, even to take you away, but he said you were probably a happy little girl and what could you want with a man like him?' Lopez smiled at her, judging his next words carefully.

'You weren't the only child, Campion. There were twin boys in Stockholm, a little girl in Venice and a pretty child in Holland.'

'Did he see them?' There was pain in her voice.

He nodded. 'Yet he used to travel in those places. He was banished from England.' Lopez shook his head. 'I know this will sound hard, but you were the special one, you were the daughter of his "angel", the only woman I think he truly loved, and you were the only one who'd been taken away from him. I think he was ashamed, too. I know he was. He was ashamed of her death, of abandoning you, and I think he was frightened to see you.'

'Frightened?'

Lopez smiled. 'Yes. Suppose the child of Kit Aretine and his angel turned out to be ugly? What price love then? Or suppose you'd hated him for leaving you? I think he wanted to treasure her memory as the perfect woman, the perfect love that could have set the world on fire. I don't know, Campion, I don't know.'

Campion lifted the seal again. 'Did he think his money was sufficient for me?'

'Perhaps.'

'I don't want his money!' She was smarting at Aretine's rejection, she remembered all the unhappy hours of childhood, all the hours that he could have spared her. She put the seal on the table. 'I don't want it.'

'You don't want his love, you mean.'

'I never had it, did I?' She thought of him. The handsomest man in Europe, the wit, rogue, poet, lover and fighter, who had abandoned his daughter to the Puritans because he could not be cumbered with her. 'What happened to him?'

'I saw him last in 1633, in Amsterdam. He wanted to settle down. He said he would write again, but not poetry. He wanted a new country, he said, a clean country, and he wanted everyone to forget there had ever been a Christopher Aretine. He said he'd make himself a grave, with a carved gravestone, and then he would make himself a farm and he would grow things, write things, and perhaps, at last, rear children. He went to Maryland.' He smiled. 'I'm told there is a grave with his name on it, but I suspect he's laughing at everyone who thinks he's beneath that stone. I think he's now a farmer, or perhaps he's dead.'

'He never wrote to you?'

'Not a word.' Lopez looked tired. 'He said he was going to Maryland to forget all the evil of his past.'

'And the seal?'

'He took it with him.'

'So he could be alive?'

Lopez nodded. 'He could be.' Lopez hated to lie to Campion. He liked her. He saw in her the strength of her dead mother, and some of the spirit of Kit Aretine. Yet Aretine was Lopez's friend, and Aretine had forced a promise from Mordecai Lopez. The promise had been solemn and simple, that Lopez would never reveal Kit Aretine to anyone, not even his own bastards, and Lopez would not break that promise. Yet he had received news from Maryland since 1633, and Lopez knew that Aretine lived. The old man smiled at Campion. 'He couldn't be a great poet, so he stopped being any kind of poet. I think perhaps he couldn't be Kit Aretine either, so he stopped trying. Think of him as a middle-aged American farmer, dreaming of the strange life he once had.'

Campion looked scornful. 'And of the children he abandoned?'

'With a fortune, if you care to take it.'

'I don't.' She was angry with a man she had never met. She stood up, unhappiness frustrating her, and picked up the Seal of St Luke. She looked at it, hating it, then put it decisively on the table beside Lopez. 'I don't want it.'

The old man watched her cross to the fireplace. She took the screen from in front of the fire and poked savagely at the dying blaze. A log collapsed in sparks. She put the poker down and turned back towards Lopez. 'Does the *Mercurius* go to Maryland?'

Lopez smiled. 'It takes weeks and weeks to reach there. Meanwhile,' he picked up the seal, 'there is this.'

She shook her head. 'Couldn't he have come to me just once?'

Lopez seemed not to hear her. He held the seal in front of his eyes and spoke casually, almost offhandedly. 'I have friends in London, men of trade who don't mind my religion. Vavasour has talked to some of them for news. It appears that Sir Grenville Cony has taken Lazen Castle for his own.' His eyes turned to look at Campion, 'Without compensation.' He put the seal down.

She was horrified. 'You mean . . .'

He nodded. 'I mean Sir Toby Lazender has lost everything. Everything. I suppose he and his mother live off charity now.'

She stared at the seal, its gold bright in the room's darkness. She knew she could not rid herself of the seals. For Toby's sake she must follow Christopher Aretine's plans. She shook her head. 'I have to collect them?'

Lopez smiled. 'With our help. I shall give that task to Vavasour.'

'Your wolfhound.'

Lopez nodded. 'I shall set a wolfhound to trap a frog.'

Lopez had sidetracked her, taking her from the anger she felt against Kit Aretine to the duty she owed to Toby and his mother. Yet she would not be deflected. Anger came back into her voice, defiance into her face. 'Will my father come back?'

The old man's voice was gentle. 'That's for him to decide. Does it matter? I'm helping you because of the debt I still owe him.'

Campion seemed to hear Matthew Slythe's voice in her head. ' "For I the Lord thy God am a jealous God, visiting the iniquity of the Fathers upon the children." ' She stared at the Seal of St Luke and knew that it was her father's iniquity that was being thrust on her. She had to take it, for Toby's sake, yet she hated the seals. She looked at Lopez. 'Keep it for me till I leave.'

He smiled. 'A few more days won't hurt. I've kept it sixteen years.' He picked it up.

She went to bed an hour later, but Mordecai Lopez lingered after she had gone. He drew back the wide curtains and thought of an old love between a Puritan and a poet; a cruel, doomed love that had burned so briefly bright and left behind this girl as dazzling as the love itself. The river heaped and fell, heaped and fell through the arches of the bridge, the turbulence shaking the long reflections of the ships' lights in the water's mirror. Kit Aretine had been his friend, his treasured friend, yet Lopez could not deny Campion's final, bitter thrust. Of father and daughter, she said, it was not she who was the bastard. Lopez stared above the bridge, stared westward into the far night, and muttered the words of an old sadness, 'My friend, my friend.'

25

London was in uproar. A witch had escaped, taken from the Tower itself, and the army searched the city with a thoroughness that was tempered by a suspicion that she had long fled. The churches were full, the preachers haranguing God to protect His people from the devil, while every murdered body found in the dawn was ascribed to the demon that stalked the streets.

Mordecai Lopez, breakfasting the morning after his long, long talk with Campion, watched soldiers searching the wharves on the opposite bank. He smiled. 'They're in for a long fruitless day.'

'Like most soldiers,' Devorax grunted.

Lopez looked at Vavasour Devorax's red eyes and sour expression. 'A bad night?'

'It didn't seem bad at the time.' Devorax drank water and made a grimace. 'I'm getting too damned old for it. So, what's to be done?'

Lopez sipped at a dish of tea. It was a luxury he could not do without. 'I want a message taken to Oxford. Can one of your men do it?'

'They do it all the time. What's it for?'

Lopez told Devorax of Sir Toby Lazender and the soldier seemed to disapprove of what he heard.

'You think she'll go to him?'

'If he wants her.' Lopez blew on his tea. 'If I were a wagering man I'd say she'll be Lady Lazender before winter.'

Devorax waited as Marta Renselinck brought food. When the housekeeper had gone he spoke savagely. 'She's a fool! She should go to Amsterdam! She'd be safe there.'

'She'll go to Oxford.' Lopez picked a tealeaf from his dish with a delicate forefinger. 'Can you get her there?'

'You pull the strings, Mordecai, and I'll dance round the damned world for you. I suppose you'll go back to Amsterdam?'

'When she's gone. Yes.'

'And leave me here.' Devorax sounded morose. He stabbed into a fried egg and watched the yolk run over the pewter plate, then scowled at Lopez's tea. 'I don't know how you drink that muck.' He scooped a mess of egg on to a piece of bread. 'So I'm to gather the seals, eh?'

'If you can.'

'I can, Mordecai, I can. It'll take time, but I can.' The

ravaged face smiled a bitter, secret smile, as bitter as the plans he had for the jewels of the Covenant. Vavasour Devorax was going to war.

Sir Grenville Cony yelped with pain.

'Sir Grenville! Still! I beg you, sir, still!' The doctor pressed down with his lancet and watched the blood flow into the silver cup. When bleeding his rich patients he always used a silver cup; it reassured them that, even in sickness, they received only the finest treatment. Doctor Chandler shook his head. 'It's thick, Sir Grenville, very thick.'

'It hurts!' Sir Grenville groaned.

'Not for long, Sir Grenville, not for long.' Chandler gave a reassuring smile. 'And it's a lovely day, Sir Grenville, a wonderful day. A boat ride, perhaps, will revive you?'

'You're a fool, Chandler, a damned fool.'

'Whatever you say, Sir Grenville, whatever you say.' The doctor wiped blood from the wound.

The door opened and Ebenezer Slythe came in. His dark, expressionless eyes looked at Sir Grenville. 'Cottjens sends his apologies.'

'Cottjens is a dungheap. Stop hovering, man!' This last was shouted at the doctor who tried to wipe more blood from the cut on Sir Grenville's upper arm. Sir Grenville pulled up his shirt and jacket, swung his legs to the floor, and groaned. His belly was in agony, had been ever since the girl had escaped from the Tower. 'So?'

Ebenezer shrugged. 'It seems Lopez is not ill. Nor is he at home.' He smiled sardonically. 'Cottjens says the bribe it took for that information will not be rendered on your account.'

'How very kind of him.' Sir Grenville sneered. He waved the doctor out of the room, backing away with his linen cloth and silver cup. 'So it's Lopez.'

'Presumably.'

'And no doubt the bitch of a girl is already in Amsterdam.'

Ebenezer shrugged. 'Presumably.'

'Presumably! Presumably! What do those watermen say?'

The men who had rowed Campion from the Tower had been found. Their story, elicited from them in terror, had not helped. Ebenezer limped to a chair. 'They took them to a coach at Bear Wharf.'

'And then?'

'Nothing.' Ebenezer seemed unmoved by the tale of failure.

'And the coach presumably took them to a ship at another wharf.' Sir Grenville rubbed his upper arm, his fat, white face scowling at the pain. 'That whoreson Jew! We should have killed them all, not expelled them! Damn him!'

Ebenezer brushed dust from his black sleeve. 'Be grateful it was only the Jew. From what you tell me, Aretine would have made a worse enemy.'

For five days Sir Grenville had lived in terror that Kit Aretine had come back from the dead. Cottjens's apologies had lifted that cloud, though Sir Grenville still surrounded himself with guards and travelled infrequently about London's streets. The frog-like face looked at Ebenezer.

'Make sure your damned house is well guarded.'

'It is.' Ebenezer, with money from the Covenant, had purchased a large riverside house in the village of Chelsea. Sir Grenville, who had made the young man his heir, did not like it, but had granted Ebenezer his independence.

Sir Grenville pushed away papers that his secretary had put on the desk. 'So what do we do now?'

Ebenezer smiled. 'There were at least four men in the rescue. One of them might be found.'

'In Amsterdam?' Sir Grenville asked scornfully.

'I was thinking of posting a reward. Two hundred pounds for any real information about her escape.'

'And what good will that do?' Sir Grenville was in a terrible mood, foul-tempered because of the bubbling pain in his stomach.

Ebenezer shrugged. 'It might lead us to her. And then we

kill her.' His dark eyes looked at Sir Grenville. 'You should have let me do it before. We were too fanciful.'

Sir Grenville grunted. 'The next time I'll kill her myself. I'll pull her damned heart out.' He nodded. 'Post your reward. You'll be swamped by fools trying to lie their way into two hundred pounds.'

Ebenezer smiled. 'I can deal with fools.'

'True.' Sir Grenville twisted about in his splayed, padded chair and looked at the two armed men who were in his garden. 'We have four years, Ebenezer, before that bitch bastard is twenty-five. Four years!'

'It's enough.'

'To find her and kill her.' Sir Grenville twisted back, his bulging eyes coming to Ebenezer. 'Because no one will get these seals. No one!'

Which was true, Ebenezer reflected. No one could get close to Sir Grenville without passing one or more of the twelve armed guards who were permanently inside the house. Not even Ebenezer could carry a weapon into Sir Grenville's presence. The seals were safe, Ebenezer knew, for he had dreamed of stealing impressions from the Seal of St Mark. He had waited for his moment, but it had never come.

Yet Ebenezer still dreamed of owning the Covenant. His sister, his bastard sister, should not have it. She would be frivolous with the money, undeserving, while Sir Grenville, Ebenezer thought, was already being left behind by the tide of history.

No, Ebenezer reflected as he walked down to Sir Grenville's boat, only he himself deserved the Covenant. He would take the money and use it to gain the power with which he could change England. He could make it a land of disciplined Saints, ruled by sober men of vision, and Ebenezer would do it with the seals of the Covenant. He did not know how, but he knew he would. It was his destiny, his mission, and he would accomplish it.

Three days later, sitting in the window of the Southwark

house, Campion heard the door open. She assumed it was Lopez, coming early from his afternoon sleep, but it was Vavasour Devorax's harsh voice that startled her.

'Your good news has arrived.'

She dropped the book, turned, and saw a sardonic look on his face. He appeared not to have shaved and she wondered if he was growing his beard again. 'Sir?'

'Mason's back from Oxford.' Devorax lowered himself into a chair. He held a bottle of brandy-wine in his hand. 'You want to celebrate with me?'

She shook her head. 'My good news?'

'Sir Toby Lazender and his mother look forward to your arrival. They wish to see you.' He poured brandy-wine into a pewter mug. 'It seems they're eager to see you.' He watched the happiness on her face. She seemed to bubble with joy. Devorax sounded sour. 'You're so keen to leave us?'

'No, sir. No.' She still felt uncomfortable in the soldier's presence. She sensed that he despised her innocence, mocked it even. 'You've been very kind, sir.'

'You mean Mordecai's been very kind.' Devorax drank, wiped his mouth. 'He'll miss you.' He gave a grim laugh. 'I think he sees you as the daughter he lost.'

'He lost?'

'Burned to death. Her and her mother.' Devorax said it brutally. 'That's why he won't live in a timber house anywhere.' He saw her expression and laughed. 'Don't feel sorry for Mordecai. It was a long time ago.'

'He never remarried?'

'No.'

Devorax frowned into the empty mug, as if puzzled at where the drink had gone. 'But don't feel sorry for him. He doesn't lack for anything.' He leaned over for the bottle.

His casual cynicism annoyed her. 'Can money replace a family?'

He stared at her, grey eyes cold, and when he spoke his voice was pitying and condescending. 'Count the bedrooms, girl.'

'Count the bedrooms?'

'God in his heaven!' He put down bottle and mug and ticked off the fingers of his left hand. 'You have the big room at the side. I understand you sleep alone?'

She blushed. 'Yes.'

'Then there's the small room at the back where I sleep, when I sleep. Then there's the other big room above here where Mordecai sleeps. Yes?'

'Yes.'

'So where, girl, do you think Marta sleeps?' He picked up the bottle again. 'Not with me, girl, I assure you. She hates me.' He grinned. 'And you tell me it's not with you, and I tell you that Marta Renselinck doesn't sleep in the kitchen.' He laughed at her. 'They've been together for twelve years now. She won't become a Jew, and he won't become a Lutheran, so they just happily adulterate each other. Are you shocked, girl?'

She hated the way he called her 'girl'. She shook her head. 'No.'

'Oh, but you are! The gallant old Jew who came to your rescue turns out to be human after all.' He seemed, suddenly, angry. He gestured at the panorama of wharves, bridge, Tower, cathedral and ships. 'Look at it all! Full of Puritans, churchmen, lawyers, all of them fat, self-important bastards who tell the rest of us how to live, but I'll tell you something.' His voice was gravelly, harsh on her ears. 'They've all got their secret, girl, all of them! And do you know where to find it?'

The ravaged face was hostile. She shook her head and he gave his humourless laugh. 'In their bedrooms, girl, in their bedrooms. So don't be shocked that Mordecai warms his bed without benefit of clergy. He's a more decent man than any of them.' He drank his brandy-wine.

She tried hard not to be rebuffed by his anger, his swearing or his seeming dislike of her. 'Have you known him long?'

'All my life it seems.' Devorax laughed.

'Did you know my father?'

The grey eyes turned to her. 'Aretine? Yes.'

'What was he like?'

Devorax laughed. 'Pretty boy, Aretine. He was a lucky bastard, especially with the women.' He shrugged. 'I liked him. He was too clever for his own good, though. Doesn't do to be clever, girl. Just gets you into trouble.'

'When did you know him?'

'In the wars. I fought for Sweden.' He touched the scar on his face. 'I got that at Lützen. Some little bastard with a sword. Still,' he smiled grimly, 'I killed him.' He poured more drink for himself. 'We're leaving tomorrow.'

'Tomorrow!' She was surprised. She knew that the search for her still continued in London; that travellers leaving the city were stopped and their coaches or wagons searched.

Devorax nodded. 'Tomorrow.' He gave her his grim smile. 'I have a travelling companion for you, someone who'll keep you safe.' He found this funny, but would not tell her more.

That night Mordecai Lopez gave her a special dinner, a farewell dinner, and Campion tried to hide the pleasure she felt at the thought of returning to Lady Margaret and Toby. Lopez saw the pleasure anyway. 'I think your Sir Toby is a lucky man.'

'I think I'm lucky.'

'You'll write to me?'

She nodded. 'Of course.'

He raised a glass of wine to her. 'I leave you in good hands, Campion.' He smiled. 'Vavasour will collect your seals. It will take time, so don't be impatient. In the meantime you are to have this.'

He pushed something over the table. For a moment she thought it was the Seal of St Luke, but then she saw it was a piece of paper. Lopez shrugged. 'That will be honoured in Oxford.'

She shook her head. 'I can't!'

'Why not?' he laughed. 'Marrying is an expensive business, Campion. You have to have a dress, you have to feed all those people, and you have to live somewhere.' He laughed at her. 'Take it. I insist! You will repay me when the seals are gathered.'

He had given her one thousand pounds. She was embarrassed, for he had already paid for a wardrobe of new clothes, but he shrugged off her thanks. 'You forget, Campion, that you are rich. The rich never find it difficult to borrow money, it's only the poor who find that hard, and they need it most. Take it. There is one other thing.'

She looked at him. She would miss him, she thought, his wry sense and gentle kindness. 'One other thing?'

'You must take it.' Like a conjurer he produced the seal. She looked at it. 'Why don't you keep it?'

'Because it's yours. You have to control part of your danger, Campion, you have to have that courage. You need it.' He smiled. 'Give it to Toby to keep, if you like, but you must have something of your father's.' He put it in the table's centre. 'It's yours. I give it to you.'

She picked it up, knowing that in so doing she had put herself back into danger. Lopez smiled. 'You'll keep it?'

'I'll keep it.'

He nodded approval and raised his glass once more. 'Well done.'

In the small hours, when the wind rippled the Thames and lifted the hair on the traitors' heads pierced on pikes above the bridge gateway, Vavasour Devorax went to Campion's room. He moved silently, like a great cat, and there was no sign that he had been drinking. He carried a lantern.

The door opened silently, greased by Devorax himself earlier in the day.

Campion slept, one hand curled, palm upwards, on the pillow beside her face.

A board creaked beneath his foot. He froze. The girl licked her lips, stirred, then was still again. The light from the lantern was low, but enough to show the Seal of St Luke beside her bed.

Vavasour Devorax picked it up.

He took it to the room which overlooked the Thames, to a table that he had prepared, and on the table was a small square of thick glass. He had smeared it with a little oil and now, using the candle from inside the lantern, he dripped sealing wax on to the glass. He pressed the seal home.

He did it again, then a third time.

The candle was put back into the lantern, and he wrapped the glass with its precious burden in a piece of muslin, then in wool, and finally put the whole into a small wooden box. It took him a minute, creeping on stockinged feet, to put the seal back by Campion's bed, and another few moments to hide all traces of his activity on the table.

A few moments later he pulled the cork from a bottle of wine and lay back on his bed. He grinned and drank to himself. Tomorrow he would take the girl to Oxford and, after that, he would play his own clever game. Not Lopez's game, not the girl's, but his own. One seal was enough. He grinned, shut his eyes, and gave himself up to the oblivion of the bottle.

PART IV
The Gathering of the Seals

26

Morning. The seagulls were screaming over the fish market at Billingsgate. Carts rumbled in the streets, the noises of a city trading and waking, a city patrolled by Parliament's army that still searched for Campion.

Marta Renselinck brought her the dress she was to travel in. 'Don't ask me why, Campion, I don't know. The pig doesn't tell me.' Devorax had sent up a cheap, coarse black dress. A bonnet matched the dress.

Mordecai Lopez kissed her on both cheeks. 'Maybe I come to your wedding, yes?'

She smiled. 'Perhaps Toby doesn't want to marry me any more.'

'You never told me he was a fool!'

She laughed. 'You come to our wedding.'

'If I can. I don't know. Take care, my dear. You have the seal?'

She nodded. It was round her neck, feeling strangely familiar and strangely odd. 'I may let Toby keep it.'

'Good.' He took her elbow. 'You have the money?'

'Yes.'

'And Marta has packed your clothes on the cart, and we've put in food for the journey. You'll be safe! And Vavasour has a companion for you, not very pleasant, but he will protect you.'

'A companion?'

'He wants it to be a surprise. Come along!'

In the yard where she had first alighted and come to the house was a small, shabby cart. It was surrounded by Devorax's men, all of them mounted, all of them armed and decorated with Parliamentary sashes. Only Mason was not armed. He was dressed as shabbily as Campion and waited on the driver's seat of the cart. Devorax saw her and grinned. 'Come here, girl! Meet your brother.' He pointed at Mason.

Mason laughed. 'Hello, sister.'

Devorax laughed. 'And what are you doing, Mason?'

'Burying father, sir!'

The men guffawed. Devorax, surprisingly agile for a man close to fifty, jumped on to the cart and then reached down for Campion. 'Give me your hand.'

In the cart was a long box. Devorax lifted the lid, releasing a reeking stench. 'Meet your father.'

Campion grimaced. In the box was the corpse of an old man. The body was emaciated in its grubby winding sheet. The corpse's hair was white and lank, the cheeks fallen about lips that were blue in death. Vavasour Devorax grinned at her. 'We call him "Old Tom". You're his daughter, and you've got papers saying that you're taking him to High Wycombe for burial. If anyone asks what he died of, say it was the plague.' He looked down at Old Tom. 'He cost me ten pounds. The price of everything's going up in this damned city.' He dropped the lid, then looked at Mason. 'You're on your own till we're out of London. Understand?'

'Yes, sir!'

'Open up!' Devorax waved at the gate. 'Lead on!'

They would cut through the city to avoid the great southern detour to the next bridge. The soldiers at London Bridge climbed on to the cart, but one view of the old man convinced them that they did not wish to search further in the filthy cart. It was the same at Ludgate and at the Knight's Bridge where they were stopped for the third and last time. Campion was nervous the third time. Vavasour Devorax and his men had ridden well ahead, out of sight, and she feared what would happen if the soldiers suspected anything. Mason was not worried. He muttered the word 'plague' and the soldiers hurried them onwards.

Vavasour Devorax waited five miles further on. Mason, with relief, changed into his soldier's clothes, buckling a sword over his orange sash and leather coat. Old Tom was lifted out of the cart and carried deep into the undergrowth. He was tipped out as food for scavenging birds and animals. Vavasour Devorax was amused. 'He served his King, Old Tom.'

'His King?' Campion was puzzled.

'He fooled the King's enemies, didn't he? You said you can ride?'

'Side-saddle.'

They abandoned the cart, using the horse as a pack-animal to take Campion's clothes, and she was mounted on a spare saddle horse. Devorax's men seemed pleased to be out in the countryside, released from London, and even more pleased when they stopped early at an inn. Devorax grinned at her. 'No point in stopping late and losing the best rooms.' He shouted for stable boys. 'Come on, girl. There's drink inside.'

She watched him that evening and saw a new Vavasour Devorax, a drunken man who blossomed in the company of the tavern and regaled them with hair-raising stories of battles old and recent. He sang songs, shouted jokes, and guarded her door that night with drunken snores where he lay on the floor outside.

They left the main road the next day and threaded their way across a fertile countryside. At one point, indistinguishable from the other places where they had stopped while men scouted the path ahead, Devorax gave an order that was greeted with a cheer. The men pulled off their orange sashes and brought out creased, white, royal favours. The sight reminded Campion of Toby. It cheered her up.

Vavasour Devorax told her that they had pierced the ring of fortresses that surrounded Oxford. They were in Royalist territory.

Campion's spirits rose all day. She had not seen the country since she had been taken to London. The crops were nearing ripeness, the woods and hedgerows overflowing with greenness, and once, after Devorax had galloped the troop up a gentle hill, she stood her horse and stared at larks that tumbled their song in the free sky.

Vavasour Devorax looked at the happiness on her face. His voice was mocking. 'Try looking ahead of you.'

She did, and saw the silver thread of the river cutting across the landscape. Clouds threw vast shadows that mottled the countryside, but by the glint of the Thames, clear in the light, was Oxford. A city of stone, lavish with spires and towers, and surrounded by a vast, sprawling earthwork. The ramparts defended the King's new capital from his enemies in nearby London. Devorax looked at her. 'Looks good from here, yes?'

She nodded, 'Yes.'

'It stinks when you're inside.' He laughed, showing his big yellow teeth. 'Come on!'

He produced a paper that took them easily past the guardposts where the road went through the huge earthen wall. Guns pointed outwards from stone platforms dug into the walls' tops. They came to a second guardpost at the edge of the city proper, and again Devorax's paper drew respect from the sentries. An officer looked at Campion. 'Who's she?'

'The damned Queen of Sheba. Mind your own business.'

Once inside the city, Campion understood why Devorax said it stank. It did. It was horribly crowded, the streets seemingly busier than London. It was a university city still, though many of the colleges, Devorax said, had been taken over by the court or by the King's army. The royal court was based here, with all its servants, courtiers and hangers-on; the placemen who followed kings as gulls followed a boat. The city garrison was huge, many of the men had brought their wives with them, and the streets seemed impossibly full. There were refugees, too, people like Lady Margaret and Toby. Devorax spoke of them, his tone managing to subtly denigrate them. 'Your friends are lucky.'

'Why?'

'The good citizens of Oxford, in their love for the King, have doubled, re-doubled, and doubled again the cost of a room. However it seems that Lord Tallis has given Lady Margaret Lazender a lavish part of his house. This way.'

He knew his way about Oxford, leading her confidently to a narrow street near the city centre. Mason pointed to a house and Devorax stopped outside. 'Put her baggage down.' He looked at her. 'This is it.' He leaned from the saddle and thumped on the door.

Campion was excited, barely able to contain her joy at the reunion. She waited for the door to open.

Devorax scowled and knocked again.

The door opened and a maidservant looked timidly at the tall, grim soldier. 'Sir?'

'Were you asleep, girl?'

'No, sir.'

'Is Sir Toby Lazender here?'

'He's out, sir. Lady Margaret's here, sir.'

Devorax nodded down at Campion's baggage, then spoke again to the maid. 'Take it inside, girl. Hurry!' He looked at Campion, standing by the door. 'In you go.'

'Aren't you coming in?'

'What for? You think I want to make polite conversation?'

She shook her head, made to feel uncomfortable again. 'I must thank you, sir.'

'True. Have you got the seal?'

'Yes.'

'Look after it.' He gathered his reins and turned his horse. 'I'll send you a message when I need you. Don't expect anything to happen soon.'

She tossed her head, offended by his offhand manner. 'I don't expect anything, sir.'

'Good girl!' He laughed. 'Never expect anything! Then

you'll never be disappointed.' He seemed pleased. 'And one last piece of advice.'

'Sir?'

'Stay away from the damned Puritans. They hate beauty.' With that he rowelled his horse, the hooves sparked on the cobbles, and he was gone. Campion was astonished, staring after the retreating troop. Had that been a compliment from Vavasour Devorax?

'Miss?' The maid was nervous. 'Miss?'

'Is Lady Margaret in?'

'Yes, miss.'

'Take me.'

She was nervous, excited, a hundred thoughts and emotions crowding her brain. She followed the maid down a long, gloomy, panelled passage and waited as the door was knocked. An imperious, familiar voice answered.

'Come!'

'Miss?' The maid held the door open.

Campion hesitated. The voice came louder.

'Who is it? Am I supposed to guess?'

Campion went in slowly, almost hesitantly. There had been moments when she had dreamed of this meeting, when the thought of Lady Margaret and her son had made the horrors of the Tower seem less real, but she had never thought again to see the aquiline face with the grey, piled hair or hear the impatient, ordering voice. Campion stood facing the garden room and smiled. 'Lady Margaret?'

'Child!' And suddenly Lady Margaret was hugging her, clinging to her, saying unintelligible things in her ear, and Campion clung to the older woman until she was pushed gently away. Lady Margaret shook her head. 'You're crying, child! I thought you'd be glad to see me!'

'You know I am.' She was crying for sheer happiness and relief. They hugged again, and then talked as though they had only five minutes to meet. Campion was laughing and crying, talking and listening, clinging to the older woman's hand.

Lady Margaret pulled off the bonnet and poked at

Campion's hair. 'You look quite dreadful, child. Didn't anyone cut your hair?'

'Dear Lady Margaret! They almost burned me alive. I didn't have time for hair!'

'Yes, dear, but we should always try to look our best when we die. First impressions are very important, Campion, and God may look on the inward things, but he's more of a fool than I think if he doesn't take a peep at the outer things as well.' She turned to a table and rang a bell. 'We shall take some wine, dear, then clean you up before Toby comes back.'

A door opened and Enid, Lady Margaret's own maid, came in. 'Lady Margaret?' She saw Campion, put her hands to her face in surprise and looked as if she would cry.

'Enid!' Lady Margaret frowned, enjoying herself. 'Have you seen a mouse?'

'It's you!' Enid ran into Campion's embrace.

Campion hugged her. 'Enid?' She wanted to cry again because of the welcome, the pleasure, the sense of being home.

Lady Margaret sniffed. 'It's hardly the Holy Ghost, Enid. Say something intelligent to Campion.' She smiled as Campion embraced Enid, waited until they had talked for a moment, and then ordered a bottle of malmsey wine. 'And after that, Enid, we'll have to do something with Campion's hair.' She frowned at the dress. 'It's nice of you to be in mourning for Sir George, dear, but I think something a little more joyful for Toby.'

Campion thought it best not to mention that the mourning had been for Old Tom. 'How is Toby?'

Lady Margaret sat down, back straight and head high. 'He swings between extreme misery when he believes you will not get here, and unseemly joy when he decides that you might. I can't think why. There are some perfectly beautiful and eminently well-born girls in this town, some of them with adequate busts. You've lost weight, dear. There's one girl in particular I tried to introduce, Lady Clarissa Worlake, but

Toby's very stubborn. I can't think why.'

Campion smiled. 'Do you really want him to marry Lady Clarissa?'

Enid had brought the wine into the room. 'She'd have killed him if he had.'

'Enid! I've had occasion to correct you in the past!'

'Yes, my Lady.' Enid smiled over Lady Margaret's shoulder, then handed them each a glass of the sweet wine.

'How's his wound?' Campion asked.

'He's lost two fingers,' Lady Margaret held up the two small fingers of her left hand, 'which embarrasses him. He wears a glove. His shoulder's very stiff, but truly his recovery was remarkable. I quite thought he'd die on the way here.'

'When will he be back?'

'I thought you were happy talking to me!'

'I am, Lady Margaret, you know I am! As happy as I could be!'

'I doubt that, child, but you said it very prettily. Toby won't be back till evening, so we've plenty of time. You must tell me everything. You can leave, Enid, that table's quite adequately dusted.'

They talked through the afternoon, still talking as Lady Margaret and Enid cut and curled her hair. Caroline, who would have done it, was staying with her sister and brother-in-law. There was only Lady Margaret, Toby, and one servant apiece in Oxford. Lady Margaret chose a dress from among those Marta Renselinck had purchased and gave it grudging approval. She gave the story of the seals and the Covenant much greater approval. 'So you're rich?'

'If I assemble three seals.'

'It's very useful for a girl to be rich.' She had refused to take Campion's money draft, saying it must go to Sir Toby as head of the household. 'You say that noisome little toad Cony has two of the seals?'

'Yes.'

'And that quite horrid brother of yours is helping him?'

Campion straightened her stomacher, looking at herself in

a long mirror. 'You haven't heard the best news.'

'Tell me, child.'

Campion turned to face Lady Margaret. 'I'm not a Slythe.' She blushed, not sure whether the truth was such good news to a prospective mother-in-law. 'I'm one of Kit Aretine's bastards.'

Lady Margaret, with her penchant for genealogy and erudition about the most extraordinary families, loved it. 'Kit Aretine! Your father! I'm so glad, dear, I'm so glad! I've often thought I didn't want Slythe blood in my grandchildren, but Aretine blood is really quite acceptable. There's Scottish blood there, but that can't be helped.'

'Scottish?'

'Sweet Lord, yes! Kit's mother was a McClure, with some heathenish name like Deirdre. A pretty woman, I believe, but definitely Scotch, though I think she lived long enough in England to lose the worst of that legacy.' She sniffed in disapproval of all things Scottish. 'So Kit's your father!'

'Yes.'

'And on the wrong side of the blanket! Well, we'll just have to ignore that. He always was a scoundrel. He was put in the Tower.'

'For calling King James "that Scottish thistle of ungendered prick".'

'You acquired some very charming language in prison, child.' Lady Margaret sniffed. 'Where is your father now?'

'In America, Maryland. If he's alive.'

'I see.' It was obvious that the mention of America did not impress Lady Margaret unduly. 'Will he come looking for you?'

'I don't know.'

'I hope his language has improved if he does. I imagine not. One can't think that the settlements are anything but uncouth.'

'I'm not sure I want him to come.'

'Don't be so very stupid, Campion. Kit Aretine was said to be the most handsome and witty of men. I've always wanted to meet him.' She stepped away. 'You look quite passable. Let me get you some earrings. And pinch your cheeks, child, you need colour.'

They sat in the garden, between shady pear trees and Campion listened to the story of Lazen Castle and of how Sir Grenville Cony had expelled the family. The Lazenders, Lady Margaret said, were ruined. Their lands were gone, their money, their home too. Charles Ferraby, the ox-eyed boy who was to marry Caroline, had withdrawn his hand. No one needed a penniless bride. Only Lord Tallis, an old friend of Sir George, had offered help.

Hooves sounded at the end of the garden, a voice called out and a gate slammed. Lady Margaret cocked an ear. 'That's Toby, dear. Hide yourself.'

'Hide?'

'Of course! You should always surprise your men, it keeps them interested.'

There was a grassy space between high bushes, a space hidden from the house, and Campion waited there through the seconds that seemed like eternity. Her heart was thumping. She felt excited, as though she was a small child playing a thrilling and secret game. She heard boots in the passage that led beside the garden to the house, the sound of a door, and then, muffled but distinct, the sound of his voice. She had a sudden, terrible memory of the Tower, of the rats scrabbling on a cold, foul floor, and then Lady Margaret's commanding voice dragged her back to this lilac-shaded garden. 'Go into the garden, Toby. I wish to talk with you.'

She heard his footsteps on the flagstones that bordered the lawn. Then silence. She waited. His voice came again. 'Are you coming, mother?'

'In a moment, Toby. Don't be tedious. Tell me the time.'

His boots sounded again, this time muffled by the grass. Campion tried to compose herself, to make her face serene and calm. She patted the ringlets of her hair, and then she could see him, his hair red in the sun, his left hand gloved. He was dressed in black. He stopped at the sundial. 'It's nearly half past six, mother!' He turned, getting no reply, and saw the blue dress beneath the lilacs.

'Toby?'

She could not be calm, she could not be serene. His strong face was showing astonishment, joy, and then they were in each other's arms, his maimed hand was about her shoulders and her face was buried on his chest. 'Toby!'

'You're here.' He tipped her face up, and then kissed her tenderly, almost in wonderment as if he did not believe it. 'Campion?'

They kissed again, this time as if they would crush the one into the other, never to let go, never again to be parted. She held on to his rough, leather armour, clinging to him as if to life itself.

Lady Margaret's voice came from the house. 'Toby!'

'Mother?'

'You might do that where your mother is not forced to watch.'

He grinned at his mother over Campion's head, then kissed again. Campion could not have cared if the whole world watched. She was home.

27

Expect nothing, Vavasour Devorax had said, yet hope as she might Campion could not have expected this.

A summer that would live for ever in her memory, a summer heavy with scent and fruit, with leaf and harvest, a summer for love.

Campion Aretine, as Lady Margaret insisted she should be called, would marry Sir Toby Lazender in one month's time. The banns were read in church and no one saw any cause or just impediment why the two should not be joined in holy matrimony. From the Tower, from the road that led to the waiting stake, her life twisted suddenly into an incessant round of parties, dancing, feasts, of people who seemed to share her happiness even though she had never met them. If her life was, indeed, a river, then it had plunged from the dark caverns of brooding terror into this broad, sunlit reach. Yet the sky above was not the seamless blue of her dreams.

She had never seen a place like Oxford. Its towers and courtyards, steeples and archways, all bore witness to a love of beauty that would have been an anathema to Matthew Slythe. All that beauty was threatened. The royal cause was foundering, the King's army on the defensive, and not even Campion's sudden happiness could hide from her the shadows that threatened Oxford. Yet that summer it was a golden city to her. She did not notice the stench in the streets, the effluence of a crowded city. She saw only a place of beauty that men had embellished and endowed with grace. She was in love.

Yet even in the broad, sunlit land through which her river flowed, a land green and scented, profuse with a thousand flowers, another shadow reached out from the past. The men who were drunk on God did not just shatter visible beauty, they had also mounted an attack on her innocence. Faithful Unto Death Hervey's dry, scaly hands had put filth within her and the filth was still there. She knew it in herself, it poisoned part of her, and she felt it on a day, late in August, when Toby was released from his garrison duties and they rode westward, alone, out into the countryside.

War seemed far off that day. The land was generous, its grass heavy and crops full. The river seemed burdened with life, edged with flowers. It was a day like the day a year ago when she had last swum in her pool at Werlatton, a day when the horizon hazed white with heat, when insects hummed in the still air, a day of perfect beauty marred only by the shadow within her.

The river had brought her here, but the water was tainted from the caves of horror it had swept her through. The current had been fast and now it was slow, yet she was still fearful. She hid the horror from Toby, pretending it did not exist, yet she feared marriage because Faithful Unto Death Hervey had put a poison in her.

Toby led her away from the Thames, their horses ambling northwards through rich fields and woods to a lush meadow that fringed a stream going south to the Thames. He tethered their horses to a fallen tree and carried a basket to a patch of grass beside the stream.

They talked as they had talked for three weeks, and it still surprised her how much they could say and how much she liked to talk with him. He amused her, educated her, listened to her, argued with her, and even the smallest thing could throw up a great conversation because they shared a curiosity about their world.

They ate by the stream, sharing bread and cold meat and drinking wine. Afterwards she lay on her back, her head pillowed by her saddle, while Toby lay on his stomach a few feet away. He looked at her. 'They'll know you're here by now.'

'Yes.' It was a subject that kept coming back. Sir Grenville Cony, Toby thought, must have his informants in Oxford. The wine had made Campion drowsy. 'Can we manage without the seals?'

'If you want to.' He was picking the tiny petals of clover and touching nectar to his tongue. 'Do you want to forget them? Throw this one away?' Toby wore the golden seal about his neck.

She sighed. 'They've caused so much trouble. I didn't ask for them. I didn't want all this to happen. I didn't ask for Ebenezer to hate me, and for Cony and for men like Vavasour Devorax.' She twisted her head to look at him. 'I didn't want to be in the Tower.' She could feel the horror inside her.

Toby rolled on to his side, wincing as his weight went momentarily on to his damaged shoulder. 'You didn't ask for it, but without the seals you'd probably be married to someone like Samuel Scammell by now. You'd probably have your own little baby Scammell with its own little Bible and its own little scowl.'

She laughed, turning her face back to the sun. 'Yes.' The stream's murmur was a background to her thoughts. 'Poor Scammell.'

'Poor?'

'He didn't ask for it either. He was harmless.'

'He was greedy.'

There was silence. The sun was bright on the inside of her eyelids. She heard the horses stirring, a fish plopping in the water. 'Do we need the seals, Toby?'

He rolled back on to his stomach, his dark red hair shading the fine-boned face he had inherited from his mother. He did not reply immediately and Campion turned her face to look at him. She loved his face. It was not, she supposed, a classically handsome face. Eyes would go much faster to a man like Lord Atheldene, but the memory would fasten on Toby. His eyes met hers.

'Two answers. I'll marry you if you're the poorest girl in the kingdom. Second answer. Yes we do. Lazen's been in the family since anyone knows. I'd like to buy it back one day, God knows when, but I'd like to do it before mother dies.'

She nodded.

He smiled at her. 'But if you tell me that you don't want the seals, that you want to be rid of Sir Grenville and your brother, then I'll throw this one away right now. I'll marry you and think myself lucky.'

'Don't throw it away.' She smiled at him. 'We'll buy Lazen Castle with it.'

He smiled. 'And you'll be Campion Lazender.'

She laughed at that. It sounded strange. She remembered how he had seen the campion flowers in her rush basket and picked the name for her. She laughed again. 'If I hadn't met you I'd still be called Dorcas.'

'Dorcas.' Toby said the name with lugubrious relish. 'Dorcas. Dorcas. Dorcas.'

'Stop it! I hate that name.'

'I shall call you Dorcas when you upset me.'

She waved a fly away from her face. 'Campion.' She said it experimentally. 'I like that name.'

'I love it.' He grinned. 'I'm just glad you hadn't picked cow parsley on the day I met you. Lady Cow Parsley Lazender doesn't sound right.'

'Or deadly nightshade.'

'Or gooseberry.'

'Lady Wortleberry Lazender.' She laughed. 'I like Campion.'

Toby plucked the seeds from meadow oat grass. 'There was a poet called Campion.'

'I know.'

'Only because I told you.' He grinned at her, then levered himself forward on his elbows so he was close to her, his face smiling down at her. 'Listen.' He thought for a few seconds.

> Lost is our freedom,
> When we submit to women so:
> Why do we need them,
> When in their best they work our woe?

She laughed at him. 'Did Campion write that?'

'He did.'

'It's not very good, is it?'

He shrugged, tickling her face with the grass stem. 'You're not supposed to like it. You're supposed to get angry with me and tell me I'm a woman-hater.'

'I'm too hot to get angry. Tell me something else he wrote and if I don't like it then I won't marry you.'

He nodded. 'Agreed.' He frowned, pretending to think again, then ducked his head, kissed her lightly on the lips, and quoted again, his eyes on hers.

> Heaven is music, and thy beauty's
> Birth is heavenly.

It was Campion's turn to pretend to think. She stared into his green eyes, then nodded. 'I'll marry you.'

'You liked it?'

'I liked it.'

'I thought you would.'

'Is that why you learned it by heart for today?'

He laughed. 'How do you know?'

'Because the only poems you know are the ones your father used to sing at Christmas, and because you left a book of Campion's poetry on the garden table and it got wet in the night.'

He grinned. 'Women shouldn't be so clever.'

'We need to be, Toby dear, considering what we marry.'

'Whom you marry.'

'What.'

He kissed her again, long and gently, and as her eyes closed he put his right hand on her stomach. He felt her stiffen beneath his touch, knew she was shrinking from him, and raised his face. 'Campion?'

She kept her eyes shut and said nothing. This was the fear, this was the thing that had been smirched. The water was tainted, the evil within her, the shadow reaching from her past.

'Campion?'

She wanted to say something to him, she wanted to give him love if he would only give her time, but they were to be married in a week and she was frightened.

He lifted his hand from her stomach, moved it gently to her face and pushed her eyelids up. The blue eyes that watched him, if not hostile, were very frightened. He smiled. 'The priest won't touch you again.'

She stared at him, her face frowning. 'You know?'

He nodded. 'I read the *Mercurius*. It's not difficult to guess.'

She thought he had not known, that the stain was hidden within her and she had hidden it from him. She had told Lady Margaret much of what had happened, though not all, and now she sat up, brushing hair from her face. 'Did your mother tell you?'

'No.' Which was not quite true. With her usual directness Lady Margaret had assured Toby that his bride was still a virgin, but she had also told him he must treat her carefully. Now Toby pushed himself up so he was sitting opposite her. 'Tell me.'

She shook her head petulantly. 'There's nothing to tell.'

'Then there's nothing to worry about.'

Her eyes met his almost in challenge, then she shrugged and, in a toneless, flat voice, she told him.

She knew it could have been far worse, but she still felt the defilement of Hervey's hands on her breasts, his breathing in her ear as his fingers groped down past her waist. She spoke of the tribunal spectators staring at her while the priest's hands slid over her body. She could feel them now, kneading and rubbing, and she knew that Faithful Unto Death Hervey had spoiled something she wanted kept clean. The stain would not go from her.

He said nothing when she finished. She had not looked at him as she talked, but had stared across the stream. Now Toby looked at her profile, wistful and beautiful, and still he waited.

She turned to him, still defensive. 'Vavasour Devorax said something odd to me.'

'What?' He was being as gentle and delicate as if he were feeling in cold waters for an elusive trout.

'He said everyone has a terrible secret, something horrible, and he said the secret is always in the bedroom. He meant it too. It all sounds so foul, as if love ends up in a squalid, dirty room with smelly sheets.'

'It doesn't.'

She had not heard him. 'Scammell pawed at me and that man you killed tried. Then there was the Reverend Hervey and there was a soldier in the Tower.' She stopped, shaking her head, and she hated the seals again for it was they that had made her vulnerable to all that lust, that had poisoned this summer's day beside a stream.

Toby lifted his hand and pushed up an unwilling chin. 'Do

you think my parents found it squalid?'

'No, but they're different.' She knew she sounded childish.

He smiled at her, shaking his head. 'It doesn't have to be squalid . . .'

'How do you know?'

'Will you listen to me?'

'Lady Clarissa Worlake?'

'No!' He laughed. 'Now will you listen?'

'Who?'

'Campion!' He startled her with sudden sternness. 'Listen! How do you think the people in Lazen found their wives, husbands and lovers?'

'I don't know.' She was miserable because of the shadow on her, childish because she was ignorant, frightened because this was the smear on the flawless sky.

'We used to talk of May Day, remember? And Harvest? How the young people and the not so young used to go off at night into the woods. That wasn't horrible! If it was, why would people look forward to it?' He smiled. 'It could be uncomfortable if it rained, but it wasn't squalid. At least a third of our marriages started that way and the church never minded. It's called love, people celebrate it. It doesn't get spoiled.'

'I never had a May Day.' She was looking at the grass, but now she looked at him accusingly. 'You did.'

'Of course I did! What was I supposed to do? Sit at home reading my Bible and deciding which of my neighbours was a sinner?'

His indignation forced a reluctant smile from her. She shook her head, still troubled. 'I'm sorry, Toby, I'm sorry. You shouldn't marry me. I'm just a Puritan and I don't know anything.'

He laughed and touched her cheek. 'I'm glad you're a Puritan.'

'Why?'

'Because no one caught you on May night or in the harvest rick.'

She smiled, still miserable. 'You caught a few, didn't you? And you caught me swimming.' She shook her head. 'If I'd known you'd seen me . . .'

'You'd have died?'

'I would have been embarrassed.'

'Poor Campion.' He smiled. 'When did you last swim?'

'Last year.' She shrugged. 'The day I met you.' She had thought so often, in the Tower, of those moments she had stolen in the stream, of the sun on her body and the water so clean about her.

Toby knelt up. 'I'm going for a swim.'

'You can't.'

'Why not?'

She shrugged, saying nothing. Because, she thought, he would undress here, and she was terrified. Faithful Unto Death Hervey had put this fear in her, a fear of her own body, of other bodies, and she was terrified of the moment that came closer, the wedding night, and yet she knew, instinctively, that Toby had brought her here to exorcise that horror.

He grinned. 'You're hot.'

'No I'm not.'

'You're hot, I'm hot, and I'm going for a swim.'

He stood up, moved a few paces to one side, and undressed. She did not look at him. She stared across the stream to where a field of barley shimmered in the heat, the grain dotted with poppies. She was being foolish, she knew, yet she could not control herself.

Toby ran into the water, a white shape at the edge of her vision, then threw himself into the stream's centre. He bellowed with delight, sending up a glittering fountain of water, and then he was standing up to his chest in the stream's centre and brushing water from his eyes. 'It's wonderful. Come in.'

'It's too cold.'

'You're hot.'

She saw the dark bruise on his shoulder, the misshapen

joint. 'Have you got your glove on?'

'Come and find out.' He grinned at her, then pushed himself downstream, swimming away until he was hidden from her by a great stand of nettles. His voice came back strong to her. 'You can come in now. I can't see you.'

'You said that last year!'

He laughed, then was silent.

She was hot. Her dress seemed sticky, her skin prickly. The air quivered over the barley, the sun was bright on poppies and cornflowers.

She wanted to swim. She remembered the pure pleasure of it, the release of a soul in darkness, and she wanted to feel the stream about her body as if the clean, cool water might wash away the defilement of Faithful Unto Death Hervey's hands. She waited for Toby to say something more, wishing him to ask her again, but he was silent. She shouted instead. 'I'm staying here!'

'Good! Whatever you want, my love!'

She waited, frowning. He said nothing more, nor did he reappear from behind the nettle stand. She waited. 'Where are you?'

'Here!'

She stood, walked to the nettles, and saw him twenty yards downstream. He grinned at her. 'You see? I couldn't see you.'

'Go further!' She waved to where the stream disappeared behind a bend thick with buckthorn and willow.

'Why should I? You're not coming in.'

'I might if you go past the willow.'

He made a dutiful face, turned, and swam a few strokes. 'Far enough?'

'Twice as far! Go on!'

He laughed and swam on, past the willow tree and into the shade of the buckthorns. She stood to see if he would come back, but he did not, so she walked back to where his clothes were thrown down and she looked, from the golden seal, casually discarded, to the sun-bright water. She wanted to go

in, she wanted so much to go in. She was hot, she had dreamed so often of this, yet she knew why she really wanted to go into the water. The shadow must be destroyed.

She walked back to the nettles. She could not see Toby in the shadow of the tree. She called out, 'Someone will see!'

There was no reply.

She walked back to his clothes, seeing the leather coat dropped on the sword, and then she looked all about her. The countryside was empty, not a person in sight, and she persuaded herself that she could swim quickly in the stream, be in and out of the water before Toby had time to come back from the trees.

One of the two horses lifted its head and stared at her, making her feel foolish. She stared again at the horizon, at the edge of a wood a half mile away, then up and down the stream. She was hot and nervous.

She had been frightened when she swam before, but that had been a fear of Matthew Slythe and his leather belt, and this time the fear was quite different as she took off shoes and stockings, undid her stomacher, unlaced her dress, and then paused. She crouched, as she used to, looking about her. Her heart beat as it used to beat, its sound loud in her ears, and then, decisively, she pulled the dress over her head and dropped it beside Toby's clothes. She fumbled at the laces of the petticoat, feeling the heat of the sun on her bare back, and then she stood, the petticoat fell, and she was naked. She ran for the water's cover.

It had not changed. It felt so clean, so cold, so good, and it reached every part of her, flooding her. She had forgotten the sheer joy of it. She ducked her head, then swam with clumsy strokes into the stream's centre, feeling the current tug at her, and her feet brushed long weeds as she turned with the water. It was good, so good, and the water was strong on her, lifting her and cleaning her. She swam nearer to the bank where she could kneel in the current, covered to her neck, and let the water flow around her.

'Isn't it good?' Toby was smiling at her just forty yards

away. He ducked his head, came up again, and swam closer. He stopped thirty yards away and she wondered whether she should run now for the bank, for her clothes, but then he stood up in the stream, the water to his waist, and grinned. 'Come and see an eight-fingered man catch a trout.'

She shook her head.

'I'll come to you, then.'

'Stay there, Toby!'

He began wading, his progress slow against the current. 'When we're married we must do this every summer. If we get Lazen back we could put a wall round some of the moat. Would you like that?'

She nodded, too frightened to speak.

He grinned, pretending not to see her crouching lower in the water. 'Of course it would be better in the Lazen stream. I suppose I could threaten the villagers with death if they came to watch us, but it seems a little extreme.' He was close now, just ten yards away. 'People will think we're very strange if we swim.'

'Stay there, Toby!' Faithful Unto Death Hervey was sliding his hands over her, Scammell was leering at her, the whole tribe of men was laughing at her nakedness. 'Don't come near me!' She was kneeling low, her arms crossed in front of her breasts.

Toby stopped. He was six or seven yards from her, smiling. 'Campion?' He spoke with infinite gentleness, and then suddenly his voice changed.

He screamed, his face screwing up in agony, and his right hand flew to his bruised left shoulder, his misshapen shoulder, and the scream became a moan of pain that stopped as he fell sideways. The current snatched at him. His head thrashed from side to side in torment.

'Toby!'

The stream was carrying him, his teeth clenched uselessly against the sob of pure pain. He scrabbled for a foothold.

Campion forgot her fear, forgot her nakedness. She rose in the water, pushed towards him, reached for him. 'Toby!'

His head thrashed. A gloved hand came out of the stream and she snatched for it, missed, but then she caught his right arm and his weight swung him away from her. She cried out as the arm slipped from her and she threw herself forward, desperate now, trying to haul his body upright, and suddenly she was aware that he was holding her, that his feet were firm on the stream's gravel, that his right hand was in the small of her back, pressing her close. Green eyes looked down at her.

'Toby!'

'Shh.'

'You cheated.' She did not know whether to laugh, but suddenly she was shivering for her body was against his and she felt his right hand stroking, stroking, and his touch was as gentle as if she was a silver fish hiding in dark reeds. 'Toby?'

His gloved left hand lifted her face and she kissed him, her eyes closed because she did not know where to look, and she put her arms about his bare waist, then hid her face on his shoulder. The fear was still there, but he seemed to be protecting her from it, and she could feel an excitement too. She clung to him, knowing that this was what she had dreamed of in Werlatton in those hopeless nights when love was a vain hope beyond her reach. 'Toby?'

'Shh.' He carried her from the water, lay her on the grass and she dared not speak nor open her eyes. She waited for the pain, even wanting it, and her hands stroked the muscles on his back as he loved her, riding over her pain, and when it was done he took her to the water again, washed her, and only then did she look at him. She was shy.

He smiled. 'Was it so horrible?'

She shook her head. She crouched low in the water. 'I'm sorry.'

'What for?'

'Being stupid.'

'You weren't.'

She looked at him. 'You cheated.'

'I know.'

She laughed, then asked the embarrassing question that

was important to her. 'Was it good for you?'

'I'm supposed to ask you that.'

'No, I mean it. Was it?'

He smiled at her. 'Never better.'

'Better than all those May Days?'

'Better than I ever dreamed possible.'

She laughed, blushing with embarrassment. 'You're sure?'

'There's only one way you'll find out.'

'How?'

'See if I want to do it again.'

She splashed him with water, looked down the stream, then back to him. 'Do you?'

They made love again, and this time she looked at him, and she held him close, knowing the shadow had been taken away. Later, after another swim in the cool, clean water, they lay on the grass and let the sun dry them. Campion, naked to the flawless sky, had her head on the saddle, while Toby, propped on one elbow beside her, traced a finger down her pale, slim body. 'You're very beautiful.'

'Your mother says my breasts will get bigger if we make love.'

He laughed. 'We'll have to measure them. You know how fathers measure their children growing with notches on a doorpost? We'll do the same with you. I can show guests.'

She laughed, turning to look at him, and loving the feeling of his fingers on her belly. She reached out with her right hand and plucked one of the dark red hairs from his chest. 'He loves me. Does that hurt?'

'Yes.'

She pulled another, still damp, 'He loves me not.'

'Stop it, I'm a tired man.'

'I can't stop now.' She tugged a third. 'He loves me.'

He put his hand on hers. 'We'll leave it at that one.'

'If you want.' She smiled at him, happy. They kissed, then lay with their arms about each other.

The Seal of St Luke lay discarded with their clothes,

forgotten for this moment, as far away as the war from this private, warm place. She tasted his skin with her tongue. 'Will it always be like this?'

'If we want it.'

'I want it.'

The stream ran clean beneath a flawless sky and Campion knew peace.

28

'The rain,' Lady Margaret announced from the window, 'will delay itself until tomorrow.' This was not an opinion, rather an order to Almighty God who, from Campion's sleepy view in bed, had different plans. The sky over Oxford was grey. September had started with bleak weather.

Lady Margaret stood over the bed. 'Do you intend to lie there all day?'

Campion shook her head. 'No.'

'It is a quarter past six, child, and I have delayed breakfast till half past.'

'I shall be there.'

Lady Margaret looked down at her. 'You're looking much better, child. Whatever my son did to you a week ago was obviously long overdue.' With that she swept from the room, shouting for Enid, calling downstairs to the kitchens, stirring the household into what would be its busiest day. She left Campion amused and a little astonished. Amused because Lady Margaret so obviously approved of her son prematurely deflowering his bride, and astonished that she herself had been so transparent. She had tried to hide the shadow across her life, and now she knew that it had been observed all along by both mother and son.

The shadow was gone, and that was proper because today

should be a day of no shadows. Today was the day that proved even the wildest dreams could come true, today she would marry.

Lady Margaret at breakfast, was less optimistic. 'He may not turn up at church, dear. I ejected him from the house last night and I have great doubts as to his sobriety this morning. He's probably fallen in love with a tapster's daughter and eloped. I had a third cousin who once fell in love with her father's chief stable-man.'

'You did?'

'I just said so.' The Roman nose sniffed at the birch tea and decided it was drinkable. 'They married her off to a particularly dull clergyman in the fens. I suspect they rather hoped she would drown, but she had nine children and became a thorn in the ample flesh of the Bishop of Ely. Do eat, child.'

The wedding dress was the most magnificent that could be made in Oxford. The petticoat was of white silk, worked all over with small flowers in pale blue silk thread. Enid, under Lady Margaret's directions, laced the petticoat tight and then picked up the wedding dress itself from the bed.

It was mostly of white satin, brilliant white, the skirt folded back at the front to show the petticoat, and the two folds held in place by rows of blue silk roses. There were no hooks or laces on the dress. Instead Enid tightened it by threading blue ribbons into the holes at the back of the dress, tying each ribbon in a large bow. The sleeves of the dress were also attached by bows to the bodice, each bow would yield to a single pull. The collar of the dress, heavy and stiff, was of silk brocade, white and cream, the weave expensive and beautiful.

There was more. The shoes, that daringly showed under the hem of her petticoat when she walked, were covered in silver satin and each had a blue flower on its toe. Her earrings were sapphire, the fillet in her hair was silver and from it hung seven yards of lace that Lady Margaret had worn at her own wedding. Lady Margaret twitched the lace into place. 'One more thing.'

'More?'

'Try not to be impatient, child.' Lady Margaret went to her workbox. 'Here.'

The lace gloves, edged with pearls, were in Lady Margaret's hands. Campion looked at them, remembering the night she had found them in Matthew Slythe's hiding place in his great chest, and she knew that these gloves had been her mother's. Kit Aretine, doubtless, had given them to his 'angel', and perhaps she had hoped, against hope itself, that she would wear them at her own wedding. They had been sent to Werlatton, the only possessions of Agatha Prescott that still survived. Lady Margaret sniffed. 'I brought them from Lazen when that odious little man evicted me. I can't think why you're crying, child.'

'Oh, Lady Margaret!' Campion wondered if her mother could see her from heaven now. She pulled the gloves on, delicate and fine. 'How will he put the ring on?'

'You still assume he'll be there? He'll just have to shove away, won't he. You don't want to make things easy for men, dear. Now. Let me look at you.'

Lady Margaret, who was proud that her son had found and was to marry such a beautiful girl, and even prouder of the fact that Campion wore her beauty lightly and not as a weapon, stepped back and looked her up and down critically. 'You can change your mind, of course.'

'I can?'

Enid laughed. 'I'll have to call you Lady Lazender in two hours, miss.'

'Enid!'

'Of course she will!' Lady Margaret came back to join in the unnecessary twitching of perfectly draped clothes. 'You're entering the aristocracy, child, and you will find polite respect a small recompense for your responsibilities.' She stepped back again, satisfied. 'You look remarkably beautiful, Campion. It's surprising what a good dressmaker can do for a girl. You may go downstairs and meet your gentleman.'

'My gentleman?'

'Did you think you were to walk up the aisle alone?'

Campion had thought precisely that. She knew that Mordecai Lopez could not be in Oxford, a letter had arrived just two days before, and she had no relative to give her away. She had steeled herself for the lonely walk to Toby's side. 'Who is it?'

'It is hardly polite to call him "it". He's gone to a remarkable amount of trouble to do this service for you and I've no doubt it's a trial to him. The least you can do is go downstairs and be pleasant to him.' Beneath Lady Margaret's tartness, as ever, was warmth, but Campion suspected that the older woman was hiding more emotion than usual.

The gentleman waited, one hand smoothing his small moustache, the face questing towards the sound of her feet on the stairs. 'Who's that?'

'Colonel Washington!'

He beamed, looking as proud and happy as if she were his own daughter. Over his eyes, but not hiding all of the terrible scar, was a velvet mask. He was quite blind.

She kissed him. 'Colonel!'

'You remember me, my dear!' He preened himself, drawing himself up to his full height which was still an inch less than Campion. He held her hands and smiled. 'It's not too late to change your mind, my dear. I'm at your complete service.' He smiled. 'I'm sure you look beautiful, you always did. I hope I don't disgrace you.'

'You look wonderful, Colonel.' Washington was in brown velvet, the material slashed to show red beneath, while round his waist was the King's sash. In one hand was a hugely plumed hat, while at his side, only decorative now, was his sword.

Lady Margaret came down the stairs. 'Ah! Sir Andrew!'

'Sir Andrew?' Campion asked.

Washington nodded. 'The King rewarded me for my blindness. A pension might have been more useful, but these days titles are cheaper.' He turned his face towards Lady Margaret. 'The carriage is waiting, your Ladyship. It will return for us.'

'But not too quickly, Andrew. Toby's had things entirely too easy. It's time he was given a little waiting and worrying.' Lady Margaret said it as though Toby had not waited and worried while his bride was in the hands of their enemies, yet it was not that which alerted Campion. There was a hint, perhaps more, of affection in her voice. She looked from the tall woman to the short man and smiled. Lady Margaret saw the smile and sniffed. 'You just hope my son is sober, child, which I very much doubt. He's probably drunk in some tavern cellar.'

Sir Andrew Washington added to the gloom. 'I hope the rain stays off.'

Lady Margaret scoffed at the thought. 'It will not rain! Come, Enid!'

When Lady Margaret had gone, Campion looked at the colonel. 'This is kind of you.'

'Not at all, my dear. Very proud, very proud. I'm just sorry it has to be me and no one closer to you.'

'Dear Sir Andrew, I can think of no one I would rather have by me.'

He liked that. 'Still, you'll have to guide me up the aisle, my dear. I'm not used to this darkness.'

'How do you manage?'

'Oh, I get along.' He smiled. 'I have a small house in Wiltshire and the servants are kind. They read to me and I can garden very well by feel. I find that I enjoy conversations more than I used. I listen, you see.' The velvet mask was turned up towards her. 'Lady Margaret was desperately worried for you. I was in Oxford during your ordeal, I wish I could have been more help.'

'I survived, Sir Andrew.'

'We prayed you would, indeed we did. My knees are still sore! Now, are you all ready for parade? Anything you have to do before we go?'

It was not far to St Mary's Church and Campion, blushing at the admiration of the crowd that gathered to watch Colonel Washington hand her into the coach, thought of the journey that had brought her this far. It had started with one seal, St Matthew, and it had taken her from the dull, coarse, black clothes of the Puritans, from their tight, bitter, envious rules, to this morning of silk and satin, of splendour and marriage. One casual meeting by a stream had led to this altar, and she thought of the one thing that had never altered in all the months. Through war and fire, through imprisonment and wounding, she and Toby had not faltered in their love.

The wedding was popular in Oxford. As the summer's campaigning drew to a close the Royalists could look back on a spring and summer of frustration and defeat. Their enemies grew stronger, the King's cause weaker, yet Campion was a symbol of defiance. She had been tried as a Royalist, as a witch, and she had escaped to the King's capital where she was reckoned as a heroine. The crowd was large outside St Mary's and, as James Wright opened the door, she faltered. James smiled at her. He had come to Oxford as Toby's soldier-servant, yet he guarded Campion whenever she stepped outside of the house without Toby.

Colonel Sir Andrew Washington took her elbow. 'Courage, my dear!'

She had not expected the church to be so full. As she warned Sir Andrew of a step at the entrance, so the music began, triumphant music that filled the church, music that soared from organ and choir, and Campion seemed to be swamped by the sound and the sight before her. The congregation had come in their Royalist finery; lace, silver, velvet, satin, silks and jewels, all lit by the candles which Mordecai Lopez's money had purchased. She turned Colonel

Washington into the main aisle, feeling the nervousness on her, smiling shyly at the faces that turned to look at her, and then she saw Toby.

He seemed tall at the choir steps. He was dressed in silver velvet, his sleeves and breeches slashed to show gold satin. He wore tall grey boots, turned lavishly above the knee to show a scarlet lining. He grinned impishly at her and for a second she thought she would laugh, such was the joy in her, but it was a joy fraught with nervous excitement. She doubted if she would be able to raise her voice to respond to the bishop, resplendent in embroidered vestments, who watched her walk towards the altar.

The bishop married them. Campion surprised herself by the firmness of her voice, even when she said the words that seemed to blend her life and her dreams. 'I, Campion Dorcas Slythe Aretine . . .'

Sir Toby, as nervous as his bride, forced the ring over the lace glove. The words of the service hardly penetrated her excitement, though she felt her heart leap when Toby repeated his vows. ' "With my body I thee worship." ' That would not have been Matthew Slythe's way, the Puritan way, for they saw nothing worshipful in the human body. They might call it 'the temple of the Holy Spirit', but Campion had learned in childhood that they saw that temple as an excreter of filth, a fleshly bag of temptation, a burden that brought sin to the soul and was well sloughed off at death. Matthew Slythe had been fond of the text that in heaven there was neither giving nor taking in marriage, but Campion was sure that there must be meadows by clean streams where lovers could love.

The Reverend Simon Perilly gave the blessing, his face beaming with joy, and then the bishop preached a mercifully short sermon before the organ thundered out again, and Campion walked down the aisle on her husband's arm. She was Campion Lazender now. She would never again be Dorcas Slythe. She had, as lovers must, made her own fate.

The first sunlight of the day greeted them as they left the

church. The light dazzled from the ceremonial broad-bladed pikes of the King's Halberdiers whose scarlet uniforms made a corridor away from the church. The shadows of the pikes were sharp on the petals strewn at their feet.

The pealing of the city's bells carried them to Merton College which, until a few weeks before, had been Queen Henrietta Maria's residence in Oxford. It was still the queen's temporary palace, even though she was abroad, and Toby had been given permission to hold the wedding feast in the great hall. He had demurred at spending so much on a wedding, but Campion had wanted them to have a ceremony worthy of the Lazenders, she wanted to defy the enemies that had tried to make her new family poor. They would have, she had insisted, a wedding to remember, so she had insisted on using part of the money Lopez had lent her.

Lady Margaret had abandoned mourning for this day. She was resplendent in scarlet, lording it over the hall where music played and where friends and strangers came for the food and wine. People eyed the bride with admiration and asked Lady Margaret where the girl had sprung from. 'She's Aretine's filly. You must remember the family? Quite excellent stock. There's a McClure strain, but well Englished.'

Campion was introduced to more people than she could hope to remember, had her hand kissed four score times and more, and even her lack of dancing skill did not matter for few people were sober enough to do it well. They danced old English dances; 'Cherrily and Merrily', 'The Friar and the Nun', and, as the afternoon turned into evening, it became more riotous as the men insisted on doing 'Up Tails All' and Campion was forced into leading the ladies in 'Petticoat Wag'. Caroline, who had come to Oxford for the wedding, shouted instructions at Campion, 'Pull it higher! Higher!'

It rained briefly at dusk, enough to give cobbles and walls, archways and bushes, a sheen of reflected light from the torches that showed Toby and Campion homeward. Toby's closest friends were now their escort, friends who were rowdy, happy and expectant. This was the one part of the traditional wedding to which Campion did not look forward. She smiled at Toby in the doorway of Lord Tallis's house. 'Must we?'

'Of course! It's always done!' He laughed.

It was for this moment that the dress was tied only with ribbons. The girls who had brought Campion home jostled her up the stairs, their hands reaching out to pluck the ribbons away. They half carried her and the men, who watched from the hall below, cheered as each pale blue ribbon was tossed over the banisters. Her right arm was naked first, then her left, and the men crowded up the stairs demanding more. The dress fell away from her as she was pushed into the bedroom, and they laid her on the bed and pulled at the petticoat laces.

The shouts of the men were close now as they pulled out the ribbons which held Toby's breeches to his coat. Caroline tugged Campion's petticoat off, leaving her naked, and Campion laughed as she struggled to get the heavy sheets and blankets over her body.

The laughter of the girls turned to shrieks as Toby was pushed through the door. He was quite naked, except for the glove on his maimed hand, and he grinned at the girls, bowed to them, as the men pushed him towards the bed. Caroline helped Campion hang on to the sheets as the men put Toby into bed with her. Sir Toby, safe with his bride, yelled at them, 'You've done your duty! Go!'

Most decided to stay, settling themselves with bottles of wine and grinning at the naked couple beneath the sheets. This was hardly a Puritan wedding, but it was a traditional English wedding, and Campion blushed when the guests said they might leave if she kissed Toby. She kissed him.

'More! More!'

They left after twenty minutes, the laggards pursued by a naked, capering Toby who locked the door when they were alone and turned to grin at her. 'That wasn't so bad, was it?'

She smiled. 'No.'

'And they'll all be waiting for us downstairs. Listen.' He knelt on the boards and thumped the floor loud and rhythmically. A huge cheer sounded from below. He grinned at her. 'What have you got on?'

'Nothing!'

'Show me.'

'Toby!'

He came and sat beside her on the bed. 'Hello, Lady Lazender.'

'Hello, Sir Toby.'

'It's time we got married in God's eyes.'

'I thought we already were.'

'That was just practice.' He pulled the bedclothes from her, bent to kiss her, and Campion, at last, was married.

Oxford was unbearable by late October. The King's army had returned, King Charles with it, and the city was crammed beyond endurance. Lady Margaret hated the crowded, stinking streets. It was decided that all of them would move north to Woodstock, close to the city and with its own small garrison of Royalist troops. Toby never forgot the danger Campion was in. If Sir Grenville could engineer her death, then the Covenant would be his for ever, yet Toby believed she might be safer in the small, guarded village than among the crowded anonymity of the city's streets.

They had one duty to perform before they left. They were summoned to an audience at court and the three of them went one windy, wet day to the crowded quadrangles of Christ Church. The crowd was bad-tempered, the soldiers who had to keep order frustrated, and it was with slow difficulty that Toby led his wife and mother through to the great hall and to the end of the long, shuffling queue of people summoned to greet the King.

Campion was curious rather than nervous. The babble of voices and the patent irritation of the courtiers had turned this public audience into something quite undignified and not at all awesome, yet when she caught her first sight of the King she was surprised by her sudden fear. He was, after all, a king, anointed of God, apart from the common ruck of men who stank in the press about him.

King Charles was much smaller than she expected, despite his high-heeled shoes and plumed hat. He was neatly bearded and stood strangely quiet and diffident in the centre of the busy throng. His eyebrows seemed raised in a perpetual expression of quizzical surprise, and if he had been anything other than the King, Campion might have taken him for one of the university doctors who still walked Oxford's streets and pretended their community had not been invaded by a court and an army.

A man carrying a tall, gold-topped staff beckoned the Lazenders forward. Sir Toby bowed, while Lady Margaret and Lady Campion curtseyed. The King nodded primly, apparently uninterested, and then the courtier who had summoned them forward gestured that they could back away from the august presence.

A gloved, royal hand was raised. Campion saw that the King wore jewelled rings on the outside of his glove. He looked at Campion and his voice was precise and clear. 'You are the daughter of Christopher Aretine?'

'Yes, your Majesty.'

He blinked at her twice and she thought no more was to be said. Then his precise, mincing voice sounded again. 'We are glad to find you more loyal than he.'

There seemed little appropriate to reply and, indeed, the bored royal eyes were already looking past Campion to the next people being ushered forward. Campion backed away, uncertain whether she had been complimented or insulted.

Lady Margaret had no doubts. 'We endure this monstrous crush of people to pay our respects and the man is rude! If he wasn't God's anointed I'm quite sure he wouldn't be invited anywhere. The man has no conversation at all, none! Except with very dreary priests. He is Scottish, of course.' She sniffed imperiously, not caring who overheard her words. 'Of course he's a distinct improvement on his father. King James dribbled and he had the most disgusting table manners. I trust my grandchildren will have good table manners. There are few things more distressing than to watch a child playing with its food. Your husband played with his food, dear, but fortunately I rarely ate with him. Ah! There's Lord Spears. He says he has a new method of grafting fruit trees. The man's a fool, but he may be right. I shall find you!' With that she plunged into the throng.

Toby grinned at Campion. 'What did you think of our all-wise monarch?'

'He's not what I expected.' She looked at the small, bearded man who was giving a faint nod at a hugely fat man who had difficulty in bowing.

'I thought you were going to wet yourself.'

'Toby! Really!'

A voice interrupted them, a harsh voice from behind. 'You must introduce me, Lady Lazender.' The voice seemed to mock her name.

She turned. Vavasour Devorax smiled sourly at her. His new beard was already an inch long. His clothes seemed as filthy as ever; still the same greasy, smelly leather jacket. He had cut his grey hair short, almost cropped like a Roundhead, and it gave his already scarred, ravaged face a more brutal look. She smiled, feeling immediately nervous. 'Colonel Devorax. This is Sir Toby.'

The cold grey eyes appraised Toby. There was the slightest nod.

Toby smiled. 'I have to thank you, sir, for my wife's preservation.'

'True.' The tone was offhand.

Toby persisted. 'Can we invite you to take supper with us?'

'You can, but I'll refuse. Lady Lazender knows my tastes run lower than dinner in polite company.' The grey eyes went to Campion. 'You have the seal?'

'Yes.' It was hidden about Toby's neck.

'Are you at the same house?'

She felt nervous, bullied by his boorish manner. She

glanced at Toby, then answered, 'We are moving to Woodstock, sir.'

He grinned. 'Don't.'

A bishop tried to squeeze past them, seeking a place nearer the King, but Devorax growled at him, reminding Campion of Lopez's description of the soldier as a wolfhound. The bishop, astonished and frightened, backed awkwardly away with muttered apologies.

Toby had been offended by Devorax's rudeness. His voice was cold. 'Why do you say "don't"?'

'Because within days I expect you to travel to Amsterdam.'

'Days?' Campion had expected to wait much longer.

'With three seals. That is, of course, if you still want your fortune.'

Campion was silent, oblivious of the noise of the crowd about her.

Toby frowned. 'How are you doing it, sir?'

'Killing people. It's usually the quickest method.'

'Sir Grenville?'

'He has the seals.' Devorax sounded bored. 'I'll come for you. If I can't come, I'll send Mason. You'll have to be ready for travel, and you'll be going to the east coast. And for God's sake pack light. You don't want to look like the Lord Mayor's procession.' He nodded at them and turned away.

It seemed appallingly casual to Campion. She had expected more drama, more excitement at the news that, at last, the seals were to be gathered. 'Colonel?'

'Yes?' He looked back, surprised.

She realized she had nothing to say. 'You're sure about supper?'

'I'm sure.' Then he was gone.

Toby shook his head. 'Is he always that disagreeable?'

'He was being positively polite.'

It was still raining as they left Christ Church, the rain a promise of the quagmires that would slow travel as autumn turned to winter. Campion was suddenly frightened. She had felt safe in Oxford, secure in a household where she was loved and guarded by a husband, and now, quite suddenly, she was faced with a new journey. She held tight to Toby's arm. They must travel eastwards, across the sea, and there would be more death before she could claim Kit Aretine's heritage.

Toby smiled down at her. 'You're frightened.'

'Yes.'

'Perhaps I can go on my own?'

She shook her head. Her journey had begun with one seal in a Puritan house. Now she would see that journey to its end, whatever her fears, and through whatever mires of blood it led. She would take St Luke to the gathering.

29

Ebenezer Slythe's offer of a reward to anyone who could give information about the escape of the witch from the Tower had yielded nothing except the usual crop of fools who thought they could lie their way to an easy two hundred pounds.

Then, in September, the Royalist news-sheet, the *Mercurius Aulicus*, simply published the news. The 'witch' who had outwitted the Parliamentarians had married in Oxford. It gave her name as Lady Campion Lazender, but the writer could not help rubbing in that, as Dorcas Scammell, she had made fools of the vaunted London garrison. Ebenezer had smiled. Did she think that by changing her name to 'Campion' she would escape her enemies?

Sir Grenville had been less cheered by the news. 'So she's in Oxford, what good is that? Do you think she's not guarded? God in heaven! She's in the middle of the King's army, and married!' He scowled. 'We have to kill both of them; legally her property is his now.'

Yet three weeks later, it seemed that the preachers of

London had been right. The age of miracles had returned to earth, had come to England where the Saints struggled to rule, and Ebenezer was a witness of such a miracle. He had prayed earnestly for God to give him the seals and now, on a Monday morning of sweeping, cold rain, it seemed his prayers were answered.

A man had come forward, a bold man who seemed unafraid of the place where Ebenezer's guards brought him. The man glanced at the brazier, at the stained table with the shackles nailed to its thick surface, and at the instruments hung neatly on the walls. He looked back at Ebenezer.

'Mr Slythe?'

'Who are you?'

'Name's Mason, sir. John Mason.'

'And you want two hundred pounds, Mason?' Ebenezer was dressed in a long, fur-edged, black cloak. These cellars were always cold unless work was in progress.

'No, sir.' Mason spoke in the short, cocky tones of a soldier. He was dressed as a soldier, though Ebenezer's men had taken his sword.

'You don't?' Ebenezer hid his surprise, making the question seem menacing.

'My colonel does, sir. He sent me.'

Ebenezer frowned. He was not used to such assurance from men or women brought to this room. He looked at his guards, both alert behind Mason, then back to the young man. 'And who is your colonel?'

'Name of Devorax, sir.'

The name meant nothing to Ebenezer. He ran a hand over his glossy, long hair that was brushed back from his pale forehead. 'Mason, I have had a dozen men here who claimed to deserve my money. The last one I was forced to punish. I bored a hole in his tongue to teach him not to lie.'

'Whatever you say, sir.' Mason was cheerfully unmoved.

'No! Not what I say, what you say. You've come about the witch?'

'That's right, sir.'

'Well? I know where she is, so don't think you'll be rewarded for that.'

'No, sir. I'm only here to give you a message, sir, and give you a small token of Colonel Devorax's good wishes.' Mason spoke as if he was reporting on the state of cavalry horses to his troop leader.

Ebenezer limped closer to Mason. He had shaved only an hour before, but already his chin was dark. 'A token?'

'Yes, sir.'

'Well?'

Mason opened a small, leather pouch that was attached to his belt. He took out a small, paper-wrapped package. 'Sir!'

Ebenezer took it, unwrapped it, and went very still. In his palm was half of a wax seal. The impression had been cut cleanly with a knife, but the semi circle clearly showed the front half of a winged ox, beneath which was the single word 'Luke'.

'Where did you get this?' Ebenezer could not hide his excitement.

'Colonel Devorax, sir.'

'Where did he get it, fool?'

'Don't know, sir. Not in the colonel's confidence, sir!'

'Who the devil is Colonel Devorax?'

'Man who wants to meet you, sir. That's my message, sir.'

'Well, go on, man! Go on!'

Mason momentarily shut his eyes, as if remembering, and then repeated the message in his clipped voice. 'Three o'clock today, sir, under the gibbet at Tyburn, sir, and Colonel Devorax says you're not to bring more than four men, sir. He'll only bring two, sir. That's it, sir.'

Ebenezer looked at the half seal of St Luke. Dear God! Lopez's seal! His mind flickered over the possibility of a trap, but he could see none. Tyburn was a well-chosen meeting place. The execution site was at a lonely crossroads outside London, amid bleak, flat land and it would be impossible for either side to bring more men without them being seen. Added to that was the breathtaking audacity with which

Devorax had cheerfully suggested Ebenezer's men could outnumber his own, as if these strangers were not fearful of the odds. Ebenezer thought swiftly. 'I'll be there.'

'Very good, sir.' Mason turned about, held out a hand for his sword. Ebenezer nodded to one of his guards and watched as the strange soldier went up the cellar steps. 'Follow him!'

Mason seemed unconcerned by his follower. He walked to the Privy Stairs and there waited in the raw, wet wind for a boat. Both men, their craft in strange convoy, crossed to the Lambeth Stairs. In the squalid street of the small hamlet Mason grinned apologetically at Slythe's man. A boy held a horse for Mason, on which he climbed and then galloped away, leaving Ebenezer's bodyguard helplessly behind.

The Tyburn gallows was a great triangle, held aloft by tall supports, and two score victims could dangle from the three great beams.

That afternoon, as Ebenezer rode towards the crossroads, he could see three horsemen waiting within the triangle. Hanging from the beams were the rotting corpses of two felons, left there as a warning against highway robbery. A crow was perched on the shoulder of one hanged man, its beak busy, while a second crow was on a corner of the huge gibbet.

It was cold. Rain swept miserably from the west, soaking the scrubby bushes and thin grass. Oxford Street, the road that led to the gallows, was greasy with mud. The cows in the fields either side of the road turned their backs to the rain and stared mournfully east to where a great pall of chimney smoke mingled with the low clouds above London.

Ebenezer reined in ten yards from the gibbet. He was irritable because of the cold, hunched inside his great, black cloak. Beneath that, fearing treachery, he wore a breastplate over leather, while two loaded pistols were in his saddlebag. Not even the rain-laden wind could scour the stench of this place. Water dripped from the dangling, bare feet of the convicts.

One of the three horsemen walked his mount towards Ebenezer. The irritation vanished, replaced by astonishment and interest, for the approaching horseman was grey-bearded, and over half his helmeted face was a thin leather mask. The man nodded to Ebenezer. 'Mr Slythe?'

Ebenezer knew this man's description. A whole army had hunted this man. 'You took the witch out of the tower!'

The man grinned. 'Guilty.' He tipped his helmet back, and then off, and peeled the mask from his face. Two grey eyes stared at Ebenezer. 'My name's Devorax. Vavasour Devorax.'

Ebenezer felt a chill of fear. He had dismissed the thought of a trap, but suddenly suspected he might now be caught in one. 'What do you want?'

'A talk, Mr Slythe, just a little talk.' A third crow flapped heavily overhead, giving a harsh cry of protest at the presence of the horsemen. It landed on one of the beams and stared at them. Devorax grinned. 'My father used to say that Tyburn crows made a particularly tasty pie. Shall we move away, Mr Slythe? Let them feed in peace?'

Ebenezer nodded and followed the evil-faced man across the glistening mud where the spectators gathered to watch the executions. There was a proposal to fill this space with tiers of public seating, but nothing had come of it yet.

Devorax had put his helmet back on and now he turned, the steel bars across his face beaded with raindrops. 'Far enough?'

The other horsemen had followed. They waited a dozen yards away.

Devorax's voice was mild. 'Thank you for coming, Mr Slythe. I thought we might do business.'

Ebenezer was still confused, still fearful, though he was reassured by the lack of menace in Devorax's voice and posture. 'Business?'

'Yes, Mr Slythe. You see I've decided to stop being a soldier. I wish to retire.' Devorax grinned. 'And I need money.'

A sudden gust of rain slashed into Ebenezer's cheek. He wiped it irritably away, still frowning at Devorax. 'Who are you?'

'I told you, Vavasour Devorax.' The soldier was leaning forward, his hands on the pommel of his saddle. 'I've served a man called Mordecai Lopez most of my life. Do you know who he is?'

'I know. Served?'

'That's right.' Vavasour Devorax took off his helmet again, hanging it by its strap on a pistol butt that was holstered to his saddle. He moved slowly, not giving alarm, and undid his saddlebag. He took out a stone bottle, uncorked it, and drank. 'You want some, Mr Slythe? It's Rumbullion from the Indies.'

Slythe shook his head, forcing himself to think clearly. He forgot the cold, the damp, and in his precise, flat voice he questioned Devorax about his long service to Mordecai Lopez. Devorax answered willingly, describing even how he had taken Campion from the Tower. He hid nothing, giving Ebenezer the address of Lopez's house. 'You can go there, Mr Slythe. He's not supposed to own a house in London so you might as well take what's there. You can share the proceeds with me.' He grinned.

Ebenezer was still not satisfied. 'Why are you betraying Lopez?'

'Betray?' Devorax laughed. 'You can't betray a Jew, Mr Slythe. They killed our Saviour, remember? You can cheat the bastards through eternity and it isn't a sin.'

That made sense to Ebenezer, but he was still not satisfied. 'Why did you serve him so long?'

'Wages, Mr Slythe, wages. He paid me.' Devorax put the bottle to his lips and Ebenezer saw a dribble of dark liquid stain the short, grey beard. Devorax rested the bottle on his saddle and stared at the gallows where the two bodies turned slowly in the wind. 'I'm getting old, Mr Slythe, and I don't want wages any more. I want a farm, and I want to die in my own bed, and I want enough money to be drunk every night and have a wife wake me for breakfast.' He seemed to become morose. 'I'm tired of the damned Jew, Mr Slythe. He pats me on the head as if I'm his lapdog. He throws me a bone now and then, but I won't be a damned dog to anyone! You understand, Mr Slythe? I'm no one's damned dog!'

The sudden, savage anger surprised Ebenezer. 'I understand.'

'I hope you do, Mr Slythe, I hope you do. I've done that Jew's dirty work throughout Europe. He's given money to armies in England, the Low Countries, Sweden, Italy, France and Spain, and I've had to be there for him. Do this, do that, and then a bloody pat on the head. God's bowels! I thought he'd give me something one day; a farm, a house, a business, but no, nothing. Then along comes Aretine's bastard daughter and what does she get? Enough money to buy out a dozen stinking Jews. She doesn't need the damned money, Mr Slythe! She's married her man, let him provide for her.'

Ebenezer kept his voice mild. 'You say the Jew saved your life?'

'Christ on the cross!' Devorax spat into the mud. 'He took me from the galleys, that's all. I wasn't nailed to a damned tree, puking out my lungs. So he saved me from a slow death in a galley. So? Do you know how many mens' lives I've saved, Mr Slythe? I'm a real soldier, not one of these pretty boys prancing around in a meadow squeaking "King Charles! King Charles!". Christ! I've seen battlefields so thick with blood that it made puddles! I've had this sword crusted to my hand with blood at the end of a day, and then slept in the open so my hair froze to the blood puddles! Jesus! I've saved mens' lives, but I don't expect a lifetime of gratitude from them. A drink or two, maybe, but not eternal worship.' He tipped the bottle again, his saddle creaking as he moved. When he spoke again his voice was grudging. 'I'm not saying he hasn't treated me fair, Mr Slythe, but I can't go on for ever. Do you know what the Jew paid me for getting the girl out of the Tower?' Ebenezer shook his head. Devorax laughed. 'Fifteen gold pieces between all of us! Do

you know how hard it is to get someone out of the Tower?'
He shook his savage head broodily. 'I expected more, I
deserved more.'

Ebenezer smiled. Something in him responded to Vavasour
Devorax. Perhaps, he thought, it was the sheer, animal
strength of the soldier, a strength that Ebenezer knew could
never be his. Or perhaps it was the stories of a sword crusted
to a man's hand, of fields of blood, stories that stirred
Ebenezer. 'So what are you offering, Devorax?'

Devorax smiled. The rain had plastered his short hair to his
skull, giving him a malevolent, even more brutal look. 'I'll
give you the seal of St Luke, plus the girl. I assume you don't
want her to live to twenty-five?' He lifted the rum to his lips,
then paused. 'You can have her damned husband, too, if you
want him.'

Ebenezer nodded. 'You'll bring the seal from Amsterdam?'

'No! It's in Oxford.' Devorax laughed. 'I stole the
impressions from her. The Jew insisted she have it, as a
memory of her father.' He laughed at the thought.

Ebenezer stirred with excitement. If the Seal of St Luke
was in Oxford, then everything could be much simpler. He
kept his voice precise and expressionless. 'And what do you
want?'

Vavasour Devorax looked down at the bottle, then
challenged Ebenezer with a sly, arrogant gaze. 'I've got
twelve men. I can't just abandon them. One hundred pounds
apiece. And for me?' He seemed to think. 'Two thousand.'
He held up a hand as if to ward off a protest. 'I know it's a
lot, but I also know how much the Covenant's worth.'

Ebenezer kept his face straight. The demand did sound
extortionate, but it was nothing compared to the yield of the
Covenant. 'Why did you approach me, Devorax, and not Sir
Grenville Cony?'

Devorax gave a short, bitter laugh. 'You'd trust a lawyer,
Mr Slythe? God's breeches! He'll twist everything and cheat
us blind! I've learned a thing or two in fifty years, Mr Slythe.

I can empty saddles faster than most men, I can tear out a windpipe with my bare fingers, and I've learned; never, never trust a damned lawyer. Do you trust him?'

Ebenezer shrugged. 'Perhaps.'

'You're getting the money from the Covenant, yes?' Devorax waited for Ebenezer's small nod. The soldier watched the younger man very carefully. 'How much does he give you? Five thousand a year? Six? Seven?' Devorax smiled. 'That's it. Seven.'

'So?'

The rum bottle tipped, Devorax drank, then grinned at Ebenezer. 'Mordecai Lopez reckons the Covenant ought to be worth nearer twenty thousand a year. That's how much that fat, bastard lawyer is cheating you. Do you think we can trust him? What do you think he'll do if he gets all three seals? Give us our share?' Devorax shook his head. 'No, Mr Slythe, it'll be a quick knifing in the night and two shallow graves. I won't deal with Sir Grenville Cony.'

Ebenezer stretched his left, lame leg. 'And how do I know that I can trust you?'

'Sweet Jesus! Do I look as if I need twenty thousand a year? Christ! I don't want to be pursued by damned parasites for ever. No. You give me enough to buy my favourite whorehouse, Mr Slythe, and I assure you of my undying devotion. And free service for you, of course.'

'I thought it was a farm you wanted.' Ebenezer smiled.

'A bastard farm.' Devorax laughed.

Ebenezer felt flattered to be humoured by this man, yet his defences were not down. 'How do you know you can trust me?'

Devorax grinned. He corked the rum bottle, pushed it into his saddlebag, and then pulled the helmet on to his head. 'Watch me, Mr Slythe.'

Devorax's horse turned, seemingly from pressure of the rider's knee, and then it went into a trot. There was a scraping hiss, Devorax's long, straight sword was free, and he

shouted at his horse that went into a spirited canter. Mud flew up from the hooves.

The crows flapped off in alarm. Devorax stood in the saddle, approaching one of the hanged men, and then his sword arm blurred into vicious speed. A downstroke sliced through the shoulder of the corpse, severing a dead arm, and, in the same motion, the sword looped up and chopped through the second shoulder. Before the first arm slopped into the mud, the second was falling.

'Hup! Hup!' Devorax shouted.

Ebenezer had heard of trained cavalry horses, but had never seen one in action. The horse wheeled, rearing as it turned, hooves lashing against enemies, and then Devorax was riding again towards the swinging corpse. 'Go! Go! Go!'

The sword was brought forward in a savage, huge stroke, driven by all the strength of the helmeted man. It cut clean through the rotting body, spine and belly, spilling liquids and decomposing entrails out of the abdomen, and again the sword kept moving in a fast, brilliant backstroke as the horse reared, the blade neatly chopping through the distended neck. The head thumped from the empty noose, falling beside the dismembered corpse.

It had been a remarkable display of horsemanship and weaponry. Devorax tipped his helmet off again, looped it on his saddle and grinned at Ebenezer. His voice was as cold as the wind. 'Think what I can do to a living body, Mr Slythe.'

Devorax cleaned the stinking filth off his blade by running it between finger and thumb, wiped his hand in his horse's mane, and then slammed the sword home. His two men grinned. Ebenezer's guards, like their master, stared at the grotesque horror that had so suddenly been chopped into the mud. The stench was appalling. Devorax trotted back to Ebenezer's side. He was not in the least breathless, as calm and composed as before his hideous display. He took the bottle from his saddlebag. 'Can I trust you, Mr Slythe?'

Ebenezer Slythe did a remarkable thing, he laughed. He

looked from the carrion on the ground to the big, ugly soldier. 'You can trust me, Devorax.' He looked back to the corpse. Already the crows were tearing at the easy pickings offered by Devorax's sword. 'How do you propose giving me the girl and the Seal of St Luke?'

Devorax closed his eyes as he drank, then tossed the empty stone bottle away. 'There's no problem. If the girl doesn't come then I have other impressions of the seal. We can fix them to paper. But she'll come.' He grinned. 'She doesn't like me, but she trusts me. She thinks I'm collecting the seals for her. The difficult thing, Mr Slythe, is not your sister, but Sir Grenville. I assume he has both seals?'

'And he guards them well.' Ebenezer was leaning forward eagerly, but the thought of parting Sir Grenville from the two seals seemed to deflate him. He shrugged. 'Even I can't get close to them.'

'You will.' Devorax seemed unworried by Ebenezer's gloom. He took a new bottle from his saddlebag and pulled out the stopper. 'I have the use of a ship, Mr Slythe. I propose that you and I meet Sir Grenville and the girl at a remote place on the coast where we will part them from their seals and sail on to Amsterdam. Simple.' He grinned.

Ebenezer shook his head. 'Sir Grenville won't travel with the seals. I told you, he guards them too well.'

Devorax said nothing. The rain pattered on his leather jacket, dripped from his boots, soaked his hair. He smiled. 'What's he afraid of?'

Ebenezer looked up at the grey clouds. 'Of someone else assembling the seals.'

Devorax's voice was patient, like a teacher with a pupil. 'Dorcas already has the Seal of St Luke?'

'So you tell me.'

'And she held the Seal of St Matthew for several months. Suppose Sir Grenville was told that during those months she had taken some wax impressions of St Matthew? That would give her two seals, yes?'

Ebenezer nodded.

'And remember, Mr Slythe, there is a fourth seal. Suppose Sir Grenville thought that Aretine was alive, that Aretine was meeting her in Amsterdam?' Devorax held up his left hand and raised, one by one, three fingers. 'Matthew, Luke, and John.' He grinned. 'Don't you think Sir Grenville would do anything to stop her? And he'd have to go himself, Mr Slythe. He wouldn't risk anyone else getting the seals from her.'

Ebenezer smiled. He saw the elegance of the suggestion, yet he also saw the difficulties. 'Did the girl take impressions of Matthew?'

The grey eyes were on him. 'No, Mr Slythe, but she tells me you possessed the seal after her.' Devorax grinned. 'Were you so honest with it?'

Ebenezer laughed again and nodded. 'I have impressions.'

'Good! So tell Sir Grenville about me. Give him the half seal of Luke and a whole impression of Matthew. Tell him you've bought me, that I'm betraying Lopez, tell him the truth except for one thing.'

'That you'll kill him?'

'That we'll kill him.' Devorax laughed. 'Give him the seals, Mr Slythe, and tell him about Lopez's house. He'll believe you.'

Rain dripped from Ebenezer's hat brim. The cloak was wet through and heavy. 'How do I persuade him that Aretine's alive?'

'You don't. I will.' Devorax smiled. 'Two days ago, Mr Slythe, the last ship of the season docked from Maryland. Two days from now I'll give Sir Grenville proof that Aretine's in town.'

Ebenezer smiled. 'He'll panic.'

'Good! He'll hear about it on Thursday morning. So be ready to move, Mr Slythe, be ready to go with him.'

'Where?'

If there was a trap here, Ebenezer reasoned, Vavasour Devorax would be unwilling to disclose the rendezvous on the eastern coast where the seals were, at last, to be brought together. If Ebenezer knew the rendezvous he could send men ahead, men to scour the place against a possible ambush, but Vavasour Devorax gladly named the building and the village where he planned to strip Sir Grenville of his seals, where he planned to take the Seal of St Luke.

Ebenezer memorized the instructions. 'I can take guards there?'

'You'd be a fool not to. Sir Grenville undoubtedly will.'

'When do we meet there?'

Devorax shrugged. 'Soon, Mr Slythe, very soon.' He nodded towards his men who waited motionless on their horses. 'I'll send Mason to you. Don't be surprised if he comes in the middle of the night. Where will Mason look for you?'

Ebenezer told him. 'How soon is soon, Devorax?'

The ugly face grinned as the soldier gathered his reins. 'Within a week, Mr Slythe, within a week.' Devorax turned his horse.

Ebenezer was unwilling to let him go. He liked being close to the strength of this man and was already wondering how he could entice Devorax into his own plans once the Covenant was his. 'Devorax! One last question.'

Devorax grinned. 'Only one?'

'How do you convince Sir Grenville that Aretine lives?'

Devorax's grin became broader. He pushed the rum bottle into his saddlebag and pulled the helmet over his head. 'That's my secret! Wait and see. You'll enjoy it!' His horse went into a walk.

'Devorax?'

The soldier turned. 'Mr Slythe?'

'I have your two hundred pounds!'

'Keep it for me! I'll collect it within a week, Mr Slythe. Within a week!' The last words were shouted back from the cantering horse that, urged by Devorax's heels, went into a gallop, scattering the crows from the butchered offal. Devorax's men swerved behind their leader, galloping beneath the rain-darkened gallows and following him westward into the murk.

Ebenezer watched them go, then walked his own horse beneath the huge beams and stared down at the horrid mess Devorax had made. Maggots writhed in the entrails. He glanced up at the second hanging man, twisting slowly, the rain dripping from the death-darkened feet into a puddle below. He considered trying to cut the body in half with his own sword, but knew his strength was not sufficient. No matter. Soon he would have the strength of thousands. Soon the Covenant would be his.

He smiled, wrenched his rein, spurred back and shouted for his men to follow him. They rode south towards Whitehall. The seals were being gathered.

30

Persuading Sir Grenville Cony was not quite as simple as Ebenezer and Devorax had supposed. Sir Grenville was no fool, he had survived too long in a troubled political world to believe that every opportunity was to be taken. He was sceptical. 'I'm an old, old man, Ebenezer. You sip ambrosia, but I smell poison.'

'You don't believe Devorax?'

'I haven't met him.' Sir Grenville stared out at the river. Rain pelted on to the surface. He turned back to the desk. 'The seals are real enough. Why did he go to you? Why not me?'

'My name was on the reward offer.'

'True.' Sir Grenville said it grudgingly. 'Yet Lopez has the reputation of being a generous man. I don't understand the complaint of this Devorax.'

Ebenezer shrugged. 'Lopez has been generous to Devorax.

He saved his life, he's employed him ever since. I don't think the fault lies with the Jew, it's with Devorax. He's greedy.'

Sir Grenville nodded. The bulging eyes looked palely at Ebenezer. 'Should we kill him?'

'He doesn't want much. Pension him off.'

Then news came that the soldiers sent to the Southwark house had been successful. Sir Grenville had feared an ambush, but instead they found Lopez's house unguarded, and its furniture, books, rugs and ornaments were being removed. Sir Grenville was pleased. 'A blow! Ebenezer! A blow against the Jew!' He laughed. 'Unless it's simply a ground bait to take us nearer the hook.' He stood up and sidled his huge belly past the desk. 'You say Devorax is taking the bitch to Amsterdam. Why? She only has the use of two seals?'

Ebenezer played his best piece. 'Devorax says that Aretine's alive. That he'll add the Seal of St John to hers in Amsterdam.'

Sir Grenville's face lost its cheerfulness. He turned aghast. 'Alive?'

Ebenezer shrugged. 'So he says. Perhaps he just meant that Lopez has the fourth seal. I don't know.' He pointed at the two lumps of red wax on Sir Grenville's table. 'We know the girl has those two, I hate to think of what will happen if Aretine is alive.'

'You hate! You've not met the bastard! Dear God! You say Devorax is taking her out of the country at this place Bradwell?'

Ebenezer nodded.

'When?'

'He said he'll let me know.' Ebenezer was playing the story by ear, but he had been pleased by the panic engendered by the mention of Kit Aretine.

Sir Grenville shouted for his secretary, 'Morse! Morse!'

'Sir?' The door opened.

'I want Barnegat, now! Tell him I'll pay double, but get him now!'

'Yes, sir.'

'Wait!' Sir Grenville looked at Ebenezer. 'You think it will be soon?'

'Within a week.'

'I want a dozen men sent to a village called Bradwell, Morse. Ebenezer can tell you where it is. They're to search the place and wait there! And Morse!'

'Sir?'

Sir Grenville ran a hand through his white curls. 'Make sure the travelling coach is ready. I'll need it within the week.'

'A week!' Morse frowned. 'But you're supposed to meet the French ambassadors this . . .'

'Get out!' Cony snarled at him. 'Get out! Do as I say!'

Sir Grenville turned and stared past Ebenezer at the great painting that hung above his fireplace. Aretine, the most beautiful man Cony had ever seen. Was he alive? Had that beauty come back to pursue him and humiliate him? The lawyer walked to the fireplace, reached up, and closed the lime-washed shutters over the naked body. 'You had better be wrong, Ebenezer. Pray God you are wrong.'

The next night, Wednesday, Vavasour Devorax came back to the city. Campion would not have recognized him. The filthy, stained, greasy clothes were gone. He had bathed, trimmed his hair and beard and then rubbed lamp-black into the greying hairs. By candlelight he looked ten years younger. He was dressed in sober, neat, clean clothes. He wore a broad-brimmed Puritan hat, in his hand was a well-thumbed Bible and his only weapon was a long, slim dagger.

His destination was close to Tower Hill in Seething Lane, and he hammered at the door of a darkened house. It was late, though many citizens would still be up. He had to hammer twice more before the door opened a crack.

'Who is it?'

'My name is God Be Praised Barlow, a Minister of the Commons.'

Goodwife Baggerlie frowned. 'It's late, sir.'

'Is it ever too late for God's work?'

Grudgingly she opened the door wider. 'You're here to see the Reverend Hervey?'

'With God's will, yes.' Devorax stepped inside, forcing Goodwife to step back. 'Is the Reverend Hervey abed?'

'He's busy, sir.' Goodwife was impressed by the tall preacher from the House of Commons. She was ready for bed, a gown pulled hastily over her nightdress and her hair wrapped in muslin.

Devorax gave her a ghastly smile. 'At his prayers, sister?'

'He's got company.' Goodwife was nervous. The Reverend Barlow was a big man and she did not like to contradict his wishes. She frowned. 'It's better you come in the morning, sir.'

Devorax frowned. 'I take no denial from a woman. Where is he?'

A stubborn look came into her small eyes. 'He says he's not to be interrupted, sir.'

'The House of Commons wishes him to be interrupted. Now lead me to him, woman! Lead!'

'You'll wait here, sir?' Goodwife said hopefully, but the tall preacher insisted on following her up the polished staircase. Goodwife stopped at the landing and tried to push Devorax downstairs. 'If you'll wait in the parlour, sir, I'll light a fire.'

'Lead me, woman! My business cannot wait!'

A voice shouted from above them, muffled by a door. 'What is it? Goodwife?'

'Master?' She shrugged. 'He'll be angry.'

'Go on, woman!'

She led him on to a wide, waxed landing. A door opened, held inches from its jamb, and a face peered at them. 'Goodwife?'

Devorax pushed past her. He leered at the face in the door's crack. 'Reverend Hervey?'

'Yes, sir.'

'I come, sir, from the Commons, with good news.'

Faithful Unto Death, who had only had time to throw a robe about his naked shoulders, frowned. 'I will be out in a moment, sir.'

Devorax quoted magnificently from the Psalms. ' "Make no tarrying!" ' He pushed the door open, forcing Hervey back, then stopped. 'My dear Mistress Hervey, my dear lady, my apologies.'

In the bed, facing him, clutching a sheet over her obviously naked body, was a dark-haired, pretty young woman. Devorax looked at Hervey. 'I had no idea you had taken a wife.' He looked again at the woman, bowed low, and swept his hat off. 'Dear lady, I have urgent business with your husband, will you forgive me?'

The woman, terrified, nodded. Her husband was a lieutenant in Parliament's northern army, she had come to this house to fetch her certificate that guaranteed her body free of a witch mark. The Reverend Faithful Unto Death Hervey, so eager was he to give satisfaction, had demanded several visits to make sure. Sometimes his devout searching of her flesh lasted a whole night. Devorax looked about the room for a robe to give her. He could see none, only her clothes on a chair. He picked up her cloak and tossed it to her. 'Wait downstairs, madam, my business will not take long.'

He turned his back on her as she pulled the cloak over her shoulders. She cast one terrified look at her other clothes, then decided discretion was the best part of valour. She scuttled past them, going to wait till the stranger left.

Goodwife made to follow her, but Devorax shut the door. He needed a witness. If the woman in the bed had not been so pretty he would have kept her as a second witness, but one was enough. 'You stay, woman.'

The Reverend Faithful Unto Death Hervey had watched this in confusion. He was gripping the edges of his robe together, in no position for bold action, but now he frowned as the big man turned the key in the lock and pocketed the key. 'Sir! You said good news from Parliament?'

'I did?' Devorax nodded. 'Indeed I did.' He tipped the absent woman's clothes from the chair and set it for Goodwife. 'Sit down.'

Goodwife frowned at Faithful Unto Death Hervey, but sat obediently. Devorax smiled at the minister. 'May I suggest you seat yourself, Reverend?'

It was a comfortable room that bore witness to Hervey's considerable success. Opposite the shuttered and curtained windows was a whole wall of books while a solid table and chair stood on a great rug before the blazing fire. The table was obviously Faithful Unto Death's desk, piled high with books and papers, and lavish with three great silver candlesticks. More candles burned on the mantel and on two low tables beside the bed. Searching for witch marks needed illumination.

This was the most difficult moment for Devorax. In his left sleeve he had concealed a length of rope which now, as Hervey's back was turned, he whipped free and looped about Goodwife's body. She screamed.

'Keep your mouth shut or I'll scrape the tripes out of you.'

'Sir!' Faithful Unto Death had turned. He stared at the huge man who yanked the rope tight about his housekeeper. Devorax's growl had terrified Goodwife, yet the soldier knew she might begin to struggle at any moment.

'You'll be dead meat if you make a sound.'

'Sir!' Hervey still clutched the robe over his nakedness. He hovered, irresolute and appalled.

Devorax's voice came strong. He was stooping to tie Goodwife's ankles, then her wrists, one to each arm of the chair. 'The business of the Commons is strange, sir, but all will be explained.'

He straightened, went behind Goodwife, and took a handkerchief from his pocket. He had her trussed now, tighter than a roasting chicken, but for good measure he gagged her. It had been easier than he thought. His threats had kept her still, and now her small, red-circled eyes stared in fright at him. He walked towards Hervey, a smile on his face. 'I come for knowledge, brother.'

'Knowledge?' Hervey backed away.

'Indeed.' Devorax smiled, reached out a hand then pulled the robe from Faithful Unto Death. Hervey clung on, but Devorax yanked it with all his power, jerking it free, then laughed at the naked, white minister. 'Sit down, bastard.'

Hervey clutched two hands over his manhood. 'Explain yourself, sir!'

Devorax's knife hissed out of its scabbard, whipped round in a blur of candle-reflected light, and pricked at Hervey's chest. 'Sit.'

Hervey sat. He crossed his thin legs and kept his hands cupped at his loins.

Devorax laughed at him. 'Do you shave your chest, Hervey?'

'Sir?'

Devorax sat on the corner of the table. Goodwife watched through wide, terrified eyes. The big soldier smiled at Hervey. 'You're not married, are you?'

Hervey did not reply. He was watching the blade of the knife with which Devorax idled. The knife blade suddenly swung towards him. 'I asked if you were married.'

'No, sir. No!'

'Finding texts in someone else's Bible were you?'

Hervey was in sheer terror. He could not take his eyes from the horridly pointed steel. Devorax's voice was amused. 'A whore, is she? Her price above rubies?'

'No!'

'Oh! A volunteer. Giving it away.' Devorax laughed. 'They'll be the ruin of a perfectly good profession one day.'

Hervey summoned his courage. He pressed down with his hands, drew up his knees, and frowned. 'What do you want, sir?'

'Want? I want a talk with you.' Devorax stood up and walked about the room, peering at books, at ornaments, glancing at Goodwife tied to her chair. He could think of no better way of proving Aretine's supposed presence in Europe than this public punishment of an avowed enemy of Aretine's daughter. He needed the witness to carry what he said to Sir Grenville Cony. He stopped, turned to the scared, naked minister and raised his voice. 'I came to talk to you about Dorcas Slythe.'

He saw pure terror in Faithful Unto Death's eyes. 'You remember her, Hervey?'

Faithful Unto Death nodded.

'I didn't hear you, Reverend.'

'Yes.'

Devorax kept his voice loud, kept it slow. 'My name, Reverend, is not Barlow. Nor do I work for that rat-hole you call Parliament. My name is Christopher Aretine. Does that mean anything to you, Reverend? Christopher Aretine?'

Hervey's pale face shook. His Adam's apple shot up and down. 'No.'

Devorax whipped round on Goodwife, the blade pointing at her. 'Christopher Aretine! Do you know the name?'

She shook her head. Her eyes watched him. He knew she had heard. Devorax strolled back to the table and perched himself on the corner. He tapped the knife blade into his palm. 'Where was her witch mark, Reverend?'

Faithful Unto Death Hervey stared at the grim face. He did not understand what was happening, but the stench of a horrid danger was all about him. 'On her belly, sir.'

'Her belly.' The knife blade still tapped into the palm. The steel edge was eighteen inches long. 'Show me on the excuse you have for a body, Reverend.'

'Sir?'

'Show me!' The blade moved like a snake striking, suddenly appearing before Hervey's eyes.

Hervey moved his right hand slowly. He pointed to his solar plexus. 'There, sir.'

'Bit high for her belly, Reverend. Did you search her breasts?'

Hervey was shaking with fear. He was not a brave man.

'I asked you, Reverend, if you searched her breasts.'

'Sir?'

'If you don't answer me, scum, I'll spit out an eyeball on this blade.'

'I did, sir! Yes, sir!'

'Why?'

'It is normal, sir, normal!'

'Explain it to me.' Devorax pulled the knife blade back. He had made the question conversational, almost reassuring.

Faithful Unto Death Hervey swallowed, his Adam's apple going up and down while his right hand returned to his crotch. 'The witch mark, sir, is a teat. One expects a teat in the area of the dugs.' He nodded vigorously, as if to confirm the truth of his statement.

Devorax smiled at him. He tossed the knife into the air so that the blade cartwheeled in the candlelight. The handle smacked back into his right hand. His eyes had not left Hervey. 'What's my name?'

'Aretine, sir. Christopher Aretine.'

'Good, good. Did you enjoy searching Dorcas Slythe's breasts?'

'Sir?' Hervey's fear flooded back. For a moment he had thought that he was turning the conversation into a reasonable course, now the torment was starting again.

'I asked if you enjoyed searching Dorcas Slythe's breasts.'

'No, sir!'

The knife blade began to describe vague circles and figures of eight before Hervey's eyes. 'I think you did, Reverend. She's very beautiful. Did you enjoy it?'

'No! I do a necessary task, sir. I search out God's enemies, sir. One does not seek enjoyment!'

'Tell that to the whore downstairs. Did you stroke Dorcas Slythe's breasts?'

'No!'

The knife blade was within an inch of Hervey's right eye. Faithful Unto Death had put his head back, but he could see the glittering spark of light looming at his eyeball. Devorax's voice was very soft. 'I'll give you one more chance, scum. Did you stroke her breasts?'

'I touched them, sir, I touched them!'

Devorax chuckled. 'You're a liar, Hervey. You probably wet yourself as you did it.' He pushed the blade forward till the steel rested on the skin below Hervey's eyeball. 'Say goodbye to your eye, scum.'

'No!' Hervey wailed and, as he did, he lost control. His bowels loosened in sheer terror and a foul stench filled the room.

Devorax laughed, leaned back with his blade unbloodied, and shook his head. 'I've seen nicer things than you fall out of a hog. Don't move, Reverend. I'm going to tell you a story.'

He stood again. The room stank, but Hervey dared not move. His eyes watched as the big man paced slowly between the shuttered windows and the bookshelves. Goodwife watched, too, her ears avid for the big soldier's words.

'Years ago, Reverend, I was a poet in this fair city. That was before scum like you turned it into a cesspit. I had a daughter and, do you know? I've never seen her from that day to this. But I know her name, Reverend, and so do you.' He grinned at Hervey. 'What do you think it is?'

Hervey did not reply. Devorax grinned at Goodwife.

'You know who it is, don't you?'

She knew. Ebenezer had recently told her that Dorcas was not his sister, but she had never known, till this moment, who the girl's father was. The Slythes, keeping to the promise they made to Martha Slythe's parents, had kept Dorcas's illegitimacy a secret all their lives. Goodwife watched, horrified, as the black-haired soldier turned back to Faithful Unto Death Hervey.

'Her name, Reverend, is Dorcas Slythe. Or was. She's married now, she's a Lady.'

Hervey's head was shaking. 'No. No.'

'I'm going to kill you, Reverend, and everyone will know that Christopher Aretine came back to take his revenge on you.' He grinned. Hervey was quivering in his own filth. Devorax raised his voice, making sure Goodwife heard every word. 'And not just you, Reverend. Tomorrow I'm going to Amsterdam, but I'll be back in two weeks and then it will be the turn of Sir Grenville Cony. Do you want to know how I'll kill him?'

Hervey summoned all his bravery, which was not much. He knew death was coming, and he tried desperately to fend it off with words. 'You're mad, sir! Think of what you do!'

'I do, Reverend, I do.' Devorax was walking slowly towards Hervey. 'And you think, as you die, why you die. You die for what you did to my daughter. Do you understand?'

'No! No!'

'Yes.' The knife blade was levelled, going towards Hervey, and Devorax's voice was as unforgiving as the winter wind. 'She is my daughter, filth, and you used her. You played with her.'

Goodwife watched. The Reverend Hervey, not daring to move or fight, had tipped his head back away from the blade. His Adam's apple was still, his eyes wide, and his lank, straw hair was on the table top. Devorax held the knife vertically above the priest's tilted face. 'I hate you, Reverend, and I'll see you in hell.' He began pushing the blade down.

'No!' Hervey shouted, and the blade went between his lips, his teeth, and he clamped his bite on them, but the big man laughed, pushed, and Faithful Unto Death's last scream was choked off as the blade went into his mouth, down, forced down, until Devorax was grunting as he pinned the head to the table top.

'You'll be dead soon, filth.'

He left Hervey there, his naked body arched above the fouled chair, one hand reaching for the blade. The noise was awful, but Devorax ignored it. He walked to Goodwife, whose eyes showed a horror equal to that of the dying man. Devorax blocked her view. 'Were you unkind to my daughter?'

She shook her head vigorously.

'I hope not, but I'm sure she'll tell me, and I'll be back in two weeks. Tell that to Sir Grenville.'

She nodded.

The noise had stopped. Blood soaked the table top, dripped on to the rug. Devorax walked to the dead man and jerked the knife free. It scraped on teeth. The lank hair, bloodied now, flapped as the head jerked up and Devorax pushed it free. He wiped the blade on the curtains, sheathed the knife, then turned again to Goodwife. 'Give Sir Grenville my regards. Tell him Christopher Aretine does not forget.'

He scooped up the woman's clothes, unlocked the door, and went downstairs. He found the woman in the parlour, shivering beneath her own cloak and one she had taken from the hallway. Devorax grinned at her. 'I wouldn't go upstairs, love.'

She looked at him, nervous.

He smiled. 'What's your name?'

She told him, then her address. Devorax tossed her clothes at her feet. 'Your husband with the army?'

She nodded.

He grinned. 'You wouldn't want him to know about this, would you?'

She shook her head. 'No. Please!'

He put a finger to his lips. 'No one will know, except you and me. And I'll find you soon.' He leaned forward and whispered in her ear. She laughed. Devorax kissed her cheek. 'And remember what I said, don't go upstairs. Promise?'

She nodded. 'I promise.'

He left her, thinking what profit she was for a night of evil, and then hurried through dark alleys until he saw Mason waiting with the horses in an entry near Aldgate. Devorax laughed as he swung himself into his saddle. Mason grinned at him. 'Colonel?'

'Nothing.' He laughed again. 'You go to kill a man and find a woman, not bad, eh? Drink?'

Mason laughed as he handed over a stone bottle which Devorax tipped to his lips. He drank deep, and felt the brandy sear down to his belly. 'God, that's good. Clothes?'

Devorax stripped off the black jacket, kicked off his square-toed shoes, and pulled on his leather jerkin, his tall boots, and finally strapped the sword to his side. He laughed again.

'Sir?'

'Nothing, John.' He was thinking how scared Sir Grenville would be in the morning when Goodwife brought the news, how the fat lawyer would be convinced that Aretine was back. He drank more brandy, then turned to Mason. 'You're to go to Mr Slythe, John.'

'Now?'

'Yes. Tell him to meet us on the coast Monday night. Seven o'clock at the latest.'

Mason repeated it.

'And tell him that if he's got no news of Aretine by ten tomorrow morning to send a patrol to the Reverend Hervey's house. He'll know where it is.'

'Sir.'

'And you're to meet me at the girl's house in Oxford tomorrow night.'

Mason seemed to think nothing of such a journey in such a short time. 'Oxford, tomorrow night, sir.'

Devorax laughed. 'The cat's in the dovecote, John. Tooth and claw! Off you go!'

He watched as Mason turned his horse, listened to the hoofbeats in Leadenhall Street, and then urged his own horse forward. He left the shoes and jacket in the alleyway, then bullied his way through Aldgate. He shouted at the guards to hurry, called the captain a whoreson piece of filth, then urged his horse into the brief, stone tunnel.

He turned left outside the gate, planning to circle London to the north before joining Oxford Street at St Giles. After a murder it was best to be outside the city gates.

He let his horse gallop across Moorfields. He could smell rain in the night wind, but he did not care. He put his head back and laughed at the cloud-shrouded moon. 'Kit Aretine! You bastard! You'd have been proud of me! Proud!'

He laughed and rode west into the night.

31

Sir Toby Lazender was tired. He had spent a fruitless day leading a hundred men in a chase beyond Wallingford. Roundheads were said to have raided a village, stripping the barns of the winter's grain, but the stories turned out to be false. He came back to Oxford tired, wet and irritated, only to find that new problems awaited him. His mother met him in the hall. 'Toby!'

'Mother?'

'There's an extraordinary man here. My dear boy, you're soaked. He insisted on talking to Campion alone. I don't like him. He was quite rude to me. You're to find out what's happening.'

Toby pulled off sword, jacket and boots. He looked up from his seat on the hall chest as James Wright took them away. 'Who is he, mother?'

'Devorax.' Lady Margaret sniffed, 'I know he saved her life, Toby, but that's no reason for drunken rudeness. He positively barred me from the room! I can't imagine that he's related to that nice Sir Horace Devorax. Do you remember him, Toby? He ran very good hounds in Somerset.'

Toby shook his head. 'I don't remember. Where are they?'

'Still in Somerset, I should think. Unless our enemies have declared war on hounds.'

Toby smiled. 'Where are Campion and Devorax?'

'In the garden room. I suspect you're leaving us, Toby.'

Toby suspected his mother had listened from the garden. He leaned his dark red curls against the hall's panelling. 'Amsterdam?'

'Yes. It appears the seals are being gathered.' She looked down at him. 'I won't stay in Oxford, Toby.'

He smiled. 'I know.' It seemed there was a small but fine house in Wiltshire that could be rented. The money had come from Lopez's loan to Campion, but Toby knew his mother's desire to go to Wiltshire arose because of a small, kind, sightless man. 'I don't suppose we'll stay long in Holland, mother.'

She sniffed. 'Devorax says there are things to arrange there, whatever that means. It will be nice to have money again.' She stopped, staring down at her son. 'I don't trust him, Toby. I'm not sure that either of you should go.'

He stood up, smiled, and kissed his mother on the forehead. 'Let me talk to him. And don't listen outside the window. You'll catch cold.'

'I can't hear the half of what he says,' Lady Margaret said imperiously. 'He mumbles and growls. You tell me. Now go on! I want to know what's happening!'

Common courtesy alone dictated that Vavasour Devorax should stand when Sir Toby, the master of the household, came into a room, but the soldier stayed slumped in the best chair, his grey eyes looking morosely at the newcomer. Toby ignored the rudeness.

'Colonel? You're welcome.'

The ugly face nodded. His beard and hair, Toby noted, were strangely streaked with black. A bottle of wine, half emptied, was by his side.

Campion came to Toby, lifted her face to be kissed, and he saw the relief in her eyes that he had arrived. He smiled. 'Hello, wife.'

She mouthed at him, her back to Devorax. 'He's drunk.'

Toby looked at Devorax. 'Do you want food, sir?'

The face shook. 'No. Do you want to know what's happening?'

Toby sat beside Campion on the settle. The candles
flickered about the room. Vavasour Devorax groaned, pulled
himself straighter in the chair and stared at Toby. 'I've told
your wife. Cony's dead, we've got his seals, and you're to
take them to Holland.'

Campion stared at Toby, Toby at the grim soldier who now
put the bottle to his lips.

'Cony's dead?'

'Sir Grenville has gone to meet his maker.' Devorax put the
bottle down. 'I don't suppose his maker will be very pleased
with what he made.' He laughed.

'How?'

'How?' Devorax laughed. 'How do you think? I killed
him. With this.' He tapped the hilt of his sword.

Toby could hardly take the news in. He shook his head.
'Didn't he have guards?'

'Of course he had guards!' The question seemed to annoy
Devorax, but then he sighed, leaned back, and told the tale in
a toneless, bored voice. 'There was a murder in London last
night. The Reverend Faithful Unto Death Hervey was also
despatched to his maker. I did it. Then I went round London
to Sir Grenville's house, demanded entry with my men on the
plausible pretext that we were the watch and wished to talk to
a man who had known the Reverend Hervey, and once inside
we did our business.' He smiled. 'The fat little lawyer fought
surprisingly hard and I ruined a perfectly good rug with his
blood. We had to blow the locks of his strongbox, and inside
were the two seals: Matthew and Mark.'

Campion was holding Toby's hand, gripping his finger
stumps beneath the thin leather glove. Toby stared at
Devorax. 'You have the seals?'

'Not with me.' He smiled pitifully at Toby. 'You really
think I'm going to ride halfway across England with half a
fortune in my pouch? Of course I don't have them. My men
have them. They're taking Lopez's ship to the place where it
will meet you.' He flourished the bottle at them. 'All is over,

children, your fortune has been secured by Vavasour Devorax.'

Toby bridled. 'My name is Sir Toby, my wife is Lady Lazender, and I trouble you to give us respect in this house.'

The grey eyes, suddenly looking not drunk at all, stared at Toby. They seemed to suggest that Devorax could slit Toby apart, but then the bearded face laughed. 'Your fortune, Sir Toby and Lady Campion, has been secured by Vavasour Devorax. Say thank you.'

Neither spoke. Devorax laughed. He looked at the bottle, decided he might as well finish it, and tipped it to his face. He wiped his lips when he had done, smearing more of the strange blackness in his beard.

'You are to meet me on Monday night. You'll have to travel east, through Epping, and you're to find a village called Bradwell.' He sneered. 'A collection of hovels near the coast of Essex. You go through the village, keeping the river on your left, are you following me?'

Toby nodded. 'Yes.'

'Just follow the coast. You'll come to a barn. You can't mistake it, it's got a ruined tower attached, as if it was a church. On top of the tower is a beacon. That's where I'll be. Eight o'clock next Monday night. Understand?'

Toby nodded again. 'Yes.'

'The nearest town is Maldon, but be careful. They're all damned Puritans over there. They'd like to burn both of you at the stake. And one other thing,' he gave then his mocking, pitying smile, 'Bring the Seal of St Luke with you.'

'Yes.'

Campion let go of Toby's hand. She frowned. 'Why are you doing this if you dislike us so much?'

Devorax shrugged. 'Do I have to like you? I was ordered to do it, remember? By Lopez.'

She looked at the ravaged face, half lit by the fire, half by the candles. 'Why do you obey Lopez?'

'Why not?' He reached down beside his chair and pulled

up a second bottle of wine. 'We all have to obey someone, unless we're the King, in which case we expect other people to get us out of the mess we've made.' He pulled the cork and looked at Toby. 'You don't mind if I drink, Sir Toby?' He mocked the title.

'You can give me a glass. I'm tired.'

'Playing soldiers?' Devorax sneered. 'The soldiers I fought with never took wine by the glass. They drank it out of the bottle.' He poured wine into the glass that Toby held out. Devorax leaned back. 'That was real soldiering, not this prancing about in fancy sashes shouting prayers.'

'Men are dying here,' Toby said.

'Doesn't take death to make a war,' Devorax said. He shut his eyes. 'It takes hatred. Savagery.' He opened his eyes. 'You know the King's going to lose?'

'Is he?'

'Oh yes. There's a new army being raised in the east.' He adopted his mocking tone again. 'The New Model Army. Saints with swords, Sir Toby. They're the most dangerous. A man would rather kill for his God than for his King. They're going to win this war.' He drank. 'I hope for England's sake it doesn't get like Germany.'

'You fought there?' Toby asked. He sensed that Devorax was mellowing, that an anger was dying.

Devorax nodded. 'I fought there.'

Campion spoke. 'You knew my father there?'

'Yes.'

There was silence. Campion hoped for more. Devorax drank. Toby looked at the fire, then back to the soldier. 'My mother says Kit Aretine was the handsomest man in England, and the wittiest.'

Devorax gave a humourless laugh. 'Like as not.' It seemed he would not say anything more, but then he leaned forward, wincing against a stiffness in the joints. 'He changed though.'

Campion was tense. 'Changed?'

'He became old. He saw too much. He used to say wit was an illusion and that you couldn't keep illusions when you were trampling in blood.' Devorax shrugged. 'Too clever for his own bloody good.'

Toby waited, but nothing more came. 'You knew him well?'

The grey eyes looked at him. The scarred face nodded. 'I knew him well. Poor bastard.' He laughed to himself.

Campion tried to urge him on. 'Did you like him?'

Devorax seemed to think about it, then nodded. 'I liked him. Everyone liked Kit. You couldn't dislike him. He was one of those men who could keep a roomful of people laughing.' The words seemed to come now as the soldier's tongue loosened. 'He could even do it in Swedish. Story after story, and we'd sit round camp-fires and nothing seemed too bad if Kit was there. You could be cold, starving, hungry as the devil, with the enemy a half-day's march behind and he'd always know how to make you laugh.' He shrugged. 'Some men have that gift. But he changed.'

'How?' Campion was leaning forward, her lips parted. Toby saw her profile against the fire and felt the familiar pang at her beauty.

Devorax wiped his lips with the filthy sleeve of his leather coat. For a second or two Toby thought he would not answer, then he shrugged. 'He fell in love. He was always falling in love, but this time it was,' he shook his head, 'different. He told me she was the second woman he'd ever really loved. The first was your mother.' He nodded at Campion. 'This one was Swedish. She was beautiful, God she was a beauty! All his women were, but this one was made on one of God's better days.' He grinned. 'She had hair your colour, Lady Campion, only she wore it short. She followed Kit, you see, and long hair's a nuisance if you're sleeping rough with an army. She went with us to Germany.' Devorax seemed far away, as if trying to relive the days of the great Swedish attacks on the northern Catholics. 'Kit said it would be his last fight. He'd marry her, live in Stockholm, but he never did. She died.' He lifted the bottle. 'And he was never the same again.'

Campion made a noise like a small moan. 'That's awful.'

Devorax laughed. 'Worse than awful. I remember it.' He grinned. 'We were in a small town and we thought the damned Catholics were miles away. They weren't. I suppose we were drunk, we often were, and the bastards came into the town that night. Torches, swords, pistols, and half the town was burning thatch and the other half was dying Protestants with the Catholics riding their horses over them. God! It was chaos! They killed a hundred that night and took off half our horses.'

Campion was frowning. 'They killed her?'

'No.' He drank again, closing his eyes as he tipped the bottle. Hooves sounded in the street, somewhere in the house a timber creaked. 'Kit was fighting the bastards. He must have killed half a dozen. Everywhere you looked that night there were enemies. They were coming out of alleys, out of houses, and he was out in the street bellowing at them, hacking them with a sword. He was on foot, but they couldn't touch him. It was nearly all over when it happened. She surprised him. She came out of their house with a dark cloak on and he thought her hair was a helmet. She suddenly appeared in the doorway and he shot her. Bang. Right through her pregnant stomach.' He shook his head. 'He said he'd forgotten about his pistol till that moment. She took half the night to die. It wasn't pretty.' He tipped the bottle again, drank, then wiped his mouth. 'That's your father's story, Lady Campion, and if you want my advice, which I'm sure you don't, then hope that you never meet him. He wasn't the same again. He wasn't the man your mother loved.'

Campion's hand was clasped around Toby's. Her face showed an awful sadness at the tale. Devorax looked at her and grinned. 'You asked. I told you.'

She shook her head, horror in her voice. 'It's terrible.'

'If he couldn't tell a girl from a soldier and hair from a helmet, then he shouldn't have had a gun in his belt.' He shrugged. 'I suppose we were drunk.' He stood up. 'I'll leave you.'

Campion stood up too. She was shocked by the story, by Devorax's callousness in his telling of it, but she would have liked to hear more of her father. 'Won't you stay and eat with us?'

'No.' Devorax pulled his sword straight. 'I have other comforts at an inn.' He grinned. 'You'll be at Bradwell?'

Toby nodded as he stood. 'Do we travel with you?'

'No. I travel alone. But I'll be waiting for you. Eight o'clock, Monday night.'

He left them, going into a street that was glistening from a fine drizzle. He carried the bottle away.

Campion watched him go, seeing him meet a mounted man who held a spare horse. They disappeared towards Carfax, leaving her horrified by the story he had told. She was frightened, too, fearing to go into the east country, the heart of Puritanism, where the seals were to be gathered. She thought of Lazen, thought of giving it back to this family that had taken her in, loved her, and of which she was now a member. She clung to Toby, appalled by all the sadness in God's world. She would go east for Toby and his mother.

Two hundred yards away, near where a great fire had just burned a part of Oxford, Vavasour Devorax tossed the empty bottle into the ruins that still smelled of smoke. He looked at Mason. 'Well?'

'Sir Grenville Cony's sent a dozen men to Bradwell, sir.'

Devorax nodded. 'And Mr Slythe?'

'He'll be there, sir. Seven o'clock. He says Sir Grenville will go with him.'

'Good.' Devorax grinned. 'How many men is Slythe taking?'

'He says six.'

'Good, good. We can take care of Sir Grenville's twelve.'

Mason yawned. 'Sir Grenville's bound to bring some more with him.'

Devorax was not worried. With his men and Slythe's he had enough to destroy Sir Grenville's guards and enough to put a small band into the village of Bradwell who could follow Toby and Campion towards the barn, cutting off their retreat. Mason looked at his colonel. 'The girl's coming, sir?'

'Yes.' Devorax smiled. 'She and her husband. Both of them.'

'They're not worried?'

Devorax shook his head. 'She thinks Cony's dead.' He laughed. 'She'll be there, John, for her father's sake.' He laughed again. He had watched the girl as he told the true story of Kit Aretine's Swedish woman. He had seen Campion's pity and distress. 'She's a romantic.' He said it mockingly then grinned at Mason. 'Come on, John. I'll find a whore for you. After Monday you can pay me!' He laughed loud, pleased with himself, for Vavasour Devorax had engineered what most would have thought impossible. Matthew, Mark and Luke were to be gathered at the sea's edge, and it was Devorax, soldier and drunk, who had made it happen. The seals would gather.

32

Toby and Campion left Oxford the next day, travelling alone. James Wright begged to accompany them, but Toby ordered him to stay with Lady Margaret instead.

Lady Margaret embraced them both. 'I don't trust that man Devorax. I don't think you should go.'

Campion smiled. 'What would you do if you were me?'

Lady Margaret sniffed. 'I should go, of course, child.'

They did not know when they would return. Devorax had told Campion that Mordecai Lopez waited for them in Amsterdam, that they must first take the seals to the bank and then, under the Jew's guidance, take the administration of the Covenant's fortune into their own hands. It would be, Devorax said, a long, hard task. Toby kissed his mother, mounted, and smiled at her from the saddle. 'Perhaps we'll be back for Christmas, Mother.'

'If not sooner,' Campion added.

'I have decided to grow apples,' Lady Margaret said irrelevantly. 'Andrew writes me that apples do well in Wiltshire.'

Campion kissed her. 'We shall miss you.'

'Of course you will, dear.'

They travelled on horseback, for a wagon could not have reached the Essex coast in the four days they had before the rendezvous. The days were becoming short, travellers were few, and the roads were wet and sticky. They rode mostly on the wide, grass verges, following a course that would take them well to the north of London.

On Saturday they were deep inside Puritan East Anglia. In the hamlets of Essex they heard, again and again, the angry call for the King to be dethroned, for the nobles to be humbled, for each man to be equal. The war was no longer about taxes and the rights of Parliament; it was a religious crusade for the overthrow of the old order. The ancient slogan of the Peasant's Revolt was heard: 'When Adam delved, and Eve span, who was then a Gentleman?'

Toby did not look a gentleman. He travelled as a soldier, sword belted over leather coat, pistol in his belt and helmet slung from his saddle. He looked like any other soldier returning from the year's campaign, a pack-horse behind him, with his wife on a third horse. Campion dressed as a Puritan. She had bought herself a pair of slab-sided, stiff, leather shoes, and beneath her long black cloak was a Puritan dress with wide, white collar and starched apron. Her hair was modestly hidden by a bonnet. She had other clothes, clothes fit for Lady Lazender, but they were hidden in the pack-horse's bundles.

If her dress was sober and her demeanour modest, her hopes were high. Mordecai Lopez had done as he had promised, he had arranged for the seals to be gathered, and she rode to fulfil her strange father's destiny. She felt little sorrow at the death of Sir Grenville Cony, none at Faithful Unto Death Hervey's end, and she believed that the killing was now done. The seals had extracted their price of blood; now they would yield the wealth with which she could restore her husband's family. She rode eagerly, not minding the cold winds and rain of autumn, the chill that brought a foretaste of the frosts to come that would harden the rutted roads into ice-sharp furrows.

They crossed Epping forest, two travellers alone in an immensity of trees. The leaves had turned, were blown by the winds to carpet their path, and sometimes, deep in gold shadow, Campion would see a motionless deer watch them pass. Once they passed a camp of charcoal makers, their temporary turf huts almost unseen till the horses were close by. The turf-clad kiln silted blue smoke among the trees. The charcoal makers sold them hedgehog meat, roasted in clay. They knew nothing of the war, except that their charcoal was fetching a good price for gunpowder.

Toby and Campion could not travel on the Sunday, for this was Puritan country and the Lord's Day was sacred. They had left the forest and were in a small-hilled country of rich earth and big, timber barns. They took the only private room in the tavern, its walls plastered with news of Parliament's victories and they were given clean straw on which to sleep.

They attended church, for to have avoided the day's three services would have attracted suspicion and enquiry. Toby, not able to resist play-acting, gave his name as Captain Righteousness Prevaileth Gunn, and said they travelled to Maldon where his wife's family lived. The preacher, an earnest young man who had prayed for the Royalists to be 'scythed mightily that their blood might fructify the land of the Saints', looked at Campion. They were outside the church, surrounded by villagers among the ancient tombstones. 'And where does your family live in Maldon, Mistress Gunn? My own mother lives there.'

Campion, not ready for the question, gaped.

Toby put a hand on her arm and spoke soothingly to the preacher. 'The Good Lord saw fit to make my dear wife simple-minded, sir. You must be gentle with her.'

The women, who had sat with Campion on the women's side of the church, clucked sympathetically. The preacher shook his head sadly. 'I shall pray for her in evening worship, Captain Gunn.'

Afterwards, eating a cold meal in the tavern, Campion hissed furiously at Toby, 'You called me simple-minded!'

He grinned. 'Sh! Dribble your food.'

'Toby!'

'And for God's sake stop looking as if you're enjoying yourself. They'll know we're impostors if we look happy.'

She cut him some cheese. 'I don't know why I love you, Toby Lazender.'

'Because you're simple-minded, my love.' He smiled at her.

They rode early the next day, crossing a land that was fertile and well watered. The sails of the mills still turned from harvest time. Many of the cottages were pargetted, their plaster outside walls moulded to show sheaves of wheat or garlands of fruit. The wind blew from their backs, carrying high clouds to the east, and rippling the surfaces of the wide streams that flowed to the North Sea. Tonight, Campion thought, she would see the sea for the first time, she would be carried on a large ship and go abroad. She felt nervous of the unknown to which the seals drew her.

This was their last day. The land flattened. By afternoon they seemed to be riding their horses beneath a sky vaster than any Campion had seen. The horizon was utterly level, broken only by a few, bent trees and the shape of a farmhouse or barn. There was a tang of salt in the air, a promise of the coast, and the first, lone screeching of gulls told them that their journey would soon be over.

The houses were poorer now and fewer. The cottages, built almost as low as the salt-marshes' tallest grasses, seemed battered by wind and rain. Tarred weatherboards clad the hovels. High overhead Campion saw geese flying in their tight pattern, their wings carrying them towards the sea and strangeness.

They stopped in the late afternoon and bought bread and cheese from a dirty, bent woman who looked at them suspiciously. 'Where be you headed?'

'Bradwell,' Toby said.

The woman shrugged. 'Nothing at Bradwell.' She peered at the coin Toby had given her, then gave an abrupt nod. It was none of her business if outlanders wanted to pay good money for old cheese.

They stopped to eat where the track was embanked against a marsh. A hundred yards away the rotting timbers of a boat stood like black ribs against the muddy bank of a creek. The water of the marsh was salt, the plants new to Campion. There was glasswort and sea-spurrey growing among the eelgrass, but to her they were as strange as this journey itself; reminders that she rode into the unknown.

She saw the sea for the first time in her life beyond the small village of Bradwell. It disappointed her. She had not known what to expect, but from the poets she had taken a picture of vast waters, of tons of liquid dashing itself against black rocks. From the Old Testament she had a similar expectation; of Leviathan, of the deep, of something massive, moving and treacherous.

Campion saw the sea far in the distance. Its surf fretted shallow at the edge of a great, spreading estuary, and between her and the sea was a mile of slick, rippled mud. The sea seemed to be a grey line, quiet and dull, edged with flashing white where the small waves broke on the glassy mud. Toby, who had seen the sea before, imagined the waters racing over the flat, mud shore, whipped up by an east wind into a savage, engulfing tide that would drown this flat land where the creeks tangled among the marsh.

Campion pulled her cloak tight at her throat. 'Is that where we're going?' She nodded towards a small building, its high gable outlined against the darkening sky.

Toby nodded. 'Yes.' Beyond it, almost unseen because its hull was hidden by the land on which the building stood, he could see a ship; its mast a tiny scratch against the sky's vastness. Journey's end in England.

'Toby!' Campion had turned, staring back at their path. Her voice was frightened. 'Toby!'

He turned. Behind them, a half mile behind, he could see four horsemen. Their horses were motionless. The west wind stirred the cloak of one man. They were helmeted, the setting sun glancing red from the barred steel. At their sides were swords. Campion looked at Toby. 'They're following us!'

Toby looked about him. The track led only to the barn on the horizon. It was the only way to go. He smiled at his wife. 'Come on. We'll be safe.'

He fidgeted with his sword-hilt, took one more look at the horsemen behind, and then led Campion along the marsh track to the place where the seals were being gathered, a building as desolate as the coast on which it stood, a building that had faced the grey sea for a thousand years.

The Romans had first built in this place. They had made a fort to fight the Saxon pirates whose oared ships would come from fog-shrouded dawns into the estuary of the Blackwater. Here the Romans had worshipped the old gods, bleeding a dying bull on to the heads of recruits in the wet pit—the rites of Mithras—praying that the god would preserve their lives in the grey waters and misted dawns.

The Romans had gone and the Saxons, pirates turned settlers, had brought their own savage gods before their conversion to Christianity. They built a church, using stones from the Roman walls, and the church, one of the first in the land of the Saxons, was a place of pilgrimage. Then came new heathens, their swords and axes more terrible than any the land had seen, and the Vikings swept the Christians from the flat, marshy land. The church still stood, but the worshippers of Thor and Odin did not know its God, and so the ancient church became a barn. It had been that ever since, an inconvenient barn, strangely built at the land's edge, a place where sheep could be penned on a bad night. There was a tower, crumbling now, supporting a tall, iron basket in which a fire could be lit to warn mariners against the killing expanse of mud on which the wind and sea could tumble and tear a ship apart.

To this forgotten church in a place where the gulls screamed above a desolate shore, Vavasour Devorax and Ebenezer Slythe brought their men. Here, too, had come Sir Grenville Cony, reassured by the men he had sent ahead that all was safe and well. His coach could go no further than the nearest farm, and from there Sir Grenville had walked. He crossed the low ridge of turf, all that was left of a Roman rampart, to see the rest of his advance guard dead or prisoners. Armed men faced him, musketoons levelled, and he turned, frantic, to see the horsemen galloping behind. Sir Grenville was taken, his men tied hand and foot, and ushered into the old building.

Vavasour Devorax, with a touch of the dramatic, had prepared the barn for the seals. The earthen floor had been cleared of debris, the hurdles that penned the sheep on the marshes pushed to one wall, and a table had been fetched from the village. About the table were five chairs, one at the head facing two on either side, and on the table were two tall groups of candles. Ebenezer, who had ridden ahead from the farm, sat smiling his treachery behind the table. A pistol rested in front of him.

Vavasour Devorax came forward. 'Sir Grenville! Good Sir Grenville!'

'Who the devil are you?' Sir Grenville's bulging eyes flicked about the room. Guards grinned as they watched him.

'My name is Vavasour Devorax.' He wore his barred helmet and, in the gloom of the barn, Sir Grenville could see little of the scarred face. He could see, though, that the tall, bearded soldier was smiling. 'I am the man who killed Faithful Unto Death Hervey. I used another name, of course, but I know you'll forgive me that. Otherwise we would not have the pleasure of your fat company. Sit down, Sir Grenville, next to Mr Slythe.'

Sir Grenville's world, that had been buttressed so long by the seals, was falling about him. No Aretine! No victory either. He had been gulled here, tricked, yet his face showed no alarm or anger. He was thinking. He ignored Ebenezer, smiling his supercilious smile beyond the table, and looked instead at the tall, soft-speaking soldier. 'We should talk, Devorax. I'm a man of business. We can reach an agreement.'

The soft-speaking soldier suddenly snarled, became vicious. 'If you don't put your fat arse on a chair, Cony, I'll rip your spine out with my bare hands. Now move!'

Sir Grenville sat next to Ebenezer. They did not talk. Devorax smiled again, his voice resuming a silky, low politeness. 'Now we wait.'

Sir Grenville, still thinking how to avoid this trap, frowned. 'For what?'

'For St Luke, Sir Grenville. What else?' Devorax laughed. 'For St Luke.'

Toby and Campion could not escape. They were met by armed men, surrounded by barred faces, and in the dusk they stripped Toby of his sword and pistol. Toby fought, doubling one man with his fist, but then he was gripped and held, a sword threatening his throat, and Campion screamed at him to stop struggling.

'How very sensible, girl.' Vavasour Devorax had come from the doorway.

Toby wrenched at the arms that held him. 'You bastard!'

'Quiet, puppy.' Devorax seemed amused. 'I don't want to have to clean my sword just because you feel heroic.' He nodded to his men. 'Take them inside.'

Campion looked at John Mason, one of the men who had rescued her and escorted her from London to the safety of Oxford. 'Why? Why?'

Mason shrugged. 'Do as he says, miss. You know it's best not to cross him.' He gestured her to the doorway.

Inside the barn, where the candles had been lit, she saw her brother and, next to him, Sir Grenville Cony. Alive. She cried out, but Devorax pushed her towards the chairs. 'Sit opposite your dear brother, girl.' He looked at Toby and sighed. 'If you struggle, puppy, I'll just have to tie you to the chair. Be sensible. Sit down.'

They sat. The guards stayed close to Toby and Campion. Devorax took the chair at the table's head, put a square, leather travelling chest on the table before him, and smiled sweetly through the bars of his helmet. 'I think we can begin now.'

Ebenezer smiled at Campion. She was trapped. The daylight had long since faded at the high windows either side of the barn. Outside, where the Blackwater met the sea, the ship snubbed at its anchors and waited for the tide to lift the waters over the mudbanks. Campion's river had brought her to this place of desolation, this place of bleak sky, land, and sea: the end.

33

Through the broken roof and windows came the forlorn sound of the gulls. The wind sighed as it bent the eelgrass eastwards. The sea grumbled where it broke at the land's edge.

Vavasour Devorax and Ebenezer Slythe smiled. Sir Grenville frowned. Toby held Campion's hand beneath the table.

Devorax took a pistol from his belt and laid it next to the travelling chest. 'Dearly beloved brethren, we are gathered here together so that two of us can become rich.' He laughed.

Ebenezer wore a black, fur-edged cloak. His own silver-hilted pistol lay beneath his right hand. He smiled at Campion. 'Welcome, sister. You haven't introduced me.'

Campion did not speak. Devorax laughed. 'It seems that Lady Lazender has lost her tongue. Let me do the honours. Mr Slythe? Allow me to name Sir Toby Lazender. Sir Toby?' Devorax gave a mocking bow in his chair, 'I don't believe you've had the pleasure of meeting Sir Grenville Cony. He's the fat one opposite you. Like you, he is my prisoner.'

A guard stood close behind Sir Grenville, as men stood close behind Toby and Campion. She did not understand, thinking Sir Grenville to be among her enemies, and Devorax saw her confusion. He laughed. 'Your brother and I have gathered the seals, girl.' The big soldier looked at Sir Grenville. Devorax seemed entirely at his ease, sprawled casually in the chair. 'Lady Lazender thought you dead, Sir Grenville, a fact that gave her confidence in me. Her assumption was premature, but not by very much.'

Sir Grenville said nothing. He simply watched Devorax. He hid his thoughts and his emotions.

Devorax turned back to Campion. His eyes glittered behind the steel bars of his helmet. 'Sir Grenville, girl, came because he feared Kit Aretine was searching for him in London. You owe me thanks, girl. I killed the Reverend Faithful Unto Death Hervey in your father's name.' Devorax chuckled. 'He died a peculiarly smelly, frightened death. Kit Aretine would have been proud of me.'

'I wish he was here now,' Campion said with bitterness.

Devorax laughed. 'Put not your trust in failures, girl.'

'My wife's name is Lady Lazender.'

Devorax looked at Toby as he might look at a tiresome child. His voice was bored. 'If you aren't quiet, puppy, I'll slit your tongue.'

Devorax's men, interspersed with Ebenezer's guards, watched in amused silence. They had drawn swords beside them, musketoons or pistols cradled in their arms. Devorax himself was utterly sober and his quiet, arrogant confidence easily dominated the strange stone barn. He looked at the dark sky through the broken roof. 'We have time before the tide will be high enough. I thought a small discussion would pass the time. You might even amuse me by pleading for your lives.' He looked slowly from Sir Grenville to Toby, from Toby to Campion. 'But we shall begin with the seals. I believe you have St Luke, girl. Put it on the table.'

Campion did not move. It was cold in the barn. She sensed the soldiers leaning forward to watch her.

Devorax sighed. 'Either you put the seal on the table, girl, or one of my men will search you for it. The choice is yours.'

Toby took his hand from Campion's. The movement made Ebenezer lift his heavy pistol, but Devorax reached out a huge hand and pressed down on the barrel. 'I think the puppy has what we want, Mr Slythe.'

Toby reached beneath his collar, pulled, and the gold seal shone in the candlelight. He looped the chain over his dark red curls, then placed the seal of St Luke on the rough timber planks. Ebenezer, smiling to himself, reached with his long, white fingers and pulled the seal by the chain towards him.

Devorax looked at Sir Grenville. 'I don't believe you came empty-handed, Sir Grenville. Your two, please.'

Sir Grenville's chair creaked. Campion could hear the sea beating endlessly on the mud of the shore. The guard behind Sir Grenville grinned, pulled back the flint of his pistol so that it clicked loudly in the stone room.

Sir Grenville blinked slowly, then moved a reluctant hand to a pocket. Devorax's pistol was pointed at him. The fat man grimaced as he fished in the tight pocket, pulled, and suddenly the seals were there. He dropped them heavily on the table.

The guard stepped back. Ebenezer reached for them, picked them up with a curious delicacy, and the seals were gathered.

Matthew, Mark and Luke were together, as they had not been in half a lifetime. Their gold chains mingled on the table, their bands of precious stones winked like tiny fire-stars. It was a fortune.

Ebenezer, his eyes dark as sin, stared at them. His mind was far ahead in the glory of power.

Sir Grenville, eyes pale and prominent, stared at them. He was thinking desperately, knowing nothing was lost as long as chairs were around a table and men talked instead of killed.

Campion stared at them. She thought of all the sadness and death they had caused, of the terror they had given her. She reached for Toby's hand and it was warm to her fingers.

Vavasour Devorax looked at the faces about the table, faces lit by the tall candles, and on his own face was an expression of satisfaction. 'Perhaps we should say a silent prayer of thanks to an absent friend. St John.'

Campion's voice was scornful. 'Shouldn't you thank your absent friend, Mordecai Lopez?'

Vavasour Devorax chuckled, a deep rumbling sound of infinite amusement. 'The girl wants me to feel guilty. My "friend" Lopez.' He looked at her with insolent humour. 'My friend Lopez is a Jew who has paid me wages for too long. He thinks a pat on the head will be sufficient for me. It isn't. I want more from life than a leather coat and a sword, girl. It's time I had some riches too!' He was becoming animated, close to the anger which Campion thought normal with this man. He leaned forward and scooped the three seals into his hand. 'This is my reward for long service, girl, this!' He shook them so that the chains rattled together.

Sir Grenville spoke for the first time. 'If you are Lopez's enemy, Devorax, then you're my friend.'

Devorax laughed. He put the seals down so that their chains trailed over the damascened barrel of Ebenezer's pistol. 'The word friend is suddenly very prominent this evening. I become rich and everyone is my friend. I don't need friends!'

'Then what do you need?' Sir Grenville was frowning, uncertainly.

Devorax stared at him for a few seconds. 'I need a certain whorehouse in Padua, Sir Grenville. It will keep me in my old age in a manner to which I have become accustomed.'

Sir Grenville had at least started a dialogue with the soldier. He nodded with a smile at the three golden seals. 'You can make a whorehouse out of half Europe with that money, Devorax.' Sir Grenville spoke patiently, equably, one reasonable man to another. 'And without friends you will have small protection against the enemies you're about to make.'

'Enemies?' Devorax said the word with a sneer. 'What enemies? You, Sir Grenville? Your corpse will be dung in this marsh tonight.' He watched the fear show in the bulging, glaucous eyes. 'Lopez? The Jew is an old man, and he knows what my sword can do. He will not seek revenge.'

Campion gripped Toby's hand. She would not show fear. 'My father.'

'Your father?' The bearded face turned to her. 'Kit Aretine abandoned you, girl, so what makes you think he'd come running now even if he could? And if he did, what makes you think he'd prefer a daughter he'd never seen to the riches of a Padua whorehouse?' Devorax laughed. 'You forget I knew your father. I knew his tastes.' He watched her face. 'Of course, if you want to save your life you could come and work for me.'

Devorax put his head back in laughter. Ebenezer smiled. Two guards clamped gloved hands on Toby's shoulders, forcing him back into the chair.

Devorax waited until Toby was quiet. He glanced at Ebenezer. 'What shall we do with them, Mr Slythe?'

Ebenezer shrugged. 'Kill them.'

Devorax pretended surprise. 'But Sir Grenville was good to you! You won't plead for his life?'

Sir Grenville looked with hatred at Ebenezer. Ebenezer smiled slowly at his erstwhile patron. With Sir Grenville dead he would inherit his wealth. 'Kill him.'

'And your sister?' Devorax was pretending innocent enquiry, 'would you not save your sister's life?'

Ebenezer looked at her. 'She's not my sister. She's the daughter of Aretine and his whore.'

Devorax smiled. 'You want her to die?'

Ebenezer nodded.

Devorax smiled at Toby. 'And doubtless you'd like to be buried at your wife's side, puppy?'

'Go to hell.'

'In my own time, puppy, in my own time.' Devorax smiled about the table. 'What a pleasant evening. A rising tide, a waiting ship, three seals, and friends. Mr Slythe and I to share the Covenant, and the rest of you to die.' He let the word hang in the cold stone barn. The wind rose in the broken rafters, died again. The waves were closer, the sound insistent.

Campion looked at the tall soldier and kept her voice as calm as she could make it. 'Toby has done nothing. He didn't ask for this. Let him go.'

'Campion!'

'No! No! Quiet!' Devorax was smiling. 'Is this love?'

Campion raised her chin. 'I love him.'

'Oh! This is touching! How much do you love him, girl?' He leaned towards her. 'How much?'

'I love him.'

'Enough to sign away the Covenant?' Devorax grinned. 'Will you put a price on it? I'll make an agreement with you. The puppy can live if you sign away all your wealth.'

He had stolen it anyway, but Campion nodded.

It was a ploy. She realized, as he opened the square, leather travelling case, that Devorax had planned this; that he had known she would plead and that he could ask his price. He brought from the case a piece of paper, an inkpot, a quill, and a bar of sealing wax. He put the paper, pen, and ink in front of her. 'Sign it, girl, and the puppy lives.'

The paper was brief. It renounced her ownership of the Covenant at twenty-five, ordering the Bank of Amsterdam to ignore the instructions that she was to receive the seals. She dipped the quill in the ink, the point scratched, and Devorax smiled at her. 'Now it's legal. Sir Grenville will tell you that it's better to have these things done legally. Isn't that right, Sir Grenville?'

Sir Grenville said nothing. He was watching Devorax who

had stood, taken the paper, and now dripped hot wax at its bottom. Devorax picked up the seals. 'St Matthew, St Mark, St Luke. There!' He held the paper up. The three wax seals shone like new blood in the candlelight. 'The Covenant is changed for the first time. Lady Campion Lazender is a pauper. You, Sir Toby, will live.'

Toby looked at the paper, at the three seals that took away Campion's wealth, and he looked at the soldier. 'She's no danger to you now. Let her live.'

Devorax put the paper on the table. 'You want her to live, puppy?'

Toby nodded.

Devorax looked at him, pretending to think. 'She gave up all for you, puppy, what will you give for her?'

Toby was fighting an impotent rage. He was trapped in this room, far outnumbered by implacable enemies. He knew that Vavasour Devorax was passing the time as the tide rose, amusing himself, but Toby could see no course but to play the big soldier's game.

'I will give whatever you want.'

'Your life, puppy?'

'No!' Campion protested.

Toby frowned at Devorax. 'Will she live?'

'She'll live.' Devorax nodded at the men behind Toby and, at the prearranged signal, they seized him. They were big men, easily overpowering him, and he could only watch as two more of Devorax's soldiers took hold of Campion. They pulled her upright and led her to the stone wall of the barn. There they stood her, her back to the stones, while Vavasour Devorax, pistol in hand, walked to face her. He glanced at Toby. 'I shall count to three, puppy, and then I will shoot your wife. If you wish to stand in front of her then my men will go with you.' He raised the huge pistol, its muzzle a gaping, black hole five paces from Campion. He pulled back the flint. 'Do remember, Sir Toby, that your wife is a pauper. She has nothing. You can let her die and you can walk away from here. You'll find a wealthy bride. There are plenty of young widows in England today.'

Campion looked at the terrible black muzzle. She raised her eyes to stare through one of the high windows of the barn. A single star glittered at her.

Devorax's voice was harsh. 'One.'

Toby shouted. He wrenched with huge strength at the men who held him, but they were ready, they were strong, and he could not release himself to attack Devorax. Ebenezer grinned.

'No, Toby, no!' Campion shook her head. He had pulled his captors close to her.

'Yes.' He smiled at her. He leaned forward and kissed her. Her cheek was cold. He kissed her again on cold, soft lips. 'I love you.'

'Two!'

The men holding Toby and Campion had arranged themselves either side of the pistol's aim. Devorax, fearing perhaps that the bullet might still strike one of his own men, moved two paces closer. The guards grinned. Devorax's voice grated, 'You can walk away, Sir Toby. You don't need a pauper as a wife.'

Toby ignored the taunting voice. He could not embrace Campion because the guards had his arms held. He leaned forward again and laid his cheek against hers. 'I love you.'

'Three!'

Devorax fired. Flame jetted from the muzzle, blossoming filthy smoke. The explosion echoed in the barn, the sound shattering back and forth between the stone walls. Toby, his back to the gun, felt a blow in the centre of his back.

The shot was a signal. Ebenezer's guards were watching, grinning, but as the sound rang in their ears they were assailed by Devorax's men. Sword-hilts raked faces, gun-butts slammed into bellies, and Ebenezer's six men were overpowered, disarmed, then kicked and clubbed down to the earthen floor.

A leather-clad arm came over Ebenezer's shoulder, clamped a hand on the pistol, and a knife blade pricked

Ebenezer's throat. Devorax's man smiled. 'Don't move, Mr Slythe.'

Devorax turned to Ebenezer. He lowered the smoking pistol. 'Why should I share the Covenant with anyone, Mr Slythe?'

The guards had let go of Campion, she clutched Toby, her arms about his back. 'Toby!'

'He's not hurt.' Devorax's voice rode over the ringing echo of the shot. 'The gun was loaded with powder and wadding. Nothing else. Let him go.'

The guards let go of Toby's arms, stepped away, and he turned, Campion still holding him, and stared at the arrogant, helmeted soldier. 'What are you doing?'

Devorax laughed. He tossed the pistol to the floor. 'Seeing if you deserve the Covenant, Sir Toby. It's yours anyway.' He took the helmet off and he laughed at their expressions. 'I'm Lopez's man. I always was, I suppose I always will be.' Sir Grenville listened with terror, Ebenezer stared open-eyed. His pistol had been taken away.

Devorax walked to the table. 'There was only one way to gather the seals, and that way was treachery, but I'll admit to a curiosity.' He held up the piece of paper with its three seals. 'You're going to be rich beyond your hopes, Sir Toby, and I wondered whether you loved her for the money or for herself. I don't think Kit Aretine would have liked his fortune to go to a greedy man.' He held the paper into the flame of a candle. It flared up, suddenly bright in the room that was misted with the smoke of his pistol. Devorax watched the flames. 'If you had not stepped in front of my pistol, Sir Toby, I would not have sent you to Holland with Lady Campion. As it is,' he dropped the burning paper, 'you both go.' He stamped the burning ashes and melting seals into the floor, then grinned at Campion. 'You're rich again. Congratulations. You're also loved, which I suspect is a greater blessing.'

Devorax opened the leather box and took from it a bottle and two glasses. He held one of the glasses towards Toby and grinned. 'I remembered your delicate drinking habits. Will you join me?'

They still stood together, holding each other, not understanding. The pistol shot still rang in Campion's ears. 'You're Lopez's man?'

'Of course!' Devorax sounded cheerful. He had poured two glasses of wine. 'When you have a good friend you don't abandon him and, believe me, Mordecai is a good man. He lost a house in London to gather these seals, but he thought it a small price for your happiness. Now, come and collect the seals, Lady Campion, and drink a toast with me.'

John Mason, grinning hugely, offered Toby his sword and pistol. Toby, still dazed, took them. He buckled the sword belt, pushed the pistol home, then took Campion's elbow and walked her towards the table. His chair had been overturned when Devorax's guards seized him and he bent to put it upright. He looked at Ebenezer's guards, each one threatened by a weapon, and he looked back to Devorax. 'I thought you were going to kill her.'

'They thought so, too.' Devorax nodded cheerfully towards Sir Grenville and Ebenezer. 'Otherwise they wouldn't have come. Think about it, Sir Toby. Think how else I could have done this.' He raised the bottle. 'I agree it wasn't comfortable for you, but I think it passing clever of me, don't you?' He chuckled and looked at Campion. 'Lady Campion, please pick up the seals. I've gone to a great deal of trouble for them and I need to get drunk.'

Campion sat. Devorax put a glass of wine before her, handed another to Toby as he sat beside her. Devorax raised the bottle. 'I give you an absent friend, I give you Christopher Aretine.'

Campion smiled, sipped, and found she was thirsty. She drained the glass.

Vavasour Devorax smiled sadly. 'He would be proud of you.'

She looked up at him. 'He would?'

'Both of you.' He nodded at Toby. 'Both of you.' Devorax

pulled the seals towards him, put them on the top of the box and then, one by one, put them before Campion. 'I'm just sorry that the last seal isn't here.'

She stared at the three cylinders of gold. 'So am I.'

'Pick them up, Lady Campion. They're yours.'

She stared at them. She did not move.

Devorax sighed. 'Sir Toby? Order your wife to pick them up. I really could not do all this again, I'm getting too old.'

Campion touched them. She fingered them cautiously, as if they might burn her, and then, decisively, she took her father's fortune. Matthew, Mark and Luke. An axe, a winged lion and a winged ox. She looped the chains wide about her bonnet and let the jewels hang bright over her cloak. Ebenezer watched. Sir Grenville watched.

The sound of the waves breaking in the night was closer now. Campion listened, remembering the poem that had comforted her in the Tower. She wondered if this was the sound of mermaids singing.

Vavasour Devorax heard the surf too, and he smiled at them. 'You'll be gone soon, we're just waiting so that a boat can get close enough to the shore.'

Campion looked at the scarred, ravaged face. 'You're not coming?'

'No.' He seemed to laugh. He looked at Sir Grenville and Ebenezer. 'I have this filth to clear up.'

Campion looked at her brother, but her question was to Devorax. 'You're not going to kill him?'

'I am!'

She shook her head. 'No.'

'No?' Devorax sounded genuinely surprised.

He had been her brother, whatever he had done, and in his defeat he looked young again. Devorax's betrayal had taken the supercilious smile from him, had taken away his newly won assurance, had left him as Campion remembered him at Werlatton; a gawky, awkward boy whom she had tried so hard to love, to protect from a world that was hard to the whole, let alone the lame. 'No. He's my brother.'

Devorax looked at her, shrugged. 'You're a fool.' He nodded. 'I'll let him live, but with a remembrance of me.' He stopped her question. 'I said I'll let him live.'

A soldier came to the door. 'Colonel? Boat's coming!'

'So soon?' Devorax put the bottle down. He nodded to Campion. 'Come on, you're going to Holland. Say goodbye to Sir Grenville, you'll not meet again.'

Campion did not. She stood up, Toby took her elbow, but she stayed a moment. She smiled at Ebenezer. 'Goodbye, Eb.'

His dark eyes looked on her with loathing.

She kept her smile. 'We'll be friends one day.'

He sneered. 'You'll burn in hell, Dorcas.'

She left her brother, guarded by Devorax's men, and she followed the tall soldier into the moonlit night. Their bags had been taken from the pack-horse and were being carried to the beach by two soldiers.

The waves sounded loud now. Campion could see the small surf as a white line that stretched in the darkness, a line that wavered, broke, thickened, moved endlessly. She pulled her cloak over the seals.

Devorax stood on the small ridge of turf that had once been a Roman wall. He was searching the sea's darkness. 'We use this place a lot.' Campion knew he spoke of the King's spies who went to and from Holland. Devorax saw something. 'Come on.'

He led them on to the beach, his boots crunching on the humped shells that marked the high-water line. Seaweed smelt strong.

Campion could see the large ship, lights dim at its stern windows while, much closer, oarsmen rowed a small boat towards the beach. The water showed white where their blades dug at the waves. Devorax pointed to the large ship. 'That's the *Wanderer*, Mordecai's ship. The crew are all his men. You can trust them.'

'Just as we trusted you?' Toby smiled.

Devorax laughed. 'Just as you trusted me.'

Campion looked up at the grim face. The moon silvered his hair, his beard, the broad buckle of the leather sword belt. 'Thank you.'

'You must be tired of thanking me.' He laughed. 'You'll forgive me, Sir Toby?' He did not wait for an answer, instead he scooped Campion into his arms and waded into the low, fretting surf towards the small boat. He called out in a strange language, received a cheerful reply, and then the boat was turned, its stern towards Campion, and Devorax lifted her inside. The bags were thrown in and Toby clambered over the transom. The wind blew cold from the Essex marshes. The waves lifted the boat, dropped it, slapped peevishly at the overlapping planks.

Devorax looked down at Campion. 'Tell Lopez I killed Cony.'

She nodded.

'And tell him what else I did.'

'I will.'

Devorax opened his pouch and tossed a square package to Toby. 'That's for Mordecai Lopez. Keep it dry and safe!'

'I will.'

Devorax reached for Campion's hand, pulled it towards him, then kissed it. 'It's a fair night for a crossing.' He released her hand. His men had already gone back towards the barn. 'God speed!'

The Dutch seamen bent their oars in the water. Spray broke on the bows and spattered back.

Campion turned. Devorax still stood in the surf. 'Will we see you again, Colonel?'

'Who knows?' His voice sounded harsh again. The boat pulled away from him. Already Campion could see a bubbling, streaked wake behind her. The oars creaked in the rowlocks.

Toby held her. It was bitterly cold on the water. To his left he could see the sea broken into a stretch of serried, small breaking waves where the tide was frustrated by the great mudbanks. His arm was tight round his wife's shoulders. 'I'm glad he wasn't our enemy.'

'So am I.' She felt the seals under her cloak. They were safe. She was taking them from her enemies, from the war, to the fortune her father had wished on her so long before. She was leaving England.

She turned again, but already the shore was indistinct. She could see the sharp, pointed gable of the old barn against the night sky, but she could not see Vavasour Devorax. She gave a strange laugh. 'He kissed my hand.'

'Perhaps he liked you after all.'

The ship's boat bumped against the *Wanderer*. Men handed Campion up the ship's waist, strong hands leaned down to pull her to the safety of the deck. The ship smelt of tar and salt. The wind slapped ropes in the rigging.

The captain, bearded and smiling, took them to the large stern cabin. It was lit by shielded lanterns and made comfortable with cushioned seats. He gave them boat cloaks for warmth, promised them soup, and begged they excuse him while he set sail.

Campion looked at Toby. She was nervous and excited at the thought of a sea voyage. They were alone. They could look back on the night, remember its fears, the kisses beneath the threatening pistol muzzle, and the strange moment when Devorax had revealed himself to be Lopez's man still. Campion smiled. 'I love you.'

Bare feet ran on the deck over their heads. Toby smiled. 'I love you.' He put the package for Lopez on the cabin table, and froze.

A name was inked on the paper: 'Lady Campion Lazender'.

'It's yours.'

For a moment she stared at it, then, with cold fingers, she tore at the string and paper. Inside was a varnished wooden box. It was five inches deep, six inches square, with an elaborate metal latch.

She did not feel the ship lurch as the anchor sucked free of the mud. She did not sense the ship lean before the land-freeing wind.

She opened the lid, and she knew already what she would find.

The box was moulded inside, lined with red velvet. Four holes had been made for the four seals, and three were empty.

In the fourth hole, its chain wound about the protruding embossed steel, was the golden seal of St John.

She opened one of the stern windows and she screamed into the night. She screamed like a gull on that desolate coast. She screamed at the marsh, the saltings, at the dark line of the bleak land, 'Father!'

Christopher Aretine did not hear her. He stood on the shore and watched the ship bearing his daughter away, taking her to safety, taking her with the love that he had so desperately wished for her. He watched till the dark shape of the boat was lost in the night.

She looked like her mother. To look at Campion was to remember the girl of so long ago, to bring back to Aretine the pain of hope and laughter, love and enjoyment, the memories. A hundred times he had wanted to tell Campion the truth, and a hundred times he had held back. Yet now she knew, and now she could find him if she so desired. She knew.

He turned, crunched over the shells and climbed the humped ridge of the turf. He envied her her love.

Aretine walked back into the barn, his eyes as empty as the sea. He picked up the wine bottle and drank, then looked at Sir Grenville. 'Time for you now, Cony.'

Sir Grenville frowned. His belly hurt, but he still hoped. 'Can't we talk, Devorax?'

The big soldier laughed. 'Devorax! You don't remember me, do you?' You only remember me when I was young, when you wanted me in your stinking sheets, when you had my portrait painted on to Narcissus.' Devorax laughed at the quaking flesh beneath him. 'Do you still have the picture,

Cony? Do you look at it and lust?'

Cony was shaking with fear.

Kit Aretine smiled. 'I came back from Maryland when the war began, Cony. I prayed you would be my enemy.'

'No!' The word seemed to be torn from the lawyer as if by a flesh-hook.

'Yes.' Aretine turned to Ebenezer, and his voice was colder than the wind that carried Campion away. 'My name is Christopher Aretine. Your sister pleaded for you. Should I let you live?'

Ebenezer could not answer. His bowels had turned to liquid. He could only remember this man hacking the corpse at Tyburn, slicing into the dead flesh with horrid skill.

Aretine turned away from them. His daughter had begged Ebenezer's life, but he was in no mood to grant it. He looked at his men and his hand gestured about the whole building. 'Kill them all.'

He walked out of the old stone building that had once been a church, and he heard the cries for mercy, the shrieking of Sir Grenville Cony. He heard the old, old sound of steel blades butchering men. He took no notice of their deaths. He walked to the ridge of turf and stared at the empty, empty sea and he thought of his daughter who had grown so straight and he felt a pity for himself. He drank.

Campion was crying, 'He's my father!'

Toby stared at the four seals, together on the table, and shook his head. 'He didn't want you to know till it was too late.'

There was an inked legend inside the lid of the polished box. 'To Campion, with what I suppose is Love. Your father, Devorax, Aretine, Kit.' Campion shook her head. 'I don't understand!'

She picked up the final seal, the seal of St John. It showed the poisoned chalice with which the Emperor Domitian had tried to kill the saint, and around the chalice's stem was the snake that had carried the poison away.

There had been a crucifix inside St Matthew for Matthew Slythe, a naked woman within St Mark for Sir Grenville Cony, and a silver pig inside St Luke for Mordecai Lopez. Her fingers unscrewed the final seal.

Inside, clasped in tiny silver claws, was her father's fear.

A small, silvered looking-glass in which he could see himself.

The ship bent into the night, and its burden was love.